About the author

Daniel Evans was born and raised in Peterborough, England where he can be found wearing a hoodie in the summer and an even bigger hoodie in the winter. His nose will be stuck in a book with the same playlist playing on repeat in his ears. *The Survivors* is his first novel.

THE SURVIVORS

Daniel Evans

THE SURVIVORS

Vanguard Press

VANGUARD PAPERBACK

© Copyright 2019
Daniel Evans

The right of Daniel Evans to be identified as author of
this work has been asserted by him in accordance with the
Copyright, Designs and Patents Act 1988.

A CIP catalogue record for this title is
available from the British Library.

ISBN 978 1 784655 41 9

This is a work of fiction. Names, characters, businesses, places,
events, locales, and incidents are either the products of the
author's imagination or used in a fictitious manner. Any
resemblance to actual persons, living or dead, or actual events is
purely coincidental.

Vanguard Press is an imprint of
Pegasus Elliot MacKenzie Publishers Ltd.
www.pegasuspublishers.com

First Published in 2019

Vanguard Press
Sheraton House Castle Park
Cambridge England

Printed & Bound in Great Britain

For Dad, who believed in this story even when I
didn't.

Acknowledgements

This book wouldn't have been possible without the help of some amazing people...

Many, many thanks to all the people at Pegasus who looked at my story and thought something could happen with it. I'm still a little bit shocked. Thank you all so much! Thank you to the editors who took my book and turned it into something... readable. I am eternally grateful.

Thank you to Suzanne Mulvey and Claire-Rose Charlton for always being on the receiving end of my (endless) emails and keeping me sane during this amazing experience.

Thank you to that one person on Wattpad who read this story and loved it even when the first few chapters were just a 1,000-word ramble. You're the best! I'm sure you know who you are. *winks*

And finally, many thanks go to my (entire) family.

Jonny. For being the best big brother anyone could want. For always being there when I need you. Always.

Gaby. For being an amazing, awesome, funny—and just the right amount of crazy a little brother could ask for. You're the best sister ever. I love you, and thanQ for everything.

Mum. For always being on the receiving end of my endless questions like: Is this how you spell this word? Is this the right word for this sentence? Does this sentence make sense to you? Thank you for being the most awesome mum in the world!

And finally—Dad. For all those long drives where we discussed AT LENGTH about things that could happen in this book, some of which are still tucked at the back of my mind, just waiting to spring back to the front. You were the first person to hear about this story, and you loved it ever since. I love you, and thank you, thank you, thank you!

I love you. All of you.

CHAPTER ONE

I was told the world ended over one hundred years ago, but that's only what I've been told. Since I haven't seen any other humans, other than our small group, I think it might be true. We don't know how or why the world ended, but it did. We are the only survivors we know.

We are on the search for people like us—survivors. I'm sure we all believe deep down, we are the only ones left. After all, who would want to live in such a desolate city? There's nothing here. We, as a small group, can just about survive.

Sometimes, it brings a tear to my eye to think that I'll never find my parents again.

I think they are dead. They probably think *I'm* dead.

This place, once part of a land known as North America, is now a ruined city. We all call this place the Estate. I don't know why, exactly, but it has a certain ring to it.

The Estate has been my home for pretty much all my life. It never used to be as bad as it is now. When I was younger, the buildings were still somewhat intact, now they're not.

Every time we think one of the buildings is going to come down, we pack our things and move to another building, and so on, and so on. We've never stayed in a building for more than three years. It would be too dangerous.

I lick my chapped lips from the scorching hot sun this morning, then I crack my knuckles, neck, and back. My thighs are starting to cramp from being in this crouched position for who knows how long, but I don't care about the pain. I can't think about the pain at this moment.

This isn't the right life for a sixteen-year-old. I never asked to live in this place—I just got stuck here.

I look into the distance with tired eyes, seeing the old dilapidated buildings every now and then. In the sunset, the buildings give off a nice orange glow, but in reality, they are an old light brown. It's the type of color that matches everything around it, making it look like one smear of color.

The building I'm on now is like the others. The roofs are the only things still intact; for now, anyway. The roof has always been my hideout—away from all the others. Away from everything and everyone. The surface of the roofs are flat, giving us the opportunity to sit or stand on them without any harm; to keep us comfortable, I guess.

Only people like me can get this high on a building. You need to scale the buildings, but the only things we can use are the ledges. You need to be quick on your feet, because if you apply too much pressure on the ledges, then they'll crumble, and you will go tumbling down.

I sometimes wonder what it would be like if it was only me in this town. I would definitely be lonely. I would probably go mad from the loneliness. I'm glad I have all the people that are surviving with me, though. I would never ask for more.

Out in the distance, I see the faintest flickering of light. The light flickers three times, then stops.

What the hell was that? I would have said back in the day, but now I just look in that direction, and turn away. I squint my eyes to see if the lights will appear again, just once, but they don't. Not even for one more time. What could that be? Instinct will always tell me that it's more survivors sending us signals, but it could have been the sun reflecting off a piece of metal or something. Of course that's what it was. I relax my muscles.

Almost every day I see something strange out in the distance, but I no longer take any notice of it.

The first time I saw something, I bugged everyone to see if we could check it out, see if it was anything, but no one would help me. Granted, I was an annoying twelve-year-old that didn't know any better than to shut up. It served me right when a boy a year older than me, walked up and slapped me across the face. Then I shut up.

It wasn't until later that night that I went and slapped him back harder, until Kyle came and pulled me off him. If he hadn't, I would have knocked him out… maybe even worse.

Kyle has always been there for me. Whenever I was upset or angry, he would always tell me to talk to him until I felt better. I'm probably the one closest to him.

When I was ten, he found me in one of these old buildings that was about to come down, and he saved me.

That was the day I lost my parents.

I remember I cried and cried until my throat hurt. Sometimes, on days like that, I cry myself to sleep thinking about my parents. In bed, I have to bury my face in my arms or hands to try and push the thoughts from my mind… but sometimes even that doesn't work.

Six years later, I still get jolted awake sweating and with tears in my eyes from nightmares about my parents. Their faces will never leave my mind. Every time I close my eyes, I see my mother's brightest blue eyes and her darkest brown hair that falls over her shoulders. I see my father's hazel eyes, and gray hair whenever I close my eyes.

I sometimes see Kyle in my father.

Vicky crouches next to me, her knees clicking as she squats. I guess she was standing up for a long time. I just didn't hear her come up on the roof.

"What are you looking at?" she whispers. The same age as me, but she sounds so much older, so much more mature.

I look over at her; her dark brown hair is cascading down her back in a loose messy braid. Her hand is on her forehead to prevent the light getting in her eyes. We could pass as siblings, but we're not. Someone once thought she was my sister because we both have the same dark hair and blue eyes.

"I just saw something in the distance. Like a flickering light." I turn to look at her, drop my voice to a whisper. "But I don't think it was anything."

She glances over at me; her blue eyes seem brighter at this time of night as she searches around my face. "You must have been up here for hours." She looks over the edge. "Don't you want to go down? I think Joel has gone out for a walk. Then we can get something to eat."

Joel. I clench my jaw at the mention of his name. I hate that guy so much. When we first found him, he could have passed as a nice guy, but when we all got to know him, he turned out to be a nasty, nasty person. I even suggested to Vicky that we should leave him out on his own and then ditch him. "No, we can't do that, Kyle will be down our throats," she said when we were on our way home that night.

Kyle is the oldest one here. The Father to us all. The nicest person out of all of us. You could talk to him for hours.

Vicky taps rhythmically on the handle of her knife with the ring I found her about a year ago. I would say that she is my best friend. She always listens to me when I want to rant about Joel and how much of a horrible person he is, and I always listen to her about her problems. We mostly have the same problems.

It's been about three years since I met Vicky. She was this small thirteen-year-old who was really scared of us at first, but when I reassured her that we wouldn't hurt her in any way, she started to relax, and she has been my best friend ever since.

"How long *have* you been up here?" Her question brings me back to the present, and I turn my head in her direction.

I shrug my shoulders. I never think about the time when I'm up here; I just climb up whenever I feel like it and stare off into the distance until someone calls me and asks if I want to come down, which is usually Vicky. No one else besides us two can climb up these buildings.

"Probably about three, maybe—at a push—four hours," I say. "I came here when the sun *just* started to go down." I try to come up with a different excuse every time I want to come up here, and they all seem to believe me.

She slowly nods her head, playing with the ring on her finger. Cheap metal, bronze, and slightly rusty, but she seems to really like it. I told her, when I first gave it to her, that I was sorry if she hated it, but she smiled, gave me a hug, and slipped it on her finger. It hasn't moved since.

She always has it on when we go scavenging for our supplies.

Vicky gets into a more comfortable position, dangling her legs over the building's ledge. "What are you thinking about in that head of yours?" She points to the side of my head, poking me the slightest bit.

I move my head to the side with a smile. "Just my parents," I say. "Also wondering if that flickering means anything."

Vicky sighs then looks over at me. "Xan, you and I both know it wasn't anything," she says. "It could have been the sun reflecting off something."

My real name is Alexander, but I never liked that name. I introduced myself to everyone as Xander, but Vicky's nickname for me is Xan. Like Vicky's real name is Victoria, but I like to call her Vicky; so does everyone else.

To answer her, I nod my head. "You're right, Vicky. I'm sorry." I look over at her. "I guess old habits die hard, huh?"

Vicky nods slowly, looking down at the roof. "I guess so."

The cool metal of the dagger at my belt is rubbing against my rough skin, but I don't mind—it's refreshing after this morning's humid air. The night is slightly better; there is a breeze, but never as cool as you want it to be.

I get out of my crouched position and sit like Vicky is, with my legs dangling off the roof's ledge. It feels good to stretch my legs after being in that position for hours.

I sigh, exhaling through my nose and run my hand through my messy brown hair, moving it away from my eyes. It's too hot to have it in my eyes; I can feel the sweat forming on my forehead already.

Vicky looks over at me with a confused look on her face, which I can see in my peripheral vision. "What's wrong?" she asks with a quiet voice, as if not to startle me.

I look over at her and smile. "Nothing, Vicky," I say. "It's just nice to be on this roof with you and have no one to bother us."

She smiles and looks down, then nods slowly. "Yeah... you're right." She slowly looks up at me. "It is nice." She continues to stare at me for a few seconds, then she looks down again and scratches the back of her neck.

We stay silent for a while, just looking out into the distance, not having a care in the world. We normally always come up here to relax; it's our escape from all the others.

For me, it's mostly an escape from Joel. He may be a year older than us, but in my eyes, he acts like a five-year-old. He is actually the one that slapped me in the face to shut me up. After that day, I just hated him. I don't think anyone blames me for it.

Vicky shuffles uncomfortably on the spot, a wincing expression covering her face.

"What's up?" I look over at her, helping her to get into a better position.

She still continues to shuffle. "Just this damn ledge," she says with a slightly frustrated tone to her voice. "I think I'm sitting on something."

I hold back a laugh that struggles to escape my mouth.

She reaches underneath herself to pull out a small stone, probably the size of a thumbnail. She holds out her hand and drops the rock in the palm of my hand. I toss it from my left hand to my right hand, examining the smooth and round surface of the rock, then I throw it far away ahead of me. It

16

makes a loud ricocheting noise when it hits some sort of metal sheet, then it goes silent.

Sometimes, Vicky and I will talk and talk about everything. We know almost everything about each other. We are the only ones that are the same age—everyone else is either older or younger than us.

I look over at Vicky; strands of her dark hair are blowing in her eyes in the warm wind. She brushes her hair behind her ear, then exhales loudly when it comes back out of place.

She slowly looks over at me, and we stare at each other for a few seconds, then she smiles at me. I smile back. I'm just about to open my mouth to say something, but I get interrupted.

"Xander, Vicky, come down from there, and come and get something to eat," Kyle's deep voice booms from below us.

I lean over the edge and peek down at Kyle; his brown—almost gray—hair is messy on top of his head. He stands there with a big crate in his hands while he looks up at us.

"We're coming," I shout down to him. "Hold on a few minutes. We'll be right down."

He nods slowly, looking inside the house. "Okay, don't be too long. Otherwise, *we* will eat all of the food."

I shake my head and roll my eyes at his comment, taking a glance over my shoulder at Vicky; she has a smile on her face from laughing.

"Come on. We better go down," I say to her.

She nods then gets up from the ledge so that she is standing right on the edge. I follow suit, fixing my charcoal colored jacket so that it's straight.

I hold out a hand for Vicky to take, to help her down, but she smirks, then shakes her head.

"Such a gentleman, but no thanks." She turns around and drops off the ledge and swiftly grabs it, slowly making her way down to the bottom.

She waits for me on the ground, and I turn around and do the same as she did.

On this building, the ledges are still perfectly intact, but I don't know how long for. They aren't breaking any time soon, that's why this building is the best for us to stay in. I won't get my hopes up, though.

I place my foot on one of the ledges, then I drop, falling for about three feet until I land perfectly on my feet. I tuck my legs in and roll, casually standing up next to Vicky.

Vicky stands next to me with her arms crossed over her chest, tapping the ground fast with the ball of her foot.

I walk up to her, stooping down so I can place my mouth close to her ear. "And *that's* how it's done," I whisper, leaning up straight.

She laughs and lightly punches me on the arm. "*Please*, I could do that with my eyes closed." She crosses her arms over her chest, jutting out her chin with her eyes closed.

I laugh. "I *really* want to see you do that." I nudge her arm with my elbow.

She laughs and looks over at me. "Oh, don't worry, I will." She starts to walk toward the building, leaving me behind.

I smile to myself as I follow her into the building.

Kyle sits on a dirty stone next to the small round table in the center of the room. He picks at a crate with the tip of his blade, being as careful as he can with it. It's like he's trying to carve an important message in the crate, and if it goes wrong, then he has to start all over again.

Vicky and I walk up to him at the table, but he doesn't acknowledge us when he's like this. He always tries to focus when he's "busy" or doing something that's somehow "important".

I lean against the table with my hands pressed firmly on the cold stone of the flat surface, waiting for Kyle to finish whatever he is doing. "I thought there was something to eat?" I look over at Vicky and she shrugs, looking around the room.

"Just wait a moment," Kyle replies even though my question was directed at Vicky. "It's almost—"

Suddenly, I hear a loud cracking sound, like someone just snapped a piece of wood in half. The sound echoes around the room, then slowly disappears.

"Ah, finally," Kyle says with a smile on his face, slowly moving his hands to the lid of the crate, pulling it up and off in one motion.

I peer inside the crate, craning my neck to see right to the bottom.

Food. *Food.* My stomach rumbles at the sight of it.

The box is filled with dried berries, dried beans and grain. It's not a lot of food, but to me, it looks like a roast chicken with potatoes on the side.

"Where did you get all of this stuff?" I ask—completely dumbfounded. "There's like… a week's supply of food in here."

"I know." Kyle presses his hands to his hips and smiles. "I found it in one of these old buildings. It was just sitting there as if someone just forgot about it."

I reach inside and pick out a handful of the contents in the crate. Vicky does the same, but she lifts up her hands to her nose, smelling the food like she's never seen it before, and exhales loudly. She picks a few berries from the pile and puts them in her mouth.

"How could we have missed this?" I ask, letting the food fall through my fingers. I pick a handful back up.

I stare at the content in the palm of my hand. I don't even know where to start. I push all thoughts from my mind and I pick out a dried berry and pop it in my mouth.

"If you weren't looking for it, you wouldn't have found it, don't worry about it." Kyle steps back so we can marvel at the amount of food in the crate. "I almost tripped over it, so that's how I found it."

"Oh," Vicky and I say at the same time.

The berries don't have as much taste as I thought they would when I placed more of them in my mouth, but they would pass as edible.

Giving up on picking out my food bit by bit, I tip the mixture in my mouth and bite down. The mixture of flavors makes my mouth feel weird, but after some time chewing, I swallow and the feeling slowly goes back to normal.

Once I've had all the food I want, I say goodnight to Kyle and Vicky and I walk to my room.

My room is not as big as I would have wanted, but since I room with Vicky, it seems even smaller. The two beds on either wall make the gap between them seem tiny compared to where the door is. The small window where our heads would be when we lay down is completely open. It lost the glass a few years back, and I don't even know how. I don't mind, though; it lets in a cool breeze on hot nights.

I sit down on my bed and untie my boots, slowly slipping them off my feet. A cool breeze seeps into the several holes in my socks, but it feels refreshing.

My room is right next door to the main room, so every time someone is up and talking, I can hear every single word they say. The walls are not as thick as you want them to be. It's quite dangerous, really; if one of these crumbles, then the whole roof will come crashing down on us.

"Why do I have to do it? Why can't Xander? He's the one that was up on the roof all day." I roll my eyes as Joel's voice fills my ears.

"Joel, please just do me this favor. It won't take you long. Just go out, grab what I need and come back. Simple." Kyle's trying to stay calm, but I can clearly hear the frustration in his voice.

I lean closer to the wall right by my bed because I know how this conversation will go.

"Yeah, come on, Joel. It won't take long," Vicky says. "If you want I can hold your hand if you're scared. Would that make you feel better?"

I stifle a laugh.

"Please, Vicky, just go to bed. I wasn't even talking to you. I *don't* even want to talk to you," Joel snaps back.

"You know what? *Fine.* At least I will get away from you," Vicky says with an angry tone to her voice.

Seconds later, Vicky walks into our room and sits down on her bed, giving me a frustrated smile. I don't smile back, because I know if I did, then it would just grate her more.

I didn't hear the rest of Joel and Kyle's conversation, but I can hear heavy footsteps walking out of the building, then the door slamming shut.

I turn back around to Vicky; she angrily tries to untie her boot laces. She kicks off her boots in one swift motion, not caring where they will end up. She slips off her jacket, so she's just left in her dark gray vest, which is starting to rip at the hems.

I slip my jacket off my shoulders, revealing my old black T-shirt underneath, and place it as a pillow at the end of my bed. We don't have real pillows here; if we did, then they would have been burned for a fire, or just generally lost, but my jacket is comfortable enough. I've been doing it for six years, so I'm pretty much used to the slight discomfort.

We don't have pajamas either, so the only thing we can sleep in is our clothes we wore from the morning. It's disgusting, really, but the only way we can get new clothes is if we found them in one of these many buildings.

I pull the knife out from my belt and place it under my pillow for safekeeping. You never know what could happen during the night.

The only light in this room is the small fire lamp sitting on the edge of my bed, and the tiny window on the other side of the room. But the window doesn't give us any light in here; it's too dark outside.

I turn to look at Vicky who is leaning back against the wall, her arms are crossed over her chest. "What was that about with Joel?" I say quietly.

She looks at me then shakes her head, breathing heavily through her nostrils. "Kyle wanted him to get something from a few buildings down, but of course, being Joel, he refused. Then I guess he gave up and left." She gives me a frustrated shrug of her shoulders, not saying anything else.

"Well, now you know why I hate him so much," I say.

She nods her head and rolls her eyes. "Yeah, I know, but I never *actually* liked him," she says. "I hate him just as much as you do."

I nod and look down at the lamp, staring at the little flame as it flickers back and forth. I use as much of the light as I can as I get myself comfortable, fluffing up my jacket so it's not flat under my head.

Vicky lies down on her bed, her head resting on her jacket. She moves her hair away from her eyes, brushing it behind her ear.

I lift up the lamp and blow the fire out.

The room suddenly turns pitch-black. I struggle to find my jacket, but once I find it, I rest my head on it and lie down. My hands are behind my head, and I'm resting on my back, looking up at the dark ceiling. From my years of sleeping in this room, I've already memorized the cracks lining right above my head.

I've memorized a lot of things whilst I've been here.

"Goodnight," I whisper to Vicky, the faint noise sounding much louder in this quiet room.

She shuffles slightly. "Goodnight," she whispers, but it sounded more like an exhale of breath, then she goes silent.

Before I close my eyes, I think about the flickering lights I saw out in the distance. Somewhere, deep, deep down inside me tells me that the lights were not just a reflection.

CHAPTER TWO

A piercing scream startles me awake.

I jolt up in my bed, whipping my hand under my jacket to grasp the knife. I jerk my head over to Vicky's bed, my eyes widening as if I just suddenly went blind.

She's sitting up in her bed, looking around frantically, visibly breathing heavily. Even though it's quite dark in here, I can still see the silhouette of her trembling body.

Once I notice no one other than us is in the room, I let go of the knife, feeling a small layer of sweat form on the palm of my hands. I wipe the sweat on my pants, curling my fingers into a fist when I feel them shake.

I get up from my bed and rush over to sit on Vicky's bed. I practically jump and land on her hard-stone bed. I pull her into my chest, and there I can feel her fast-beating heart. I wrap my arms around her shoulders, letting her nuzzle her face in my chest.

"Shh, it's okay, Vicky. I'm… I'm here now," I whisper to her. "I'm here."

She sniffs, and I know that she has been crying. I squeeze her tighter, but not too tight as to suffocate her.

She starts to shake, and her breathing has become a fast, but quiet, panting. "I-I'm sorry." She lifts her head off my chest slightly so she can wipe at her eyes. "I didn't mean to wake you up."

I rub her arms reassuringly, shushing her again softly. "No, you don't have to be sorry." I move a small strand of her hair out of her eyes. "Do you want to talk about it?"

She shakes her head slowly, wiping the tears from her eyes with the back of her hand. She looks into my eyes, and even in the darkness of the room, I can still see the pale blue irises of her eyes.

"Thank you," she whispers.

I squeeze her again, then look back to her. "No problem. It's what best friends are for, right?" I ask, giving her a little nudge with my arm.

She laughs quietly, wiping away a tear from her eyes. Her hair falls over her face in big strands, and I brush one away from near her eyes and place it behind her ear.

"Are you all right now?" I ask her.

She nods her head, wiping more stray tears from her face. "I will be," she says. "Thank you."

"No problem." I let go of her shoulders, slowly starting to get up from her bed.

She pulls me back, her hands resting on my arm. "Xan... can you stay with me... until I fall asleep, at least?" she whispers.

I smile as I nod my head slowly. "Of course I will," I whisper.

She leans her back on the wall near her bed, and I sit next to her, holding her arms. She rests her head on my shoulder, still slightly shaking. I kiss the top of her head, mumbling something that I'm sure she didn't understand.

I stroke lightly on her arms to calm her down, and she eventually stops shaking.

*****

Hours. That's how long I've been awake. It's still pitch-black outside, and I can see the stars and night sky outside the small window in our room.

Some point during the night, we both managed to lay down on her bed, our heads resting on her pillow. My arms are around her middle, keeping her pressed against my chest. I can only hear her light breathing as it slowly brushes against my skin, my neck, my chest. I turn my head to look down at her, her head is pressed firmly on my chest, and her mouth slightly ajar.

She's fast asleep.

I can't seem to close my eyes and drift off to sleep. It seems like such a struggle. I can still hear the scream that startled me awake. It echoes and bounces around my skull, even as I try to force it out with another thought, but to no avail.

I wonder what her nightmare was about. Her parents? Her time alone in the Estate? Me? I shrug off the thoughts and slowly remove my hands from around her body, softly grabbing her shoulders to gently move her head to the other side of the pillow. I really don't want to move, but I need to stretch my arms and legs.

I brush a strand of hair away from her eyes, pushing it slowly behind her ear. I tentatively make my way off the bed and creep my way to mine. I sit down on the cold, hard stone, hoping I'm not making too much noise. I grab my boots from the floor, slipping the worn leather on my feet, tying up the laces. I grab my jacket from the end of the bed, smoothing it out, then I slip it on my shoulders and around my torso.

I grab my dagger, wiping some of the dirt away from the blade with the hem of my T-shirt, then I slip it into my belt.

I rise from my bed, making my way to the main room, trying to be as quiet as I can so I don't wake anyone up, but then I see Kyle sitting at the round table, using the tip of his knife to pick out dirt from under his nails. He hasn't heard me yet, so I stop trying to be so quiet. I slowly make my way to the round table, sitting down on the hard seat.

He doesn't acknowledge me as I slide into the seat in front of him. I look up at Kyle to see his face as expressionless as anything. "Hey," I say softly.

He licks his dry lips and looks up at me. "Hey," he whispers back, but it didn't sound normal, not like him at all. It sounded like… a stranger.

"Are you okay, Kyle?" I ask, trying to look up into his gray eyes. His head is so low that his chin is almost touching his chest.

Something's not right, but I don't know what. Kyle never gets upset about anything. Even when I slapped—and almost knocked out—Joel, he stayed calm, and didn't raise his voice, or even have a scowl on his face.

Kyle nods slowly. "Yeah, I... just couldn't sleep. I've been up for a little while." He's trying to sound happy, but the pain is still there. I can hear from the slight croak of his voice, that I know he's trying to hold back some tears. I brush my long, messy hair out of my face, playing with my thumbs, not saying anything else.

The metallic sound of Kyle's dagger echoes through the silent room, making me wince. I look down at the small blade attached to the worn leather handle of his knife. It's slightly rusty and it's losing its sharpness.

I get up from the chair and walk over to the crate full of the food from last night. It's still filled with all the berries and grain—no one must have eaten any. I grab two makeshift bowls that Kyle made and fill them to the brim with the food from the crate. The bowls are not the deepest that you would want them to be, but at least they hold *something*.

I slowly make my way back to the table, balancing the two bowls in my hands. I place the bowl in front of Kyle, and he stares intently at it as if it isn't real. I sit back down on the stone and pick out a few dried berries. They seem to have lost more of the flavor since last night, and I don't even know how that's possible.

After I've eaten half of the food in my bowl, Kyle still hasn't even touched the mixture in his bowl. He keeps picking up a pinch of it, then dropping it back into the bowl, changing his mind.

I move the bowl slightly closer to him. "Kyle, you need to eat something." I try and keep my voice as quiet as I can so I don't wake anyone up.

Kyle clears his throat. "I'm not very hungry." Even though he cleared his throat, his voice still sounds hoarse.

I exhale loudly, trying not to get frustrated. "Well, it's there if you get hungry, Kyle. I'm going back to bed." I get up from the stone table, and I tip the grain back into the crate. "Good night." I'm not really going to bed, I just needed an excuse to leave the table.

I turn my head in Kyle's direction before entering my room.

Vicky is still asleep as I walk into the room. I decide not to wake her up, since we normally wake up an hour from now.

I crouch in front of her bed, lightly brushing a lock of her dark hair out from her eyes. She looks so peaceful while she's sleeping; it's almost like she didn't wake up in the middle of the night screaming from a nightmare.

Vicky stirs in her sleep, and I slowly move my hand away, but then I see her eyes flutter.

"Xan?" Vicky whispers. She squints her eyes as if she's struggling to see me.

I smile. "Yeah, it's me," I whisper back.

She looks over to the window on the other side of the room. "What time is it?" She rubs the sleep out of her eyes, still trying to sit up.

"Probably around five o'clock." I give her another small smile. "You can go back to sleep for another hour if you want."

She nods slowly, laying her head back on her jacket, then she's out like a light.

I get up from my position, slowly making my way to the small lamp that lit up the room last night. I struggle to light the lamp, because normally Vicky lights it up for us. *She's*

27

normally the first one up, and *she* normally struggles to wake me up.

After a few more attempts, the lamp blazes with sudden light so that I have to squint my eyes.

I pick the lamp up gingerly, as if I am about to drop it, and make my way to the back of the building. We always supply our stock at the back of the buildings, so it's out of the way, and so we can still grab it easily if we wanted.

The old musty scent invades my nose as I walk into the room. It's always cold in here, or maybe it's just the eerie silence that makes it cold. I can't tell any more. I've been in here too many times to try and figure it out.

My heavy breaths sound like an explosion going off in this dark room. I instantly shut my mouth, silently breathing through my nose.

I pull a small black backpack out from the old bookcase we put our supplies in, and I struggle to slip it on my back. I have nowhere to place the lamp, so I'm trying to juggle the lamp and the pack at the same time.

"Need some help there?" a deep voice booms from behind me, and it startles me.

I whip my head to see who the voice belongs to, and it's none other than Adam.

I mentally roll my eyes.

Adam is an "all right" guy… when he's not talking. He's kind in his *own* way. He's not as rude and arrogant as Joel is, so I'm thankful for that.

Adam is the type of guy that likes to rip the sleeves off his T-shirts to show off his biceps—which he's trying to do now by crossing his arms over his thick chest.

Compared to me, Adam is *huge*. His arms make mine look like flimsy sticks, but since I became a Scavenger I started to develop *some* muscles. Although mine are nothing compared to his.

I puff out an irritated breath. "No, I'm fine," I say through gritted teeth.

"Are you sure? You seem like you're struggling." He takes a few steps closer to me.

I let out another breath of frustrated air. "Fine, if you want to help, take this." I shove the lamp in his direction, almost making it extinguish. He takes it with a smug smile, obviously proud that he won.

I slip the backpack on my shoulders, letting it rest comfortably on my back. I grab another one and slip it over my head so it rests diagonally against my back. I look back over to Adam, who is staring at the little fire intently, making his bluish-green eyes glow.

I hesitantly take the lamp from his hand so I don't burn myself, and Adam snaps back to reality, smiling widely. "Thank you," I say.

He smiles again, running a slow hand through his dark blond curls. He scratches his stubble growing chin, staring at the floor. "So, are you heading out now?" he asks.

I nod, fixing the packs so they are more comfortable on my back. "Just like every single day since I started."

This is how our conversations go: he asks me if I need help, then he insists on helping, then we exchange awkward small talk.

He's harmless, really; he never talks back to us, and he always does what he is told, but he does have his moments. Typical eighteen-year-old.

"How's Lara doing?" I ask, trying to fill the time in before I wake Vicky up.

Adam looks confused for a second, then he suddenly realizes I'm talking about his sister.

Adam may be pretty, but he *can* be dumb sometimes.

Lara helps Adam out with his job, which is to fix up the building we are staying in. It includes putting up wood panels and stuff like that—stuff I'm not good at. I'll just stick with being a Scavenger.

"She's all right, I guess." He shrugs. "How's Vicky?"

I nod my head. "Yeah, she's good. I'm going to wake her up soon."

"Doesn't she normally wake *you* up?" he asks, squinting his eyes at me.

I laugh and nod my head slightly. "Yeah, she does, but I just couldn't sleep."

"Yeah, me neither. I guess you heard the blood-curdling scream too, then?"

I look down and bite my lip. "That was Vicky screaming."

Adam struggles to find words. His face shows that he is sorry for what he said, and I just nod to reassure him.

"Is she all right now?" he asks, and I nod slowly.

"Oh, *there* you are, Adam. I've been looking for you *everywhere*." Lara's voice fills my ears, then I hear her footsteps as she saunters into the room.

I crane my neck to look over Adam's broad shoulders to see Lara's small figure approaching us, a dark expression covering her face.

"Well, you obviously didn't look *everywhere,* Lara, because I'm right here," Adam snaps back, an irritated look crossing his face.

Lara lets out an exasperated sigh, slowly looking over at me, trying to keep her face impassive as she forces a smile on her face. "Hey, Xander," she says, trying to sound calm.

"Hi, Lara," I say back with a small smile. "Did you sleep well?"

"Like a baby," she replies, keeping her frustrated smile on her face. Lara's smile suddenly falls as she turns to face Adam. She crosses her arms over her chest, showing some of her muscles.

Well, that's a Builder for you, I think. All muscles, leaving the rest of us to look like, well… this.

"Adam, come on, we need to start working. You know the rules: once we are both up, we need to start working. You don't want Kyle to kick you off this team, now do you?" she says menacingly, making *me* back away from her. She may be two years older than me, but she sounds like she could be in her late twenties—looks like it too.

Adam gives her a tight shake of his head, not opening his mouth to say any more. I think he knows better than to.

For the only two Builders, you would think they would get along better, but no. They *always* jump down each other's throats. If this is how *all* siblings get on with each other, then I'm glad I don't have a brother or sister.

Lara and Adam could be twins, because they both have the same dark blond hair and bluish-green eyes, but I don't think they are twins; they've never said if they are or not. I definitely know they are siblings, though.

I pretend to look at the invisible watch on my arm, feigning being late for something. "Oh, would you look at that. I need to get going... right about now, actually." I swiftly walk toward the door, brushing past Adam and Lara along the way.

I turn around to look at Lara and Adam's faces which are staring at me with the same type of expression. "I'll leave you two to talk." I nod and turn around.

Before I even leave the doorway, they are back to their heated argument.

I hold back a laugh.

When I get back into my room, Vicky is still asleep. I slowly make my way to my bed, plopping the packs down on the hard stone as quietly as I can.

I slowly sit down on the bed, my knees *click, click, clicking* as I make contact with the bed. I scowl at my legs for making too much noise, but then I look over at Vicky and my frown fades.

How can she sleep so peacefully when she's sleeping on *rock*? I swear that's what these beds are made out of. Every morning I wake up with an aching back and limbs. I don't even have a blanket. But, at least I have something to rest my head on. I can't complain about that.

I pull myself onto the bed so my back is resting against the wall. I pull my knees close to my body, resting my head against the wall, trying to be as comfortable as possible.

Then I slowly close my eyes.

*****

A hand violently shakes my shoulder, forcing me to open my eyes.

Vicky stands by my bed, leaning close to me so our faces are a few inches from touching. She's smiling, a smile I've woken up to every morning. I can't help the smile that appears on my face.

I must have fallen asleep for a while, because Vicky's face is illuminated by the natural light of the sun.

Our roles are reversed again—*She's* waking *me* up.

"Morning, Sleeping Beauty," she says softly, as if not to startle me.

"Morning," I say back, rubbing some of the sleep out of my eyes. "I guess it's time to go, then?"

"You know it is." Vicky stands up straight, gathering her hair in her hands, splitting it in three sections, braiding her hair quickly. Once she's done, she ties it off with a strand of synthetic leather that was clenched between her teeth.

I swing my legs off the bed, grabbing one of the two small backpacks that I left on the end of my bed. I swing it on my back, adjusting the straps so that they are tighter, slightly more comfortable. Vicky does the same, and within a few minutes, we are both ready to go.

Vicky walks over to the back of the room and pulls out two bandanas, throwing mine to me. She tries to throw it as if it will hit me in the face, but I catch it without a second thought, and Vicky sticks her tongue out at me.

I smile and adjust the black material around my neck loosely. Vicky does the same with her red bandana, pulling it down to rest around her neck.

We always have these just in case of a sandstorm—we never get caught in the middle of one, but Kyle says to wear it "just in case."

Kyle always says for us to take these backpacks. It's mostly in case we find anything of value, or if we get injured, then we have a small first-aid kit each, but really the packs mostly just weigh us down. If we didn't have them on, then we could both run a lot faster, but Kyle insists, so we don't argue. We don't want to be kicked off this team. Scavenging, climbing and running are the only things that I can do, the only things I *want* to do in this place.

When we walk out of the room, Lara and Adam are fixing one of the pillars holding up the ceiling. I always get nervous whenever they work on something as sensitive as the pillars, but I have to trust them. It's in their title; they are Builders, after all.

"Lara, can you stop being annoying for *one* minute?" I can hear the frustration pouring out of Adam's voice.

"I wouldn't be annoying if *you* got it right for once in *your* life," Lara snaps back at him with the same amount of frustration.

Sometimes it's funny watching these two try to co-operate, and it makes me glad that I don't have any siblings.

"That's rich coming from you. One of the pillars that you worked on snapped yesterday. And it wasn't until I used these"—he flexes his biceps, making Lara roll her eyes—"to fix them back up. Now, if you'll excuse me, I have work to do." He slowly goes back to hammering some nails into the wooden pillar. Lara turns around, discreetly punching the palm of her hand multiple times with her right, all while mumbling insults and curses under her breath.

I look over at Vicky, we both stare at each other, having a full on conversation with our eyes. We are both saying the same thing: *I'm glad we don't have any brothers or sisters.* Then we would say something like: *Is that how we sometimes act?* Then we would both laugh.

I walk over to the crate full of the food. I pull out a pouch made of leather pouring a generous amount of the content into the bag, tying it off when it is full to the brim. I secure it to my belt, making sure that it doesn't slide off when I'm hopping from building to building.

The food is mostly for lunch, but I normally will just take a few seeds or whatever and eat when I get hungry. Vicky is more organized than I am; she always waits until lunch to eat some of her food. She does that with the water as well. I always drink half of it, then dump the rest of it on my head and around my neck to cool myself off from the heat. By the time we get home I'm dry, it normally dries straight away.

I grab two water bottles from the box underneath *more* boxes, and I hand one to Vicky, she slips it inside her pack, as I do.

As we make it to the front door, Joel comes hurrying out of his room, with his jacket half on his shoulder and half not. His navy-blue bandana hangs loosely around his neck. His blond hair is sticking up everywhere. Overslept. Again.

He yawns, rubs his eyes, and tries to fix his jacket at the same time. "Come on," he says through a yawn. "Let's just get this day over with so I can go back to bed."

I roll my eyes, slightly shaking my head. Unfortunately, Joel has the same job as Vicky and I do, being a Scavenger. Maybe this is some test Kyle is giving me so that I'll start to grow accustomed to him, but that will never happen. Not in my world, anyway. In my world, there is no Joel, there is no Estate, and there is no Wastelands—which is what we called the place in the distance. Most importantly, in my world, we will *all* live normal lives. Normal teenage lives. I don't know what that's like.

When we go out, Joel never stays with us. He always wanders off by himself, and we just have to let him. It's good, really—the further away he is from me, the better.

Kyle walks out of his room, rubbing his eyes with the back of his hand like a child would. He grabs a bowl from the side and fills it with food. Then he goes and sits down at the table in the middle of the room; just like he did earlier. Just like earlier never happened. Almost like he's… trying to forget it.

I would too if I was in his situation.

I let Vicky and Joel out first, glancing behind me, giving one last look at Kyle before slipping out of the front door.

CHAPTER THREE

The heat of the sun is starting to give me a headache, and yet, we haven't even made it ten steps out of the door. It sometimes is really tedious doing this job, because we have covered *every* building within a five-mile radius.

Thankfully Joel has left Vicky and me alone. He always does, but it is nice for it just to be Vicky and me, because then we can talk without anyone eavesdropping.

Vicky nudges me in the side. "Hey," she says. "What's wrong?"

I look over at her. Her blue eyes searching my face, for anything. She always knows *one* way to get information out of me.

I sigh audibly. "It's just we have covered *every single* building in this area. I'm starting to get bored."

She laughs and nudges me again. "There's a way to fix that," she says, giving me a small smirk. "Let's go *further* out, but not so much as to end up in the Wastelands."

"Don't worry," I say, "I'm sure when the time is right, we will *all* go out to the Wastelands."

"Maybe you're right," she says, tugging on my arm. "Let's go up on the roofs and look for anything we can keep."

Vicky looks at the building to our left. She seems to be examining it, which is what any good Scavenger would do, anyway. We never climb up buildings that look too old. We don't want to take the risk of one coming down on us.

When I take a closer look at the building, the first things I spot are the ledges, and the windows that occupy them. Most of the windows in these buildings are either covered in rock and dust so it would be impossible to see through them, or they are so small that you can't even fit your hand through.

I stalk my way to the building, grabbing hold of the lowest ledge that I can find, applying the most downward force I can muster. I look back over to Vicky, she searches my face for any problems.

"I think we are good to go," I say. "Just try to be as light on your feet as possible." I tap the ledge three times.

Vicky lets out a loud breath of air. "*Please,* that's my specialty." She grabs hold of the first ledge she comes into contact with, and hauls herself up, clutching the next ledge higher, then higher.

When she gets halfway up without difficulty, I start to pull myself up, placing my foot down gingerly onto the ledges. I climb higher, and higher, careful with the ledges at my feet, and my hands. Then I pull myself up, swinging my legs over the edge.

Vicky sits along the roof's edge, swinging her legs from side to side. She looks over at me, then smiles. "Took you long enough," she says.

"Yeah, well"—I turn around and sit on the ledge—"*some* of us haven't even woken up yet. So, don't blame me if I'm a *little* slower than usual."

She laughs and nods her head. "What do you think we will find today?"

I shrug. "I don't know. We could find anything. But not too much stuff otherwise it will just slow us down."

Vicky slaps me hard on the back, making me wince slightly. "Come on, Grandpa, we need to get going."

I slowly get up from the ledge, wiping some of the dust from my jacket and pants. "Hey, don't forget *you* were just like this only a few days ago. So, don't go calling *me* Grandpa."

I laugh thinking about that day; I had to pretty much *drag* her out of bed, and she was dragging her heels outside, and I almost scooped her up in my arms and carried her with me.

She laughs, removing the dirt from her jacket. "Whatever, Grandpa. Let's go."

I shake my head, pulling the black bandana around my mouth, letting it rest on the bridge of my nose. Vicky does the same, but she tightens it more around the back of her head.

I stare at the roof of this old building, and I find nothing but a few rocks and dust.

With a sigh, I take off running to the other side of the roof, pressing a single foot on the raised ledge, and I leap across the gap. For a moment, I am flying, completely lost as the wind brushes against my long hair. The feeling stops as soon as my feet land instinctively on the hard surface. I tuck and roll, and I press my hand firmly on the roof to stop moving.

I turn my head just in time to see Vicky jumping across the gap, her arms are spread from her body. Then, as if to propel her forward, she pushed her arms out in front of her, then she lands on the roof.

As she regains her balance, I stand straight up and dust off my jacket and pants. The bandana tied around my head protected any unwanted dust and sand from entering my system.

"Man, I love doing that!" Vicky hollers, sounding muffled behind her bandana.

I laugh and wipe away a light sheen of sweat from my forehead. "Tell me about it. I don't think I've had that much adrenaline before."

My eyes scan the flat surface of the roof before Vicky can respond to the sentence. But the only thing on this roof is dust and a few small pebbles. I'm starting to doubt there is even anything—

Before I even realize it, I'm in a crouched position again, looking at something intently. This is no rock, and it's definitely not a clump of dust, either. No, it seems to be metal. A perfectly round piece of metal. I pick the article up gingerly, as if it would singe my fingers off, but it doesn't. In fact, the only thing I feel is a rough surface of dust and sand.

"What do you see? Is it anything important?" Vicky says behind me. I don't respond to her, but after a few seconds, I feel her crouch next to me, slightly leaning in to get a closer look.

"What the hell is that thing?" I don't answer her question, instead I slide my dagger from my belt, and hold it tightly in my right hand. With the tip, I start to pick away the hard exterior of this object.

Underneath the caked dust, I can see the slightest shimmer of silver. I scrape away the remainder of the dust, and finally I notice a man's head looking to the left. Then I realize—

"It's a coin," I say under my breath, grazing my thumb across the warm metal. I slide the dagger back into my belt.

"What is it?" Vicky mumbles.

I bring the coin closer to her. "It's a coin, Vicky," I repeat, this time louder.

"Oh," is all she says. She takes the coin from my hand and studies it closely.

I remember my dad used to have a few of these coins, and when I used to sit next to him, he showed me all these different styles of them. Most of them were from different countries. He once told me that people used to buy things with this type of money. That was back before the world is how it is now. We never needed coins, or money, because we traded our supplies for stuff we needed.

It was stupid, really; you could only trade clothes for clothes, food for different food, different metals for other types of metals, and so on.

Now, we have to find our supplies. The clothes on my back now, I found them only a few months ago. Every time I grow out of clothes, I have to work tooth and nail to find new ones.

That's why I'm a Scavenger. Otherwise, the clothes I'm wearing now would just get ruined. Thankfully, these clothes on me now are slightly big for me, so I have a few more years to grow into them.

"Xan?" Vicky snaps me back to reality.

"Yeah? What did you say?" I blink rapidly to get her face to focus.

"No, I didn't say anything, it's just that you blanked out for a few minutes."

"Oh, I was just… thinking."

Vicky places her hand slowly on my shoulder. "You do that a lot, you know?" she says and I nod, laughing lightly. "About what?" she whispers softly.

"Just about this coin. I think my dad had a few. He showed me them when I was really young. This just reminded me of that time, I guess."

"Do you want to keep it, or should I just throw it over the edge?" Vicky says as she hands me over the coin.

I take it slowly, rubbing my fingers around it's—now hot— exterior. "No, it's fine, I'll just keep it." I place it inside my pocket and rise from the position. My knees click painfully, even Vicky winced. How long was I in that position?

"Come on. Let's head in that direction," I point to a cluster of buildings in the distance, "and see if we can find anything new."

She nods. She doesn't even wait for me before she takes off in the direction of the buildings I pointed out. I smile, and make sure my bandana is fit snugly before following shortly after her.

With the momentum, I can easily jump from roof to roof without difficulty.

I watch as Vicky jumps across a roof a few meters ahead of me. Strands of her dark hair fly behind her as they come into contact with the wind.

But then, as she takes off from the building she just ran from, I can tell that her jump wasn't long enough. Her foot slips from the ledge, and she falls from the roof. Thankfully, she grabs the roof just in time to avoid falling from a great height.

When I land on the building she is hanging from, I skid to a stop, turning my body sharply enough to make something crack, but I don't care, because Vicky is the one that needs the help.

I grab her small hand, just before her fingers slip from the ledge. She grabs onto me like a vine wrapped around a tree, and she doesn't let go.

"Hold on!" I yell at her. She doesn't reply, but the expression on her face tells me that she heard me.

I start to pull her up. She plants one foot on the ledge, then pushes herself up.

Still holding onto her, I slip, and start to fall backward. Vicky falls with me.

My back slams onto the roof painfully, then Vicky lands on top of me, causing the air from my lungs to be whisked away. We stay in this position for what seems like a while but may have only been seconds. Me, trying to regain some of the air, and Vicky trying to regain composure.

"Are you... all right?" I say, once I get my voice back.

She nods her head slowly. "Yeah." She swallows, hard. "Thanks." Strands of her dark hair fall over her forehead, and down the sides of her cheeks. And as I follow the contour of her hair going down her cheek, I suddenly feel Vicky's eyes upon me. As my eyes shift position, we are both locked in a stare which neither of us has felt before. Our eyes seem to penetrate right through each other. As quickly as that moment came, it goes as Vicky places her hand on my chest and pushes herself up.

"No problem," I finally manage to choke out.

She's so light that I didn't even feel pressure on my chest or stomach. She sits on the roof, breathing heavily. I guess traumatized by what just happened.

I sit up, staring at her for a few seconds. "Do you want some water?"

She nods her head slowly, but clearly avoids eye contact. I slip my pack off my shoulders and unzip it. I fish out the bottle of water and hand it to her. She unscrews it slowly and tips the liquid into her mouth.

Once she's finished, she screws the lid back on top of the bottle, and hands it back to me, looking at the floor constantly as she does so. I drop the bottle into the pack and zip it back up, then I swing it back on my shoulders, and start to turn around.

Why won't Vicky just look at me? She hasn't looked at me directly in the eye since we locked eyes back on the floor.

With a loud sigh, I rise from the floor and dust off my clothing. "We'll go whenever you're ready," I say bluntly. I walk over to the nearest ledge and swing my legs over as I sit down. I scoop out the coin from my pocket and run my fingers and thumbs over the shiny exterior.

Vicky sniffs from behind me. I would go and comfort her, but what's the point when she won't even look me in the eyes? So instead, I bow my head and continue to graze my finger along the metal.

"That's it," I mutter angrily to myself after a long time. I slam the coin back inside my pocket, swiftly rising from the ledge. In a few strides, I'm standing right next to her.

In those few minutes, she's managed to pull her legs close to her body and hug her arms around them.

I slowly crouch in front of her.

She still won't lift her eyes.

"Vicky, look at me." She hesitates at first, but then she lifts her eyes. Her eyes are glassy. A single teardrop could fall down her cheek at any minute.

She still isn't looking into my eyes, in fact, she is looking at the space between my eyes, avoiding them completely. Well, it's a start.

"Vicky, we have to go." She looks down again, then slowly nods her head. I offer a hand to help her up, but she shrugs it away. I drop my hand to my side out of frustration. "Let's walk around on the ground. It will be safer."

She doesn't wait for me to finish the sentence before she is climbing down the side of the building. I watch as her head slowly disappears behind the structure.

I take a minute to calm down, and let off a bit of steam, because I don't want to climb down this building if I'm taking my frustration out on the ledges—because then they will definitely come down.

I close my eyes and take a long, deep breath in through my nose, and out of my mouth. I slowly walk over to the ledge and peer down below. Vicky has her arms crossed over her chest and is looking around at nothing in particular.

I turn around on the ball of my foot and start to climb down the side of the structure.

When I make it to the bottom, I dust off my jacket and run my hand through my tangled dark hair.

Vicky stands about a meter away from me, her arms still crossed over her chest, staring at the same medium sized rock below her. She *still* won't look at me.

"Okay. Let's start in these houses," I say, pointing to the few houses around us.

Vicky nods wordlessly and trudges to the closest house, crunching broken shards of glass and other debris and rubble.

"Okay, then," I mutter to myself. I stuff my hands in my jacket pockets and walk to the house opposite the one Vicky chose, kicking some rock and dust along the way.

I reach behind me and unzip my backpack just a sliver, so I can drop items in there easily.

The first thing I notice in this house is the table in the center of the room. It is exactly like our house, only with the exception of broken glass and ceramic littering the floor. The wallpaper has been completely ripped off the walls, leaving the old light-brown hue underneath it all.

Portraits of families have been completely smashed beyond repair.

I gingerly pick up one of the frames, careful not to cut my fingers on the sharp glass. I wipe away a thin layer of dust that was forming on the image.

In the picture, a man and woman stand behind two young children—a boy and a girl. They are smiling in front of this house, which once, believe it or not, actually looked decent.

Where are they now? Did they leave? Die? The kids in the picture don't look familiar. They definitely don't live with us.

Maybe they did die.

I place the picture frame on the side slowly as if not to wake anyone up in this empty house.

I walk into, what seems like the kitchen, but I can't be too sure because *every single* item that was once in the cabinets is now littered on the floor.

I check around the ceilings for any signs of cracks or chipping, but I find nothing; it's all perfect. So, the structure of the building is almost perfect, but the contents inside the building aren't? How is that even possible?

I crouch down next to the closest cabinet and open up the wooden doors. Dust flies out like a raging sandstorm, and I'm glad that I have my bandana around my nose and mouth, but, somehow, I still feel the small particles creep their way behind the fabric. I cough loudly, waving my hand from side to side as if to blow away the dust.

After all of that, I find nothing in the cabinet.

"Damn it," I mutter to myself, slamming the door loudly, making more dust fly around. I rise from the floor, ignoring a stabbing pain in my neck. It was probably when I whipped my head around to help Vicky back on the roof. I rub it slowly, trying to ease some of the horrible tension that's starting to build there.

I rummage through the cabinets, opening them up faster than I should.

When I open the next cabinet, something black catches my eyes. It's sitting right at the back, but it's too dark to see anything. I reach my hand forward, then the thing moves. I jerk my hand back and wipe away the dirt on my pants.

I'd recognize the small black body and long tail anywhere. A rat.

"Gross," I mumble, watching it scurry away to a dark corner.

The light catches something in the darkness. I can see a glint of light from the corner of my eye.

A small unwanted packet of plastic water bottles sits unguarded in the dark cabinet. I reach forward, grabbing hold of the plastic wrapped around the bottles, and pull it into the light.

A light layer of dust covers the plastic, and I wipe it away with the palm of my hand. I pull my knife from my belt, and, with one slice down the center, the entire wrapping is off.

I stuff the two bottles of water in my backpack and rise from the floor. I walk around the main room for a while, until I can no longer find anything that could be useful. The only things that I could find are a few half-empty bottles of aspirin, some iodine, a few pieces of fabric, and some bandages.

I walk up the stairs, jumping over the huge gaps among them, and finally, after some precision, I make it to the landing.

Even though the outside of this building is quite large, the upstairs only has two rooms and one bathroom. I walk as lightly as I can to the first room I can see, but I can still hear the floorboards creak under my boots.

I push open the wooden door and peer inside. The only things in this room are an upside down bed frame and a set of drawers.

I hop over the few cracks and splinters in the floor and make it to the front of the drawers. I tug at the handles, but they don't open up easily. Out of frustration, I rip the front of the drawer off its hinges, and I drop the useless wood to the side, slowly pulling out one of the drawers.

Something silver catches my eye, and I would be able to recognize it instantly if it wasn't covered in layers of dust.

A nice little dagger.

I pick it up carefully, admiring the weight, and sharpness. My index finger picks up the dust as I run it along the smooth surface. I slide the knife in my belt, walking out of the room. I don't want to put the knife in the backpack, because it could tear open the fabric, so it's probably best if I keep it in my belt.

The door to the next room is locked. I keep trying to move the doorknob, but it won't budge. I push my shoulder to the flat surface of the wood, to see if it would give purchase, but to no avail.

I push myself away from the door and make my way to the bathroom, grabbing the wall as soon as I see that there is no floor to the bathroom. Different sizes of broken wood line the circumference of the bathroom floor.

A hardly audible creak can be heard from behind me. My fingers wrap around the handle of my knife. I turn around, whip my knife from my belt, and point the tip to my so-called "attacker".

"Whoa, whoa! Calm down," Vicky says as she lifts her arms up to surrender. "It's only me."

My arm drops to my side. "Damn it, Vicky. You scared the hell out of me." I slide the knife back in my belt.

"Hey, I'm sorry. I didn't mean to scare you. Well, maybe I did a little." Vicky steps forward and wraps her arms around my torso. I wrap mine around her middle.

At least she is happier.

"What are you doing in here, anyway?" I ask.

"I finished in the house I was in," she says. "I got bored. I wanted to see if you needed help."

"Thanks."

"No problem."

She lifts herself off me and looks up at me. "Feel better now?" I nod my head, and Vicky steps back slightly.

"Come on, let's get out of this hellhole before something else jumps out at us," I say, walking side by side with Vicky.

Vicky jumps over the gaping hole in the stairs with ease. Whereas I have to grab hold of the wall to jump down the steps.

We both laugh when I slip and almost fall over.

It seems all of the events from the last hour have disappeared.

*****

A building that's been under construction stands in front of us. Metal bars and poles crisscross the entire structure. To me, it looks like a huge climbing frame for adults. While to everyone else, this whole thing just screams "DANGER!" over and over again.

I start walking toward the building, ignoring the warning buzzing in my ears.

"What are you doing?" Vicky says, grabbing hold of my forearm, pulling me back.

"Doing my job," I laugh.

Vicky hesitates, but says nothing.

"Don't worry, I'll be careful. I've done it many times before."

"On a scaffolding?" Vicky asks, watching me go.

"Well... not *exactly* scaffolding, but close to it." I smile, continuing forward.

I walk toward the closest bar, gripping the hot metal tightly in my hand. I pull myself up. I stop as the metal creaks, but it doesn't move an inch.

When I make it halfway to the top, I can feel the humid breeze brushing through my hair.

When I look at the metal closely, I can see that there are some pieces sharper than others. The metal poles look like they have been here for years, rotting away from the heat.

"Do you want to come up?" I shout down to Vicky.

She shakes her head quickly, too quickly. "No," she says. "It won't hold both of us."

"Suit yourself."

With one of my hands, I brush away some dust and grime growing on the pole. I wipe the excess on my pants.

"Did you find anything?" Vicky shouts from below. I peek down, and I see Vicky standing there with her hand shading her eyes looking up at me.

"No," I shout back. "Nothing."

"Do you want to come back down? It doesn't seem that safe."

"Yeah. Be right down."

I slowly make my way down, trying to ignore the horrible noise the metal is making.

I try not to look down. Heights never bother me. In fact, it gives a kind of rush knowing that I am standing above everyone else. Not in a ruling way, but a way that I can see what others can't. It's almost… peaceful, I guess.

My gaze moves down, and I look at the wooden platform just a few meters away from my feet.

I look back at the bar I am holding onto. The rust is starting to flake under my hands, causing my grip to falter slightly.

Then the metal snaps.

A gasp escapes my lips as I start to fall backward.

Just before I hit the wooden platform, a sharp piece of metal gets lodged deep in the side of my torso.

It's the last thing I remember before the darkness surrounds me.

CHAPTER FOUR

A white-hot pain rips through my entire body, snapping my eyes open. The world around me seems to slow down. The air around me starts to turn thick as I struggle to breathe—in, out. A flash of light crosses my vision, but I take no notice of it.

"Xander!" Vicky shouts from below me. Her voice sounds distant, like she is deep underwater, trying to shout my name, but it only comes out a mere echo. I think she says it again, but I can't tell.

Darkness has almost taken me fully. I fight hard to keep my eyes open just a few more seconds, but as the seconds tick by, I can feel myself dropping, dropping, drop—

A blurry figure is crouched next to me.

A cold hand touches my face, but I hardly feel it.

The sun behind the figure makes it look like a silhouette, staring down at me.

Vicky.

Vicky has come to help me.

I think she says my name again, then again, but everything sounds distant—even my own thoughts sound like an echo.

She grabs my face between her hands, keeping my eyes on hers. I don't want to look anywhere but at her—I can't; her grip is too tight.

I can just make out the blue irises of her eyes, before darkness takes over.

*****

I go in and out of consciousness. My head lolls to the side, then to the ground. I can see that I am moving, but I am unsure how; my feet appear stationary. It is all very confusing. I'm half being dragged, and half moving myself, but I can't feel my legs.

An arm is wrapped tightly around my waist, and another arm is clutching my wrist, tightening as I start to tumble slightly.

Vicky.

Vicky is moving me.

Vicky is saving me.

The pain in my side throbs to the sound of my heartbeat.

Thump… thump… thump…

Each *thump* gets louder every time I take a step forward, then another.

I look down at my side; a thin piece of metal is protruding out of my body, dripping with blood. It blurs as I continue to stare at it.

My eyes close. The pain is too much to bear. Too much. Too much of *everything.*

Stop.

I want everything to *stop.*

"Xander." Vicky's voice still sounds a thousand miles away—away from *me.* "You need to stay awake. You can make it. Please. *I can't lose you.*"

Those were the last words I heard before the darkness took over once again.

*****

I jolt awake from a sharp pain in my side.

Everything around me is starting to come back into focus, but my head still feels groggy. Every single sound feels ten times louder than it usually does. My limbs feel like lead, keeping me down even when I fight to get up.

I can tell that I am lying on my bed in my room. *How did I get here?* I think, cautiously, but then I suddenly remember: *Vicky saved me.* Vicky is the one that got me back here.

A hand pushes me back down on the bed, and I tiredly comply. I look over to see who the arm belongs to; Drew. One of the two Medics. Drew's ash blond hair hangs loosely over his forehead, almost covering his dark brown eyes. He looks tired, clearly hasn't slept in ages.

"Xander, just relax. It will hurt even more if you keep moving." Drew's calming deep voice fills my ears.

I look down at my side, and I realize that my shirt and jacket have been discarded. Only red can be seen on the side of my body.

Blood is a strange color; it's darker than you think it is, and the metallic smell that's emanating off it is nauseating. It's hard to look directly at my wound.

The crimson of the blood almost makes my olive skin look darker.

Drew grabs a few things from the box which has all the supplies that Vicky and I found a few months ago. He walks closer to the entrance, slightly leaning back to look out of the door. He's really tall; he stands quite a few inches taller than me. I don't know how old he is, but at a guess, I would say late twenties, maybe.

"Liv!" Drew shouts, making me wince. "Come in here! I need your help!"

A few seconds later, Olivia—Liv—comes walking into my room, a frustrated look on her face. *What's she so angry about?* She removes an elastic from her wrist and pulls her dark hair away from her face, tying it into a high tail behind her head. The heat from this room causes small specks of sweat to form on her dark skin. I can see them as the light shines across her forehead.

"Sorry, Drew, but I was trying to calm Vicky down. She really wants to see Xander." Liv talks as if I wasn't listening,

51

as if I wasn't in the room as they have this conversation. Why won't they let Vicky in? It's only a wound in my side. I want to see if Vicky is okay.

"No, don't worry. I just needed help with the bandages," Drew says calmly.

"Okay, sure," Liv says, with a sweet smile on her face. "Can you pass me those latex gloves?"

Even though Liv is putting on a cheery demeanor, I can tell that she has been up for hours, because of the countless bags under her eyes, and the slight slump of her shoulders as she leans down to inspect my side. That's the same for Drew as well, but Drew is good at covering it up.

Liv throws Drew an old rag from the box. Drew tips a clear bottle of rubbing alcohol onto the rag; soaking it.

I grit my teeth as Drew wipes away the dried blood from my wound, clearing away some of the fresh red liquid as he does so.

When he finishes, he grabs some tweezers and starts to pull away some of the metal still stuck inside my body. I groan in pain, fighting the urge to punch him in the face.

In Drew's mouth is a thin needle with a long piece of thread hanging down. Great. He's going to have to stitch me up, isn't he?

"I would grit your teeth hard if I was you," Drew says, hovering over me with the needle in his hand.

He pushes me back on the bed, and I squeeze my eyes shut, all the while gritting my teeth. He hands me a leather belt, motioning for me to place it between my teeth. I do, biting down hard on it.

He comes closer to me with the needle.

*****

After an agonizing ten minutes of torture, Drew has finally finished with stitching me back up.

52

He wipes away the blood with the alcohol one last time, before wrapping my middle with a clean white bandage.

I pull the belt away from my teeth. Bite marks are permanently indented in the fine leather. I completely ruined this belt.

Drew notices the belt, hiding a smirk. "Did I hurt you *that* much?"

I shrug slowly, dropping the belt on the floor.

I carefully try and touch my wound, but Drew stops me, moving my hand away. "Don't try and touch it, it will just cause more pain."

I nod. "Thanks, you two." My voice sounds hoarse—unlike me at all.

They both nod, starting to pack the stuff back inside the box. As soon as they exit the room, I hear Liv speak up. "You can go in now, Vicky," is all she says.

Vicky storms into the room like a child that was told no by their parents. She wraps her arms around my neck, pulling me up off the bed slightly.

"Xan, I-I was so worried. As soon as they kicked me out of the room I got so scared. Are you okay?"

I place my hands on the first place I can find, which is her waist, and I hold her tighter. "Don't worry, I'm okay now, just a little bit achy and shattered as hell."

Vicky cups my cheeks hard and stares at me intently. "Why did you climb up that building?" she demands. I can see a few tears shimmering in her eyes, threatening to escape.

I open my mouth to say something, but nothing comes out. All I can feel is the tightness forming at the back of my throat, and if I attempt to say something, it would sound hoarser than before. I don't even know why I climbed up that building. I guess I just thought there could be something really important there.

I hear footsteps walk into our room. I peer over Vicky's shoulder to see who it is. The two Stockers. These two take all our supplies and organize them, putting them neatly in the bookcase at the back of the room.

They are twins.

But the only problem is that they are both mute.

They both have fiery red hair and green eyes. The only way I can tell the difference between them is by the way they dress.

Vicky and I both think that they are about thirteen years old, because they are both quite short, and they have young, healthy faces, despite the few freckles they have lining their noses and cheeks.

They never told us their names, because they couldn't, so Vicky and I gave them nicknames.

The one on the left we call Ponytail because she *always* has her hair tied up, exposing more of her face.

And the other one we call Blinky because she blinks more often than she should.

Blinky grabs the two backpacks from Vicky's bed, and Ponytail grabs an empty box from the ground. Blinky starts to pull the stuff we found from the backpacks, placing the water bottles and food in the box as well.

"Thanks, guys," I say once they finish. They both wince at the sound of my voice, but Ponytail nods her head, making her tail bob up and down as she does so. Blinky nods and gives us her signature blinks. Then they both leave, slowly closing the door behind them.

"You know, you're going to have to stay in bed for a few more days," Vicky suddenly says.

"No, I don't. I can make it. I can do my job," I say, trying to get off of the bed. A sharp pain explodes in my side. I can't help but scream out in pain, the sound scraping against my throat painfully.

Vicky rushes over to my side and pushes me back down. "Don't move, Xander. You'll just make it even worse."

"Ugh!" I groan. "I can't just stay here."

"You can, and you will," Vicky says calmly, almost a whisper. Her voice soothes me and my aching head.

"I'm going to be so bored here." I shake my head, glaring at my lap as if it would help the situation—it doesn't.

"Here—" Vicky throws something into my lap, and I cover up being hurt. "Be imaginative."

I stare at the browning object sitting in my lap with furrowed brows. I poke at it with my index finger as if it will suddenly jump up and attack me. I curl my upper lip as the old, musty smell lingers in the air and around my nose.

"What the hell," I say, "is that thing?"

Vicky steps closer, arms crossed over her chest. "A book, you idiot."

"This is a *book*?" I hold the so-called "book" in front of her, eyes wide as I stare at her, then the book. "This is a poor excuse of a book."

The front and back covers and spine have been completely ripped off so I have no idea what the title is, or what it could be about. The only thing keeping these ripped-beyond-repair pages together is a thin layer of glue where the spine should have been.

"Yeah, I know," Vicky replies. "I found it under my bed, so yeah…"

I drop the book on my bed next to me, rubbing my fingers together slowly, trying to keep my face impassive. "Thanks for the gift," I say sarcastically. "Truly, I love it." My voice still sounds sarcastic. "But that might be the most disgusting thing I've ever held in my hand. Sorry."

"Well, if you want to be bored." Vicky shrugs. "Suit yourself."

"What time is it?" I change the subject, looking out of the small window.

"About six in the morning. I need to go soon." She sits down on her bed, hugging her legs tightly to her chest, slowly wrapping her arms around them.

"How long was I out?" I ask quietly, almost afraid to ask the question out loud to someone—anyone.

"A few days." She barely whispered the three words.

"Did you at least fall asleep in these past few days?" I ask, slightly sitting up in bed, groaning when I feel a slight pain in my side.

Vicky doesn't say anything for a while.

Then, "No," she says. "I didn't." She grabs the empty backpack and slips it on her shoulder. "Every minute that ticked by were the worst of my life. Every hour I would look at you and think, *is he going to wake up today?* And when I first brought you in here, they kicked me out of the room. It took them two *whole* days to get that damn piece of metal out of your side." Tears start to form in her eyes, but she doesn't let them fall. She looks away from me. "So, no, Xander, I *didn't* get to sleep. At all."

I open my mouth to speak, but I don't get time.

"I have to go. Kyle already told me to go twice," she says, strapping the pack tightly on her back. She walks straight for the door without casting me one last look.

"Vicky, wait!" I shout, but it's too late because Vicky has already walked out of the room.

*****

I stare up at the cracked ceiling, thinking about Vicky's words before she left.

Every minute that ticked by were the worst of my life. Every hour I would look at you and think, is he going to wake up today?

A tear falls down my cheek thinking about those words. I can't stop picturing the tears that were welling up in her pale eyes.

The ceiling starts to become blurry around the edges, and I blink away the tears that were starting to form. I watch as the ceiling becomes sharper.

I don't know how long I have been staring up at this cracked ceiling for, but it must have been a while because the room is starting to get slightly darker.

"Hey," someone says from the door.

I sit up straight, seeing Kyle in the doorway. "Hi."

"Can I come in?" he asks cautiously.

"Of course," I say, leaning my back against the wall.

"I thought you might want this." Kyle hands me a bottle of water.

I take it with a smile. "Thanks." I unscrew the lid, tipping the warm liquid in my mouth, letting it soak my sandpaper-dry throat.

"So, how are you feeling?" Kyle asks as he sits down on Vicky's bed, folding his arms in his lap.

"I would be lying if I said I was feeling better," I say.

Kyle nods but says nothing for a moment. "Just to let you know that you are going to have a few more days to recover." He brushes away some hair from his eyes, crosses his arms over his chest.

I nod, but what I really want to say is that I can't stay cooped up in this room all day long, but I know Kyle, he will strap me down on this bed if he has too.

"Okay," I say eventually.

We don't say anything for a while, but I can't help watch Kyle look around the room.

"I don't like the fact that Vicky is out there alone," I say. "Anything could happen to her." *Like something almost* did *happen to her.* "And it's not like Joel will come to her rescue."

He looks me directly in the eye. "Me neither," he says. "But just between you and me, you and Vicky are the best Scavengers that I have. Joel's kind of crap at his job."

I laugh at what he said about Joel because it's true; Joel *is* crap at his job. He never comes back with anything important. And if it's a good day, he might come back with a small bottle of medicine. Overall, he *never* scavenges, period.

"Xander?" Kyle snaps his fingers in front of my face. "Did you hear what I said?"

I shake my head. "No, sorry. Can you repeat it?"

"Do you want anything to eat?"

"No. Thanks."

Kyle rises from Vicky's bed and makes his way to the entrance. His shoulders are slightly slumped, and he is dragging his feet along the ground. He too is tired.

I don't get why everyone is so tired. They can all sleep. Even Ponytail and Blinky looked tired. It just doesn't make any sense.

"Kyle, can I ask you something?" I say before he can walk out of the room.

He turns around and walks to the foot of my bed. "Sure. What is it?" he asks quietly.

"Why—" I swallow hard, trying again. "Why is everyone so tired? They look like they haven't slept in years."

He chuckles slightly. "Because everyone is worried about you, Xander."

I don't have anything to say back to him. Everyone was worried about *me*? Surely people have more important things to worry about than me.

Kyle turns around slowly making his way to the door. I watch his broad figure exit the room, leaving me completely dumbfounded.

CHAPTER FIVE

"You stupid idiot."

I smile to myself as Lara and Adam talk to each other; the same way they do almost every single day.

It's the only entertainment I have right now.

I'm currently propped up in my bed, my back resting on the wall, while my eyes are closed; pretending to sleep— pretending to do *anything* other than listen to Adam and Lara.

The throbbing in my side has lessened slightly, but there are a few passing hours where I feel a pain explode in my flesh. If I apply some pressure on my side, the pain dies down a bit.

"Will you *shut up* already?" Adam hisses back at Lara. "Xander is trying to sleep, if you can't see."

Lara makes a sound at the back of her throat, then continues with what she was doing. The two are in my room fixing a large crack in the wall opposite my bed. I said it would be fine, but with them being the Builders, they said that they need to fix it as soon as possible.

It's really boring without anyone to talk to. With Vicky gone, I have to stare at the blank wall just in front of me, because everyone else is working, or somehow busy.

When Vicky came home last night, she completely avoided eye contact with me... she didn't even say goodnight to me.

"No, Adam—wait! You need to do it like this, not *this*," Lara's voice fills the silence in the room.

"Yes, but this way worked last time. Don't you remember?" Adam says back defensively.

"Well, trust me, this—"

"Guys. Please," I say, with my eyes still closed. "I'm begging you to stop arguing." I crack open one eye, and I see them both looking at me intently. "Is this how you always speak to each other?"

They both look at each other, tilting their heads slightly. "Sometimes," they both say.

Both of my eyes open fully. Sometimes? *Sometimes?* Every time I am with them, they find one way to argue; it may be something big such as a pillar coming down, or something really small where one of them drops a rag on the floor.

"We're sorry for waking you up, Xander," Adam says calmly.

"No, don't worry about it," I say back, propping myself up higher in my bed. "Since I'm awake, can you guys... talk to me, or something?"

"Sure," they both say at the same time.

"Oh, tell us what happened on that day, then, if you don't mind telling the story," Adam says, still fixing the wall. "We still don't know the full story behind it."

I tell them everything, from when I found the coin, to inside the house, then I tell them about the building under construction, and then me almost dying. The only things I leave out are when Vicky almost fell off the building, our locked eyes, and then our small argument.

I run my fingers along the coin. I took it out when I told them about it. The caked dust and sand still gives it a rough texture, but I've held it too long in my hand for it to be called uncomfortable.

I look down at my torso. They discarded the bandage. They told me that the wound needed time to "breathe", or some crap like that, so all I can see is the white thread of my stitches. A slight purple ring has formed on the outside of my wound, leaving the center of it to be a nice, deep red, slowly turning a light pink over time.

They still won't let me put my shirt on, and last night I was so cold that I was shivering and covered in goosebumps—even *when* they gave me a blanket to cover myself with.

I watch Adam place all of the tools back inside their box, and straighten up, clicking his back as he does so.

"We're done, Xander," Lara says, breaking through my thoughts.

"Okay. Thanks, guys," I say. "I'll see you later."

They both nod, gathering their things, and exit my room.

*****

My lone dagger sticks perfectly in the wall opposite me. I don't always attempt to throw my knives, but I have nothing else to do.

I flip the small silver knife that I found back in the house between both of my hands. The caked dust on the knife almost makes it look more menacing, and I don't even know why. I flip the knife so that I'm holding onto the blade, and then I flip it back around.

I hold the knife in front of me, studying the way the handle of the dagger sticks out of the wall in front of my bed. Then I throw the knife.

Vicky walks into the room as soon as the knife lands in the wall, almost catching her face. Her eyes squint as she shoots daggers at me.

"Sorry," I murmur more to myself than her.

She exhales loudly and pulls out both daggers, then she tosses them to me, both landing in my lap, the sound of them clashing together is the only sound traveling around the room. Unless the awkward tension can make a noise, then the knives were the only thing making a sound.

What *is* her problem? I didn't say anything to her…

Every minute that ticked by were the worst of my life. Every hour I would look at you and think, is he going to wake up today?

Her words ring inside of my skull as I watch her move over to her bed. Of course she will be a little short with me; I almost died. I would have died if she wasn't there to help me—to save me.

"Vicky," I call out to her, but she doesn't respond. "Vicky, what's wrong?" Even though I know what is wrong with her, I want to hear it come out of her mouth. I want her to say the words to me. "Please tell me."

Her back is turned to me as she is sitting on the edge of her bed. "Nothing," she lies.

"Don't say it's nothing, Vicky. Tell me what's wrong."

Before she can reply, Alfredo, but we like to call him Alfie, walks into the room, carrying a big tray with two bowls on top of it.

"Oh, I am sorry. Am I interrupting something?" he says in his thick Italian accent.

"Well—"

"No," Vicky interrupts me, "you're not, Alfie." She rises slightly from her position, casting a fake smile in his direction. "Don't worry about it."

I watch Alfie place the tray down slowly, almost like he feels the weird tension in the room. He wipes a thin layer of sweat from his tanned skin with the back of his hand.

I stare down at the food, feeling hungrier with every second that ticks by.

"I almost died out in the Estate, and now you want to kill me with your food?" I say sarcastically, trying to lighten the mood.

Vicky smirks just slightly, but then it falls, quickly.

Alfie exhales loudly. "Eh! *Tu sei un bastardo.*" He waves his hands around furiously. I can't help but laugh at his sudden outburst. Then he stomps out of the room, giving one last huff before slamming the door shut.

"What's wrong, then?" I ask.

She shakes her head. "Nothing, Xander. It's nothing; I promise. I'm just tired. It's been a long week. A very long week."

"Yeah, you're right it has," I say, looking down at the ground. "I spent most of it unconscious, so…"

"That's not funny, Xander!" Vicky gives me a stern look.

I look down. "Sorry," I mumble. "When was the right time to say something like that?"

"There isn't a right time to say that." She inhales deeply, lowers her voice. "You could have died, Xander."

"I know… I'm sorry."

The silence that follows is deafening, you could hear a pin drop. The only sound that I can hear is the soft conversations of the people in the house.

"Are you going to go up on the roof?" I ask quietly.

She shakes her head slowly. "No, it won't be the same without you there as well."

"Fair enough, but I don't want you to be cooped up in here all day with me." That's a lie, because I would give up everything in a heartbeat to be with Vicky. I just don't know if she feels the same.

"It'll be fine," she replies quietly.

"Fine."

I notice Vicky staring at the wound on my side, then her eyes travel up to a scar on my chest, then finally to my eyes.

My mind wanders back to when Vicky was hanging from that building, that terrified look on her face. And when I fell backward, how she fell on top of me, and the fact that she didn't look into my eyes for a while after that.

I just don't understand *why* she didn't look at me directly.

Vicky reaches over and grabs one of the bowls on the tray. She sits down on her bed, with her legs tightly up against her chest, slowly eating the food.

I reach over slowly, being careful with the wound in my side, and I grab the only bowl left.

"When will you be able to walk again?" Vicky asks quietly. She was so quiet that I hardly heard her.

"Hopefully tomorrow," I say. "Drew is coming here later today to check the stitches."

Vicky winces slightly at the word *stitches* but other than that, she agrees. "Does it still hurt?" Her voice has risen slightly.

"Sometimes," I reply. "Only if I think too much about it." I raise one of my shoulders for a half-hearted shrug.

Vicky nods, raising her hand to place a speck of food in her mouth.

"How was work?" I ask. We don't think of it as "work" per se, it's more like second nature; we just get on with it.

She raises her shoulders slightly. "It was all right," she says. "I didn't find much. I haven't been able to for the past few days..." She said the last few words quietly, almost like she didn't want me to hear them in the first place.

I nod slowly. I don't know why it is so difficult to talk to her; she's my best friend. I should be able to talk to her about anything. I guess my injury *really* hit her hard.

I turn my head toward the door at the sound of a slight knock.

Kyle stands there; his arms behind his back, slightly leaning against the door frame. "Sorry to interrupt your conversation, but—" He turns to face her. "Vicky, I just wanted to inform you that you are allowed the day off tomorrow," he says smoothly.

"How come?" Vicky places the bowl next to her on her bed.

"Well, since Xander is going to be able to start walking again tomorrow, I would like you to help him around. Help him on his feet, stuff like that."

Vicky glances over in my direction. My eyes flick to hers, but then her eyes snap back to Kyle.

"Sure," Vicky says, her eyes flick to me, then back to Kyle again. "I'll help him."

*****

"How's my favorite patient doing?" Drew says as he enters the room.

"I'm your *only* patient, Drew," I say. "And I've been better. There's not much to do when you're lying down in bed twenty-four hours a day."

"Well, today, you are hopefully going to be able to walk again," Drew says. He places a small box on the foot of my bed and walks closer to me. He kneels down, his knees clicking as he does so. He grabs an old gray rag from the box and a small bottle of rubbing alcohol. He tips the clear liquid on the rag; soaking it.

As he places the cold, wet rag on my skin, I don't feel anything—only a cold, tingling sensation, but as soon as he starts to rub against the wound, I can feel the sting.

He squints his dark brown eyes at my wound as he works. "Try not to move too much if you can, Xander," Drew says, suddenly holding a pair of small scissors, and a pair of tweezers.

"Okay," I say quietly, trying not to tense as the cold metal touches my skin.

Drew pulls up one of the small stitches with the tweezers, then he cuts the thin, white thread away.

After about five minutes, he finishes with my stitches. I think Drew was talking to me, keeping me distracted, but I didn't hear any of it. I must have blanked out while he was cutting away the thread.

"All done," he says. He wipes a light sheen of sweat from his forehead, brushing a lock of his ash blond hair from his eyes.

"Thanks, Drew. I don't know what I would do without you," I say, gingerly touching the wound on my side, feeling the line that is now my scar; a permanent reminder of the day I fell.

"Let's not go down that road, Xander." He laughs. "And it's no problem. Anytime." Drew nods, and walks out of the room.

It's weird seeing a wound that once was gushing blood now completely dry, and somewhat clean.

Vicky throws me my plain black T-shirt. It hits me in the face and lands softly in my lap. I slowly look over at her.

"You might want to put that back on," Vicky says, with a smirk glued to her face. She crosses her arms over her chest and looks at me with her eyebrows raised.

"What?" I ask, staring at her and the T-shirt in my hands.

"Are you going to put it on, or am I going to have to help you put it on?" she says.

I smirk. "Do you want to help me put it on?" I ask sweetly, tilting my head to the side slightly, all while trying to hold back a laugh. "Because, you know, I think the wound made me lose feeling in my arms."

Vicky does a scoff, and a laugh at the same time, and shakes her head. "Just shut up, and put the shirt on, will you?"

I let out a small laugh. I slip the T-shirt over my head, and down the side of my torso, being careful when it meets the scar.

I slowly swing my legs over the side of my bed, and gingerly press my feet to the ground. I see Vicky watching my every move, seeing if something will go wrong.

"Xander, it's only been a week," Vicky says sarcastically. "You haven't lost your legs completely."

I shoot her a look. "Yeah, well, it feels like it's been a whole year." When I put pressure on my feet, I start to feel them go numb in a matter of seconds.

I place my hands on the bed and push myself up.

When I stand up, I feel like I've forgotten how to walk. I take one step, and I tumble forward.

Vicky catches me before I fall. One of her arms is snaked around the good side of my waist, while the other is pressed firmly on my shoulder.

"Are you all right?" Vicky whispers as she looks up at me.

"Yeah," I say slowly. "Thanks."

"No problem." She guides me back to my bed, and just like that, I am back on the surface where I was for a whole week. I can't take being on this surface any longer.

I notice Vicky's arms are still wrapped around me. I glance over at her; her face is lowered so that she is staring at her boots.

"Are you ready to try again?" Vicky asks quietly, still staring at the floor intently.

I stare at my legs for a few seconds. I don't want to fall down the instant I stand back up, and I don't want to stay on this bed any longer. I guess I only have one other option.

"Will you help me?" I ask, slowly looking back over at her.

"Of course I will," she says, smiling. "Know that I will always help you, Xan."

I can't help but smile, trying not to let her see the red creeping its way up my throat. "Thanks."

Vicky stands up, letting go of me as she does. She grabs my left hand, swinging it around her neck. Then she slips her other arm around my waist. I stand up slowly, being careful not to put too much weight on Vicky, but also being careful not to crash to the ground.

I steady myself, testing each foot carefully. I can stand, that's a start, but I don't know if I can walk yet.

Vicky takes a tentative step forward, her eyes flickering to me, and the floor. When I take another step forward, a sharp pain shoots up my leg, and I wince.

After an agonizing few steps, I finally make it to the front room. Some people are sitting around the table in the center of the room, and a few are standing around, talking.

When I make it two steps into the room, people stop what they are doing, and they all turn their heads to look over at me.

"Hey, Xander's up!" Adam shouts. People laugh and cheer, and I hide a smile.

Adam walks over to me and swings my arm around his neck, the same way Vicky has. They both sit me down on a seat at the table in the middle of the room, which Ponytail kindly moved out of the way for. I nod to say thank you, and she nods back, retreating backward slightly.

Vicky stands behind me, and Adam stands next to her, then he slaps me on the back. "How are you doing, buddy?" he asks, leaning down slightly so he can talk in my ear.

I nod slowly. "Getting better, thanks."

"That's good to hear, we were afraid you were going to have to stay in that bed, forever." He brushes a strand of his curly, dark blond hair out of his eyes.

Every single person walks up to me one by one, and asks me that same question: "How are you doing?" "How are you feeling?" "Do you need me to do anything?" On and on. It keeps going on for a while. I'm thankful for it though—it shows that they all care.

Joel is the last person to walk up to me, he gives me a small, curt nod. "Glad to see you're up," he says in a bored voice, and I give a small nod back, then he walks away. He said those words to me like he was *told* to say them. I can tell he didn't want to say them to me.

I turn around to look at Vicky, and she looks down at me and raises her eyebrows, then shrugs.

I sit with my hands under my chin, wondering what everyone has been doing for that week while I was in bed.

CHAPTER SIX

As it turns out, the week was the same as if I was never even injured, except for the fact that everyone didn't sleep much— they wouldn't tell me that, but I know, because Kyle told me.

"They're all still worried about you," Kyle said when everyone went to sleep that night. I even wanted to go to sleep myself, but Kyle said that I should talk to him for a bit.

"Why are they? I'm fine now; I'm awake, *and* walking," I said, raising my voice with every passing word.

"Keep your voice lower, please." Kyle looked behind him at all the doors around the room. "Some people think that it was *your* fault that you got injured."

My eyes darted toward the direction of Joel's bedroom. *That damn idiot,* I thought. *Of course it was him who said that.* I curled my hands into tight fists.

I took a deep breath in through my nose. "By 'some people' I think you mean *Joel,* right?" I spat out his name as if it was something revolting I had in my mouth.

"Technically… yes, it was, but everyone was saying how ridiculous that sounded, and—"

I held my hands out to cut him off. "It's fine, Kyle, don't worry. This is just how Joel is. I don't really take it personally. He's just an idiot."

Kyle shook his head slowly. Then he looked around the room. "It's late," he whispered. "You should go and get some rest."

I pressed my hands on the table firmly to help me get up, then I swung my legs out from the chair, and stood up.

"Goodnight," I said to him before I entered my room.

It took him a while before he replied, "Goodnight."

*****

I sit down on my bed slowly, trying my hardest not to wake Vicky up.

I untie my boots and place them both next to my bed on the floor, then I swing my legs up, and rest my head on the jacket.

"You're up late," Vicky whispers. I jerk my head over toward her bed, my neck aches slightly from the fast movement, but I take no notice of it.

Vicky is lying on her side, her arm is under her head, and she stares at me. Even though it is almost pitch-black in the room, I can still see the blue of her eyes; they almost seem to shine.

I lie on my side, facing Vicky. "I was talking to Kyle," I whisper. "What are *you* doing up?"

Vicky exhales through her teeth. "I just couldn't sleep," she says.

I place my arm under my head. "Do you want to talk about it?"

Vicky looks down at the ground, swallowing hard. Then, says nothing.

"Vicky?" I try to get her attention. "It might help if you tell me. Remember you can tell me anything."

"I keep seeing you," Vicky whispers eventually.

"What do you keep seeing?" I ask, still trying to keep my voice as low as possible.

Vicky sniffs slightly. "I..." She swallows again. "I keep seeing that day you fell, Xan. Every time I close my eyes, I see you fall from that building. I can't stop hearing the scream when that piece of metal got stuck inside you." She pauses. "Inside your body."

I wince slightly. All of the events after I fell are a blur, a smear of color and sound that I don't recognize.

Vicky's sniffs pick up speed now. I swing my legs over the bed as quickly as I can and shuffle over to Vicky's bed. She sits up slowly and turns around so that she is facing me. Then I wrap my arms around her and she buries her face in the crook of my neck.

"It's okay," I reassure her. "I'm okay now." I stroke her arm reassuringly.

She suddenly stops sniffing… again. She sucks in a sharp breath, then she slowly gets up from my chest, and wipes her eyes with the back of her hand.

"Are you okay now?" I ask, brushing away a strand of her hair.

She nods her head slowly. "I still don't think I can sleep," she says quietly.

"That's fine," I say. "We can stay up. It will be like when we were little."

Vicky looks over at me and shakes her head. "You don't have to stay up with me." Her voice lowers with every word.

"No, I don't have to, you're right," I say. "But I will."

Vicky looks down at her lap and smiles. "Thank you," she says quietly.

*****

I can finally get back to my job. It's been about a week since I started walking, because they (by "they" I mean Drew) wanted me to heal perfectly. There were a few times where I climbed up on the roof with Vicky without Drew knowing.

The same thing happened when I went up there; I saw the three flickering lights. I didn't tell Vicky I saw them; I don't want her thinking I'm going crazy, so, instead, I just pushed it out of my mind, and pretended that I didn't see anything.

I sit with my elbows resting on the table in the main room, and I pick out the dried berries from inside the bowl, pushing past the grain to get to the ones at the bottom.

"You're going to be hungry later if you just pick out the berries," Vicky says from the other side of the table.

I raise my head and shrug. "I'm not really in the mood for grain." I push the bowl a few inches away from me. "Do you want to finish my food?"

Vicky shakes her head. "No thanks," she says. "But I'm sure you can save it for when we go out."

"Okay, that's a good idea," I say, placing the bowl on the counter behind me. I rise from the table and walk into my room.

The T-shirt that I'm wearing is the same one I wore when I got stabbed with the metal. There is a giant rip, and blood stains the fabric.

I can't use this T-shirt any more; it's too ruined. It's a shame we only have one set of clothes in this damn place. I would kill to change my clothes or even have a *decent* shower. If we *really* needed to wash ourselves, we would have to use a few bottles of water because, in the Estate, we don't have running water. You wouldn't believe that we once did— many, many years ago.

I walk over to Kyle's bedroom, knocking quietly on the old wood.

At first, he doesn't answer, but then he says a quiet, "Come in."

I slowly turn the doorknob and push open the old wooden door.

"Hey, Kyle," I say quietly. "Do you have any spare T-shirts that I can have? I can't use this one, any more."

Kyle places an object on the foot of his bed and gets up from his sitting position, then he pulls out a small box from under his bed. He starts to pull out random objects until he finds what he's looking for.

"Do you think this will fit?" Kyle presents a black T-shirt to me. It look's slightly bigger than my ones, but I think it will do.

"I'm sure it will." I walk closer to him and grab the fabric from his hands. "Thanks."

"No problem," he says back.

I stare at the article on the foot of his bed, slowly picking it up. "What is this thing?" I ask. I can see the slightest piece of silver underneath the caked dust.

"I'm not really that sure," he says. "I found it a few days ago. It was just lying around outside."

I push out the dried dirt and dust, wiping it clean with the hem of my T-shirt. The silver is shinier than I expected it to be. The two flat sides of it are sharp, connecting at the center to create a point.

"It's an arrowhead," I say, still staring at the piece of metal.

"Really?" Kyle asks, leaning in to get a closer look.

"Yeah, look. This part was probably a piece of the shaft, and this part is obviously the arrowhead… it's interesting." The shaft of what was once the arrow has been snapped, leaving a sharp, jagged piece of metal behind. "Where did you say you found this?"

"Just outside the house."

"Oh," I breathe.

"Yeah, exactly."

"Anyway, I'd better get going. I need to change," I say, handing the object back to Kyle.

He pushes it back over to me. "You keep that. I don't have any use for it."

"Are you sure?" I ask.

He nods slowly.

"Thank you for this," I say. "And thanks, again, for the T-shirt." I slowly walk out of his room, admiring the way the sides of the arrowhead are still very sharp. I slip the article in my pocket and walk into my room.

I place Kyle's T-shirt on my bed, and I start to remove my old one. Even though I don't have to be careful any more, I always seem to slow down whenever it comes to my side—I don't want to split the remaining few stitches.

"Oh, sorry, I didn't realize you were getting dressed," Vicky says.

I look over at her, she hangs near the door frame, deciding whether to enter or not. "No, don't worry. I was just changing my shirt," I say.

Vicky walks over to her bed, but I can feel her eyes burning into my back, staring at a scar I got a long time ago.

"It looks like it's getting better," Vicky says.

I turn around and see her staring at the scar on my side. I gingerly touch the center of it, trying not to wince. "Yeah, I guess it does."

Vicky reaches over and runs her index finger along the line of my scar. I suck in a silent breath of air. She looks up at me. "Does it hurt?" she asks, quietly.

I shake my head. "Not any more," I whisper.

Vicky removes her finger quickly. Too quickly, startling me. She steps back a few steps. "W-we'd better get going. Don't want to be late." She grabs her boots from the floor, and her jacket, and swiftly walks out of the room, slamming the door shut as she does so. The sound echoes around my head until I can't take it anymore.

I stare at Kyle's T-shirt on my bed. I shake my head a few times to remove the weird encounter Vicky and I just had, slipping the black fabric over my head. I don't care about the wound on my side… there are more important things to worry about, not just a scar on the side of my body.

I slump down on my bed, grabbing the boots from under my bed, forcefully trying to slip them on my feet. I slow down tying my laces, because I don't want to snap them. I yank my jacket and slip it on my shoulders. I slip my dagger inside my belt, securing it tightly so it doesn't fall out. I grab my black bandana and tie it loosely around my neck, making sure it is tight enough.

I walk over to the door and slowly open it up. Vicky sits at the table, and when she sees me, she smiles. I smile weakly back.

"Hey, I packed you some of the food," Vicky says as she hands me the small woven bag full of food.

I take it carefully, and I strap it on my belt. "Thanks." I nod slowly.

"No problem," Vicky says back, as she ties her red bandana around her neck. "Are you ready to go?"

"Yeah, I guess," I say. "Where's Joel?"

"He left about ten minutes ago." She shakes her head when she sees the expression on my face. "Don't ask, because I have no idea why."

I nod, and we make our way to the door. I grab the backpack just before we exit the door, and I slip it on my shoulders.

I don't know why Vicky is suddenly back to her normal self. It's almost as if she didn't run out of our room, not even five minutes ago. I push it *all* out of my mind and focus on the one thing I actually *woke up* for.

Scavenging.

*****

The heat of the sun bakes my neck as we walk from house to house.

Vicky is talking animatedly about the things she found back when I was still in bed. It may not have been a lot that she found, but she is still excited about what she *did* find. She uses her hands to gesture about every word she is saying.

I'm trying my hardest to listen to what she is saying, but the only thing I can think about is when she touched the scar on my side.

"—don't know what to do. What do you think I should do, Xander?" My ears suddenly perk up to what Vicky is saying.

"The, uh… the first thing you suggested, I guess." I have no idea what Vicky said to me. I don't even know if she gave me more than one option to choose from.

Vicky suddenly stops me with an arm across my chest. She turns around to look at me—blue eyes staring deeply into mine. "Are you in there, Xan?" She points to the side of my head, but I back away, grabbing her forearms.

"Stop it," I warn, dropping her forearms as she laughs away. We continue walking.

"What should you do, sorry?" I ask, keeping my eyes trained on the broken rubble lining the floor.

Vicky sighs. "Oh, you know, I was wondering… if I should ask Joel out?"

My head snaps over to her direction. "WHAT?" I shout, my throat burning.

Vicky punches me hard on the arm. "I'm joking!" she shouts back and laughs. "But that's what you get for not listening to me."

"I'm sorry, Vicky. I'm just really tired," I say. "What did you originally say?"

Vicky laughs. "I was just wondering if you wanted to start on the roofs, and I will take the ground, how does that sound?"

I nod my head slowly. "Sounds good," I say. "Have fun." I start walking toward the closest building.

"You too!" Vicky shouts back as if I was a mile away.

I grab the ledge and heave myself up. I look up and down with every ledge I press my foot against. I try not to heave myself up too hard, even when I feel my hand slipping from the edge.

I look behind me, and I see Vicky walk into one of these houses, adjusting her backpack as she does so.

I push and pull myself up, and over the edge.

The sun blinds my eyes as I look out into the distance. I use my hand to cover my eyes, but as I look on, I can see a slight red glow through my fingers.

77

I pull out a bottle of water from the backpack, and I tip the lukewarm water into my mouth, trying not to down the entire bottle.

When I've quenched my thirst, I drop the bottle back in my pack and zip it back up slightly.

I rise from the floor, ignoring the way my knees click like I'm an eighty-year-old man. I check around on the floor on this roof, and I find nothing but dust and rubble.

I slowly walk over to one side of the roof, and I stretch my legs and arms. I run fast to the other side of the roof, planting one foot on the raised ledge, leaping across the gap. Just like that, I'm flying again, feeling the warm breeze brush against my face, my arms, my hands—everywhere.

I don't always imagine I'm flying, because when you fly, you eventually have to land, then you're back to reality.

When I land on the roof, I skid to a stop, pressing my hand on the hard surface before I fall forward. I stay in a crouched position when I'm looking around on the roof. My eyes scan the whole perimeter of the surface.

Nothing, I think, shaking my head. I run to the other side of the roof, and I leap across the gap, flying over the unknown below.

I do the same thing for every single building: run, jump, scan. Run, jump, scan.

It isn't until the *fifth* building that I actually find something.

I crouch down, picking the object up carefully. This isn't covered in dust and dirt like I thought it would be. I scoop the arrowhead out of my pocket, and I press the objects close together. They are the *exact* same. The new arrowhead seems to be cleaner, so, *whoever* left it here, obviously lost it recently.

That's crazy, I think to myself. No one else is in the Estate other than us.

I drop both of them in my pocket, rising from my position. The sun feels hot against my head, and I wipe away a light sheen of sweat from my forehead with the sleeve of my jacket.

I climb down the side of the building, and when I make it to the bottom, I think about the two arrowheads in my pocket.

"Hey, did you find anything good?" Vicky says when I see her next. We are both hanging around outside a building that we are both thinking of exploring.

"No, nothing good," I say, but I feel like I'm lying to her. "What about you? Did you find anything good?"

"Not really." Vicky shakes her head. "Only a few things. Nothing important."

I nod my head slowly. "Shall we look inside this house? I know you're *dying* to explore inside here." I point out the building to the left.

"Yeah, come on, then." She starts to walk inside the building, gesturing for me to follow her.

When I first walk inside the building, I am hit with a wave of different smells; mildew, sweat, dirt and what almost smells like… rotting corpses. No, that can't be right. Can it?

Vicky seems to notice because her upper lip curls up in disgust. "What the hell died in here?" she whispers.

I laugh. "I'm not sure, but it smells like the dead bodies are growing *new* dead bodies."

Vicky glances over her shoulder at me and laughs.

The house, in general, seems pretty empty. Old chairs and a table lie upside down in the center of the room. A few pictures have been smashed, the glass littering the floor everywhere you step. The wallpaper has been ripped off, leaving a few chunks behind.

We both walk inside the kitchen, and believe it or not, this room seems to be the tidiest, despite the dust and dirt lining the floor.

Vicky starts looking through the cupboards near the floor, and I start with the ones at the top. Every single door I open up, a storm of dust flies out, but there are supplies in here that I thought would *never* be in this house; bandages, pills, rubbing alcohol, hypodermic needles, everything. Everything that we could possibly need.

"Jackpot!" I whisper-shout. I slip the pack off my shoulders and open it up fully. I grab everything I come into contact with, and soon, I'm even *scooping* the things out of the cupboard, into my backpack.

"Drew and Liv are going to be so happy when we get back," Vicky says as she stands next to me.

"I know. At least they—" I'm cut off by the sound of glass shattering.

Vicky and I glance once at each other, and then to the source of the noise. I zip the pack up and slip it on my shoulders, still staring at where the sound came from.

I slide my knife out of my belt, holding it out in front of me. We both slowly walk out of the kitchen.

Vicky points to the closed basement door a few meters away from us. "It sounded like it came from down there," she whispers in my ear. "Maybe it's just a rat."

I crouch down next to the door to the basement, holding the knife tighter in my hand, making my knuckles white. "Stay behind me," I whisper.

She crouches behind me, slowly placing her hands on my shoulders. Her breathing picks up speed. I can feel the rise and fall of her chest against my back. She's so close to me that I can feel her warm breath on the back of my neck.

I undo the open lock, slowly sliding out the padlock. I grab the handle of the door, and in one motion, I yank it upward.

I point the business end of the dagger at whatever is in the basement.

As soon as the dust clears, my eyes open wide to what is in here.

We are staring at the faces of more survivors.

CHAPTER SEVEN

I don't know how long we've been staring at these people; a minute? Two? An hour? Ten years?

They stare at us wide-eyed. Vicky's grasp on my shoulder tightens, causing my back to arch slightly. Her chest presses against my back, keeping us close together.

A woman, probably the same age as Kyle stares at me with wide, green eyes. Soot, grime, and dirt covers half of her hollow face. Her light brown hair is pulled into a messy ponytail, and strands of her hair hang loose over her eyes. Her mouth has made a perfect O as she continues to stare at us.

A little girl is next to her; she has the same amount of soot and grime all over her face. Her dark blonde hair is tied in two plaits down the sides of her face, but she stares up at me with wide, light brown eyes. Her face is just as hollow as the older woman.

I can see the fear clearly written across both of their faces, but I would have thought that since we have been staring at each other, for what feels like hours, they would have calmed down slightly. I reach my hand out slowly, but they back away quickly.

I guess not.

It's only now that I manage to find my voice. "It—it's... okay," is all I manage to say to them. I don't know who I'm trying to calm down; them or myself.

I see the mother staring at the tip of my not-so-subtle dagger. I retract the blade, and tuck it inside my belt, making sure that the blade is not within eyeshot of the new survivors.

"It's okay," I repeat, holding my hand out to them. "We won't hurt you." My voice stays light and soft, but inside my head is screaming. We just found new survivors! Something we have *all* been looking for, for *years*!

I calm my own voice inside my head and inhale through my nose—smelling the rotten smell of corpses—and out of my mouth.

The duo stare at my outstretched hand, then back up at my eyes. I nod my head slowly.

The older woman presses her calloused hand into mine slowly. Her hand feels extremely dry, almost like holding a roll of sandpaper.

I pull her slowly into the light. She uses her hand to block the blinding glare from her eyes, and when she's fully out, her eyes squint, but her hand goes back to her side.

If the basement was unlocked, then why didn't they leave? Maybe they were scared to, my mind marvels. Maybe they thought they were alone, so that's why they didn't try and find survivors.

"What's your name?" I ask softly, trying to keep my voice the same pitch.

The woman doesn't answer my question, instead, she looks at the younger survivor, and grabs her hand, slowly pulling her behind her back.

"Mine's Xander. This is Vicky," I say. "What's yours?"

She opens her mouth to speak, but no words come out. She coughs, covering her mouth with her hand. Dust flies out. "M-my n-n-name i-is... Sera," the woman stutters.

"Sera, don't be afraid, we are just like you. We too are survivors," I say with a smile.

Sera smiles and looks down at the little girl standing next to her. "This... this is my daughter, Cassia."

I smile at Sera and kneel down to Cassia's height. "Hi, Cassia. My name's Xander." Her wide brown eyes search around my face, resting on my eyes. "How old are you?"

"Umm...," Cassia starts, playing with her fingers. "I'm... ten."

"Ten? Wow! You're almost an adult," I say with a big smile on my face.

Cassia laughs lightly. At least they aren't scared of us any more, I think.

Cassia suddenly reaches forward, pressing her cold, small hands against my cheeks. I smile. "Are you... real?" she all but whispers, the sound passing through dry lips.

I nod, my smile slowly fading. "I'm real, Cassia," I whisper. "We are real."

She lets go of my cheeks slowly, and I start to stand back up.

I turn to Sera. "Do you have any major injuries? Scratches? Burns? Anything you might want checking?"

Sera checks her arms, then shakes her head. "No... nothing major. Only a few cuts and scrapes." Sera's and Cassia's voices sound really hoarse. I wonder how long it has been since they had some water.

"How long have you guys been in there?" Vicky says, pointing to the basement door.

Sera and Cassia both look back. "About a week," Sera says, wiping something out of her eye. At first, I thought it was a tear, but she wiped it away so quickly, I didn't get a chance to get a good look at it.

"Is it just you two?" Sera asks.

We shake our heads. "No, there are a few more people that are living with us," I say.

"How long have you lived there?" Sera asks.

"Quite a few years," Vicky and I say at the same time, giving each other a sidelong glance.

"Would you like to come with us?" Vicky asks. "We have clothes, food, fresh water. We even have a couple of doctors!"

Sera shakes her head. "Oh, no. That's very kind of you two, but I don't want to be an inconvenience."

"Nonsense," Vicky says. "We would love it if you could stay with us."

Sera shrugs slowly. "Well, if it's all right with you. Thanks."

"No problem," Vicky says.

"Come on," I say. "I think it's time to meet the others."

*****

"Everyone!" I shout. "Come into the main room! Now!"

Sera and Cassia stand next to Vicky at the entrance of the room, while I stand a few feet in front of them.

"What the hell, Xander?" Adam says. "You don't need to scream your damn head off."

When Adam and Lara walk into the room, both of their eyes open wide, almost popping out of their sockets as they stare at the two survivors behind me.

A few seconds later, Kyle, Ponytail, Blinky, Drew and Liv, and finally, Alfie walk into the room. I hear someone gasp aloud, but I couldn't tell who it was.

"Guys—" I grab hold of Sera's shoulders and bring her slightly closer. "This is Sera, and this is Cassia."

No one says anything for a while. All their mouths are ajar, and their eyes are wide with wonder and amazement.

Say something, guys, I want to say out loud, but I can't. *You're going to frighten them.*

I notice Liv's eyes searching down Sera's body, taking in what she is wearing, the state of her skin, everything. Everything that makes Sera cower away behind me.

Okay... it has been over two minutes, and nobody has said anything, I think, angrily.

"Someone say something, please," I finally say, trying to get their attention, all the while keeping my voice calm and soft.

Alfie walks up to them before I was forced to pull someone forward. "*Ciao*," he greets. "My name is Alfredo, but you can call me Alfie." He offers a hand to Sera, and she takes it with a smile. Alfie shakes her hand not-too-softly, making Sera almost wrench away.

"Hi," is all Sera says. She looks down at the ground, shuffling uncomfortably on the spot.

I push Sera and Cassia forward a few steps. "Sera, this is Lara, Adam, Kyle, Drew, Liv, and you've already met Alfie."

Sera points to the two red heads standing near the back. "What are their names?"

I shoot a quick glance over at Vicky, her eyes open widely, and she shrugs. "Uh... this is Ponytail, and that is Blinky." My voice was at the right volume so that only Sera and Cassia could hear me.

Sera shoots me a confused look, but I shrug it off to say I'll tell you later. She nods slowly.

"So, Sera," Kyle starts, stepping closer. "Where did you come from?"

"We're not really sure," Sera replies.

"So, you were here this whole time?" Kyle looks over at Vicky and me. "I wonder why we didn't see you before."

I look down, embarrassed. "Uh... well—"

"It's because we were hidden," Sera interrupts me, "in our basement."

"You were hidden?" Adam steps up. "From what?"

"Uh, well..."

"That's enough questions for today, guys," I interrupt, turning to look at Sera and Cassia. "I think it's time to get cleaned up. Don't you?"

They both look down at their clothes and nod their heads quickly.

"Liv, can you help them get cleaned up, please?" I ask, turning around to face her.

"Sure," she replies. "Come on, girls. Let's get that crap off your face."

As soon as Liv says that, Sera starts to run her index finger across her cheek, noticing that a thin layer of, indeed, *crap* has come off her cheek.

I swing the backpack off my shoulders, throwing it to Drew. "There's a few medical things in there for you, Drew."

"Thanks, guys," he says, opening the pack, revealing the stuff. "This stuff will keep us alive for a few months... hopefully." He looks up at me as he says the last word, raising his eyebrows slightly.

"What are you looking at me for?" I ask while laughing.

Drew shakes his head. "No reason." He laughs and brushes a few strands of his growing hair out of his eyes.

I look over at Vicky. She shrugs. "It's true," she whispers.

I shake my head while I laugh. "Shut up."

We both laugh and walk into our room.

When we sit down, Adam walks into the room, and sits down opposite me, on Vicky's bed. I look over at Vicky with a confused look on my face.

"Xander, are you sure about those two? Did you ask them questions?" he whispers, leaning closer to me.

"Adam, what the hell are you talking about? Of course I asked them questions. What, did you honestly think that I would let them in here without even knowing their names?" I say, pointing a few times at the door.

Adam scratches the back of his neck. "Okay, keep your voice down. Are you sure they're cool? I don't want to wake up tomorrow seeing that everything I own has been stolen."

I laugh. "Adam, seriously. It's a grown woman and a ten-year-old girl. What are they going to do to you?"

Adam shakes his head. "I don't know, but, believe me, ten-year-old girls can be very vicious."

I look over at Vicky and we both burst out laughing. "What, are you telling me that you're scared of Cassia?"

Adam shakes his head quickly... too quickly. He slowly rolls his broad shoulders. "N-no of course not. I just want to be prepared in case they... I don't know... attack me, or something."

I can't help but laugh because it's funny, and it's funnier because Vicky is laughing with me, and it makes Adam look quite mad.

"Adam, don't worry that pretty little head of yours. They are *both* harmless," I say, finishing the conversation.

"Whatever, Xander, but don't come running to me if Cassie—or whatever you called her—comes running at you with a dagger. Okay?"

I pretend to shoot him with my hand. "Gotcha." I wink.

Adam rolls his eyes as he gets up from the bed. He slowly walks to the door. "Thanks for calling me pretty," he says before walking out of the room.

Vicky laughs. "He is such a baby."

"I know." I laugh. "Adam's a baby dressed in a huge eighteen-year-old's body."

Vicky laughs lightly, then places a lock of her hair behind her ear. "I wonder why Sera and Cassia were hidden in the basement in the first place."

I shrug. "I'm not sure," I say. "But, wouldn't you want to hide for the rest of your life if you were the only person in the Estate?"

Vicky lifts one shoulder. "I guess," she whispers. "But, maybe they were hiding from *someone.* Not just because they were alone. It was just slightly weird, that's all."

"Vicky, if they were hiding from someone, we would have found them." I get up from my bed, and I sit next to her. "We don't *really* know for sure how long they were in there for. They did say a week, but that could have been a lie, just so we wouldn't ask a lot of questions."

I don't know why everyone is so worried about having new people with us. It was the exact same when we bought everyone else in. Sera and Cassia shouldn't be treated any different just because we haven't found anyone for a long, *long* time.

The survivors in the next room are now *just* like us.

"I know what you mean, Xan, but remember; there are only a few rooms in this building, and they are *all* taken," Vicky says. "And what about jobs? It takes a while to get used to the jobs we have here."

I slump, suddenly feeling very tired, very stressed. *Maybe we should all go to the Wastelands, instead,* I think.

"I'm not sure that we'll be able to, Xan," Vicky says suddenly.

"What?" I ask, furrowing my brows.

"You said that maybe we should go to the Wastelands."

I tilt my head slightly. "Did I say that out loud?" I ask.

Vicky nods her head, then laughs. "You're so weird." She punches me on the arm.

Before she can punch me again, I grab her fist and hold it above her head. "Were you going to punch me again?" I ask sweetly, my grin growing larger.

Vicky stares at me for a long time. "I was thinking about it." She looks up at her fist, then back to my eyes. "Then again… I don't want to knock you out or anything."

I laugh then stand up, still holding onto her hand. "You'll have to be able to reach my face first." I stand a few good inches above her. Her face is just about level with my neck.

She pulls her wrist away from my grasp. "Yes, but, I have a good aim for here—" She slaps me in the stomach.

I double over slightly. "Yeah… good point. I'll keep that in mind."

"Good." She smiles. "Glad that's settled."

"Come on," I say. "Let's just get something to eat."

*****

Everyone sits around the table. Well, everyone apart from Sera, Cassia, Liv and Joel.

We are all chewing on the grain, oats and dried berries, no one uttering a single word. I am kind of thankful for it, though; I like the silence; it's peaceful, and, then, of course, it gets interrupted.

"Hey, guys, sorry I'm late," Joel says as he enters the house.

I exhale a silent irritated breath of air between my teeth.

"Where have you been? You were supposed to come back a while ago," Kyle says with a slightly frustrated tone to his voice.

"Oh, you know, I was out and about," Joel says, grabbing a bowl from the side and filling it with his hands. "Doing my job." He said the last part so quietly, that I almost thought he didn't say anything at all.

I look over at Vicky, and she rolls her eyes. I nod my head as if to agree with her, slowly looking back down at my bowl.

Joel swings his pack over his shoulder, smacking it down on the table.

I curl my upper lip, leaning back slightly. "Joel, do you mind? We are trying to eat. We don't want to see your sweaty backpack. I would actually like to keep my food in my stomach." Some people snicker, but I don't smile; I keep my face as emotionless as possible.

The look Joel gives me after that could kill, and I swear— I swear, I felt a knife pierce through my chest.

"If you're not careful, *Xander,* this"—he lifts up the pack, pointing it in my direction—"might end up somewhere very unpleasant."

I push my bowl to the side, almost making it tip over the edge, and I lean forward. "Is that a threat, Joel?"

Joel drops the pack to the ground, making a loud noise. "Maybe it is. Maybe it isn't. Maybe we will never know."

I curl my hands into tight fists.

Vicky places her hand on my leg, and I look over at her. She shakes her head, mouths *don't* like she knows what I might do—like she can read my mind.

I can actually feel the awkwardness from each person traveling around the room. You could almost reach forward and tear it apart with your bare hands, or cut straight down it with a knife.

Adam shifts uncomfortably on the spot next to me, taking a quick glance over at Drew. I can see it in the corner of my eye, even when my gaze is locked on Joel's.

"Okay, okay. That's enough, guys," Kyle interrupts. "Xander, why don't you go and calm down." Kyle looks over at me and nods encouragingly.

I scowl at Joel. "Gladly." I push myself up from the table loudly, not really caring if I startle anyone.

Vicky's concerned blue eyes are the last thing I see before I slam the door shut behind me.

CHAPTER EIGHT

It was childish, really. I should never have slammed the door shut in front of *everyone,* but when Joel said that to me, something inside my head just snapped. I'm almost positive I would have punched his smug face if it wasn't for Vicky calming me down with just one touch to my leg.

My hands shake at my sides, as if ready to strike a certain person, and I stuff them under my legs, calming them down slightly.

The door opens not even a few minutes later; Vicky glances over at me, smiles, then looks down to the floor. She closes the door quietly behind her, lingering there for a few seconds before taking one step forward.

I don't dare look up again. I can't handle the embarrassment that is probably written all over my face; so instead, I keep my face emotionless.

I was so caught up in my own thoughts, that I didn't even hear, or feel Vicky come and sit next to me. She's so close to me now that her arm is pressed up against mine; she doesn't seem to notice, so I don't say anything.

I intertwine my hands together, pressing my thumbs together firmly, making them turn a shade of white.

"It's not your fault, you know?" Vicky's voice is calm, quiet... almost inaudible. She looks over at me. Smiles.

"But," I whisper, keeping my face impassive, "why do I feel like such an idiot?"

"Because Joel pestered you." She turns her body to look at me straight on, the grin dropping from her face. "Xander, this isn't your fault. If you would have punched Joel, sure, you might have felt better, but it doesn't mean anything will be solved. You could come out worst of the two of you, and I don't want to see that happen to you."

What she is saying is true, so I don't know why my anger sometimes gets the best of me.

"Thanks, Vicky." I laugh, then swing my arm around her shoulder. "What would I do without you?"

Vicky laughs, then jabs her finger in my good side. "Probably something dangerous."

I scoff quietly. "*Please.* 'Danger' is my middle name."

"If you say so, Xan. You don't want *this* to happen again, do you?" she says, grazing her hand along my healing wound.

I look down at her hand pressed against my side. "I don't know." I look back over at her. "Sometimes it's nice for someone to worry about you."

Vicky turns beet red, then looks down quickly. "Well, someone has too!" she says a bit too loudly.

I hold my hands up in a mock surrender. "Hey, calm down, it was a joke," I laugh.

We stay silent for a while. I don't know exactly how long for, but it probably was a while because all of the lights from the main room have been turned off.

I exhale loudly. "Come on, I think we should get to sleep. You know how hard it is to wake me up."

Vicky laughs. "Don't remind me." She gets up from my bed and smooths out her shirt. "If you don't get up on time, I am going to throw water on your face, I hope you know that."

I smile. "Got it."

Vicky rolls her eyes, then sits on her bed. "Goodnight," she says quietly.

"Night," I say, before turning the light off.

*****

I'm dreaming that I'm running around in the Estate. Vicky runs with me; her hair blowing behind her in dark, long strands. She is running a few feet in front of me, so I'm left trailing behind her, staring at her back as she runs faster, pushes harder. We kick up sand and dust with each tread on the hard-packed earth, and it fills my mouth and eyes.

I'm sweating from exertion, but I don't stop and I don't slow down. I can't. My legs are the only thing that I can't take control of. The world around me blends into one color; a long expanse of light orange and dark yellow which is slowly turning white under the light of the scorching sun.

I don't know how long it took me, but it's only now that I realize where we are heading; we are running full speed for the Wastelands.

The old buildings disappear behind us as we run straight into the desert. I can feel the shift from the hard stone below my feet, to the soft, soft sand below me.

I can feel sweat rolling down the back of my neck as I look at the expanse of orange and yellow. It's so beautiful, so natural that it looks like a painting I've never seen before.

I take a glance over my shoulder, and there I see how wide the Estate really is. It's incredible. Hardly any words can describe this amazing, ancient place.

Dust and rocks fly around my boots as I skid to a stop.

Now I can *finally* control my own legs. It's almost as if they *wanted* me to go to the Wastelands. Like they *wanted* me to venture into the unknown.

"This is what you wanted, wasn't it?" Vicky's voice sounds distant, an echo that carries on for a long time; almost like what I heard when I got stabbed.

"It is. It really is," I reply, sounding like I'm underwater.

A sudden whistling sound can be heard from a few miles away, and I start, whipping my head from side to side. My eyes scan around the empty expanse, trying to find the source of the noise.

The world slows down as I hear a blood-curdling scream.

And that's when I see the arrow impaled deep inside Vicky's chest.

I wake with a start.

I sit up in bed, sweat dripping from my forehead, down to my legs. I look over at Vicky; she is sitting up in bed, with a bowl of grain and oats in her lap. She looks worried—terrified, even; the same look she wore when she got shot with the arrow. I squeeze my eyes shut, pushing those thoughts from my head.

"Bad dream?" she whispers.

I nod slowly. "Yeah." My voice comes out a whisper through dry lips and a sore throat. My tongue feels like sandpaper, scraping around my mouth.

"Do you want to talk about it?"

The arrow inside Vicky's chest flashes across my eyes. My breath hitches inside my throat, and I close my eyes, *willing* the thoughts to go away.

I shake my head. "N-no. Sorry."

Vicky gets up from her bed to sit next to me. "Hey, you don't have to be sorry. I'm always here for you if you need to talk. Always."

I nod. "Thanks, Vicky."

"No problem." She reaches over and grabs a bowl full of food. "Here, eat this. You must be hungry."

"A little bit." I nod my thanks as she passes me the bowl and a bottle of water—something to soothe this dry throat of mine.

"I'll be in the main room when you're ready to go." Vicky reaches for her jacket and boots, holding them over one shoulder.

"Thanks, again," I say. "I'll be done in a few minutes."

"Take your time. There's no need to rush." She smiles before closing the door behind her, the soft *click* echoing around the small room.

I slowly pick at the grain and oats in the bowl. What I wouldn't give to have a *real* breakfast; one that actually fills me up. One that actually has a *taste*. Not one we found lying around inside a crate that could have been there longer than we were.

I take a swig of my water, then I go back to eating, all while thinking of the nightmare I just experienced, even though I try my hardest not to, it just keeps coming back to me.

It makes me want to scream out—in pain or frustration or stress or anger, I can't tell anymore.

I may not be afraid of dying, but I am afraid of Vicky dying—the person that matters most.

*****

My trusty knife rubs against my skin as I walk in rhythm with Vicky.

The morning sun feels like it's singeing my hairs off; one by one. I run my fingers through it, brushing it back so it cools my forehead slightly. *And* so it's out of my eyes. It hardly does the first thing. I just leave it, continuing forward.

Sweat rolls down my neck and escapes through the hem of my T-shirt. If I wasn't wearing a black top and a dark jacket, I'm sure I would be much cooler, but no.

Every few minutes, flashes of my dream—nightmare—run across my vision, making my breathing stop, then start, faster, harder. It's making my palms sweat.

And Vicky has no idea.

She doesn't know that she died in my dream. Should I tell her? Will she be scared of me? She'll more than likely be angry with me, but I don't know why she would. Maybe she will understand. I don't know. I don't *know*.

The scariest thing is: the arrow that killed Vicky is the same arrow that Kyle found, and like the one I found around in the

Estate. I must have had it on my mind for a while if it turned up in my dream—my nightmare.

The arrowhead suddenly feels heavy in my pocket, almost like it wants me to fall to the ground. It's like it knows it killed my best friend in my nightmare. It burns against my leg, and I try to ignore it.

"Xander?" Vicky says. "Are you all right?"

I slowly look over at her, trying to act nonchalant even though my head is screaming. "Yeah," I lie, sounding like a whisper.

She exhales loudly, almost like she heard the lie pass my lips. "I guess you're still pretty shaken by that dream, huh?"

She knows me too well.

I can never lie to her.

I nod slowly, finally admitting it. "I guess I am. It was pretty… traumatic, to say the least."

"You still don't want to talk about it, do you?" Her voice is a whisper as it fills my ears.

I shake my head, wanting, *begging* her to change the subject.

"I think it's time we had some lunch," Vicky says as she climbs up to the roof of one of these buildings, getting herself comfortable.

We never fail to eat on the roofs; it keeps us, and our food away from the dirt and rubble on the ground.

Once I've climbed up the same building, I swing myself around and sit on the edge, making sure my legs dangle over the ledge.

I brush off the backpack, pulling out two bottles of water. As I start to fish out the last bottle of water, my finger gets caught on something cold and thin. I furrow my brows as I pull it out slowly, trying to remember when I snatched a silver bracelet that is too small to fit around my wrist—*any* male wrist.

The realization hits me faster than I thought it would; I picked it up because it reminded me of Vicky. It was the only good thing I found that day. It was the only thing that caught my eye. I can't believe I *just* remembered it was in my backpack.

Vicky notices my slowness, and halts eating from her pile to look over at me.

I untangle the chain from my fingers and hold it out in front of her. "This is for you," I finally say, smiling. "Sorry if you hate it." I said the last part as a joke, knowing Vicky will get what I'm talking about; it's what I said when I gave her the ring. It's going to be what I say every time I get her something nice. It's a running joke we have.

Vicky laughs lightly as she tentatively reaches out and grabs the bracelet from my fingers. "Xan... it's... it's beautiful." She looks over at me, then wraps her arms around my neck. I rest my hands on her waist. We hug longer than necessary, and I feel Vicky's arms tighten slightly around my neck. "Thank you."

"No problem," I say. "Anytime."

Vicky lifts herself up from me, smiling widely, and puts the bracelet on her left wrist. "It matches my ring," she says, still twirling it around her wrist.

I look at the ring on her finger. I remember when I first gave that to her. She was so happy with it that she almost kissed me on the mouth, but she stopped herself. I would be lying if I said I wasn't *slightly* disappointed afterward.

I slip the leather pouch from my belt and I pull out some of the food that I stored for today. They taste as bland as they always do. I break apart a dried piece of the berry between my teeth, pulling it apart with my tongue.

The afternoon sun brightens up the sand in the Wasteland drastically, blinding me. I squint against the bright, bright light, looking further out. Just a few buildings down to the right of me is a particular structure that is almost completely broken beyond repair. Vicky and I didn't even dare to try and find stuff in that place.

If I squint hard enough, I think I can see Joel a mile or two away from us standing on a roof, staring out in the Wastelands. He's not doing anything—just staring. I don't actually blame him for taking a small break; it's boiling hot out here today.

I wipe the sweat off my forehead, the heat almost agreeing with what I said inside my mind.

Once I finish the amount of food I want, I pull out a bottle of water and sip slowly on the warm liquid, trying to soothe my parched throat. I tie the bag back to my belt, leaning back slightly, bracing my hands on the roof, letting the sun warm my face.

"You're not hungry?" Vicky asks, getting my attention.

Without looking at her, I reply, smoothly, "I don't have much of an appetite right now."

Vicky doesn't say anything after that. What *do* you say to a person that says they don't have an appetite?

"Well, the food is always there if you want it, I guess." She has a nonchalant way of speaking, but I can tell, deep down, she is slightly frustrated. We've known each other for too long for me to call it a miss. Maybe it's because I didn't tell her about my dream. Maybe it was the tone of my voice. I don't know.

"Do you think it was wrong of me?" I hear myself say, opening my eyes to look over at her.

She stops eating, placing the bag next to her. "What was wrong of you?" She wipes her mouth even though nothing was there in the first place.

"The thing with Joel?"

"Oh." Vicky looks down at her lap, then shuffles slightly on the ledge. "I don't know," she says. "I mean, sure, he *does* deserve to be punched, but it wouldn't solve anything. He'll just end up punching you back. Harder."

"Well—"

"Do you remember when he slapped you when you were twelve?" Vicky interrupts me.

"How could I forget?" I smirk to myself remembering the time I slapped him back harder—and I mean *harder*. I can still hear the noise of my hand meeting his jaw.

"See, that smirk right there. You're remembering the time that you slapped him, aren't you?"

I laugh. "Of course. How could I forget that pure, precious moment?"

"It would be just like that if you would have punched him. He will do it back *twice* as hard."

"It would be worth it, though," I say as Vicky turns to look at me. "I could wipe that ugly smug smile off his face."

Vicky laughs, looks down. "I don't think you would be able to punch his face hard enough…" She shakes her head. "But that's not the point."

"Can you believe that when we first met him, we were *nice* to him?" I say, curling my upper lip in disgust.

Vicky's face lightens up, just like she remembered something really important. "Can I tell you a secret?"

I lean forward slightly. "Always."

Vicky leans down to look at me straight in the eyes. "A little birdie told me that she had a crush on Joel when he first came here."

I laugh a little too loud. "Wow! That's hilarious, and kind of gross at the same time."

"Tell me about it."

"Who was it?" I ask. "Liv?"

She shakes her head.

"It couldn't have been Ponytail or Blinky, so… was it Lara?"

Vicky smirks and nods her head slowly. "Yeah."

I shake my head despite me believing it. "What was she *thinking*?"

"She definitely doesn't like him now. In fact, she *despises* him," Vicky says, brushing a strand of hair behind her ear.

"Is there *anyone* that actually likes him?" I ask, already knowing the answer.

"Well, I think Blinky and Ponytail do. I saw Joel talking to them, and they were laughing—silently, of course, but they were still laughing."

"That's not like them to like someone like him." I furrow my brows, not believing what Vicky says, but, somehow it does sound plausible. "Maybe they were just being nice. You know how kind Ponytail and Blinky can be."

Vicky shrugs, not saying any more. I don't continue with the conversation. Instead, I look out into the distance again, letting the sun warm my face.

"I'm bored," Vicky suddenly says after a while. I look over at her. "Do you want to go back? I'm tired, and I just want to get back to my bed and sleep."

"Let's do one more house and then sure, we can go. Then you can sleep 'till your heart's content," I say back.

Vicky huffs, and says a quiet "Fine" under her breath.

We both decide to just search through the house we are sat upon, since we are both too tired to go looking for a house we haven't found yet.

Surprisingly, the door to this house is locked. It must have locked behind us when we left it that time. The doors are never, and I mean *never,* locked.

"Are you sure it's locked? It might just be stuck," Vicky suggests. "We just did this house only a few weeks ago."

"No, the doorknob would turn if it was just stuck. I can't move it left or right," I say, trying to push the door open, but to no avail. I drop it out of frustration, uttering a curse under my breath.

I slide my trusty knife from my belt, and I start to pick at the stubborn lock of this old door, muttering incoherent sentences under my breath.

After an *agonizing* few minutes, I finally manage to snap the lock off, it landing with a *clank* against the hard ground.

"Finally!" I holler, sliding my knife back inside my belt.

I almost wanted to give up about thirty seconds after I started, but Vicky said no. She has a good way of telling me what to do.

The house looks exactly the same as the others. Haven't people ever heard of decorating? Old pictures of the families have been smashed to the point where I can't actually see the faces any more. Most of the wallpaper has survived, but some of it has been ripped by what looks like the claws of an animal.

I shake my head, pushing the thoughts from my head.

"If you take upstairs, I'll start searching down here," I say, making Vicky nod her head.

"Sure," she says, before taking the steps up two at a time.

I search around the room for anything we can use. I walk over to a closed set of drawers, slowly pulling open the creaky, and somewhat dusty top drawer. Inside are a few papers, nothing interesting. No juicy information. Only business types of letters. One is a letter addressed to an employee talking about the risk of redundancy because the company went bankrupt. This person obviously didn't have time to mail it before... well, *this* happened.

I find myself reading most of the letters in here, even though my head screams for me to stop, that it is *none of my business,* but I can't seem to stop. I push away some of the blank papers, trying to find more letters when something underneath them shines silver. I pull it out slowly.

At first, I thought it was another knife, but it isn't. The handle has a very intricate design carved into the metal; it is bigger, *bulkier* than the blade, but comfortable to grip. I feel my hand letting go of the handle only to grab back onto it. It feels nice to hold.

I think I remember my dad used to have one of these lying around in our old house. He always used to pick dirt from under his nails with it. I think I only saw him use it properly a few times in his life.

The article I'm holding in my hand is a letter opener. I think, at least.

The sides of the blade aren't as sharp as the tip. When I press my finger on the tip, blood starts to flow out like a red, sticky river.

I hiss as I retract my finger, wiping the crimson liquid on my pants as I do so.

I slide the letter opener in my belt and I start searching around the room for more things to take back home.

Nothing. Not even any medical things. I can't leave here with only *one* thing. I decide to play it quick and easy. I yank one of the papers from the drawer I found the letter opener in and I stuff it inside my pocket.

I didn't get time to read this letter.

I'll read it later if I have the chance.

I run up the stairs two at a time, finally making it to the landing.

"Hey, Vicky, do you have any Band-Aids?" I ask, inspecting my wound, feeling it throb slightly. "I cut my finger. It hurts like a—Vicky?"

Vicky doesn't respond to my question. I look inside a bedroom, and I see Vicky standing there, staring at something intently, moving her head from side to side.

Then I notice what she is staring at; she is looking at herself in a mirror. A very large mirror at that. It's big enough that it reaches the ceiling.

"I think that's a *little* too big to bring back home, don't you think?" I ask sarcastically, stepping closer to her. My arm brushes hers as I step up next to her.

"No, you idiot. I was just looking. I haven't seen my reflection for... I-I don't even know how long for."

I peek at myself in the mirror. What I see takes me aback slightly. I see a face with a prominent jawline, almond-shaped eyes, and a small to medium-sized nose. The darkness of the room makes my olive skin look darker. I look older than a sixteen-year-old. That's probably because I have hair that falls messily over my forehead, and stubble growing on my chin, cheeks and throat.

Mine and Vicky's blue eyes are the only things that seem to shine in this room.

"Huh. So, *that's* what I look like now?" I say, interrupting the silence. "Boy, do *I* look like a mess." I run my hand through my hair, messing it up even more than it already was.

Vicky looks at me through the mirror, her eyes narrow slightly, almost like she is going to tell me off for something.

Vicky spins on her heel to look at me properly. "It's probably because of this," she says, running her hand across my jawline. "You look older than your age."

"You're right." I stare at Vicky for what seems like a while, but it may have only been for a few seconds, then she slowly looks down.

She turns around and looks back at herself in the mirror. "But have you seen *my* hair? It's like I just got out of bed." She lifts her braid up, letting it fall behind her back.

"That's not true. Your hair always looks perfect," I say, picking up her braid, running her soft hair through my fingers.

Vicky smiles, looks down, brushes a few strands behind her ear. I slowly drop her braid, my hand brushing her back softly.

"What was it you wanted?" Vicky asks quickly, turning around to look at me, slightly backing away.

"Just a Band-Aid, if you have one."

"Oh, yeah, sure. I think I have a few," Vicky says as she slips the pack off her shoulders. She pulls out a first-aid kit and pulls out one long strip that is my Band-Aid.

I reach my hand out to take it, but Vicky retracts her arms, shaking her head.

"It's fine, I'll do it for you." She unwraps the paper, then pulls my hand toward her. "Damn, that looks bad. What the hell did you cut yourself on?"

I pull the letter opener from my belt and show her it, noticing there is a dot of my blood on the tip.

Vicky nods, not saying anything else. Her fingers slowly unwrap the packaging, carefully placing the material over my wound. "Typical you."

"What?" I ask, laughing as I look down at her.

"You always find *one* way to hurt yourself." She looks up as she works, then back down.

"Maybe I just like it when you fix me up."

Vicky doesn't look back up at me, but I see her smile even though she tries to cover it up with her hair.

The injury is still gushing blood, emanating a metallic smell that lingers around the room. She wraps the material around my finger once more, then after a few seconds, I feel my finger throb like my heartbeat—faster than usual.

"Thanks," I say, smiling down at her. "Lifesaver."

She smiles back, packing away her stuff. "Hardly." She laughs. "You're welcome."

I decide to break the silence again. "Do you want to go back now?"

Vicky looks over at me and nods quickly. "Yes. *Please.*"

"Lead the way."

*****

When we get back, two people are sitting around the small table in the center of the room.

I almost didn't recognize them.

"Sera? Cassia? Wow, you two look really different," I say, stepping closer to them.

Sera and Cassia are both dressed simply in black pants and gray T-shirts, boots on their feet. Sera has let her light brown hair fall loosely over her shoulders, almost making her look younger. Cassia has her dark blonde hair tied in one high ponytail, exposing her young, now-healthier face.

Liv has done a great job at scrubbing away the dirt on their faces. I need to remember to thank her later.

"You two look... like... us," I say.

"Thanks, Xander," they both say at the same time, smiling.

I smile back. I'm just about to open my mouth to say *you're welcome,* but I don't get a chance to.

"Well, well, well. Look who it is." Joel's deep voice fills my ears.

I freeze, staring at Sera and Cassia, who both are staring at Joel with wide eyes. I finally manage to find my voice. "Why don't you two go get some rest in your room?" I say to them kindly, smiling even though I don't want to at the moment.

They both nod, then rush over to their room.

My smile fades. I take a deep breath in, then out, slowly turning around, preparing for what is to come with Joel.

"What? No snippy comments today then, Xander?" Joel says, stepping slightly closer to me.

I look around the room, then shrug half-heartedly. "No crowd. No point."

Joel laughs, a little too loud at that. "You think you are so funny, don't you?"

I shrug again. "That's for other people to decide, not me."

I can hear shuffling where my room is, and I don't need to move my head to know who that is. Vicky.

"You know what, Xander? I am sick and tired of your sarcastic comments." Joel is coming closer and closer to me with every passing word.

I can feel my hands tighten into fists at my side, and I don't know if Joel can see it or not.

"You want to punch me, don't you?" he says, smirking. *Yeah, to wipe that ugly smirk off your face,* I don't say, even though I want to say it. I so *desperately* want to say it.

I don't say anything. I can't. Nothing will come out of my mouth. The only thing I am aware of is the pounding in my head, getting louder, louder with each second that ticks by with both of us staring at each other.

So, I do the only thing that you *can* do in these situations.

I turn around and walk away.

"That's what I thought," he mumbles, following me to my room.

I stare at Vicky, then look down at the floor.

"Drop it, Joel," Vicky says, and I look up at her, smiling. "Just leave him the hell alone for once in your life."

"You're weak," Joel says, completely ignoring Vicky. Then he does something I never thought he would do—he pushes me. Hard.

I stumble forward, eyes widening. I suddenly freeze.

If you would have punched Joel, sure, you might have felt better, but it doesn't mean anything will be solved.

Vicky's words ring in my head as I continue to stare at the floor, all while ignoring Joel's insults behind me. He pushes me again, harder this time. I grab the wall to keep myself from stumbling.

You could come out worst of the two of you, and I don't want to see that happen to you.

Then something inside me… snaps.

I whirl around, and my right arm swings on its own accord.

Joel staggers to the side as my fist makes contact with his jaw. My hand stings, but I take no notice of the pain. He presses two fingers against his mouth, smearing a thin layer of blood there.

"Finally!" he says, letting blood fly freely from his mouth. "I've been waiting for you to do that." His teeth are stained with blood as he smiles a wide, menacing smile that almost splits his face in half.

My eyes widen as Joel wraps his arms around my middle, pushing me against the wall. The air escapes my lungs as

Joel's body crashes against my chest. His fist makes contact with my bad side over and over again, making me see black at the edges of my vision.

"Joel, stop!" I can just about make out Vicky's voice as she shouts over the sound of Joel's fist against my side. He pulls me away from the wall, hard, smashing my back against the table. A chair flies away somewhere, but I take no notice of it.

I feel the edge of the table cut into my skin as Joel pushes harder, using his whole weight. His hand closes around my throat, pure, burning hatred lighting up his eyes as his grip tightens, tightens, tightens—

Then, just like before, something again snaps inside me.

I manage to yank my arm out from its position, pushing Joel away from me as hard as I can. He staggers backward, almost dazed for a moment as he tries to grapple for something to keep him upright.

Then, with one swing, I punch him straight across the jaw, ignoring the pain that my knuckles are causing me. A pain, similar to a white-hot pain explodes in the flesh of my hand.

Kyle materializes from nowhere, grabbing hold of Joel's arms, trapping him against his chest. He spits blood from his mouth, almost near my boots.

I turn my head to look at Vicky, who has tears in her eyes, and some are dripping down her cheeks. I think she reaches forward for me, but I look away.

Everything turns silent. My breaths are the only thing I can hear, the only thing I can *feel,* and I do the only thing that comes to my mind.

I run.

CHAPTER NINE

My mind races, and my side throbs the faster I run.

The rubble on the ground crunches and crumbles under the weight of my boots as I push hard against the ground, trying to get as far away from everything as quickly as possible. The wind whips against my face and I desperately try to wipe away the sand still in the air, still filling my eyes, my mouth, my *lungs*.

I don't even know where I am going. I don't even know where I am; my mind can't process the things around me. Everything feels and looks like a blur—a smear of light that seems to be one color. I don't know how long it takes me to realize that it's my tears, burning the back of my eyes.

The sun has fully set now, making the buildings in the Estate darker, almost scarier, like they could just swallow me up and I'll never be seen again. The stars and the crescent moon provide the only light for me to orient myself around. The hard rubble becomes tightly compacted together on the streets, making it harder to step around easily; making it harder for me not to trip and fall over.

I slow down to a jog, then a fast walk, then I stop, hunched over, sweat dripping from my forehead, my chest rising and falling.

The tears in my eyes blur my vision, and I blink several times to remove the sting, the blur of color, the small particles that I can't seem to name.

I don't remember screaming. I don't remember hearing anything but the slight vibration tearing at my throat. Then the next thing I felt was a ripping in my vocal cords, cutting straight down my chest. I can't seem to focus on one sound;

not even the wind as it brushes around me, moving my hair and clothes in every direction.

The pain in my side doesn't subside, doesn't make this any better. I can feel the throb of my heartbeat right where Joel punched me, over and over again. I slowly lift up my shirt, and my own assumptions are correct; a big blue and purple bruise has formed. My scar rests right in the center of the ugly mark. The bruise looks obvious in contrast to my olive skin; it's like looking at a black object in the middle of a white background; you can spot it from miles away.

I gingerly lower my shirt, resting it softly over the bruise. The material rests against the mark on my back, and I wince, trying to ease the pain. I slowly reach back, pressing my index finger against the mark. A small amount of fresh blood comes off on my finger, but the rest of it feels dried, keeping my wound together.

I walk over to the closest building, sliding down the nearest wall, being careful with my back. The rubble on the ground dig into my legs as I sit on the hard floor, but I don't care about the pain. I try to calm my racing heart as I rest my back against the wall, slowly leaning my head back against it.

I look up at the stars in the night sky and think about one thing, and one thing only.

Will I be punished for what I did to Joel?

*****

The wind brushing against my face is surprisingly cold. The wind is *never* cold; it always blows hot air around the buildings, and it always leaves me sweating buckets.

I tug my worn jacket tighter around my shoulder, cursing when it rips at the seam on my back.

"Great," I hiss through gritted teeth. I pull the ripped jacket off my shoulders, tossing it away, out of my line of sight.

Why does everything bad have to happen to *me*? Why me?

I pull my knees close to my chest, wrapping my shaking arms around them, hissing when my elbow brushes against my bruise.

I wish I never left Vicky. She must be worried sick. I almost feel like I want to get back up and go home, but then I remember Joel, and I stay in place, pulling my legs closer to my chest.

I was sure by now I would have got used to Joel's attitude, his way of speaking to others, and just genuinely… his face. He has been this way since I was twelve; the time he slapped me, but surely a thirteen-year-old would know better.

Obviously not.

The shine of the moon snaps me back to reality.

I have no idea what time it is, but I am almost positive that everyone is in bed asleep, no longer worrying about that idiot that ran out from a fight, from *everyone*.

Tears stream down my face, dripping on the hem of my T-shirt when I don't wipe them away. I don't know why I'm crying, but I feel an ache in the pit of my stomach and in my chest. This is the worst type of sad, because… I can't seem to explain why. I can't seem to explain why I have a sickening feeling in my stomach.

I wrap my arms tighter around my knees, and I bury my head in-between them.

Then I close my eyes.

*****

Something small and sharp hits the back of my head, interrupting my dreamless half-sleep.

The sun has just started to rise above the horizon, giving the Estate a purple and orange glow. The buildings around me turn from a dark brown to a lighter shade, and for a small, single moment, I get lost in the color of them. The sun slowly rises some more, but I look away, cursing when something sharp hits me in the face again.

I run my hand through my hair to detect what might have hit me, but I find nothing. Whatever hit me must have been *tiny*.

I look over to where I felt it come from, my eyes squint immediately after what I see is coming toward me.

Sand.

A damn sandstorm.

I jerk my head to look the other way, lifting up my T-shirt to cover my mouth and nose, begging the sand to stay away from my mouth, my nose, *everything*.

I wish I snatched my bandana before I ran out. I even dropped my backpack, so I have nothing to rely on; nothing to keep me alive in this situation.

I just hope whatever will happen to me will be quick and easy.

The tiny particles invade my eyes, even though I am squeezing them shut with all my might. I raise my hand to cover the sand from my eyes, but even as I do it, I can feel the sand creep past my fingertips.

The storm picks up speed now.

I wish I never got rid of my jacket.

I'm such an idiot.

This stupid sand is coming from the desert that separates the Wastelands and the Estate.

I scramble to my feet, blindly pushing myself to the front door of this house. My hands glide along the surface of this old wooden door until I stop at the rusted metal handle. I twist it with more force than necessary and I stumble inside, kicking the door shut behind me. I fall and land hard on my chest, causing some air to be knocked out of my lungs.

I lower my T-shirt, breathing in the—almost—fresh air.

I feel too weak to even move my arms or legs. The sand really hurt; it felt like it was being shot straight through the other side of my body. The worst thing is: it would probably hurt less if it *was* shot straight through my body.

The sand has somehow managed to create another layer of skin above my own. I have to dig my fingernails under all the caked sand to remove even a small fraction of it.

I cough up some sand, and it sprinkles from my neck and face, landing on the floor.

I place my hands under my body, pushing myself up, ignoring the way the sand irritates my skin under my clothes. I flip myself onto my back, sending a jolt of pain up my spine and I slowly sit up. Using my right hand, I rub the sore spot on my back, easing the growing tension.

I search around the room, squinting as my eyes adjust to the darkness.

I slowly get up from the floor, and when I stumble forward, I grab onto the first thing I come into contact with. I push myself toward the kitchen, begging my legs and feet to work properly.

I grab hold of the door frame before my feet give way and I crash to the ground. Rubble, glass and everything else you can think of is littered on the ground. I can't even see the floor, I don't know what color it is under all this debris.

Glass cracks and shatters under the weight of my heavy boots as I make my way to the lower cabinets. I swing one open and peer inside. A thick layer of dust has covered the entire space inside the cabinet, but something manages to catch my eye; a shimmering as the light reflects on it. Water bottles. I reach forward, pulling out the packet of water.

I don't plan on drinking all of it, and I don't really want to bring it back home. I'm going to use it to get rid of all of the sand in my hair and body. Maybe, if I'm lucky, I might be able to find a new pair of pants and a T-shirt, but I won't get my hopes up just yet.

I swing the bottles under my arm as I walk to the stairs. Some of them strain and creak, but they don't give out. When

I make it to the landing, I walk straight for the bathroom, not caring what the bedrooms will have in them, yet.

I place the water on the side near the bathtub, carefully trying to cut open the packaging with the tip of my knife.

In total, I have six medium-sized bottles of water. I hope this will be enough.

I strip off my T-shirt, shaking off the excess sand, watching with satisfaction as it falls to the ground. The sand managed to get stuck on my chest and stomach, and I don't even know how—I had total coverage for my front.

I shake my head. *Don't be stupid, Xander,* I think, staring at the shirt in my hand. *Sand gets* everywhere.

I untie the laces of my boots, shaking out the sand. I place them tiredly near the direction of the door, keeping them away from all of the sand on the floor.

I undo the clasp of my belt, slowly removing my pants, again, shaking off the sand.

I place both articles of clothing on the side and step into the bathtub. I grab hold of one of the bottles, unscrewing the lid. It takes a lot of restraint not to tip the water into my dry mouth. Instead, I lift the bottle above my head, letting the warm water drip down on my head.

It feels weird to have water on my body, after not having any for what feels like forever. I rub and run my fingers through my mass of dark hair to remove some of the sand. When the water hits the faded white acrylic, it sounds almost like what I imagine water or rain hitting a glass panel would sound like. The water seeps into the many cracks in this tub, disappearing forever.

Once my hair has been completely soaked and is sticking to my forehead, I grab another bottle of water, and I repeat this action with my chest, stomach, and my legs, scrubbing harder than necessary.

I tip one last bottle of water above my head, for good measure. I rub my face vigorously, scraping away some of the caked sand on my eyelids.

I step out of the tub, slowly and carefully lowering myself on the edge, dripping wet. I stand straight back up when the bathtub creaks under my weight. I decide to just stand against the wall.

It is so silent in this room that I can hear the *plink, plink, plink* of the water dripping off my arms to the ground.

With a frustrated sigh, I push myself off the wall. *I can't just stand here and wait for myself to dry,* I think, searching intently for some sort of towel to dry myself with.

The only thing I could find was a ten-by-ten-inch cloth that is starting to turn yellow, but the only good thing about it is it's dry. I run it across my body, picking up every last drop of water still on my skin.

When I dry my hair, the cloth is soaked and dripping with water within *seconds.* So, I decide to let my hair dry naturally.

I grab my T-shirt, and with all my might, I hit it against the wall, shaking off every single bit of sand that might be stuck there. I do the same with my pants.

I walk around this empty house half-naked looking for any more clothes to put on. I wouldn't mind even if it was just a tank top.

This house must have belonged to a woman, because the only clothes I could find are tiny T-shirts, very, *very* short shorts, and shoes that are the same size as my hands.

If this woman left all of her clothes, then where is the woman? Dead? Did she run away? People don't just up and leave without any of their belongings. They take the essentials, sure, but they don't leave *this* much stuff.

The only thing that could be useful in my situation, is a thin black scarf. This could be useful in another sandstorm—if, and when, I get caught in another one. I hope I don't.

If you look really carefully at this scarf, you can tell that it belongs to a woman, but you wouldn't be able to tell if you just glance at it. I'm really only thankful because it's black—it would be useful when I want to hide in the dark.

I halt dead in my tracks when something catches my line of sight. Despite its ragged shape and the fact that it's leaning heavily on the wall to the left, it's still intact. This bookcase has seen better days, but it still has a few titles adorning its shelves. I tread my way toward it, eyes never leaving the worn book spines.

My fingers slowly glide over the worn gold lettering of the titles. I don't recognize the books; Dad never told me about these ones. Some are even in a completely different language. A few are fiction, I can tell, but a few are non-fiction or biographies—telling us the story of a famous person that no longer exists.

The owner of this house was obviously a book lover.

I snap the book shut I had in my hands and slip it back inside the bookcase, causing the old, musty smell to invade my nose. It doesn't smell as bad as the one Vicky gave me. These ones smell, well, *nice,* somehow. It's a welcoming kind of smell; one that isn't harsh on your nostrils.

I slip my T-shirt on my body, smoothing it against my slightly damp skin. I pull on the pants, clasping up my belt, making sure that all of my daggers and stuff are still tied to it. Then, I tie up my boots. Finally, I wrap the black scarf around my neck, letting it fall naturally across my chest and shoulders.

I down the last bottle of water and I place the empty plastic on the ground. I cough when some of the water goes down the wrong direction, and I had to spit to calm my raging throat.

A sudden thought races through my mind. Has everyone gone back to their jobs as if nothing happened the night before?

I guess they should, really. They can't all stop what they are doing for a stupid boy that ran away without uttering a single word. I didn't even look at any of them—I just bolted. I can't really remember what happened the second I ran out of the door. I can't tell if anyone called my name. Maybe Vicky did. Maybe she ran after me. She may have even grabbed hold of my hand to stop me, but I wouldn't have felt it.

I don't know why my mind falls so easily to false hope. Maybe it's sometimes better to think about that, other than all the bad things that could happen in this type of situation.

The next time I look around at my surroundings, I'm downstairs near the front door. I was so caught up in my own thoughts that I didn't realize I managed to walk downstairs without tripping, without even looking as I went down.

I take one last look around the room before heading for the front door. The doorknob creaks and screeches when I turn it to the right, but the sound stops as soon as the door is open, wide open, letting in a warm breeze. It wipes past my head, brushing my hair away from my forehead.

I take one step out of the door and I suddenly stop, frozen in place, eyes wide with shock. My breathing stops; so does my heart. It starts again. *Th-thump… th-thump… th-thump…*

A person stands at the house opposite me. At first, I thought it was a completely new survivor, but that thought sounded ridiculous before it even properly entered my mind. Then I see the long dark braid cascading down their back.

Something crunches under my boot, but I don't look down. I can't look down. I can't. I *can't.*

She turns around slowly. Her facial expression can only resemble mine. Her red bandana is wrapped around her mouth and nose, covering half of her face.

Then I see her bright blue eyes as they pierce straight into mine.

CHAPTER TEN

She latches onto my neck before I can even comprehend what is happening. I didn't even see or hear her take those few steps to get to me. When I saw her, all my tears came rushing back, flooding my eyes—making them blur to the point where I couldn't wash them away.

She pulls me down to her height, and it's only then that I let my arms tighten around her waist. Her face is completely hidden in my chest. My head is resting softly on her shoulder.

I squeeze my eyes shut, letting a few tears to fall on the ground behind Vicky.

I can feel her warm breath hitting my chest as it passes through her bandana.

All the feelings of loneliness slowly disappear as my grip on Vicky tightens, her arms tightening around me.

I don't know why, but I feel like a rock has been lodged deep inside my throat, blocking my airway, causing me not to utter a single word, but I want to. I *really* want to. I want to say how sorry I am for running away. I want to explain why I let my anger get the better of me.

More importantly, I want to tell her how happy I am to see her.

Maybe we don't need to say anything to each other. We've both learned new ways to speak to each other by just our eye contact and body language. I guess that's the good thing about having a best friend; you know what each of you is thinking— even if you don't show it on your face.

Vicky knows when I'm in pain—because she can see it in my eyes, but I tend to hide my pain behind a smile, then everyone else around me thinks I'm okay. It is so much easier to pretend you are okay, when in reality… you're not.

We may not always be with each other, but we will always be there *for* each other.

*****

We sit on the floor by the entrance of this house.

We both ended up hugging for what felt like an hour, but it could have been longer. I don't count the time when I'm with Vicky; when you count the time, it always seems to go quicker for me, and I don't like it when that happens.

Vicky hugs her knees close to her chest. She pulled down her bandana, letting her breathe in the fresh air. She pulls her backpack off, letting it drop near her feet on the floor.

She exhales. "Do you want to tell me what happened?"

I slowly look over at her, then back to the floor. "I ran."

She shuffles slightly as she looks down, but she can tell I haven't finished speaking, so she doesn't say anything, yet.

"I got… too angry with Joel, and I just… snapped, I guess."

She shuffles again and moves herself to look at me full on.

"When I ran out of the house, I thought everything would just disappear behind me. Like, every thought and feeling would just dissolve if I ran fast enough, if I pushed hard enough on the ground."

Vicky places her hand on my leg, using her thumb to rub in circles on the same spot. "I'm really sorry, Xan."

I laugh slightly, even though it isn't even funny. "When I finally stopped running, I slumped down next to a wall and tried to sleep it all off, but I never even got close to sleep."

I notice Vicky still hasn't taken her hand off my leg. She runs her thumb across it again, calming me down.

I lick my dry lips. "Then that stupid sandstorm hit."

Vicky's grasp tightens the slightest bit, and if I wasn't paying much attention, I probably wouldn't have noticed. "I saw that, too," she says. "It looked really bad."

I nod my head, agreeing. "After about... maybe thirty seconds of being in the sandstorm, I couldn't even feel my arms or legs. Sand covered half of my face, leaving me blind for a while. Then I managed, *somehow*, to get into this house—" I point to the building behind us. "Then, I think I tripped inside." My gaze lands on something in front of me. I'm looking but not really *seeing*.

I'm touching but not actually feeling.

"I'm really sorry that happened to you," Vicky whispers softly, scooting closer to me. "How did you manage to get the sand off you?"

Somehow, I feel the sand irritate my skin. I feel the little particles creep their way into my flesh, and, yet, I'm all clean.

I shake my head as if I don't remember anything, but I remember every single thing that happened, so I keep talking.

"I found bottles of water in the house. I went upstairs, stripped off my clothes and scrubbed away all of the caked sand. I think this house belonged to a woman because it was full of women's clothes. That's where I found this scarf." I ruffle the material and let it drop naturally. "I brought this down in case I got caught in another sandstorm."

Vicky pushes a strand of her hair out of her eyes, then slowly reaches up to run her fingers over her bandana.

"Then I found you, I guess," I finish, nudging Vicky on the arm softly.

She smiles, nudging me on the arm. "So... if I wasn't on my job today, you would have stayed hidden, away from all of us? Forever?"

I shake my head. "No." My mouth twitches slightly at the corner. "Because I knew that you were going to find me, one way or another."

Vicky saw my little smile. I can tell because she blushes and looks down quickly.

I sling my arm around Vicky's shoulder, pulling her closer to me. "You know? I'm glad I have someone like you; someone that *actually* understands me. Someone to keep me out of trouble."

Vicky laughs lightly, slightly leaning into me. "Me too, Xan." She brushes something off her lap, picks at a piece of thread. "I'm glad we found each other back when we were little. It seems like such a long time ago…"

It's like my life is flashing before my eyes; I'm seeing the first time I met Vicky. The buildings around me almost look like they are dissolving, switching the scenery to when we were little.

I'm standing in the alleyway of two houses; there are broken pieces of rubble, glass and everything else you can think of on the floor. I hear footsteps in front of me. There is no light in this alley, so I can hardly see what I'm stepping on.

A sob, panting, and what almost sounds like scratching can be heard in my right ear.

I clutch the dagger from my belt harder in my hands, my knuckles turning white. You would probably think it's dangerous to give a thirteen-year-old a knife, but trust me, we need them.

A tin can clatters to the ground a few feet ahead of me, rolling around to somewhere unknown to me. My eyes widen as if it would help see in the dark, but it doesn't. The scrambling of feet sounds at the same place as the can.

I pull the dagger from my belt and hold it out in front of me, my hands shaking uncontrollably. I can feel the sweat forming in the palm of my hands as I tighten my grip on it.

After a few seconds, I hear something crash to the ground, and a small "Ow" as it passes through dry lips.

Any normal person would think it was just a rat, but the quiet whimper afterward made me think otherwise.

There is just enough light to see the person. It's a girl. A young girl. Strands of her long dark hair fall over her eyes as she scrambles away from me. I keep moving forward to try and calm her down, but to no avail.

She only stops when her back hits a wall behind her.

Her knees are close to her chest, making it look like she is crushing her ribs.

"P-p-please... d-don't... hurt me." Her voice is barely above a whisper, but from the slight croak, I can tell she is holding back a sob.

"It's okay," I whisper, slowly lowering myself to her level. "I won't hurt you. I promise."

She slowly pushes a few strands of her long hair out of her face, and there I can see the color of her eyes. They're blue. Pale blue. The same color as mine.

She looks as if she could be around my age, but she looks slightly smaller than the average thirteen-year-old.

Soot, grime, dirt and ash covers her face and arms. I don't know what she was looking for in this alley, but I'm positive that she has been here for a long time.

"My name is Xander," I say, holding my hand out in front of me. She looks down to my hand, then to my eyes. Her pale blue eyes shining in the moonlight. Her eyes are searching around my face for anything. She doesn't seem to see anything. "What's your name?"

She slowly but surely presses her hand into mine, and I close my fingers around hers giving her a kind smile. I slowly pull her into the moonlight.

She smiles back. "I'm Vicky."

Within seconds, the whole scene just disappears in front of my eyes. Vicky is still sitting next to me. My arm is still draped over and around her shoulders. She rests her head against my chest, and I pull her closer to me, the memory still fresh in my mind.

The whole memory must have been a few seconds to Vicky, but to me, the whole thing seemed like an hour.

So, I act as if nothing happened.

"Me too," I say finally, pulling her even closer. "I'm glad we found each other too."

*****

Since it's still early, Vicky and I decide to scavenge for a while and enjoy being alone in the peace and quiet. I mean, Vicky is supposed to be scavenging today, but the rest of the guys don't know about her finding me. Not yet, anyway.

I am dreading going back to the house, though. Sure, I *am* excited to sleep in my own bed and eat some food, but I am not looking forward to all the questions that will be asked.

I don't think Vicky is really doing her job, because she keeps avoiding going into houses, and to be fair, I *am* distracting her with a conversation. I don't think she minds, though.

We keep making up scenarios of what would happen when I get back home. They mostly involve Joel, and what he will say if and when I get back home, but will Joel have the brains to punch me again? Since I *did* technically punch him first?

I snap back to reality when Vicky suggests we sit down and have something to eat. We both climb up the nearest building, situating ourselves on the hard ledge.

It feels good not to have a backpack to carry around, and I do feel sorry for Vicky since she has to carry hers. I did offer to carry it, but of course, being Vicky, and being as stubborn as she is, she kept it on.

Vicky holds her bag of leather full of grain, oats and berries in front of me. I shake my head.

Vicky exhales. "Xander, just please, you haven't eaten for a while." She shakes the bag slightly. "Take a handful. Hell, take half." She shakes the bag again. "You must be starving."

"Kind of." I smile. "Thank you." I reach my hand in the bag, pulling out a palm full of the mixture. I slowly put it in my mouth, bit by bit.

"Don't mention it." She looks on in the distance, and slowly picks out a few berries, crushing them in-between her teeth.

The Wastelands at this time look so exotic, nothing like what it normally looks like. The way the sun shines on the desert floor makes it look brighter. Very inviting. If only we could go out there… I push that thought from my mind, knowing exactly what the reaction from everyone will be like if I mention it.

There is nothing in the Estate for us; we never find more survivors. (Except Sera and Cassia, of course.) And we have pretty much ransacked most of the houses here.

"You're going to have to face them sooner or later," Vicky says after a while.

I look over at her, sighing silently. "I know," I exhale loudly.

Vicky takes a drink of her water, then hands it to me. I take it slowly, thanking her.

"It might not be as bad as you think." I know Vicky is lying, but she says it anyway—she doesn't want to see the same thing happen to me, and I don't like seeing her upset; it breaks my heart.

"Maybe," I say quietly. "But have you even *met* the others? They will bombard me with questions."

"Then you will just have to answer them." She looks at me. "They won't judge you."

I snort. "Joel will," I say. "In fact, I can almost *guarantee* what he will say to me."

"Then"—Vicky shrugs—"if the worst comes to the worst… you can just punch him again."

I smile as I think that scenario over.

"I was joking, Xander! Don't you *dare!*" Vicky shouts, lightly hitting me on the arm.

"But you would feel so much better once it's over and done with," I say, trying to block Vicky's punches.

"Just don't, Xan!"

"Fine!" I laugh. "I won't. I promise."

"Good." Vicky packs away her food and water, pulling the pack tighter on her back. "Let's get this all over with."

I nod my head. "Be prepared to catch me when Joel knocks me out. Shall I keep my arms close to my chest so it's less weight?" My voice sounds sarcastic.

Vicky shoots me a hard glare. "Don't think about him, right now. Let's just get home, and sleep all of this off. Okay?"

"Fine," I mumble, beginning to climb down the building.

Giving up half way, I drop and roll to a stop, pressing my hand on the hard ground. I wait patiently for Vicky with my hands in my pockets, tapping my foot repeatedly on the ground.

Vicky jumps down more gracefully than I did, and together we both walk toward our house.

*****

"Remember, Xan," Vicky says, "keep your chin up, and put on your most I-don't-give-a-crap-about-what-you-think look."

I raise my chin up higher than necessary, and Vicky lets out an irritated breath. "Lower your chin, you idiot."

I smile as she grabs hold of my chin, and slowly (but forcefully) lowers my chin.

"Squint your eyes slightly."

I squint my eyes, just as she said.

She tilts her head to the side, examining me slightly. "Beautiful," she says sarcastically.

I roll my eyes, looking down at the ground.

We are standing one house away from ours, and we have our voices at just the right level so only we can hear.

We slowly walk toward the house, and I prepare for the many questions that are *bound* to be thrown my way.

CHAPTER ELEVEN

Kyle is the first person to walk up to me as I enter the house. He wraps his arms around my shoulders, completely crushing me in a bear hug. He was sitting at the round table at the center of the room, absentmindedly picking food from one of the wooden bowls.

"What the hell is wrong with you, Xander?" He lifts himself up from me, grabbing hold of my shoulders tightly. "Why did you run away?"

"You know why, Kyle," I whisper, looking down at the ground.

He nods slowly, still looking at the floor. "Come on." Kyle guides Vicky and me over to the table. The only other people in the room are Sera and Cassia, looking healthier than before.

Cassia rushes up to me, quickly wrapping her small arms around my waist. I smile down at her and pat her back softly.

"Are you okay now, Xander?" Cassia asks quietly. "H-he looked like he really hurt you."

Oh, no. She must have seen him punch me.

"I am," I say, half-meaning it. "Thank you, Cassia."

She releases me slowly and smiles.

Sera stands up, pressing her hand to my shoulder, giving me a kind smile. I smile back. She takes Cassia's hand and walks out of the main room.

Vicky and I both sit down slowly, Kyle in front of both of us. I bring my chair closer to the table, the sound echoing around the room loudly.

"Here." Kyle pushes his bowl half full of food in front of me. "You must be hungry."

"I'm just going to go to my room," Vicky says, pushing herself up from the table. Kyle nods, saying goodnight to her before she lifts herself off the table.

I want to stop her, to tell her to stay, but, instead, I just watch her leave, giving her a smile when she turns around to look at me over her shoulder.

I slowly pick up a berry from the pile, ripping the smallest speck from it you possibly could think, then I swallow. I can feel it glide down my throat, making me hack uncontrollably.

Kyle asks if I'm okay, and I just nod my head, keeping a frown plastered on my face.

"Do you... feel like telling me what happened?" Kyle's voice sounds lighter and softer than normal, less deep... more caring. This is the same type of voice he uses whenever I used to speak with him—when he used to tell me everything will be okay; back when I was little.

I shake my head; I don't feel like speaking at all today. I don't like answering questions when they only involve *me*. And I'm sure everyone thinks that the whole thing was my fault. I certainly do, anyway.

"Where is *he*?" I ask, despite not wanting to speak.

Kyle knows exactly who I'm talking about; I can see it on his face—the little twitch from the corner of his mouth. "*He* is still out." He cranes his neck to look out of the front door. "But if I were you, I would go to your room before he comes back. You don't know what he could do to you."

I roll my eyes, shaking my head quickly. "I can't act as if I'm afraid of him, Kyle—because I'm not."

Kyle closes his eyes, a small grin twitching behind his thin beard. "I know, Xander, I know, but you never know *what he could do to you.* Maybe try and talk to him. Maybe you can end up finding a good side of him," he repeats, sounding firmer this time.

Kyle's right; Joel could do *anything* to me. He may even be plotting out a plan to attack me as we speak, but the "good side" part of him. Never.

I grip the edges of the table firmly in my hands, turning my knuckles white. I ignore the pain. "Well, what do you expect us to do, Kyle? Get along? Skip around outside? Braid each other's hair?" I stand up, my chair grating against the floor loudly. "We are *never* going to get along, Kyle. *Never.*" I push myself from the table, stomping my way to my room, slamming the door shut behind me, the old wood rattling against the frame.

I don't walk over to my bed. I don't even look at Vicky as I enter my room.

I don't turn around when she calls my name.

Instead, I walk over to the storage room at the back of the house, trying to find solitude in a place where I feel everyone is asking too many questions—even if they are just in my head.

As I enter the room, the musty smell invades my senses, causing my upper lip to curl in disgust. The room is just how I want it: empty. Even Blinky and Ponytail aren't in here. They normally *are* in here—it is their job to be in here. I don't even know where they are, and, to be honest, at the moment, I don't really care.

I press my back against one of the corners, sliding down until my knees are pressed tightly against my chest. I wrap my arms around them to keep me in place. The cut on my back pulls painfully. I try not to wince.

The room isn't as dark as it was the last time I was in here—when I had to carry a lamp around. I can see the shelves with all our supplies; they are obvious. It takes up a whole wall. You would have to be blind to miss all our supplies.

I look around the shelves, scanning each and every item on them carefully, then I see it. My backpack, with my black bandana tied loosely on the strap.

Someone, probably Vicky, bought it back in here when I…
ran, I guess.

The eerie silence of the room is starting to send a cold
shiver up my spine, causing my back to arch. It almost doesn't
let me hear the voice drifting into the room.

"Oh, *there* you are, Xander."

I whip my head over to the source of the voice.

Adam stands there, a big box full of tools in his hands. "We
were wondering if you were ever going to come back."

I don't say anything.

Of course, my peace and quiet had to be ruined, didn't it?

Adam walks over to the shelves, carefully sliding the box
in whatever empty space he can find. Once he's finished, he
stands about a meter away from me, bouncing up and down
on the balls of his feet. He crosses his arms, uncrosses them.
Puts his hands in his pockets like he doesn't know what to do
with them.

"Mind if I sit?" he asks quietly, shuffling on the spot.

I stay silent, jabbing my thumb into my knee until it hurts.

He slumps against the wall to my left and slides down it.
He pulls his knees about a foot or two away from his chest,
slowly placing his forearms on his knees. He rests his head on
the wall behind him, letting out a loud sigh.

I hear him inhale loudly. "If it makes you feel any better, I
won't ask you any questions. I know you wouldn't like that."

I stare at him after that, but he looks away before I can read
the emotion in his blue-green eyes.

"How did you know that I don't like it when people ask me
questions?" I ask, harsher than I intended, furrowing my
brows.

Adam shrugs. "Because… I'm the same, Xander. I *hate* it
when people ask me questions about myself. I don't know
why, but something lodges inside my throat whenever I'm in
that type of situation, and there is no way out of it."

I stare wide-eyed at my knees. I didn't know Adam and I were so much alike. On the outside, we are like strangers, but on the inside… we could pretty much be brothers.

Adam brushes something off his knee. "I know you may not believe it because I'm so… outgoing, and, somewhat crazy, but it's true. All of it."

"But why do you always seem so confident in yourself?" I look down and slowly shake my head, not believing a word of what he is saying.

"I just put on that type of demeanor, so people wouldn't ask questions." He looks over at me, then the door.

"Questions about what?" I ask, lowering my voice slightly.

"Anything," he says, shrugging. "Believe it or not… I'm actually quite a shy person."

This time, I *actually* laugh.

"I know you don't believe me, Xander, but think about it; if you are a shy person, wouldn't some people ask why? I don't like that. That's why I seem so confident." He starts to get up. "It's all an act."

He starts to walk away.

"Wait!" I call out to him and he stops, turning around on the ball of his foot. "Why did you tell me this stuff, Adam?"

He shrugs. "I don't know." He looks away for a second, then back to me. "Because we're friends, right?"

Since when? "Of course." I smile and nod my head. "We're friends. And don't worry; your secret is safe with me."

He nods his head before leaving the room, giving me a small thumbs-up.

"Ah, Adam. Have you seen Xander? I can't find him anywhere." I strain my ears at the voice of Vicky, sounding worried with every passing word.

Adam doesn't say anything, but I know—I know he told her I'm in here.

I hear footsteps for a second. Then nothing at all. Vicky freezes as she sees me in the corner of the room. I probably look like I'm crushing my ribs beyond repair.

She unfreezes quickly, almost as if she knew she was staring. "Hey," she whispers.

"Hey," I whisper back.

"Are you okay?" She comes closer to me.

I nod my head. "I am. Now."

She presses her back against the wall and slowly slides down right next to me, our arms and shoulders pressed together firmly.

"I was going to go up to the roof," she says after a while, looking over at me. "Do you want to come up as well?"

I turn my head to look at her. I smile. "Of course."

Vicky taps my knee three times—hard—and says, "Come on. We better go before it's too late." She uses my knee to push herself up and uses the wall to support her back.

As I get up, my joints click with every inch I move. Vicky and I both wince at the same time.

I don't pass Kyle on the way out, but I do pass Adam, who gives me another small thumbs-up. I smile and nod back.

Just before I walk out of the door, Joel walks in. He freezes just after the door frame, glaring at me with so much hatred that it feels like it's cutting me in half. I glare back. A big purple and blue bruise has formed on the side of the jaw where I punched him. His lip is slightly split and the blood has scabbed over.

"He's not worth it, Xan," Vicky says, trying to direct me out of the door.

Joel's shoulder collides with mine as I pass the door frame, and I breathe multiple times through my nose and out of my mouth to try and calm myself down. If it wasn't for Vicky's hand around my shoulders, I would have been angrier.

I'm glad Vicky's always there to help me calm down—even when I sometimes can't calm myself.

*****

We both lay flat on our backs, looking up at the night sky. There are a few stars in the sky, shining down on us, making the roof glow slightly.

My chest rises and falls slowly as I breathe in the cold fresh air. I'm glad I'm back with Vicky. Although I must admit, I do like being alone; but I wouldn't pass up the opportunity to be with Vicky, not at all.

"I forgot to ask," Vicky blurts out, moving her head to look at me. "What happened to your jacket?"

I look over at her, intertwining my fingers, resting them on my chest. "I threw it away."

"Why?" Vicky asks.

"It ripped."

"How?"

I sigh. "I tried to pull it tighter around my shoulders, and the seam at the back completely ripped open."

"Man, that sucks."

"Tell me about it." I shake my head and look back up at the sky. "So, I guess the jacket was shrinking."

Vicky laughs. "Xan, don't be stupid. You and I both know that you are getting broader. Right here—" She points to my shoulder. "And here—" Then my chest.

"I think it's time to find new clothes. I think I'm outgrowing some of these," I say, trying to look down at my chest.

"You and me both, brother," Vicky says quietly, stretching out her plain T-shirt.

"I wish the Estate went on forever, then we can find more clothes to wear," I say.

"I know, but it doesn't."

I sit up, turning around to face her.

132

She props herself up with her elbows, giving me a confused look.

"Don't call me crazy for saying this," I say. "But… what if we all go to the Wastelands? I mean, what is there for us here in the Estate?"

Vicky looks down. "Food, shelter, water. The list goes on, Xan. None of the others will go with you."

I shake my head. "You don't know that." I cross my legs. "Think about it; we could all get away from this, and, plus, we will be able to see if there is life out there." I point my thumb behind me, out to the Wastelands, turn my head to look. "It's worth a try, I guess. Right?"

Vicky sits up fully, crossing her legs just as I'm doing. She looks out into the distance, thinking it over. "It would be nice," she says. "We have always spoken about the Wastelands and what could be out there." She looks over at me. "But what do we do if nothing is out there?"

I shrug. "We come back. What have we got to lose?"

Vicky shakes her head and looks out to the Wastelands again. She stays silent for a few seconds. "Nothing. We have *nothing* to lose," she whispers.

"That settles it, then." I rise from the floor, brushing off the dust from my body. "I'm going to ask Kyle if we can go out to the Wastelands."

CHAPTER TWELVE

I don't see Kyle as I enter the house. In fact, I don't see anyone.

Everyone has gone to bed.

Vicky and I creep our way to our room and I slowly close the door behind me, hearing the faint, satisfying *click* as the lock falls into place.

"How do you think I should ask him?" I whisper as I sit on my bed. I can't really see Vicky, but I know she is looking at me and hearing what I'm saying.

Vicky exhales. "I don't know," she says. "Maybe you should just say it how it is."

"But I can't really walk up to Kyle, kick down his door and say, 'Pack your bags, we are moving to the Wastelands,' can I?" I say, getting into a more comfortable position.

"Well," Vicky starts, "you could say something *like* that, minus the kicking the door down part."

Sometimes I wish we could just be at the Wastelands right now, it would be so much easier. Sure, we don't know what is out there, and we don't know what would happen if and when we *do* go there, but it wouldn't hurt to at least *try*. Would it?

Maybe nothing is out there. Maybe the desert just goes on for a while until, I don't know... we end up in another state or something. We wouldn't be able to survive out there for long without food or water, and once we are out there I'm not turning back.

Not for anything.

"I-I'll figure something out, Vicky," I say. "I need to get some sleep; I haven't for a while."

"Don't remind me," Vicky whispers, shuffling to lay down. "Goodnight."

"Night," I reply.

I don't know why, but a part of me *wants* to go ask Kyle, but the other part of me *doesn't.*

Bad scenarios of what would happen out in the Wastelands play on repeat over and over again in my head, then they stay there until I have to shake my head to get rid of the memory, but sometimes even that doesn't work.

I just hope when we do go to the Wastelands, my nightmare doesn't come true.

*****

The sunlight pierces straight through my eyelids as I turn over to lay on my side. I try squeezing my eyes shut hard, but even that doesn't work. I turn my body so that I'm lying flat on my back, pressing my forearm against my eyes. As I peek under my arm, I see Vicky standing there, arms crossed over her chest, looking down at me.

"Good morning," she says sweetly, with a hint of sarcasm in it. Ugh! It's too early for sarcasm.

"*Ugh!*" I mumble back to her.

Vicky laughs. "Are you going to get up and ask Kyle, or are you going to stay in bed all day?"

I turn over so that my back is facing Vicky. "Stay in bed all day," I mumble. My voice sounds thick and scratchy with sleep, and I have to cough to get rid of the noise.

A forceful hand spins me around. Vicky's hand slams into my shoulder as my back hits the bed. Her face is only a few inches away from mine.

Now I'm awake.

"I don't think so, Xander," Vicky says, smiling. "You are going to get up from this bed, put on those boots, walk up to Kyle, grow a pair, and ask him."

I'm taken aback, but I'm laughing all the same.

"Okay, okay," I say, laughing. "I'm up." I press the palm of my hand to my eyes, rubbing the sleep out of them.

"Good," Vicky says, hitting me on the shoulder a few times. She lifts herself up from her position, giving me a better view of her face. She reaches down and tosses me my boots. My head must still be quite foggy because I didn't feel the boots hit my chest. "Put these on. I'll meet you outside."

Vicky starts toward the door.

"You know, you could ask—" I start to say, but I don't get a chance to finish.

"Nope." Vicky closes the door behind her.

The rest of my sentence dies on my tongue as I stare aimlessly at the wooden door.

She can be so stubborn sometimes. She is so much like me.

I slip on my boots, tying up the thick laces, pulling them tightly—tighter than necessary, making sure they won't come undone.

I rub the sleep out of my eyes, smoothing down my mass of thick hair.

I get up from my bed, running over the sentence I made up to ask Kyle. I walk toward the door, waiting for the rejection that I'm sure is going to be Kyle's response.

*****

When you want to ask Kyle something, the best way is to wait until he is in a good mood. Today, I think he is.

He just laughed at a joke Adam came up with. Something about him almost getting stabbed by Lara with a screwdriver, or something of that nature. Adam seems to be getting into the story—the joke, because he is using his hands to gesture all around. Even Vicky is laughing.

Lara is there also. She is trying to defend herself by saying that she tripped, and the screwdriver just *happened* to be in

136

her hand, but everyone just ends up laughing at her, and in the end, she laughs too.

Vicky glances back at me and secretly motions for me to come in. I slowly make my way toward the table, not really wanting to disturb the conversation.

"Hey, Xander. You're finally up," Kyle says, gesturing to the empty chair around the table.

Adam slaps a hand on my shoulder. "How are you doing, buddy?"

I've started seeing Adam in a new light since he told me about him being shy, and not liking it when people ask him personal questions—or any questions at that.

I smile. "I'm doing good, thanks," I say. "How are *you* doing?"

Adam laughs. "Other than almost being stabbed by Lara, I'm doing just fine, thank you for asking."

Everyone erupts into laughter.

It's moments like this that I feel guiltiest for wanting to pack up and leave. Everyone seems to be having so much fun. I don't want to put them in danger.

I look over at Vicky. She mouths the word *tell him* slowly while her eyes are slightly wider than normal. All I can do to respond to her is nod my head slowly.

I inhale through my nose, carefully closing my eyes. *Just do it, Xander*, I think, angrily. It's not like he will stab me through the heart. It's only a suggestion. Just say it!

"Kyle, I need to ask you something," I say over everyone's conversations.

The room suddenly goes so silent. My heart almost seems to stop as I slowly open my eyes. Everyone's eyes are on me. I can see Vicky smiling from the corner of my eye, and I hit her softly under the table. Her smile suddenly falls as she hits me back, harder.

"Hey, Lara. Break's over. How about we go and finish with that pillar we were doing?" Adam says cheerfully.

"Yep. Let's do it," Lara replies just as happily.

"See you later, guys," they both say at the same time before walking out of the room as quickly as they possibly could.

"What was it you wanted to ask me?" Kyle says after a long awkward silence.

There's no easier way to say it, Xander. So just say it! "I-I... I think... I think we should... we should all... go to the Wastelands." I mumbled the last part of the sentence. I couldn't even understand it in my own ears.

"You think we should *what?*" Kyle asks, furrowing his brows.

I glance in Vicky's direction; she gives me a nod of encouragement.

I swallow hard, removing the rock in my throat. "I think we should all go to the Wastelands." I continue to stare at the table, not wanting to meet eye contact with Kyle at all.

Kyle shuffles in his seat, letting out a few breaths.

Great, I think. Here it comes. I should just leave now before Kyle kicks me out.

"Well," Kyle begins, "I've given it some thought, and I think we *should* go out there."

I slowly raise my head, my eyebrows furrowed together tightly. "What did you just say?"

Kyle laughs, pressing his hand to his chest. "I agree with you, Xander. I think we should go to the Wastelands. I've been thinking about it for a while now. Not as much as you, probably, but I've still been thinking about it."

Did I just step into an alternate dimension? Kyle said *yes. Yes!* I did not expect him to say that. Every single time I asked him that question, he's always said no. Even Joel slapped me because I suggested something like that. I can't wait to see the look on Joel's face when we actually start heading toward the Wastelands.

"But," Kyle suddenly says, "we leave today."

I look over at Vicky, her face probably matches mine: shock.

"Okay," I say, smiling widely. "We leave today."

*****

I stuff whatever items I had in my bedroom into my backpack, and it's not a great amount. Two bottles of water. The scarf I found back in the house. My bandana. The two arrowheads, and the clothes on my back. That's it. No jacket, no extra T-shirts or pants, or even a change of footwear. I doubt anyone will have any more items than I do.

"It's weird," Vicky suddenly says, snapping me back to reality. "Never in my life did I think I was going to leave this place behind."

It's true; I never thought I was going to leave this place either. After I turned thirteen, I stopped caring too much about going out to the Wastelands. What was the point of caring when no one would listen to a word you said? Sometimes not even your best friend.

"Yeah," I say. "I-I know. It's really weird, isn't it?" What's even weirder is that Vicky and Kyle almost seem as excited as I am about leaving. I wonder what caused the change of heart.

Vicky slowly walks over to me, leaning her elbow on my shoulder. She has to reach up high because I stand about a foot and a half taller than her.

"Is that all you're taking?" she asks, peering inside the small backpack.

"*This* is all I have," I say, cocking an eyebrow. "I doubt you have more stuff than this."

"No, I don't. But at least I have"—she tugs at my shirt—"a jacket."

I bat her hand away softly. "Th-that wasn't my fault, Vicky."

139

Vicky laughs a little too loud. "No? So, whose fault was it? The jacket's?" She leans closer to me.

I slowly nod my head. "Y-yeah, it was the jacket's fault."

Vicky laughs again, making me smile. "You're such an idiot." Shaking her head, Vicky slowly walks back to her bed. "I wonder what is waiting for us out in the Wastelands..."

I don't know why I gasped, but I did, and I don't know why I gasped louder than necessary, but I did.

"This is what you wanted, wasn't it?" Vicky's voice sounds distant, an echo that carries on for a long time; almost like what I heard when I got stabbed.

"It is. It really is," I say, sounding like I'm underwater.

A sudden whistling sound can be heard from a few miles away, and I start, whipping my head from side to side. My eyes scan around the empty expanse, trying to find the source of the noise.

The world slows down as I hear a blood-curdling scream.

And that's when I see the arrow impaled deep inside Vicky's chest...

My breath hitches in my throat as I stumble back, eyes wider than saucers. I drop whatever is in my hand and it clatters to the ground, but the noise isn't even audible to my own ears.

I think Vicky is trying to say my name, but I can't hear anything. Nothing... nothing.

Nothing.

I stumble onto Vicky's bed, but I hardly noticed with all the fog clouding my mind, and I can't seem to shake it out.

Vicky grabs hold of the sides of my face, and she says my name again... *"Xander,"* she says to me. *"Can you hear me?"* she says to me.

I can hear you, I want to say to her, but my throat closes. Something lodges inside that I can't seem to swallow down.

I stare deeply at the bottomless blue pits of her eyes, and maybe it's my mind playing tricks on me, but I think I see tears forming in her eyes, making them glassier and glassier with each passing second.

My eyes seem to drift on their own, and I have no idea where I am looking.

"Xander," Vicky says. "Xander, look at me." My eyes slowly drift back to hers on their own accord. She still has a tight grasp on the sides of my face, and it doesn't even look like she wants to let go, and, to be honest, I don't want her to let go.

My vision starts to go black around the edges, my head starts to go fuzzy, every sound becomes a mere echo in my ears.

I can just about see Vicky looking over her shoulder and shouting something, before the world goes completely dark.

*****

"Xander, can you hear me?"

The world around me is white.

"Xander, can you *hear me*?"

A burning bright light blinds my eyes.

"He's not waking up."

Pain stabs me in my left temple.

"Give him some room to breathe, guys."

Too much pain.

Too much *pain*.

Their voices sound so distant, almost like they're not even there in the first place—they sound so artificial.

Something in my eyes is starting to focus. Everything is starting to become clearer, sharper.

I can see faces, worried faces. They are everywhere, only a few inches away from mine.

I can feel the cool air filling my lungs.

"Xander?" someone says, probably Vicky; I can recognize the voice anywhere.

My eyes open wider, taking in each and every light with a burning sensation working its way to the back of my head.

"Xander!" This time, it was definitely Vicky who said that, because she then wraps her arms around my neck, pushing me back down on the bed. I snake my arms around her back, pulling her closer. "I was… so worried about you, Xan." Her voice is barely above a whisper, but I squeeze her tighter to let her know I heard.

When Vicky removes herself from me, I look to the side of my bed to see Drew squatting down, inspecting something on my face.

"We've got to stop meeting like this," Drew says and I laugh, a noise that sounds hoarse coming from my mouth. Drew slowly stands up. "He's going to be okay, guys."

Everyone visibly relaxes.

Vicky comes and stands by the side of my head, resting her cold hand on my shoulder.

"Why did you faint, Xander?" Kyle asks, coming slightly closer to my bed.

"I-I don't even know." I shake my head to try to remember something. I remember the dream, the piercing scream that I heard from Vicky; it still haunts me to this day.

"Drew, do you know why he fainted?" Adam asks. "No one just faints for no reason, right?"

"You're right, they don't, Adam," Drew says, scratching the back of his neck. "My guess is that you didn't have enough food in your system, so your body just started shutting down. Other causes of fainting are low oxygen to the brain." He taps the side of his head for good measure. "Before we leave, I want you to eat that whole bowl of food on the side of your bed and drink this whole bottle of water."

After my weird memory, I don't remember taking in any oxygen; my breath seemed to have almost stopped by itself. Shock overtaking me probably.

After Drew and Liv leave, there is only Adam, Lara, Cassia, Sera, Kyle and Vicky. No sign of Ponytail or Blinky, or even a sign of Joel, which I'm thankful for.

"Maybe we should postpone this—" Kyle starts to say, but I interrupt him.

"No! No! I'm fine. I just need to eat this food and drink this water and I'll be back in no time. I've waited almost five years, I don't even want to wait another five minutes."

Kyle holds his hand in front of him. "Okay, okay. Fine. Once you've eaten and rested for a few minutes... we'll leave."

I breathe in deeply. "Fine."

*****

Never in my life did I think I was *actually* going to go out to the Wastelands. The idea seemed so absurd to the others—it even started to sound absurd to me, too.

Until today.

Finally, today is the day where we are going to go out to the Wastelands.

I tighten the straps on my backpack and follow Vicky out the door, peeking inside my old room before the door fully closes.

A part of me is sad, and a part of me is happy to leave. When I start to think about the memories of the house I grew up in for... who knows how long, I get upset, and I'm sure everyone else does, too. But when I think of all the new memories we will make out there, it lifts my spirit.

"All right!" Kyle shouts over all our conversations.

I am too nervous to even speak, and I don't even know why I'm nervous. I should be happy, I should be excited. I kept bouncing up and down on the balls of my feet. Vicky even has to stop me by grabbing hold of my shoulders, telling me everything will be okay.

143

Kyle continues. "There are too many for us *all* to go out there. So, one person from each job is going to come now, and in a few days or weeks, we will come back for you if it's safe. Who's up first?"

Adam and Lara are the first ones to walk up to Kyle. Adam seems to be the one to volunteer to go out there.

After about two minutes of the same thing, I just sit down at the table in the center of the room for probably the last time in my life, hopefully.

"Okay, I think that's it," Kyle finishes.

So, the people that are coming with us are Kyle, Vicky, me, Joel, Adam, Drew, Ponytail and Blinky. Kyle said that he needed both Ponytail and Blinky with us to "carry extra stock".

Sera and Cassia are better off staying here with Liv and Lara. I wouldn't be able to live with myself if something happened to them if they got in danger with us.

"Alfie! You are going to stay here with the girls," Kyle says.

"*Grazie,*" Alfie says back, walking over to the girls.

"Wait, so why is Xander, Vicky *and* Joel going out there?" Liv asks, stepping closer to Drew.

"Because they know the Estate like the back of their hands; we would be lost without them," Kyle says, stuffing a few items in his pocket.

We all walk up to the remaining people in the group and hug them goodbye.

I guide Liv away from the rest of the group, listening to them say goodbye to each other. "Liv, I just wanted to say thank you." I look back over at the group, seeing them hug each other with sad smiles on their faces. "Thank you for cleaning up Sera and Cassia."

Liv shakes her head, her dark hair swaying back and forth. "That's no problem, Xander. You know I'm always here to help."

I smile as I pull her into an embrace, her thin arms wrapping around my back softly. "Take care of them," I whisper, training my eyes to the floor.

"Always." She lifts herself from me, smiling kindly.

Sera crosses the room to get to me, and I incline my head to the left, indicating I want to speak to her. She seems to understand.

"Are you okay, Xander?" Sera's eyes are concerned. "Is everything all right?"

I nod my head a little too fast. "Everything is fine. I just want to make sure you'll be okay with Liv, Lara and Alfie."

Sera nods her head, smiles wide. "We'll be fine. It might be fun; we can get to know each other better." Sera looks over at the trio who are staying behind. "Cassia seems to have taken a liking to Lara." She nods her head and I follow where her gaze lands.

Lara has Cassia next to her, her long arm wrapped tightly around her shoulders, smiling widely down at her.

I smile sadly because I know that this might be the last time I see them.

Suddenly remembering, I move my hand to the back of my belt. "I have something for you," I say quietly, watching as Sera's interest piques. I slide the letter opener out of my belt and hold it out in front of her.

She looks up at me with worried eyes.

"It's okay." I move the object closer to her. "This is for you. It can keep you safe."

She reluctantly takes the opener from my hands, running her finger across the intricate design on the handle. "Thank you. But... why would I ever need this?"

"It's just in case of an emergency. We all got something when we first got here." I point to each person in the room, showing Sera that they all have some type of dagger in their belts.

145

She looks over at me and I point to my belt, showing her my dagger. "I even have one and I'm sixteen."

Sera nods slowly, placing the opener in her belt. "Thanks again."

I smile and walk back over to the rest of the group.

I hug Lara last. She rests her hands on my shoulders, her dark blonde hair falling over her green-blue eyes. "Make sure that the next time I see you, you're in one piece, okay?" she says.

I laugh. "I wouldn't count on it. You know me."

She laughs and gives me one last hug.

I walk over to Kyle who is standing by the door. He turns to look at the group. "Okay, guys. Are you ready to go?"

We all silently nod, seemingly exhaling the same nervous breath of air.

I look back at the group and wave before the door shuts behind me.

As everyone starts walking forward silently, I turn back around, giving one last, long look and a small smile before walking away from the place I was happy to call home.

CHAPTER THIRTEEN

The desert of the Wasteland is just starting to come into view as we walk farther out of the Estate.

Nobody is uttering a single word. Probably nerves, maybe excitement. Maybe some other emotion that they are keeping locked inside their heads. The only sound we are all making is the *crunch* of our booted feet against the hard-packed ground.

Vicky is walking next to me, the same way we always do when we are scavenging out here, but I guess we don't have to do that any more.

I feel sorry for the girls and Alfie because they have to stay and wait for us to come back for them. I hate to say it, but knowing Vicky and me, we will probably end up forgetting about them, but I know Kyle won't. He doesn't forget about anyone.

Kyle is at the front of the group and I'm at the back with Vicky, trying to ignore the horrible tension cramping in my foot. They've left about a two or three-meter space between us; probably so we can chat, and no one will interrupt us.

That's a very nice thing they did for us; if we could actually talk to each other.

"This is ridiculous," Vicky suddenly says, turning to look at me. "You haven't said a word in ages. What is wrong?"

I'm taken aback by her tone of voice, but probably since none of us has spoken a word, any sentence would seem harsh.

"Nothing, I was just thinking," I say slowly, carefully. "I was just wondering how long we've been walking."

"Physically, probably about ten minutes." A pause. "*Mentally*, probably about ten years."

I laugh because it's true—when no one speaks, it seems like time stops and the world around you slows down.

"Can you believe this is really happening?" I keep my eyes trained on the rock, dirt and cracks passing below the steps of my boots.

Vicky kicks a pebble in front of her, and we both watch as it bounces around until it stops. "I *can* believe it," she says. "But I think it will seem more real when we actually get out of the Estate." Vicky lifts her hands and gestures to the buildings around us. "It just feels like we are at work."

"But think about it." I nudge her with my arm. "No more being a Scavenger. No more waking up at dawn. The list just goes on and on." I laugh. "We are free to do what we want. Finally."

Vicky shrugs. "Yeah, but I'll miss being a Scavenger." She turns to look at me. "Won't you?"

I shake my head slowly, thinking it over. "Not really." I can't tell if I'm lying or telling the truth.

"But you were the original Scavenger," Vicky snaps, obviously thinking I was telling the truth. "How could you say you won't miss it?"

I do remember the day Kyle gave me the job of being a Scavenger. The first time was the scariest; I didn't know what I was doing. Then Vicky came, and she made it a hundred times better. Then Joel came and made it a hundred times *worse.*

So instead, I say, "You know what, Vicky? I'm lying, I *will* miss it. My head... my head's just all over the place at the moment."

Vicky places a reassuring hand on my shoulder. "I understand, Xan. You're tired. You're worried. You're nervous." She pauses. "But I'm nervous, too."

I smile widely, slinging one arm around Vicky's shoulders. Her hand wraps around my waist, and I squeeze her tighter.

"I'm glad I have someone who understands my weirdness." I lean closer. "We can be weird together."

Vicky laughs. "You can say *that* again."

"Hey, I wonder when we are going to reach…" I don't bother finishing the rest of my sentence, because we have entered the Wastelands desert.

*****

We are caught in the middle of a sandstorm. It's not as bad as the one I experienced by myself, but it's still painful to the point where I want to rip my skin off my body.

The black material of the scarf is wrapped tightly around my mouth, half-protecting me from the harsh particles pricking me in the face, in the arms.

My eyes are squeezed shut, causing *every single* thing around me to be pitch-black, and I'm being careful where I walk, because I don't want to accidentally bump into Vicky— or anyone, for that matter. I'm almost positive if I keep my eyes shut, I'll end up tripping over something; maybe even my own feet.

I slowly turn my head so that I'm facing the way we came from, and just in the distance, I think I can just about see the houses of the Estate.

"We need to find shelter!" someone shouts over the raging wind.

I feel something latch onto me. I look down and see Vicky's arms wrapped around my forearm. She's holding on so she doesn't get separated from me.

I swing my arm around her shoulders again and pull her closer. She's trying to hide her face from the sand in my shirt, but it doesn't work.

The tiny stabs of pain shoot up and down my arms, making them go numb until I can't feel my arm wrapped around Vicky's shoulders. I can't feel *anything.*

"Are you okay?" I try to shout to Vicky over my scarf and the wind.

"Been better, thanks," she shouts back. "You?"

"Been better." My breath feels hot under my bandana, and it makes me uncomfortable in this raging heat.

We just need to keep going. If we stop now, we'll never go again, and I think that might be the truth.

*****

Eventually, sometime during our trek, we find a small shelter to rest for the night, because I doubt any of us wants to keep walking in this sandstorm.

None of us would survive it.

When the last person—me—walks into the shelter, everyone lowers their bandanas. Exasperated breaths and the raging wind are the only things we can hear.

Everyone's still breathing heavily, covered in sand.

No one is saying a single word. I don't even blame them.

"Hey," I say, laughing, turning to face the others, "now you guys know how *we* feel."

Vicky snorts, covering her mouth with her hand to avoid bursting out laughing, and even—even Joel cracked a smile. He looks down, smile dropping with it.

After a few seconds, everyone else starts to join our laughter.

"Yeah, you're right, Xander," Kyle says. "We didn't realize it was this hard. We're sorry."

"Don't worry about it," I say, walking over to the corner. "You'll get used to it after a few hours." I gesture between Vicky, Joel and me. "We did."

This is the first time I even *looked* at Joel without scowling or curling my upper lip in disgust. He didn't seem weird about the fact that I just used him to make a point. I guess he forgot about our fight.

My semi-permanent bruise is a reminder that I made a mistake that day, and I'll never be able to take that memory away—no matter how hard I try. It won't leave me, even when I wish to pull it out of my mind with my bare hands.

I lean against the stone wall of our shelter, crossing my arms over my chest, coughing up some sand that managed to get lodged at the back of my throat.

Vicky comes and stands next to me.

"Well," Adam says quietly, getting our attention, "this is awkward."

Always leave it to Adam to lighten the mood, even when we all feel down.

Adam claps his hands together so loudly it startles me. "You know what? I'm gonna make a fire, 'cause why the hell not?"

"I'll help you," Drew says.

I can tell by the tone of Drew and Adam's voices, and their body language that they can feel the weird tension in the room. I mean, who can't? You can literally cut through the tension with a knife.

Vicky and I both sit against the wall, our heads are pressed against the stone, listening to the conversations between our group of friends.

Sometime during all of this, Adam and Drew both came back with a few sticks, and some dry things that I couldn't recognize since they were covered in sand.

They are all currently fighting over how to light the fire; Adam is suggesting rub two sticks together, while Drew is suggesting to use one.

I ignore the rest of the argument when Vicky turns to look at me. "I thought this trip was going to be fun." She looks over at the argument. "It hasn't even been a day and they are already jumping down each other's throats."

I pick up a handful of sand, letting the particles run through my fingers like fine talcum powder. "Yeah, I know. I'm getting sick of this. Hold on." I turn to look at Drew and Adam. "Hey, guys? Can you pick a way to light the fire *before* we all freeze over?"

Drew grins. "Yes, we can, Xander." He snatches the sticks from Adam's hands. "And *this* is how we are going to do it." He proceeds to use one stick to ignite the fire, and after a few minutes, the embers catch light, and, with some patience, the fire is roaring.

"It's about time," Vicky whispers so only I can hear. I grin.

I guess the fire wasn't really for warmth, I think it was something to look at before we all die of boredom, and it was something for Adam and Drew to do. I guess that's what this journey will need—just some patience. We all need to wait to get what we want, and what I want is to get out of this desert and find whatever the hell might be beyond this area.

I hope after all of this waiting, there is *something* for us in the Wastelands.

The fact that we are in this shelter now tells me that there might be something for us, because if we weren't here, Kyle would have believed that there was nothing, that it was a waste of our time.

I probably would have believed that too.

"What are you thinking about?" Vicky whispers, getting closer to me.

"Everything," I whisper back. It's not really a lie. "I'm thinking about everything, and how could I not? I mean, we are in the *Wastelands,* Vicky. *The Wastelands.*"

"I know, it's kind of surreal, isn't it?" Vicky whispers back, staring intently at the roaring fire in front of us.

I stretch my legs out in front of me, the same way Vicky's legs were the first time she sat down. "You're right. It doesn't feel real." My hand rests next to Vicky's, right between our legs, the back of our hands pressed together. Then something peculiar happens: her fingers lace with mine, and her palm presses against mine.

My body is alive with something I haven't felt before. I squeeze her hand and she squeezes back.

I don't know why, but I keep seeing parts of my nightmare flash across my vision, and the scariest thing is: we are only a few meters away from where the arrow impaled Vicky's chest.

A barely-silent gasp escapes my mouth, and it's too late to stuff it back inside.

"Hey." Vicky squeezes my hand again. "Are you okay?"

I look over at her, my lips parted to say something, but no sounds come out of my mouth.

No, I'm not, is what my mind wants me to say. *I just don't know how to tell you, Vicky.*

"Yeah," I managed to breathe out after a short time. "I'm fine."

The sandstorm has died down, and a low breeze can be heard as it passes through the small spaces in the shelter. It's scary, and at the same time, calming.

No one is speaking; we are all mesmerized by the fire that we haven't seen for a while. The heat from the fire is so strong that I can feel it through my boots.

Adam is sitting right next to the fire. He is using the flames to heat up his dagger, and then he stabs it into the sand, causing a popping sound to come from it.

Vicky's hand tightens around my own, and I look over at her. She's fast asleep.

How long has my mind been wandering? Maybe Vicky was just so tired she couldn't stay awake. My mind is too busy to fall asleep.

Everyone is lying on their backs; some are leaning against the wall. I look at the fire for a while, watching the way the orange and yellow light illuminates the darkness around us. The cracking and popping from the wood is the only thing I can focus on as my mind floats around the space.

I'm so tired that I didn't even feel Vicky's head loll onto my shoulder and her hand tighten around mine. I rub my thumb against the back of her hand to calm her down, and it seems to work.

I rest my head on top of hers and try my hardest to fall asleep.

CHAPTER FOURTEEN

When I opened my eyes I expected to see the sun, instead I saw the moon. Which is nice, but it also reminds me that we still have a few hours until we can actually start doing something. This is the best time to travel because it is cooler outside than it was earlier. I wouldn't be able to get these guys up and going for the life of me.

I wouldn't allow myself to fall asleep because I was positive that was going to have *that* dream again. The same one that will haunt me forever. The one that will pull me under until it's the only thing I can think about for the rest of my life.

I look down at mine and Vicky's intertwined fingers, then at her face. She looks so peaceful. Her face is relaxed, no crease on her forehead or even furrowing her brows. Her long dark hair falls over her face in a few strands, covering a part of her eyes, down to her lips.

I'm tempted to brush her hair away from her face, but I refrain from that thought, instead placing my hand in my pocket.

I slowly detach our hands, pushing myself up from the floor, mentally cursing when my joints click with every inch I move. Vicky shifts, just a little bit, just enough for me to suck in my breath, halting my movements completely. She relaxes again, snugging against the wall behind her. I exhale.

I walk over to the entrance, leaning against the rock that is still holding up the shelter.

I look back to the group, glancing at each and every member as hard as I can. It's difficult to see since the fire has gone out and is now a big clump of dark gray ash.

I shiver as the wind brushes up and down my spine.

It's weird looking back at somewhere you have lived for your whole life and being in the place where you have dreamed about being since you were twelve.

It's not as glamorous as I thought it was going to be. Well, honestly, I expected a lot of things that we didn't have in the Estate. Showers are one of them. More survivors are the other thing.

It's very weird when you play out scenarios in your head, and then they turn out differently. What's *even* weirder, is when you play out scenarios and they turn out exactly the way you thought. That's only happened to me a couple of times; most of them including Joel and what he will do, and some are what Vicky would say to me.

There are no lights out in the Estate, but I can just make out the black shapes of the buildings. What I never noticed before was that most of the buildings are the same height.

I'm going to miss Scavenging. I was lying when Vicky asked if I would miss it or not. The thing I'll miss most is feeling free when I'm leaping across the buildings. It never felt like "work" when I was with Vicky.

I lean my head against the cool rock, crossing my shaking arms over my chest, letting out a long breath that I didn't realize was trapped at the back of my throat.

A hand slowly rests on my shoulder, and I don't need to look to know who is standing right next to me, chest pressed against my side.

"Hey," Vicky whispers, removing her hand from my shoulder.

"Hi," I whisper back. "What are you doing up?"

"I just couldn't sleep." Vicky lifts up her right hand and rubs her fingers over the spot where my hand was only a few minutes ago. I don't think she even realizes she's done it, but then suddenly she freezes, shoving her hand in her pocket.

I pretend as if I didn't see anything.

I don't know why, but it felt natural to hold Vicky's hand. The shape of our fingers and palms seem to have molded together as one. When I curled my fingers around hers, I was sure she would wrench away from me, moving to sit somewhere else.

But she didn't.

She stayed with me, her hands still clutching mine.

I can still smell the intoxicating smell of smoke emanating from our skin and clothes. I like the smell—it's very distinctive, you would recognize what it is as soon as it runs up your nose.

Vicky shivers, hugging her arms close to her body, squeezing to stop shivering, but it doesn't work.

"Are you cold?" I ask, keeping my voice as low as possible.

Vicky nods. "A little bit."

I uncross my arms, wrapping one around Vicky's shoulder, bringing her closer to me. She nuzzles her face in the side of my body and stops shivering.

"Is that better?" I ask, trying to look down at Vicky's face.

She nods, doesn't say anything else as she presses her nose into my shirt.

After a few minutes, I decide to speak up. "Do you want to start the fire again?"

Vicky shrugs. "It's up to you," she says. "I'm not sure how to start a fire, so…"

"It's fine, I'll do it," I say, looking at her again.

Vicky nods slowly. "Okay."

I let go of Vicky at the same time she steps away from me. We both turn away from the entrance and walk over to the pit, trying to be as quiet as possible as we crouch down on the floor.

The gray ash stains my pants as I kneel down to start the new fire. I pile up the same amount of sticks we used last night, and I grab a new stick, trying to remember what Drew did to start the fire. Something about rubbing it against something? I wish I'd listened when Drew was arguing with Adam, but I couldn't because I was too distracted by the hand that was interlocked with mine.

I feel Vicky kneel next to me, resting her hand on top of my shoulder.

"How the hell are you supposed to do this?" I ask, angrily gripping the stick in my hand until my knuckles go a dangerous shade of white.

I hold my breath as Kyle shifts in his sleep.

Vicky slowly grabs hold of the stick, prying my hand away from it. "Give it here."

I give up, loosening my grip on the stick, my knuckles turning back to their normal color.

"I think they did it like this..." Vicky slowly places the stick on a log underneath the pyramid of twigs and sticks, then quickly spins it around with two hands, causing a small line of smoke to form. After a few minutes of doing that, the small fire grows until all of the sticks catch light and we are warm again.

I pull my dagger from my belt, poking at the sticks and twigs, watching with satisfaction as the sparks rise slowly toward the ceiling. I spread them out more, seeing the fire grow slightly bigger, then smaller within a few seconds.

We both lean against the same wall we slept on, staring at the fire in front of us, savoring the heat on our tired faces.

Without thinking twice about it, I grab hold of Vicky's hand, slowly lacing my fingers with hers.

She squeezes my hand before I drift off to sleep.

*****

It wasn't the hand shaking my shoulder that woke me up. It wasn't even my name being called—it was the gentle touch of my hair being moved out of my eyes.

Vicky kneels beside me, smiling such a kind and genuine smile that I can't help but stare at her for a few seconds, my eyes traveling every fraction of her face. Her hair is dropping from the sides of her face as she leans over me, her hair almost grazing my skin. She places a strand of her hair behind her ear, but since she is leaning over me, it falls back to its original position.

"Morning, sleepy head," she whispers, running a hand through her hair again.

"Morning, early bird," I say back, my voice sounding hoarse and dry.

Vicky smiles wider but doesn't say anything about my voice. "Come on, everyone is already waiting outside for you."

I sit up and look around the room, seeing a very empty, and very quiet shelter. The fire has gone out again, leaving clumps of ash scattered around the pit, making the sand that was once there black. I notice there is still a single burning ember in the ashes; I stare at it as I rub the sleep from my eyes.

I didn't have that dream again. I think holding her hand and her being close to me made me less worried, because I knew she was safe.

Vicky pulls my arm to help me get up from the floor, and I rub the remaining sleep out of my eyes, wanting to fall back down and go to sleep.

I look around the shelter, making sure that I didn't forget anything, then, seeing nothing, Vicky and I both slowly walk out of the cave.

"*And* he's awake," Adam says slowly, pointing to me. "Took you long enough, Xander."

I shake my head. "Sorry, guys. I didn't sleep very well last night."

Kyle steps forward. "Well, forget about it." He passes me a bottle of water. I take a big swig of it. "Now we can actually go out to the Wastelands in peace."

Vicky and I both glance at each other, smirking before following the guys the rest of the way.

*****

My feet are blistered. My whole body is covered in sweat by the time we reach the sand dunes. I don't have the energy to walk up these—none of us do. It came to the point where Vicky had to pull me up with her, and I don't even know how she suddenly got this extra power.

I lost all my energy before I even realized it.

"Just leave me, Vicky," I say to her when we just start to pull ourselves up the dunes. "Just—" Sand in my throat. "Just—leave—"

"Don't be stupid, Xander," she says back to me. "I'm not going to leave you, *none* of us are going to leave you, Xan. We can't—we can't leave you." She said that last part so quietly that I thought I just dreamed it. "Come on! Up! That's it! You've got it! You're almost there. Just a little bit more—"

Now, we are all in a straight line, all trying to walk up these hellish sand dunes *without* tripping over our own two feet.

My feet sink into the soft particles below me, but I use that to my advantage; I propel myself forward, ignoring the screaming feeling my feet are giving me as I push harder. I wipe the sweat off my forehead and continue forward.

My feet almost give up on me when I reach the top of the dune, but Vicky is keeping me held up.

"I'm sure there is something just beyond this point." Kyle uses his finger to point to the extra sand dunes ahead of us. "I'm sure there is."

"If we just keep on standing here, it'll get worse," I say after a while, getting everyone's attention. "Otherwise we—mostly me—won't be able to keep going. So, let's go!"

160

Everyone slowly starts walking down the slope, leaning back slightly to avoid stumbling forward. Which is exactly what I do.

When we get to the bottom, I see a flat piece of sand, something that looks easier to walk on. It looks like it goes on forever. Unless the heat is making me go crazy, it looks like it has some shade, but it seems like miles and miles away from us.

A sudden grating noise snaps me back to reality. A sort of metal against metal type of noise. I cringe a second too late. I turn around slowly, not caring about the others as they speed ahead of me.

What I see sends a shiver down my spine. Different emotions run through my body that I can't even name. Every thought has dropped from my mind onto the sand, and they are sinking into the particles as the seconds tick by.

A group of four people—men by the looks of them—are standing in a perfect line. All wearing the darkest clothes you could possibly think of. Bandanas wrapped tightly around their mouths and heads, only showing their dark, dark eyes. They raise what look like medium-sized swords, all pointed at... me? No, *us*. They don't look friendly. They look like they want to kill us. They probably *will* kill us.

My mouth drops open.

My breath hitches in my throat.

And I snap.

"Run!" I shout to the guys, my voice cracking. I turn around just in time to see the four shadowy figures charge down the slope, weapons pointed directly at us.

Everyone has stopped walking, despite my loud command, and they look at me dumbfoundedly, but as soon as they see what is chasing me, chasing *us*, they all widen their eyes and run.

I grab hold of Vicky's arm, pulling her with me to keep her running at the same speed as me. My dream will *not* come true. Not today. Not *ever*.

I can't look back. I can't look back. I *won't* look back at them.

Vicky and I run past some people, but I can't focus on anything, only getting to that flat expanse of sand.

A sudden whistling sound can be heard.

My heart stops and I'm pretty certain I'm already dead. But my feet are still moving. They are still getting Vicky and me away from the figures.

Then the arrow whizzes past my head, knocking me to the ground. A strangled gasp escapes my lips as I land hard on the sand, on my chest, and I think, *this is it, this is it, this is it*—

This is how I'm going to die.

"Come on!" I'm hauled up by my backpack by someone, and I don't even know who. They push me forward. My hand grapples for Vicky's, and as soon as my fingers touch hers, I know she is safe, she is *safe*.

She is with *me*.

I am not dead. *She* isn't dead.

We push in front of everyone else, eyes fixed on the horizon, only focusing on the sun as it—

And then suddenly I'm falling, hard.

My heart is in my stomach, and the world is a blur for only a second. I land hard on my side, and the darkness around me blurs for a long moment. I don't hear anything but the buzzing in my ears and my heartbeat as it slows down... down...

For a pure, solidifying moment, I think I've come to my devastating end again, but then I see the sand and my worries dissolve. Only slightly. The darkness shifts, light slowly pouring in from somewhere I can't quite see.

I'm not dead. I'm *not* dead.

And neither is Vicky. We are both lying on a huge bed of rock. A small layer of sand covers said rock, making it look just like the desert. I pull myself up, rubbing at my sore spot. I help Vicky up, and she winces.

"Who... the hell... were *they*?" Vicky asks, frantically trying to catch her breath.

"I... don't know," I say, wiping sweat off my forehead, trying to catch my breath as well.

Suddenly Kyle, Joel, Adam, Drew and Ponytail jump down, getting into a tight formation, visibly shaking and breathing heavily. They fall down more gracefully than we did. They must have seen us fall down, into this place.

My eyes scan the whole group with furrowed brows, because I know something is wrong. Something *very* wrong.

I lean closer to Vicky. "Where's Blinky?"

Vicky's eyes jerk to every single person around us. She shakes her head fast. "I... I don't know. Was she with us?"

"I think so. I'm sure I saw her with us." I shake my head, despite myself. "I... I can't tell." I look up. We landed in some kind of hole. A man-made hole. It's the same height, maybe more, as me. I can't see over the side, but I could easily try. The light pours in from the top. I can see the sky just as well as if we were standing in the desert. I reach up, grabbing hold of the sand, and I haul myself up, and over the side.

What I see sends my heart pounding in my ears, a rock in my throat, hands that can't stop shaking as I keep myself half-over the ledge.

Blinky is being pulled away from us by those shadowy figures. She tries so hard to get away, but they won't let her go—no matter how hard she thrashes in their grip.

My legs won't move. I can't move. *Nothing* will move.

They pull her up, one of them holding onto her legs, the other holding onto her arms. She's thrashing around, desperate to get away. The other two have their swords pointed at her chest, inching closer and closer.

And I still can't move.

No, is the only thing my mind says. *No, no, no.*

163

I don't know when, or how, but I managed to hoist myself up onto my knees, my hand stuck inside the soft sand.

I rise from the floor, but I'm too late, because Blinky's muffled screams suddenly stop as one of the figures stabs her through the chest.

CHAPTER FIFTEEN

A strangled scream escapes my mouth as I watch Blinky's body go limp in the figure's arms.

Get up. Get up, now!

I need to get to them. I need to stop them. They can't get away with this. They *can't. They can't, they can't.*

Get. Up!

One of the shadow figures throws Blinky over his shoulder, making her limp arms drop down his back. After a few seconds, I see a stream of red run down the length of his garments… and I lose it.

I burst forward, ready to throw my hands around the man's throat, but I get pulled back by the hem of my T-shirt, almost making it rip off completely.

Someone wraps their arm around my waist, pulling me down the hole. I'm dazed for a minute, trying to figure out where everything is. Then I see everyone's faces staring straight at me. They slowly ease me down, but I push them away, scratching against the wall to get up there again. To help. To do *anything.*

Kyle pulls me back, seizing hold of my shoulders, forcing me to look at him. "What are you trying to do, Xander? Get yourself killed?" he hisses, only a few inches away from my face.

I push him away, hard. "I can't let them get away with what they did, Kyle." My voice breaks, and I bite my lip to avoid breaking down in front of everyone. Instead, a strangled sob sounds at the back of my throat.

I can't get the look of horror on Blinky's face out of my mind. I can hear her scream as it rings in my ears.

And I can't help the tears streaming down my face.

But I don't care.

Vicky pushes her way to get to me. She spins me around, hugging me so tightly I can almost feel every broken part of me being fixed back together. Almost.

"I-I can't… I can't f-face P-Pony—" I can hardly finish her name, but Vicky knows exactly who I'm talking about. "I'll… I'll break if I see her, Vicky."

"You don't have to if you don't want to," Vicky whispers back, squeezing me even tighter.

I hear Ponytail crying and my heart breaks. My knees go weak, and I don't know how long Vicky can hold me.

Vicky helps me stand up straighter, bringing me around a corner, away from the others.

I can't help it—I fall to my knees. "I…," I start, breathing heavily. I can feel the rock growing inside my throat. "I just… *sat* there." I swallow hard, tears streaming down my cheeks. "I just sat there and watched as they stabbed…" I close my eyes and swallow again. "As they stabbed her through the heart." I've never felt this type of pain before. It's weird. It's different. It feels like someone is ripping my heart out of my chest.

Vicky kneels in front of me. She cups my face between her hands, forcing me to look at her, but I can't. "Xander, look at me. Please." My eyes travel up to her glassy blue eyes, and my vision blurs. "This isn't your fault. You did all you could."

"I could have saved her." My eyes fill with more tears, making this rock in my throat grow. "I could have saved her, Vicky."

Tears stream down her face. "I know, Xander." She brushes hair out of my eyes. "You would have been a hero," she says. "But you could have died just as easily, and I wouldn't be able to live with myself if anything ever happened to you." She slowly lets her forehead rest against mine, and I let the tears take over. I can't do anything else.

Vicky wraps her arms around me, pulling me to her before I can respond, but in my condition, I don't even think I could say a single word—to her or myself, it doesn't make a difference.

We both hug each other as tight as we possibly can, because we have nothing else to do. There is nothing we can do that will bring Blinky back. Nothing. I can't even imagine what is going through Ponytail's mind right now.

And the worst thing is: I didn't even know Blinky's real name.

*****

I was the first one to stop crying.

We are both still kneeling on the ground, neither mustering up the courage to move, to meet the others, to do *anything* but listen to each other breathe.

I don't know how long we've been in this position, but it must have been a long time because I can't feel my legs. It feels like tiny needles are pricking their way up and down my flesh, exploding in one place as I move slightly, then another. It doesn't even compare to what I feel everywhere else.

"When do you want to go back to the others?" Vicky whispers softly in my ear.

"I don't know," I whisper. "I don't know if I can face Ponytail, yet."

Vicky lifts herself from me and looks me in the eyes. "You won't know if you don't try."

I nod slowly and we both rise from the floor, wincing when our legs almost give out and we almost crash back to the ground.

"You okay?" Vicky whispers.

I nod, half-meaning it, and we both start walking back to the others.

I try my hardest not to look at Ponytail. I am positive that I will break down then and there if I see her face, because I will just be seeing Blinky in another form. Literally.

Thankfully, from where I am standing, Adam blocks the view of her, but if either one of us even moves an inch, I will see the red hair and green eyes of Ponytail.

Don't move, Adam, I plead silently. Please, don't move. Please, please, please—

"Why did those... *men* in the black clothes just stop and turn around?" Adam asks, crossing his arms over his thick chest. He still hasn't moved, and I don't dare to look up from the ground. I *can't* look up. If I see *anyone's* face, it will remind me that this is all my fault.

I can see Kyle shrug in the corner of my eye. "Maybe they got what they wanted."

"Us?" Drew asks. Even though I can't see him, I can already tell what his face will look like—and it won't look happy.

"*One* of us," Kyle corrects.

I stiffen at his tone, and Vicky grabs my hand and runs her thumb against the back of my hand. I can already feel myself drop from one single touch.

Either Kyle doesn't care about Blinky's death, or he is just taking it differently from the rest of us. I would probably say the latter; Kyle isn't heartless. When I came back from running away, he almost crushed the living *daylights* out of me with a hug.

We've all known Blinky too long to say we don't care that she died. It is just hard to make friends with someone who can't speak back to you. Who can't do anything but blink at us when we say something to her.

I squeeze Vicky's hand and let out a long breath that was trapped in my throat.

"But that's ridiculous," Adam says as he steps forward, leaving a clear view of Ponytail.

I stiffen to stone and keep my eyes locked on the ground.

Vicky squeezes my hand twice to get my attention, but I can't even think straight.

Don't look up! I shout inside my head. *Don't look up, Xander.* Don't. *Don't—*

"Why would they only take *one* of us when they could have easily killed all of us?" Adam continues.

"So, what? Are you complaining now?" Joel says bitterly, making me slowly close my eyes. "Do you want to go out there and help them finish the job?"

"Hey, watch who you are talking to, buddy," Adam says, pressing a finger to Joel's chest, making him stumble back slightly.

"What are you going to do about it, Adam?" Joel says, stepping forward. Wrong move, Joel. Why would he try to pick a fight with someone who is twice his size, and can probably knock him out with a flick of his finger?

"I'll tell you what I'm going to do about it, *Joel,*" Adam says, towering over Joel, hands curling into fists.

"Okay, okay, guys. That's enough," Drew says, stepping between both of them. "Fighting won't get us out of this hell, so just shut up and walk away from each other."

With a few huffs and a few grunts and curses under their breaths, they both walk away from each other.

Drew inhales, exhales, shakes his head. "Right, so, what are we going to do? We can't just stay here all day."

I finally decide to lift my head, but not to look at Ponytail— to look around. I need to see where we *actually* are. Right now, I have no idea where the hell we are. I have no clue how far we are from the Estate. Are we even in the Wastelands any more?

"We could go *that* way," I say, interrupting whatever argument Kyle and Drew were having. Right behind us is what looks like a tunnel of some sorts, but the top ceiling is half-made up of rock and half of sand.

169

The tunnel just seems to be an endless expanse of black.

"Yeah, because we *all* want to walk into darkness together, Xander," Joel says.

I didn't even realize he was even listening to me. "It was just a suggestion, Joel." I try not to roll my eyes as hard. "You could always stay here and wait for those guys to come back."

"And also," Joel says, completely ignoring me, "I don't want to be walking anywhere near *this* guy." He jerks his thumb over to the direction of Adam.

"Joel, seriously, what is the worst he could do to you?" Kyle asks, getting as frustrated as I am with him.

Adam steps up. "My knife might just 'accidentally' end up in his back, I don't know..." He shrugs.

"I would like to see you try, pretty boy," Joel bites back.

Adam snorts quietly, starting to pull out his dagger from his belt.

I rush forward, pulling his hand back down. "Don't even bother trying, Adam." I look over to Joel, who has a smug smile on his face. "He's not worth it."

Adam's nostrils flare as he slides his knife back into his belt, then I let go of his arm. "I wasn't *actually* going to stab him in the back," he whispers when Joel walked away from us. "I just wanted to see him scared."

"Look, Adam, as much as I want to see that happen to Joel..." I trail off, closing my eyes. "No one else should die; not now, not ever. Okay?"

Adam nods his head, rolls his shoulders backward. "Fine, I'm sorry."

I nod and don't say anything else.

"Okay," Adam says after a long time of silence. "So, who's going to be the first one to enter the Tunnel of Death?"

I scrunch up my eyebrows at the name.

Joel laughs, a sound that should be kept inside his throat. "No one? What a surprise. Nice suggestion, Xander. *Real* nice."

"Fine," I say, stepping forward, glaring at Joel. "I'll go through it—"

"No!" Kyle interrupts, lowers his voice. "If anyone should go through, it should be me." He looks around at everyone, then the tunnel. "I'll go through," he repeats, almost like he's trying to convince himself of something. "Don't wait up."

We all watch silently as the darkness completely swallows him whole.

*****

Never in my sixteen years of living did I ever think I was going to be sitting in an unknown place in the Wastelands, tucked next to my best friend and people I am glad to call my friends.

It didn't even occur to me that there might be random places that we *still* don't know about. We don't know a lot of things about the Wastelands; we've only seen it from a great distance.

I sit with my back against one of the walls down this (hell) hole.

Vicky shifts uncomfortably on the floor next to me, brushing away some rocks and dust, then finally settles back down, blowing out a sigh as she does so.

The back of her hand keeps brushing against my own, and I don't know whether to grab her hand or not.

Ponytail's quiet tears can be heard and it breaks my heart, piece by piece, until I can feel all the remains in the pit of my stomach. It *was* all my fault; I didn't stop those figures in time. I just watched as they pierced her through the heart, and the most I could do was scream at them.

I think Joel is trying to comfort her, but I can't see because I refuse to lift my head and look.

"Drew, can you *stop* that?" I say, finally having enough.

Drew had been pacing back and forth between all of us, muttering things like, "I wonder where he is," and "Shouldn't he be *back* by now?"

"How am I supposed to stop?" he says. "Kyle has been in there for *ten* minutes."

"How are you supposed to know that?" I ask, rubbing at my eyes. "You have no method of telling the time."

Drew shakes his head. "I counted the time off in my head."

Joel snorts.

Vicky looks up.

I continue to stare.

Adam bursts out laughing. "Wow!" he says. "That is *sad.*" He pats the seat next to him. "Come on, Andrew, take the load off. Kyle will be fine. He *is* a big boy now."

Drew runs his hands through his growing ash blond hair, still staring at the dark tunnel as if it will suddenly come alive with light.

Then Drew turns around slowly, staring at Adam with furrowed brows. "D-did you just call me Andrew?"

"*That's* what you're worried about?" Adam says back.

"No, I'm just—"

"Kyle!" I say loudly, making everyone's eyes snap over to the dark tunnel. His form is just starting to come into view. He raises his arm to cover the sudden light probably burning through his eyes.

"Hey, guys," he says, coming closer to us.

I rise from the floor, marching over to Kyle. "Well?" I start. "Did you find anything?" My voice is eager, too eager.

"Well... not really," Kyle says. "For starters, it was too damn dark, so I couldn't see a single thing."

"Then why were you taking so long?" Drew asks.

Kyle turns to him. "I was taking small steps because I didn't want to step on anything, or trip over anything. I got bored after a while and turned back. It seems to go on for a little while longer."

I peer over Kyle's shoulder and stare deeply into the darkness. "We should still go through," I say, turning back around. "I'm not waiting here for us to get killed off, one by one." A pause. "Who's with me?"

*****

All right, here we go; one step at a time.

In the end, everyone decided to follow me through the dark tunnel. Joel said no, but it was six against one, then he eventually gave up and followed us, no matter how much he huffed and muttered under his breath.

Even though I can't see, I can feel Vicky's presence next to me. I definitely know it's her, because suddenly she grabs my hand and interlocks our fingers together.

I squeeze her hand and she squeezes back. I won't lose her in this dark, dark tunnel.

I'm not sure how long we've been walking, but in my head, it doesn't feel like a long time. It might not have been. But it still might have been at the same time.

"What," Adam starts, "the *hell* is *that*?"

I wasn't sure where he was looking, but then I suddenly see it. It slaps me in the face. It punches me in the stomach. It burns into my eyes.

Light.

It's so dim that I'm not even sure if it is really there. I could have hit my head on a hanging object while I was walking through this dark hell.

The closer we get to it, the more I realize I wasn't actually imagining the light. Adam *was* right.

We decrease our speed every other step we take forward. Vicky's grasp on my hand gets tighter, but it doesn't hurt; it somehow feels more reassuring; I know she's here with me— right next to me. Safe.

173

At first, I didn't feel the pain reaching to my nose, but when I started to rub it, it got so much worse.

I'd bumped into a body.

"Sorry," someone, I think Adam, mumbles more to himself than to me. It wasn't even his fault.

Everyone stopped walking, all at the same time.

"Did you ever see this, Kyle?" Drew whispers from somewhere in the group.

"No," Kyle whispers back after a while. "No, I didn't. I didn't get this far."

I think the light is coming from the ground, but I can't be too sure; I'm still trying to wrap my head around the fact that we are in a tunnel under the Wastelands, far away from home, far away from… everything.

"What? Do we just… go through?" Adam asks, all signs of sarcasm gone from his voice.

"I guess we do," Kyle says. Even though it's dark, I can still hear the shrug of his shoulders, the uncertain look on his face. "Okay, so, who's going to be the one to go through first?"

"Why don't *you* want to go this time, Kyle?" I ask, stepping closer to who I think might be Kyle.

"Because, Xander, I went through the tunnel first. This is on you guys," he says, stepping out of the way so I have a better view of the light.

"You know what, guys?" Adam says, stepping closer and closer to the light. "I'll go through." I think he turns around to face the light, but I can't see anything besides the broad silhouette of his body. He breathes in, out, let's out a low whistle. "See you on the other side, suckers," he says.

Then the ground swallows him whole.

Drew, Joel and Ponytail go through the hole one by one, leaving Vicky, Kyle and me in the tunnel.

I grab Vicky's hand before she has a chance to step forward. "Be careful," I whisper.

"You too." She squeezes my hand, and I feel her slip away from me.

Kyle squeezes my shoulder. "Your turn," he says. "Enjoy the ride."

I laugh. "Don't be too long up here."

"Just go."

I step forward, then another step, then one more.

I can see the light at the bottom of this hole. I can see everyone's feet. It's not a very deep drop. At least, I don't *think* it's a very deep drop...

I take that one remaining step forward and I sink, then I'm sliding.

It was a slope of sand, not very steep, not very easy to climb back up.

Vicky walks up to me, pulling me up with her hand. "You okay?"

I nod my head, exhale a breath. "Yeah," I say. "Thanks." I wipe away all of the sand from my pants and T-shirt, shaking out all of the irritating particles.

"Glad you could finally make it, Xander." Adam's voice sounds so much louder in this quiet room, but he doesn't seem to care.

I don't reply to what he says, instead I take in everything that is around me. Darkness. Nothing but darkness, darkness, darkness. The one dim light is coming from a lamp in the corner of this room. I can see everyone; they are all staring at the dark as much as I am.

I am so immersed in the weird place, that I don't even feel Kyle drop down the slide, coming to stand next to all of us.

"What a load of *crap*," Adam says louder than necessary. "I was expecting something more glamorous than this."

Me too, Adam, I think, staring around the room. *Me too.*

My heart almost stops as we hear laughing, and it wasn't from one of us—it came from the darkness. It's a deep type of

175

laugh, one that carries on in this space long after the person stops.

I pull the dagger from my belt, holding it out in front of me. Everyone else does the same and, somehow, I'm not really surprised.

"They look so bloody scared." My heart races at the sound of the deep voice. It's been so long since I've heard a British person's accent that I almost forgot what they sound like. The way they pronounce every single word properly.

Something comes into the light. Slowly at first, but then it picks up speed.

It's a boy, probably around my age. He has dirty blond hair, with a few streaks of brown in it. His hair is long and covers most of his forehead and goes down over his eyes. It looks messy but styled at the same time—slightly overgrown. I can't tell what color his eyes are, but he has a thin face with a sharp jawline and hollowed cheeks.

It's a survivor, another one.

Another *survivor.*

Looks like we weren't the only survivors.

The boy walks closer to us, crosses his arms over his chest, and I knew I would never forget the next words that pass through his lips.

"Welcome to the Wastelands."

CHAPTER SIXTEEN

Ten, one hundred, one thousand blinks later and I still don't really understand what this boy just said. The words weren't foreign to me, but it felt like they just went in one ear and out the other.

Wastelands. Wastelands? *Welcome to the Wastelands.*

As soon as the words passed his lips, I was sure he was joking, just messing around with us, trying to get a reaction out of us, but his face is completely emotionless; no twitch of his mouth, no amusement in his eyes. He looks like he is waiting for us to respond to what he said. I guess we weren't the only ones that call it the Wastelands.

One, two, three seconds pass.

He uncrosses his arms.

Four, five, six.

He puffs out a loud breath of air, audible to all of us. "Do not all talk at once."

Whatever comment I was going to say next gets stuck in my throat and dies.

The boy steps forward, giving us a better view of his figure; his clothes aren't as worn and frayed as I thought they would be—they are simple, a thin light gray T-shirt that falls below his hips but stops just before his thighs, made out of a material I can't quite recognize. A cotton-like material is on one of his hands like a glove, but the other is completely bare. His pants are plain black, nothing special about them, and he has frayed leather boots on his feet. He is very thin and tall—his clothes are almost hanging off his body.

He studies each one of us carefully, eyes lingering on Vicky for longer than necessary. I pull her behind my back, and he smirks to himself, turning away to look at someone else.

The boy laughs out loud. "Well," he says, "if you are not going to talk, then I guess I am going to have to show you." He turns away from us and starts walking over to a series of... buttons, maybe? I can't be too sure what they are. I didn't even see them in the first place.

He breathes out a loud sigh and pushes a few of the buttons, making a small *click* sound around us.

Lights. *Lights*?

They have electricity?

The lights flicker all around us, making me blink and squint my eyes until I decide to shut them hard. After rubbing my eyes with the balls of my hands for a few seconds, I see something that sends my mouth to the floor and my heart to pound in my ears.

People.

Survivors.

Weapons... pointed at *us.*

My eyes scan over each individual in the spacious room; around fifty or so people are staring straight at us, not saying a single word, but all wearing the same expression; anger, hatred, confusion, all wrapped up into one look. Their gazes are almost as sharp as the instruments wrapped tightly in their vice-like grips.

The boy walks back to the center of the room, standing a few feet in front of the people. I seem to find my eyes drifting of their own accord; a male, head-to-toe in the same type of black clothing as the first boy, holds a medium-sized silver bow, the razor-sharp tip pointed directly at *my* chest. His bandana is wrapped tightly around his mouth, and a thin black hood is over his head, covering most of his features.

Unless it's just the lights, but his eyes seem to be darker than all of the articles of clothing on his body.

I feel my hand tighten around the dagger as I pull Vicky fully behind me. I'm *not* going to let that arrow be the death of Vicky. It has to go through *me* first.

"Okay," the boy huffs, "obviously you are in shock and cannot say a single word, so"—he steps forward—"I am just going to start talking."

The room goes quiet for a single moment, and the only thing I can hear is the beating of my heart slamming against my chest.

"We," the boy continues, "call ourselves the Wastelanders, and yes, I know what you are thinking, *Wastelanders? What a creative name*, but that name has stuck with us for centuries."

Centuries? As in before the world ended?

"This"—he waves a hand behind his back—"is just half of what there really is."

There's *more* people? I'm still trying to wrap my head around the fact that we weren't the only survivors left. There are *more*. I guess the end of the world didn't destroy *everyone*. I wonder if there are more people out there… somewhere.

I keep my eyes fixed on the guy in black with the arrow pointed at me, and no matter how hard I try, I can't seem to break the eye contact. He's looking at me with so much hatred that I'm sure it hurts more than if that arrow went straight through my chest.

I was so caught up in staring down the guy with the bow and arrows, that I didn't even hear the rest of what the other boy was saying. It must not have been important, because all of the faces on the Wastelanders are the same: bored. A pair of Wastelanders are having their own conversation altogether, completely ignoring the blond boy talking to all of us.

"Just shut the hell up already, Will," a girl's voice pipes up, causing a few of the Wastelanders to snicker.

I search the whole area, but I still can't find where the girl is located among all the people.

179

The boy holding the bow slides the arrow out from it, tucking it behind his back, where I'm sure there is a quiver full of those arrows. The bow-wielding person steps forward, pulling the bandana from his mouth in one swift motion.

I lean back, eyes wide with shock.

A girl.

The person with the bow is a *girl,* not a *boy.*

She must have been the one to tell the boy, I think she called him Will, to shut up. She looks to be the same age as Will, which means she must be the same age as Vicky and me.

"You're boring the life out of them with all this information," the girl says, still coming closer to the rest of us. "Back yourself up and give them room to breathe." She jerks her thumb behind her, and I suppress a laugh, recognizing it to be similar to something I would say.

Will laughs, holds up his hands, and backs away slowly. "*O-kay,*" he says, laughing. "No need to bite my head off."

The girl grins a small grin as Will retreats. It's the sort of smile that is genuine—maybe these two are close friends who have a lot of banter, which kind of reminds me of a couple of people I know well. As if she read my mind, Vicky shuffles behind me, placing a hand on my forearm.

An older woman steps forward, seemingly out of nowhere, arms crossed over her chest. Her long dirty blonde hair falls over her shoulders messily, stopping just before her ribs start. She looks to be the same age as Kyle and Sera, but I can't be too sure. The woman has that type of scrutinizing look on her face, one that you can't call a miss.

"What are you people doing here?" Her British accent is as thick as Will's, and when she talks, her voice is slow—careful, even.

"Look—we don't want any trouble," Kyle says and I slowly look over at him.

"And they speak," Will says loudly. "Finally."

"Silence, Will," the woman says without turning around.

"Yes, Mother," Will says quietly behind her, retreating slowly.

I turn my face to look over at Vicky, mouthing the word *Mother* with a furrow of my brows as she locks eyes with me.

"Carry on," Will's mother says, tilting her head slightly.

"We just had to find a place to hide," Kyle continues. "We got attacked."

"By whom?" she presses, keeping her face neutral.

"Some... figures in black just up there." He points to where we were only a few minutes ago, but it feels like hours ago. "They killed... they killed one of our friends."

I wince, suddenly feeling numb. My hands start to shake. My heart starts to race. I can't seem to focus on one single thing around me.

The murmurs that follow next are deafening. Everyone is talking to someone. We, and Will's mom, are the only people that are being quiet.

"Silence!" she shouts over the roar of conversation.

The whole place quietens down like a drop of a hat.

"Those figures you saw?" the woman continues. "We call them the Shadows. They are dangerous, and they have been threatening us for *God* knows how long. You are lucky to have escaped them."

"Well, it's not like we *all* escaped them," I hear myself say, all eyes turning to me. "They killed one of our friends."

Vicky presses a warm hand to my arm, tightening as the silence follows.

"And we are sorry about that. Truly," the woman says, sounding genuinely sad. "But we have lost approximately one hundred and fifty-one of our men to those savage Shadows, and we keep fighting, no matter what."

I zone out of the rest of the conversation, diverting my eyes back toward the girl; she's talking to Will, subtly pointing at us, saying a few things, shrugging at what Will says back.

But then she does something else—she pulls down the hood from her head, letting her long golden blonde hair fall behind her back and over her shoulders.

Her eyes find mine, and suddenly I'm trapped, unable to look away. It's too late to look away, now; she's already caught me looking at her. I'm too far away to see what color her eyes are, but without the hood and bandana, they look less dark—friendlier, somehow.

She looks down and my mind snaps back to reality.

"Well," the woman says, starting to sound bored, "if you are seeking refuge, then we must at least know your names."

None of us speak for a few moments.

"Okay, I will start this off." She steps forward, giving us a better view of her face; she's not as wrinkled as I thought she would be, but she doesn't look young. "My name is Johanna. This is my son Will." Will jerks his head up and waves a haphazard hand in our direction. "Now, what are your names?"

After a beat, Kyle steps forward. "My name is Kyle."

"I'm Drew."

"Adam."

"Joel."

"Vicky."

And finally, I step up. "I'm Xander."

"*Xander,*" Johanna echoes. "What an interesting name." She taps her fingers against her chin. "Do you spell it with an ex or a zed?"

"What's that got to do with anything?" I snap back.

She shrugs. "Just trying to make conversation. You know, since you are hardly saying a single word to any of us?"

"How do you expect us to say a word to you?" I say, sounding harsher than I expected. "You didn't exactly roll out the welcome wagon." I gesture behind her, pointing and waving at the many weapons that are *still* pointed at us.

Johanna looks behind her, frowns, looks back at us, shakes her head and turns around completely. "My good friends," she shouts. "We have guests." She points to the crowd. "Put those pointy instruments away and show some respect."

Who is this woman, and how can she just tell people to stop? Is she important? A leader in some way? My eyes can't help but notice the medium-sized dagger tucked inside her belt; it's clean, looks like it hasn't been used for a while. Maybe she didn't have to use it here.

The only sound I can hear is the grating of metal against metal as the arrows of the archers are sliding out of their bows.

It seems all of us visibly relax.

All of the tense muscles in my body drop until they feel like running water, flowing freely around my body.

But I can still feel the Girl's—which is what I've decided to call her—eyes on me. You know that feeling you get when you *know* someone is subtly looking at you, but you aren't directly looking at them? That's the feeling I have now, and I have to try to ignore it.

She's pretty—beautiful, even, I'll give her that. But the way her eyes seem to emanate hatred toward me, almost makes me want to shrink away in fear, re-thinking everything I thought about her.

"Come," Johanna's voice breaks through the silence. "Let me show you nice people around."

That's right, time to meet the other half of the people that are apparently *somewhere* in this place. Well, according to Will and his mom, at least.

Kyle was the first one to follow Johanna. The rest of us slowly follow, taking tentative steps forward toward the Wastelanders. As we walk away, their gazes remain on us. I can hear small laughs and whispers, something like "They are so small," and "Can you see how *skinny* they are? They look like they haven't eaten in *years.*"

The latter part is true, very true. We haven't eaten for a long time, and I don't even know how long it has been since I have had a *real* meal, other than grain and dried berries.

I ignore the gazes from all of them, except for Will and the Girl, whose eyes are still on me, and only me. I meet their stares, and I can't look away. I can't, I can't, I *can't*—

"If you will all follow me," Johanna says, "I will show you the Mess Hall."

The Mess Hall? God, how big *is* this place?

I turn my head just enough to see behind me; Vicky is standing next to me and the Wastelanders are right on our tail. As Johanna walks, the Wastelanders clear a path for her, making us walk past them. They are on both sides; there is no way to escape their gazes.

A burly Wastelander with tattoos snaking up his arms smirks an evil grin at me. Behind him is the Girl and Will, talking silently and looking over at us, nodding and looking around. I slowly look away. Obviously they weren't being subtle whilst talking about me.

Some male Wastelander whistles twice as Vicky walks past him—one quick, one long. She blushes and looks down, flipping her hair over her shoulder to cover her face. I try to shoot a look at who whistled, but I can't see who it was.

Vicky and I are at the back of the group, hardly able to hear what Johanna is talking about, but it doesn't really matter, because the place is pretty self-explanatory.

It's a dining hall, period. That's all it is. There's nothing special about it. The only special thing about it is what they call it—the Mess Hall.

It's a large, dark room, that smells like everything except for food. Tables and chairs line most of the center of the room, giving us a small amount of room to walk around.

As I weave from table to table to get to the other side of the room with Vicky, I spot a few more Wastelanders behind a wall with a square-shaped hole in it, which obviously is where they get food. The people behind the wall who are watching us with their big kitchen knives raised, frozen in place, must be the cooks.

I lean down to Vicky's height. "I hope we get used to that smell."

Vicky laughs quietly, grins, and says, "You and me both, brother."

As we exit the Mess Hall, I can't help but look inside the different rooms we pass; people seem to be having fun, shouting, laughing, arm wrestling, having *fun* in a way I never knew was possible.

"After we have finished showing you around," Johanna says, "I want you all to meet us in the Mess Hall." A pause. "We will be waiting there for you."

We pass a few more rooms, see more people from a distance, watching as they give us dirty looks, and finally after what feels like hours, we come to a stop in front of an old doorframe with a browning, ripped curtain separating us from whatever is inside.

"This is for you seven," Johanna says, eyes roaming around each person. "There are two rooms; one for boys, one for girls. Do not fight over the space."

We all stare at the curtain that separates us and our new living spaces.

I push myself forward, ready to pull the curtain back and step through the door when Johanna stops me with a hand to the chest. "But first"—she looks down at me—"I think it is time for a shower." She looks at everyone else. "Don't you?"

CHAPTER SEVENTEEN

The water from the showers is indeed perfect.

It's hot, it's refreshing, and most importantly, it's clean.

The only problem is, it only lasts five minutes.

"It's to save water," they said to me.

"At least it's always hot," they said to me.

"You will get used to it after a few days," they said to me.

There is no timer anywhere on, or near the showers, so we have no idea when the water is going to stop. We just have to assume it's going to stop in the next few seconds and try to be as quick as we can.

That's hard to do, since I haven't had a proper shower for one, ten, *sixteen* years of my life. Once the five minutes is up, you can't even turn the shower back on, you have to wait an *hour* for the water to be ready. I kept asking why, but the only answer they would give me is that they need to save the water. I think because this place is so big, they need to ration the water as much as they can.

I rinse whatever type of soap they gave me from my hair, rubbing it away from my eyes as best I can. The soap is quite irritating, but I'm not complaining—at least I have something to clean myself with. I haven't had that luxury for *years*.

Once I've finished, I tilt my head back, letting all the water fall on my face, then I tilt my head back down, letting the water bead on my neck, down my back, and I do that until the timer stops.

I can feel the water slowing down, getting less and less powerful with each passing second. It goes slightly colder as the water slows down. It's not cold enough to be uncomfortable, but just enough to notice.

Three.

Two.

One.

The shower is off.

The others are still using the showers. I can hear the water hitting the floor at different rhythm's. It's a weird noise—calming and at the same time, maddening.

There are exactly four cubicles—I'm in the end one. The walls that separate the different cubicles almost reach the ceiling, but a sliver is visible at the bottom, letting all of the water spill into my space.

As soon as I saw the showers, I closed the door, stripped off my clothes, and jumped right in. I didn't say that I was having one, I didn't give anyone time to react. I didn't even stop and turn around when they called my name.

The steam from the showers makes it difficult to see the floor as I blindly reach for the nice, white clean towel hanging on a hook just next to the door.

The cubicles themselves are quite large, big enough for me to move around easily, but not so big as to seem like I'm having a shower out in the open. Comfortable is the right word to use; I felt comfortable.

My hair seems longer as I brush it away from my eyes. Darker, too; so dark that it almost looks black.

At first, it hurt when I washed away the dried blood from the wound on my side, but after a few more seconds it didn't hurt any more. It's amazing how one scar can bring back so many memories, ones that you know you will never forget; ones that will haunt you forever. A constant reminder of the time I almost died.

The material of the towel feels weirdly soft, softer than I expected it to be when I wrapped it around my waist.

I don't bother to dry myself, yet. I want to savor the feeling of water on my skin before I forget what it feels like. It's different, somehow, the feeling of this water on my skin, compared to the water I used back home from a bottle of water. It feels better, cleaner, healthier; like it's actually meant for humans.

Unless I'm just imagining it, I swear the rest of the showers turned off at the same time.

"Whoa—man!" Adam shouts from his cubicle, which just so happens to be right next to mine. "That was the *best* shower I've had in *years*!"

I don't know what it is about the steam, the condensation running down the walls that makes me feel at home, like I'm back in the Estate. It makes me feel happier. Maybe it's just knowing that there is an actual *shower* to use and not just a bottle of water.

I can still remember the time I had to use a packet of water bottles to wash away the sand when I ran away from everyone; when I punched Joel, and he punched me back, harder. The bruise left by Joel throbs as I think about it over and over, playing it over in my mind. I can still see the blood as it stained his teeth. It's almost like the image has burned into my memory, forcing me to think about it every time something as simple as a scar comes into my line of sight.

I remember not hearing anything after we fought.

But most importantly, I remember the tears in Vicky's eyes, the pain in her face, the way she tried her hardest to get Joel off me.

The way she shouted my name...

Three taps on my shower door startle me, snapping me back to reality. I suck in a startled breath as I take a step back, away from the door.

"Hey, Xander?" Adam says, waiting a few seconds before continuing. "What are you doing?" A pause. "Are you even still in there?"

"Which question do you want me to answer first, Adam?" I shout back to him, wiping water from my forehead.

I hear Adam laugh. "Neither," he says. "I just wanted to know in case you fainted, or something."

Ever since Adam has told me about him being shy, he's been friendlier to me, like we've been friends for years.

"That's really nice of you," I say back, trying to keep my voice emotionless. "But I would love it if you *don't* talk to me while I'm naked."

Adam laughs again. "Got it." He shuffles around outside. "We are all ready to go. Are you coming?"

"Yeah, I'll be out in a bit," I say. "Just go without me."

"Are you sure?" I hear Kyle chime in.

"Yeah, just go," I say, tightening the towel around my waist. "It's only down the hall, it's not like I'll get lost." I shrug even though they can't see me.

A few beats pass before someone replies.

"Okay, fine," Drew says.

"We will be waiting in the room," Adam says.

"Don't be too long," Kyle says. "We need to meet that woman—Johanna, I think her name is."

"Yeah, okay then, guys," I say. "I'll be out soon. Just give me a few more minutes."

"Okay," they all say at the same time before shutting the door behind them.

I breathe out a sigh as the silence continues and continues.

The only audible sound that I can hear is the *plink, plink, plink* of the water hitting the floor at a constant speed, drilling into my head as if looking for something, somewhere to settle on my mind.

Feeling satisfied, I pull the white towel from my waist, but I pull it up in time to avoid it getting wet on the shower floor. I drape the towel over my head, drying the big mess of hair on my head.

Once I've done that, I pull on my pants, buckling up my belt, making sure my knife is nice and secure before doing anything else.

I stuff my old T-shirt in my back pocket before unlocking the shower door. I don't see the point of putting it on; it's old, and let's be honest, I've been sweating in it, and I don't want to put it back on my clean body.

I open the door.

It takes me a moment to adjust to the sharpness of the room, having been so used to seeing steam in the cubicle, I have to squint to avoid a headache.

It goes as quickly as it came.

I shiver as a gust of cold wind brushes against my skin, and I wonder, for a moment, where it might have come from.

When I first came into the shower room, I didn't notice many things; I just saw the shower and I got in. It didn't even occur to me that there would be anything other than a few showers in here, but no—there's also a mirror.

I don't know what made me walk over to it. Maybe it was the fact that I've only seen my reflection once in God knows how long.

When I wiped away the condensation, the first thing I saw—which is the only thing that stood out—is my bright blue eyes. I run my hands along my face, noticing my skin is slightly lighter than its usual olive tone, but maybe it's just the lights playing tricks on my eyes.

I brush my hair down with my fingers, styling it back to the position it was originally. I breathe out a puff of air through my teeth, my hands still fighting their way through my unruly dark hair. My hair isn't as long as you would think it is. That's because I used to cut my hair with my knife. Stupid mistake, I know, but it saved me from having hair as long as Vicky's.

Irritated, I untangle my fingers, slowly turning away from the mirror, ignoring the way my face seems to have gotten hollowed, my features more defined. I need to eat something, right now.

Walking over to the door, I have a strange feeling of wanting to have another shower, just to be sure, just to make sure I'm clean—but I am; I'm already clean.

My hand barely touched the rusted doorknob, before the old wooden door swings open and I start, staring with wide eyes.

I crash into the body that stepped through the frame.

"Hey, watch where you're going." The Girl's voice has never made me angrier before.

I can just make out the top of her blonde head. "You're the one that crashed into *me*," I say, getting angrier, looking down at her face. "Maybe you should watch where *you're* going, yeah?"

She takes a few seconds to realize how little I'm wearing. Her eyes travel from my legs, to my torso, to my face, her eyes still full of hatred.

Suddenly, I realize she's not empty-handed. She's carrying a pile of clothes, more than likely for us.

"Here," she says bitterly, shoving the pile at me. "Johanna wanted me to give you these."

I take the pile from her hands, noticing she has her bow and quiver slung around her back. The string of the bow and strap of the quiver are the only things visible on her chest. I look at her eyes, seeing what color they really are; they are hazel, almost green.

She turns away before I can take a better look.

"Well," I say, breaking the very awkward silence, "I'm going to leave."

The Girl sarcastically smiles, if that's even possible. "That would probably be a good idea."

I scoff, and, even though I'm not proud of it, I slightly nudge her as I walk out of the room.

I hear her mutter something under her breath, then laugh quietly.

I turn toward the bedrooms, and I can't help but notice how she looked back at me before closing the bathroom door behind her.

*****

The first thing Adam said to me was, "Damn, you took your time. What the hell were you doing?"

"I ran into that blonde girl." The one that looked at me with enough hatred to stab me through the heart. "She gave us these."

All the boys had the same idea as me: don't put your T-shirt back on but keep your pants on.

I throw the top article of clothing to Kyle, which turns out to be a dark gray shirt, the same type that Will and the rest of the Wastelanders were wearing.

I throw one to everyone.

When Adam tries to put his on, it hardly fits the shape of his torso. "Huh," he exhales, staring down at his chest. "Well, it will have to do."

I leave the last one for me. A light gray piece with a hood, softer than anything, which is really surprising. The whole shirt is sleeveless, completely exposing my arms.

I walk over to my bed, which is the smallest thing in the world, but at least I don't have to sleep on rock. I haven't actually tried it out yet, but I can't wait to feel what the mattress will feel like under my body.

I grab my bandana from the old wooden bedside table, which only stands on three legs, and just in case, I tie my bandana around my wrist, making sure my dagger is secure on my belt before walking out of the door, everyone else following suit behind me.

When we got out of the shower, Vicky and Ponytail decided to have one. I don't even know if they realized that the Girl was in there with them.

The girls walk out of their room at the same time we walked out of ours. I let everyone go first, and I wait near the back for Vicky. The girls are wearing the same thing we are. Vicky is in a dark gray, almost black shirt, and her hair is the same—tied into a plait down her back; the same length as always.

"Wow," I say. "You look… like… a Wastelander." I must admit; Vicky does look different. The way the material hugs her body makes her look more… dangerous, somehow. Dangerous in a good way, though.

"Likewise," Vicky says back, tugging the hem of my shirt. "Gray suits you. You should wear lighter clothes more often." Her eyes narrow slightly. She reaches forward, pressing a single finger to my chest, where a hole has been ripped near the center of my shirt, exposing a small fraction of my chest.

I shrug. "It came that way when she gave it to me."

"Fair enough." Vicky laughs, lifting one shoulder for a small shrug.

I nudge her with my elbow, smirking slightly as I say, "We better catch up with the others."

CHAPTER EIGHTEEN

No one looks up as we silently slip inside the Mess Hall.

The whole room is filled with the Wastelanders, talking loudly as they fork food into their laughing mouths. I'm in total shock as I see one group of people near the back of the room *throwing* food at each other and laughing. No one even notices they are doing it.

We spot our group right in the center of the rowdy Wastelanders, all of them looking as uncomfortable as they probably could be. Our group looks tiny compared to the others; they are all skin and bone while the others are pure muscle. The only exception is Adam; he looks like he actually could fit into this place.

Johanna doesn't stop talking even when we come into her line of sight, right near the back of our group.

"—does not matter if you just arrived here," she says, intertwining her hands on the table. "Every one of us has a part to play. We all have specific jobs for you, and we hope you will learn to get on with them." She smiles such a fake smile at each person in the group that it makes me want to wipe the smile off her face.

They have jobs here? So, it's not just a place where you can do what you want, and everyone will be fine about it? I guess they are more like the Estate then we thought.

Johanna grabs a small piece of paper from the Girl who is sitting to the right of her, and Will is sitting to the left of her. Both have their arms crossed over their chests, faces as impassive as they could be. "The three of us have come up with a job for each of you."

Johanna drops the paper on the table in front of her, and I try to take a peek at it, but she tugs it closer to her, almost like she's trying to hide it from us.

"Okay," Johanna says, eyes scanning over the carefully written words. "Adam." He quickly jumps to his feet. "You will be assigned with Tessa to be a Security Guard down by the entrance—the place we first met you."

Of course they will assign Adam to be a "Security Guard" down near the entrance; they wouldn't expect him to be anything else—and we don't either. Adam has that type of protective physique; he looks like he could crush rock with his bare hands.

Johanna points out who Tessa is, and I crane my neck to take a look at what she looks like. Long light brown hair and even lighter brown eyes. Pretty. Very, very pretty. She is standing just a few tables away from us, talking and laughing with a few people at the table next to hers.

"*Damn.*" Adam runs a hand through his hair, fixes his tight-fitting shirt. "Don't mind if I do—" Then he's off, slowly walking over to Tessa, who still hasn't even looked his way. He runs another hand through his dark blond curls, messing them up slightly just before Tessa looks up and smiles, holding out her hand for him to shake.

I nudge Vicky with my elbow, leaning in closer to her, nodding my head in the direction of Adam and Tessa. "*This* should be good."

Vicky smiles, her nose creasing slightly at the edges. "You know what's going to happen, don't you?"

I puff out a breath of air, lean back. "Of *course* I do." I look back over to the pair. "It's Adam; he'll swoop in and try to steal her heart. Probably crash and burn along the way. Then she'll probably come back to him because of his... charm, I guess."

"Sounds about right," Vicky agrees, and we turn our attention back to Johanna.

"Joel," she says, and he lifts his head up from looking at his lap. "You will be working with Zach down in Engineering, fixing things that need to be fixed, building a few things— stuff like that." She points out someone in the distance, who I'm assuming is Zach. He's extremely tall, with long graying hair tied into a ponytail behind his head, head-to-toe in nothing but black.

Joel nods his head, says nothing as he walks over to Zach and a few more people.

Johanna continues to list out our names and the jobs we are going to do; Kyle will end up working with a few people as a Medic, stitching up a few of the wounded, healing the sick— something he never wanted to do, but, being Kyle, he said yes. I think he wanted to ask to be a leader with Johanna, which is what he was in the Estate, but he couldn't bring himself to ask. I don't think anyone would dare to ask for that kind of role.

Johanna said for Drew to be something called a Runner, which involves running around the Wastelands, trying to find signs of life, new territory and anything that could be useful. Very much like being a Scavenger. But Drew protested and asked to be a Medic, then after some badgering, Johanna gave up and said yes.

I hope I get the job to be a Runner.

Because Johanna has no idea what Ponytail can do, she got stuck with the job of being a Cook, working in the kitchen with a few others.

Ponytail seemed okay with it.

"Vicky," Johanna says, smiling at her. "You will be working as a Weapons Cleaner with Will."

Will turns in her direction and very clearly winks at her.

I clench my jaw so hard it actually feels like it's going to break.

Vicky looks down, smiles, says, "Okay," gets up from her seat, and walks away with Will. She looks back at me, but I turn my head in the opposite direction, avoiding her gaze completely.

And it kills me.

"And finally," Johanna says, making me turn to look at her. "Xander." She silently reads whatever my job will be.

I silently hope: Runner, Runner, Runner.

Runner.

"You will be assigned as a Hunter."

I try so hard to hide my disappointment. I can't really tell if I failed or not.

"And you, my dear boy, will be working with this young lady right here," Johanna continues, wrapping an arm around the Girl's shoulders, giving her a small squeeze, which the Girl just smiles at.

I almost fail to hide my anger as the Girl's hazel eyes stare deep into my soul, and she doesn't even try to hide the fact that she *is* staring openly at me.

So instead, I swallow the protest stuck in my throat and say, "Okay."

I try to ignore the small smirk the Girl gives me before she gets up from the table and walks away.

And I follow behind her.

*****

Now that I know that the Girl is a Hunter, the bow and arrows are starting to make sense.

We don't say a single word to each other as we pass several hallways, go through different doors, pass some Wastelanders who don't even glance our way.

She stops so suddenly that I almost bump into her. The door she stopped at is old—very old, in fact. She turns the rusty doorknob, and I cringe as the whole thing squeaks on its hinges.

I step forward slowly, suddenly stunned at what I see inside.

197

Weapons.

Weapons everywhere.

On the walls, on tables, some are even sprawled across the floor. I think I even see a small pile of them in the corner.

A nightmare, I think, stepping forward. I have just walked into a nightmare.

But I don't turn back.

I shut the door behind me.

Swords, knives and spears of all different sizes line one wall. The only place on this wall that I can find without a sword or knife on it is where a door is, leading to a place I don't know. I see another door near the corner of the room, which I'm assuming is filled with *more* weapons.

"Remember, Vicky, you have got to be *gentle* with them, they are *weapons,* not toys that you can just throw around."

I relax my tense muscles as the familiar British voice invades my ears.

"Yes, I know they are *weapons,* Will." I grin from ear to ear at the sound of Vicky's voice. "And I'm *not* throwing these knives around." She exhales loudly. "Why can't I do it like this?"

"Because it is dangerous, and—oh, hey, guys!"

Vicky and Will are standing at a table, a cloth and a small dagger in Vicky's hand, and Will's hand on hers. Because Will towers over Vicky quite a bit, he had to stoop down to keep his head level with hers, his face almost pressed against hers.

And I almost shatter my teeth.

Vicky steps away from Will as soon as she sees the look on my face, but if only she could read the emotions in my eyes at this distance.

"What are you guys doing here?" Will stuffs his hands in his pockets, shuffling uncomfortably on the spot.

"I'm looking for a bow to suit him." The Girl jerks her thumb behind her back at me. "I was wondering if you could help me."

Will looks in my direction, hesitates for a split second, eyes searching my face. "Oh—y-yeah, yeah, of course I can." He crosses the room, leaving Vicky behind, stops short in front of a wall full of bows of different colors, sizes and materials.

Will pulls off a simple black bow, curved at the limbs, medium-sized. He hands it to me and I take it as if it's made of glass, like it will shatter into a million pieces when in the hands of the wrong person.

It's too beautiful, too perfect for someone like me.

Will hands me over a quiver full of arrows, the same glossy black texture as the bow, and I stare at them as if they aren't real, like this is a dream I'm about to wake up from.

Wake up.

Wake up.

"Xander?" Will says and I look up, staring at him with wide eyes. "Are you going to try it out?"

I snap out of my daze like a flick of a switch. "Oh, yeah, yeah, yeah," I say quickly, shaking my head. "Here, could you hold this for a second?" I shove the bow to him before he can reply, and he holds it out in front of him. I slip the quiver onto my back, securing it, making sure it's comfortable enough. I make sure I can grab an arrow smoothly.

I take the bow from Will's hand, thanking him with a small nod of the head.

I start to reach for an arrow when Will stops me with a touch to the arm. I back away as if his touch burnt me.

Will doesn't notice my sharp eyes on his retreating arm. "I would not do it in here if I were you." He points to the door with the swords on the wall. "Go in there."

And I do.

I slowly walk toward the door, the Girl a few feet behind me, and I open the door slowly.

Darkness.

I only see darkness.

Nothing but pitch-black emptiness.

The Girl pushes in front of me, says something sarcastic under her breath, flips a light switch on. Each of the lights turn on individually, slowly brightening the room. The sudden bright lights blind my eyes for a moment as I see what is inside the room.

Targets.

Dummies.

Things hanging from the ceiling, which have giant holes and rips in them. You can clearly see where the arrows and knives have impaled the targets, completely destroying them.

We step inside, the door slowly closing behind us, and I have no idea how it happened, but I don't care, because I can only focus on the things in front of me.

"*Now* you can try it out." The Girl steps closer to me, but I can't see her. She's behind me, but her voice sounds somewhere else; almost different as if I wasn't really paying attention.

I slide an arrow from my quiver, stretching my arm up to pull it out, my hands fumbling with the top of the arrow.

I remember reading a book with an archer as the main character. The story didn't interest me because the author made it seem like the character knew *exactly* what he was doing, even when he'd never touched a bow in his life. I try to mimic what the character was doing in the book, seeing if I can remember if I'm holding the bow right. I rack my brain because I read the book years ago. *Come on, Xander. It's not rocket science.* My thoughts sound frustrated inside my head.

"You *do* know how to shoot one, don't you?" the Girl asks.

I press my lips into one thin line, shaking my head. "Of course not." I shrug. "I never had the opportunity to learn." I stare down at the black bow for a few seconds, feeling the smooth, smooth texture. "Who built this, by the way?"

"The Engineers did," she replies, sounding more frustrated by the minute.

"Oh." This must have taken years to build. It's so smooth, such a strange material that I'm sure it didn't take one day to build this thing I'm holding in my hand. The girl doesn't say anything for a while, just watches as I admire the weapon. "I still don't know how to shoot this thing."

"Here."

Suddenly I feel her close, too close, her arms touching my arms, her chest pressed against my side. "Like this," she says. "Relax your muscles, you're too tense."

I swallow hard as her hands find mine, helping me notch the arrow onto the taut string.

"Okay," she says, backing away slightly. "Pull the string back to your jaw." She lifts her hand, making a show of examining it.

I do and suddenly wish I hadn't; the string is too tight, too powerful, but I don't release it. I can't. I feel the string cutting into my fingers, making me more and more uncomfortable with each passing second.

"Keep the arrow in the center of your vision." Her voice is just above a whisper, sounding kinder than she normally does. "Lower your elbow slightly." She doesn't give me time to before she slowly lowers it for me, pushing it so softly that it feels like air.

Her hands slowly move to my side, pushing so I'm straighter. "Keep your body rigid, but straight." Her palm is placed where my scar is, and she has no idea about it.

She lets go of me so I can shoot, stepping back to cross her arms over her chest, looking bored suddenly. "Go on, then. Shoot."

I ignore her sudden demand and take my time, moving the arrow to the point where I think the center of the target is. If I keep the arrow on the center of the target, more than likely it won't hit dead center when I release. So, I move the point slightly to the left.

I suck in my breath as the string slips through my fingers.

The arrow flies toward the target and I'm so dazed that I don't even know if the arrow hit the target. I don't even realize how much pain I'm in until I start to think about it.

My arm is stinging, and I almost drop the bow to the ground.

I bite back a groan of pain when I clutch at my arm in agony. "Why does… my arm… hurt?"

The Girl laughs quietly. "You're such a baby." She's still laughing even when she says it. "It was only the string whipping across your arm."

I take some time to find the arrow, my heart slightly dropping when I can't find it on the target, not even near it. I find it protruding from the wall behind it, about five feet away from the actual target.

Embarrassing.

How embarrassing.

"What the *hell*?" I say, pointing to the arrow in the wall. "I never even got *close* to it."

She scrunches her eyebrows at the arrow, shaking her head slightly. "Huh," she says slowly. "It looks like"—she swallows—"you're going to need a bit more training."

The suggestion is so obvious that I actually start laughing, out loud. "Of course I need more training," I say, pointing to my first and worst shot in my life. "I don't think you will want me as a Hunter if I can't even shoot the damn animals."

She crosses the room to get to me, staring at me in the eyes for a few seconds. Her eyes are so hazel, such a soft, strange color that I almost forgot what I just said to her. She looks up slightly, making her eyes seem greener, somehow. Beautiful.

"You've got to calm down, okay?" she says, her eyes never leaving mine. "Getting angry at nothing will not solve your problem. I can help you get better at archery."

I shake my head, step back. "Archery just isn't my forte."

The Girl doesn't move. "It wasn't mine, either. Until I trained, of course."

I hesitate for a second. "How good are you?"

She looks down. "I-it doesn't matter how good *I* am, Xander." She steps back slightly. "This is about you, okay?"

"Please," I whisper, "show me."

She looks down again, bites her lower lip, pulls the bow from her back, and in just a few seconds, she pulls the arrow from her quiver, lines it up with the bow and shoots.

Like she has done it a million times.

The arrow is just next to the center, but it still manages to slap my shot in the face.

I blink. "Wow," I breathe, still staring at the silver arrow stuck inside the target. "H-how—how… did you—?"

"Practice," she says, lowering the bow, "and patience." She slides the bow onto her back. "Which is exactly what you need to have if you want to succeed in archery." She steps closer to me, lowers her voice slightly, just above a whisper. "It doesn't just happen overnight. Nothing really does."

I can't meet her eyes; I keep staring at the arrow inside the target.

"So," she says, coming into my line of sight, "every single day, I want you to train with me until you can"—she looks over at the target, hiding a smile—"at least *hit* the target."

I'm taken aback; this is the first time she actually made a joke. Even though it was mocking me, it was still a joke.

I shoot her a dirty look, trying to hide a smile creeping onto my face.

She can't hide the smile she has plastered on her face. "Okay, so, tomorrow, this time." She turns around and starts to walk away, slowly looking back. "Don't be late."

I almost expect her to turn her head around and say, *Or I'll throw water on your face,* but she doesn't… because only Vicky would think to say that to me.

"Hey!" I call out to her and she stops, but doesn't look back. "I… still don't know your name." I don't really want to keep referring to her as "Girl".

She looks back slightly. "Kara."

Then, she walks away.

CHAPTER NINETEEN

When I walked out of the training room about five minutes after Kara, I didn't see Vicky or Will cleaning the weapons. I didn't see anyone. It was so silent that I could even hear my own heartbeat as it pounded against my chest. I don't know what it is about this place that sets my heart racing, but I really don't like it.

I swing the bow onto my back, making sure it's secure before walking out of the weapons room.

When I went to retrieve my arrow from the wall, it managed to get stuck inside whatever the walls were made out of, and I didn't even realize that I was strong enough to do that. It left the tip of the arrowhead slightly bent, but other than that, the rest of the arrow was fine.

A few younger Wastelanders nod in my direction when I pass them in the hallways, and I ignore the pounding in my chest from thinking they were going to do anything else to me. I guess that's what makes my heart pound—the Wasters, with their overpowering size and sharp eyes.

The Wastelanders are so different to us from the Estate; they *look* like survivors—tatted clothes, long hair, battle wounds and scars (from what? I don't know,) and hollow cheeks and faces from not eating enough food, even though they have cooks to prepare their meals, some of them look like they are about to keel over.

I follow some people, staring intently at their backs as they make their way to the Mess Hall—hopefully.

They do, and I'm immensely happy. *I need to find my* own *way around,* I remind myself, thinking about the maze of hallways and sharp turns.

I spot Vicky sitting at a table with Adam and Tessa and some other Waster I've never seen before. They are all talking and smiling at each other, despite the frown they are receiving from the other Waster on the table.

I casually slide into the seat next to Vicky's, nudging her side lightly, making her smile. "Hey," I greet her, making her smile wider.

"Hey," she replies. "How was training to be a Hunter?"

"It was... painful, to say the least," I say, causing Vicky's eyebrows to scrunch up. "Don't ask." I shake my head, thinking about the way the string snapped against my forearm.

The way Kara's arms were pressed against my side...

Vicky shrugs, nods her head, turning back to her food. "Aren't you getting anything to eat?"

I shrug. "I might later," I say. "I don't really have an appetite at the minute."

I stare at the brown mess on her tray, trying to unravel the curl of my top lip and I fail. The food doesn't look appetizing whatsoever; it looks like something you would spit out after chewing it a few times.

"What the *hell* is in your tray?" I ask, still staring at the contents.

Vicky swallows the food in her mouth, swirls the rest with her spoon. "I don't even know," she says, scooping more onto her spoon just to let it drop back in her tray. "I heard some people in the kitchen call it 'stew', so I'm just going to go with that."

"Yum," I say, dragging out the word. "*Please* tell me there are other options."

"Unfortunately, no." She lifts up her spoon, pointing in the general direction of all the Wasters. "See?"

She's right, all of them have that weird "stew" in their trays, and they seem to enjoy it.

"Oh, well," I say, turning back to her. "Food is food, right? I probably wouldn't care if it grew legs and walked off my tray."

Vicky laughs, spooning more of it in her mouth as if she doesn't care what it looks like.

I turn back to Adam and Tessa; they are both talking intensely to each other, sitting rather close to each other. Adam's hand rests on the back of Tessa's chair.

Because I'm me, I kick him under the table, causing him to stop talking and say a quiet "Ow," which he almost breathes out.

"Oh, I'm sorry, Adam," I say, my voice dripping with fake sympathy. "Was that your leg?"

Adam glares at me, but I only smirk at him, slowly turning to face Tessa. "Hi," I say. "I'm Xander." I offer a hand to her, which she takes, shaking it once.

"Tessa," she says back, her light brown eyes gleaming.

"Oh, Tessa?" I tilt my head. "You're the girl Adam keeps talking about?"

Now it's Adams turn to kick me under the table, but I just smirk wider, trying not to burst out laughing.

Tessa blushes, looks down. "Yeah." She turns to look at Adam. "I guess I am."

Adam awkwardly laughs, brushes some hair out of his eyes and looks down, avoiding eye contact with her. He slowly looks up at me, and I mouth *you're welcome* with a smile. He glares at me. I smile wider.

"Well," I say to Tessa, still smiling, "it's nice to finally meet you."

"It was very nice to meet you too, Xander," she says, continuing her conversation with Adam.

I turn back to look at Vicky; she's shaking her head. "Adam is going to kill you. You know that, right?" Her voice is barely above a whisper, just loud enough so I can hear her.

"Yeah, I know." I shake my head. "But it was funny, you've got to admit that."

Vicky laughs, looks down. "Maybe a little."

I turn my body to look at the only other boy sitting at the table with us; he's wearing the same type of shirt that I am, only a dark, dark gray. His hood is up, covering up half of his face. A very interesting tattoo snakes up one of his arms, disappearing in the sleeve of his shirt. The ink looks very intricate, almost like the Waster is asking a question only he knows the answer to.

I think I've stared at him too long, because he suddenly looks over at me, shifting uncomfortably in his seat. "Should I just leave, or are you finished staring at me?" he asks me, staring at me with dark eyes that almost look black. He has a scar that travels from his cheek to his jaw. It's still red, quite a recent injury.

I stammer for a total of one, two, three seconds. "O-oh, y-yeah—I-I'm sorry... I didn't mean to stare at you, but your tattoo"—I point to his arm—"is quite extraordinary."

"Oh." He looks down at his arm, runs his hand over it. "Thanks, I guess." He shrugs. "I've had this quite a while. I just tend to ignore it."

I look down at his arm again, seeing the swirls and concentric circles lining the length of his arm. Why would he want to ignore it? He has an amazing piece of art etched onto his skin, surely he should be proud of it.

I push the thought out of my mind, holding out my hand. "I'm Xander, by the way."

"I know who you are." He takes my hand, shakes it once. "You're the new guys." He looks around, then back to me. "Everyone seems to talk about you."

I furrow my brows. "Why?"

He shrugs, goes back to his food. "It's probably because we haven't had any new survivors for years."

"Oh." The two letters pass my lips even when I shut my mouth.

"Yeah, I know." He grabs his tray, slowly shuffles off the seat to stand up.

"I'm sorry," I call out to him. "I didn't catch your name."

He laughs, the sound deep in his chest. "It's probably because I didn't throw it." He nods. "I'm Thomas."

I smile as he walks away from the table.

"He seemed nice," Vicky says, getting my attention.

"You think?" I watch as he leaves the room.

"Yeah." Vicky shrugs. "I mean… it *was* pretty hilarious when he snapped at you."

I laugh. "I honestly didn't expect him to say that to me."

"I can't blame him, though." Vicky looks over at me, smiling a small smile. "You *do* have a tendency to stare at people a *second* too long."

"Oh," that two-lettered exhale again.

"But, hey," she says, and I turn to look at her, "we all still love you, so don't worry."

I wrap my arm around her shoulders, giving her a small squeeze. "That's what I like to hear."

I spot Kara a few tables next to mine and she doesn't look happy; she's scowling at me. She suddenly turns away, continuing a conversation with the Waster next to her as if she wasn't staring at me not even a second ago.

I look down, up, to the side, back to Kara; she doesn't look back at me.

I sigh as my stomach rumbles, bringing me back to Earth, and I sigh. "Screw it," I say under my breath. "I'm going to get something to eat." I slide off the chair, away from Vicky. "You don't have to wait for me if you want to get some rest."

Vicky shrugs, rests her chin in the palm of her hand and doesn't say anything else as she swirls her food around in her bowl.

I turn around, walking toward the huge hole in the wall—the place where they serve us our food.

Ponytail is behind the wall, her red hair tied high into a—you guessed it—ponytail. Her green eyes staring at mine with something unreadable. It definitely isn't a happy-to-see-you look. I'm not really surprised, though. I'm surprised she hasn't jumped through the hole, knocked me down to the ground, and strangled me until I'm unconscious. But she hasn't. She just looks unreadable.

I look down, swallowing the growing rock inside my throat, slowly blinking away something stinging in my eyes.

I slide the tray I picked up in front of her and she scoops a generous amount of the brown "stew" inside it.

I smile my thanks, but she doesn't do anything back—only looks away as if I'm a stranger; like she hasn't known me for years. Like I didn't take her and her sister in when they had nothing.

I turn around, walking back to our table without uttering a single word.

Ponytail may be mute, but she isn't deaf. She heard everything I said, everything about the death of her sister being my fault, about the fact that I just sat there, staring hopelessly as they drove that sword in her chest. She must believe me; she *believes* that I didn't help her, and now she looks at me as if I'm a monster.

I *am* a monster.

A monster that should have been on the receiving end of that blade instead of Blinky.

Vicky must have said something to me, because she starts to get up from the table, giving me a smile before she walks away.

With a slight buzzing in my ears, I watch her go, keeping a frown plastered on my face.

I grab the cold metal spoon, but I've suddenly lost my appetite. Like if I take a bite of this food, it will come up so quickly that I'll almost die.

With the Mess Hall emptying and the food in my plate that I still haven't touched, I get up from the table, making my way to the exit.

I push the bow more comfortably on my back as I walk down the hallway, not seeing a single person pass me along the way. I'm grateful for the quiet hallways. I don't really want the Wastelanders to see the expression on my face, to think I am weak in some way.

Where do people go when they've finished their food? Surely this place can't be *that* big, right? I haven't actually explored anywhere, so I don't really know. There could be another place just like this around the corner and I probably wouldn't notice.

I pass a room, stop dead in my tracks and I actually back up a few steps.

Kara.

Kara in a ring.

Kara fighting.

Kara *winning*.

I lean against the door frame, arms crossed over my chest as I watch her circle some lean Waster who is twice her size and twice her height.

And she does it without a look of fear on her face.

I step inside the room.

The lean male Waster lunges forward, arms out, but Kara sidesteps just in time, ducking down only to kick the Waster's legs from under him, sending him crashing to the ground with a loud *thump*.

The crowd around the ring goes wild.

I can't do anything but stare.

When the Waster regains his composure, finally lifting himself up from the floor, Kara grabs his arm and twists it

211

behind his back and he groans in pain. When he tries to pull away, Kara only pulls harder, then suddenly the Waster screams out in agony.

She must have shattered his arm.

The screams from the crowd deafen me.

The man falls to his knees, and she follows with him, maintaining the grip on his arm. Her teeth are clenched tightly, almost as if she is struggling with the man she has trapped under her body.

He taps furiously on the ground with his free arm and she finally releases him, making him fall to the ground, clutching at his broken arm, still crying out in agony.

I back away, suddenly hitting the wall. I wish for it to just collapse and I would be out of this room quickly. But nothing happens. Where did the door go?

An older Waster grabs hold of Kara's hand, raising it above her head. "Who's next to challenge our Champion?" he shouts to the crowd. Some of the people around the ring chant some people's names I don't recognize.

No one steps up and I'm not surprised. No one wants to have their arm broken by her.

In the Wastelands, their standards must be low.

Fighting: boys and girls—normal, apparently.

Everyone is suddenly staring at me.

And my breathing stops as I see the man holding Kara's hand pointing at me.

I shake my head furiously, desperately trying to crush the wall at my back, to get the hell out of this room. I try to find the door, but I can't feel anything.

When Kara sees who the man is pointing at, I swear—I swear I see the color drain from her face. She shakes her head. "Him?" she says, turning to the man next to her. "The new guy?" She shakes her head again. "This won't be a fair fight."

"What do you think, folks?" the man shouts. "Who thinks the Champion should fight the new guy?"

The crowd responds with a loud series of screams and hollers.

And I want to crawl into a ball and hide.

I feel someone push me forward until I stumble into the ring. I see blood. Dark, dried blood. Blood from a person that didn't deserve to be here. I don't deserve to be here.

No one deserves to be here.

I get up from the ground, moving to stand my ground, staring at nothing but Kara. My chest expands to twice its size with each lungful of air I breathe in, out. In, out.

I slide my bow and quiver off my back, passing them in the direction of a younger Waster who takes them quickly, tossing them both behind him without looking to see where it will end up.

She slowly gets into her stance, a look of fear on her face. Fear? I don't concentrate on that. I copy her stance, my eyes flicking to my legs, then her legs to see if they are the same width apart.

We start circling each other.

The chants from the crowd almost freeze my bones solid. They stop me from turning to look at the people around the ring.

"Kill him!"

"Break his arm!"

"Don't stop until he's unconscious!"

I think she hears them too, because she swallows hard and bites her lower lip, visibly taking a long breath of air into her lungs. Her chest deflates slightly as she lets the air go. She cracks her neck, rolling her shoulders backward, forward.

She's ready.

But I don't know if *I* am.

There's no time to try and figure that out.

She blocks whatever move I was about to make, punching me in the jaw. I stumble to the side, clutching at my now-broken jaw, probably. The noise of the crowd starts to ring inside my ear, and I can't hear anything else other than a buzzing getting louder.

I hear, more than feel, my nose crunch. I feel the blood pouring down to my mouth, and I grab at it in agony, cursing to myself.

One hand on my nose, the other hand cupping my jaw, and I see her coming toward me. I try to move away, but she grabs my arm, twisting it behind my back, and I think *this is it*. And it didn't even take long.

I wait for the pain. I wait for the shattering of my bone. I wait for agony, for white-hot pain. I wait for something, *anything* to happen.

It doesn't come.

Nothing comes.

My back is pressed against her chest, and I can feel her heart racing. I can hear her breathing fast against my neck.

"I'm not going to hurt you, Xander," she whispers in my ear. "I just need them to *think* I am."

I try to look like I'm in pain. I spit some blood from my mouth.

"We need to drag this out a little longer," she continues. "Just… keep the crowd satisfied, somehow."

I know how to do it. I've got a plan.

I use my free arm to reach back, quickly grabbing hold of her other arm before she can react. I pull her in front of me, making her drop my arm, and I hear her gasp.

She's resting against my chest and I gently pull her arm behind her back. "Convincing enough for them, huh?" I say, keeping my voice as low as possible so the crowd doesn't hear it—or see it.

"Umm…" She looks around the group crowded around the small ring. "Not yet."

I hiss in pain as she drives her elbow into my side, and I drop her arm, quickly clutching at my side to soothe the pain.

She kicks my legs from underneath me, the same way she did with the other Waster, and I fall down hard on my back.

Now it's my turn.

I swipe my left leg to the side, taking her right one with it, and she suddenly falls on top of me. I didn't think that part through.

The air suddenly gets knocked out of my lungs so hard that I start to see black at the edge of my vision. I think I'm trying to get air in my lungs, but it only sounds like I'm wheezing, like I'm gasping for air that is no longer surrounding me in this ring.

Her blonde hair falls down the sides of her face as she pulls herself up from my chest, looking into my eyes. Her hazel-green eyes are wide as they search around my face. "You are going to pay for that," she says quietly, her eyes never leaving mine.

"Oh, now I'm scared," I whisper sarcastically, quirking a half-grin.

"Yeah, you better be." She pulls herself up quickly, grabbing my arm, turning me so that I'm resting on my stomach. My arm is behind my back again.

"Told you, you would pay for it." Her face is near my ear, keeping her voice low.

"End this now, please," I say, begging my voice to stay quiet.

"Are you getting tired, all of a sudden, Xander?" she asks sarcastically, pulling my arm slightly tighter.

I laugh even though I tell myself not to. "No. Only as much as you probably are."

"Fine." She leans down closer to me, but I can't see anything other than the dark ground. "When I tap you on your side, I want you to scream out in pain, got it?"

I can't do anything but give a small nod.

The crowd's screams suddenly come back as I try to focus on what Kara is doing.

"Break his arm!" they chant. "Break his arm! His arm!"

Then, she taps me on the side so softly that if I wasn't paying attention, I probably wouldn't even notice.

And I do what she said: I scream out in pain.

But Kara doesn't do anything, other than pull my arm just a tiny bit harder.

All I can do is listen as the crowd goes completely insane at Kara's victory.

I stay like that, on the ground, waiting for all the Wastelanders to finally leave me alone.

CHAPTER TWENTY

I don't know how long it took for all the Wasters to desert, but it felt like a lifetime.

The older Waster who grabbed Kara's hand right after she beat-up the lean guy is the last to leave. "Congratulations on another perfect fight, Kara," he says as everything goes silent. "You really showed *him* who was boss." I can tell by the way he says *him* that he is talking about me.

I'm the only other person in the room.

Kara awkwardly laughs, kicking something on the ground. "Thanks, Ty," she says. "Do you think I should have gone easy on him?"

The man named Ty scoffs. "Pff, of *course* not." He laughs quickly. "How else are they supposed to learn?"

Kara is silent for a long moment. "Yeah," she says. "I guess you're right." She pauses. "Thanks again, Ty."

I try not to breathe. I try to hold my breath as long as I can.

"That's no problem, Kara," Ty says, walking away. "Get some rest. I hear you have to train him to be a Hunter."

Even though my face is pressed against the ground and all I can see is black and smell blood, I can feel him pointing at me.

"Yeah, but it's not all that bad," Kara says. "He's not difficult to teach."

I try to steady my breathing, making sure my back isn't rising and falling as fast as I think it is.

Ty laughs again. "Well… fair enough, but get some rest anyway." He starts to walk away. "I'll see you tomorrow, okay?"

"Okay," Kara replies. "See you tomorrow."

I exhale as soon as I hear the door shut behind the man.

A long time passes.

"You can get up from the floor, now."

I disregard the demand in her voice, pressing my hands underneath my body, pushing myself up, ignoring the pain exploding in my nose, jaw and limbs.

The blood from my nose stains the floor in a tiny pool of red. I stare at it as if it isn't real, like it was already there when I got pushed into the ring. It now matches the rest of the blood stains on here, from moments like I have just experienced.

Kara's eyes widen as she takes a better look at my nose. "Oh… God," she breathes out. She crosses the room and grabs my jaw, pulling my face closer to her, inspecting my nose closer. "What have I done?"

I pull away from her tight grasp. "I'm fine," I lie, turning around. "I'll be fine, Kara."

She spins me around with a touch to the shoulder. "Don't be stupid, Xander," she says. "We have to take you to the Infirmary."

"You're overreacting now, Kara." I step away from her, intent to get out of this room quickly.

She follows me. "It could be broken for all we know."

I actually laugh out loud. "I *highly* doubt it's broken," I say. "Maybe when you clocked me in the face, my nose just got cut or something."

Kara looks down, studies her fists, drops them like she just burnt herself. "I can't believe I actually…" She trails off, whispering to herself. She shakes her head. "Come on," she says. "You either come with me to the Infirmary now, or I'll pull you by your hood. Choose."

I smirk to myself as I follow behind her, grabbing my bow and quiver from where the young Waster threw them on the floor.

"Good choice," she mutters under her breath, brushing some loose hair behind her ear.

I roll my eyes, shake my head and follow behind her.

I count the number of people that stare at me when we pass each other.

Two male Wasters, one taller than the other, both have long hair.

Two.

A group of Wasters that actually stops laughing and having fun to watch me pass them.

Six.

A male and female, a couple, all over each other. They *too* stare at me.

Eight.

A total of *eight* people stare at me with looks of pity—and the walk to the Infirmary isn't even that long.

The door to the Infirmary is the cleanest I've ever seen. A blinding shade of white, and a medium-sized red cross sits right in the center of it.

Kara knocks on the door—three light taps and then she waits, stepping backward, keeping her arms at her sides.

I study a small crack in the floor as I hear the shuffling going on inside the room. A few voices that I can't really hear sound from the other side of the door.

I snap my head up as I hear the door open, revealing none other than Drew.

"I should have guessed," he says, looking at me, smiling, "that *you* would be the one to get yourself injured first."

I smile as I walk inside the room. "It's only because I miss your company, Drew," I say, sitting on a chair next to an old wooden desk. "I miss seeing your pretty face."

Drew snorts, grabbing a few things from the desk, turning around to Kara. "He didn't hit his head, either, did he?"

Kara shakes her head, doesn't crack a smile. I think Drew meant that question as a joke, but Kara *still* didn't laugh or smile even if she knew it *was* a joke.

Drew's old wooden chair grates against the floor as he scoots closer to me, holding a soaking wet rag close to my face, inching slowly, slowly toward my nose.

When the rag touches my skin, I actually flinch. Not so much as to comment about it, but enough for Drew to notice it.

The blood from my nose ran all the way down to my mouth, almost gluing it shut with the warm red liquid. I had to pry my mouth open to be able to breathe.

Kara looks so ashamed that I actually feel bad for her.

"How did you even manage to do this?" Drew's voice is quiet, but loud enough so that we can still hear him.

My eyes flick over to Kara, and she swallows hard. She opens her mouth to speak.

I interrupt her. "I-I fell down... hit my nose too hard." I try to stop glancing over at Kara. "It's a good thing Kara was there." I see her stiffen. "If she wasn't there, I would have been in a whole different situation."

"Well," Drew says, cleaning the last of the blood, dropping it on his desk, "it's not broken, but your nose might still bleed slightly, but that's fine, just wipe it away."

"Thanks, Drew," I say, standing up. "You truly are a life-saver."

Someone scoffs, and I whip my head to the noise.

A middle-aged man is standing in the corner, and I didn't even realize he was there; he was so quiet. His long blond hair is tied tightly into a ponytail at the back of his head, exposing all of his face. His nose is the biggest part of his features, it looks like it doesn't even belong there. His face is unshaven, very messy looking. His bushy eyebrows drawn together scornfully, squinting his dull brown eyes at us.

Obviously, Blondie isn't the "friendly" type.

He crosses his arms over his chest. "He couldn't save anyone's life even if they showed him how to."

Drew looks down, scratches the back of his neck as he ignores his insult.

I step closer to Blondie, so slowly. "Are you kidding me?" I keep my voice low, menacing. "You have no idea what Drew has done to save people's lives."

Blondie snorts. "Yeah, sure."

"He saved my life once." My voice rises just slightly.

"Xander—" Drew starts to say, but I cut him off.

"He fixed me up. You have *no* idea what Drew is capable of."

Blondie laughs out loud. Head back, mouth open.

I cringe, wanting to stuff that noise back inside his throat.

"Yeah," he says, still laughing. "I'll believe *that* when I see it."

I take a quick glance at Drew who is still staring at the floor. I smile, slowly pulling the hem of my shirt up, exposing the scar on my side to Blondie and Kara.

They both lean forward.

"Oh, my…," Kara mumbles under her breath.

Blondie is still staring at it, memorizing it, studying it, his eyes following the line that runs down the center of the whole thing.

Blondie's mouth parts as if to say something, but no words come out, only a faint sound of breathing could be heard.

I pull my shirt back down, making Blondie's mouth snap shut. I take a step toward him. "Do you want to know how I got that scar?" I don't give him time to respond. "A piece of *metal* got stuck deep inside my side." I keep my voice low, even. "If it wasn't for Drew," I glance back at him, "I would be *dead.*"

I feel both the Wasters flinch slightly at the word *dead.*

I take a step closer. "If I ever hear you talking about Drew like that again," I say. "I will personally make your life as miserable as you're making Drew's."

I don't know why I regretted the words as soon as they passed my lips. Blondie deserves this. Drew doesn't deserve to be treated like this. So, I don't know why I feel sorry for Blondie as I step away from him.

I see Blondie's Adam's apple bobbing as he swallows hard. His face remains expressionless, but I see something else in his eyes. Maybe fear? Maybe hatred? I can't really tell. I don't really care.

"Thanks again, Drew." I keep my eyes locked with Blondie's, even though I'm talking to Drew. "I'll see you later." I slowly turn to leave, eyes never leaving the older Waster's.

"O-o-okay, sure," Drew stammers, shifting in his seat. "I-I'll see you later, Xander."

I slam the door shut as Kara and I pass it.

I smile as we walk down the hallway. "Thanks for taking me to the Infirmary," I say, turning to look at her. "I had fun."

*****

My new bedroom is surprisingly empty as I walk inside. Adam must still be on Security duty with Tessa. Joel must be with the Engineers, and I have no idea where Kyle could be.

Kara went back to her living quarters when we came back from the Infirmary, reminding me about tomorrow and what time we will start training.

I replied to her with a not-so-quiet groan.

I fling my bow and quiver off my shoulder, shoving them under the bed, feeling relieved when I can't feel the heavy metal across my back, pulling me down.

I pad my way across the room, flinging the door open, causing a small draft to crawl up my skin and I shiver.

In two long strides, I make it to the bathroom, but I don't even have time to touch the handle before someone opens it from the opposite direction.

I almost stumble back, but I catch myself just in time.

"Oh—I-I'm so sorry, Xan," Vicky says, eyes wide. She steps forward, one arm out as if to catch me. "Are you okay?"

I find my balance. "Yeah, I'm fine. How are you?"

Vicky shrugs, crosses her arms over her chest casually. "Yeah, I'm fine." Her eyes drift from my eyes to my nose, and she steps even closer. So close that our chests are almost touching.

I swallow hard and I'm definitely sure she heard it.

"What happened to your nose?" She reaches up as if to touch it, but I step back, grabbing her forearms lightly.

"It's nothing, Vicky." I drop her arms. "I just got pushed into a fighting ring earlier, then someone kicked my ass, it's not a big deal."

"Who did this to you, Xander?" she asks, stepping closer to me, but I step back.

I didn't think it was Kara's fault what happened to me, she looked like she wouldn't have punched me right in the nose, but with everyone around, they wouldn't let her pass until I was unconscious on the floor.

She is the Champion after all.

I don't think it's fair to push Kara under the bus. Instead, I shake my head. "No one did this to me, really."

Vicky laughs, but it doesn't sound genuine. "That's B.S., Xander, and you know it is." She steps even closer. "Who. Did. This. To. You? Why won't you just tell me who did it, Xander?"

I sigh. "Because it doesn't *matter* who did this to me, Vicky. What matters is that I'm still alive and breathing." I move around her to get to the bathroom, but she pushes me back with her arm.

She's even closer to me, our faces an inch apart. "Don't make me punch you, Xander," she says, not joking any more. "Tell me!"

I shrink back slightly at the volume of her voice. "It was Kara, okay?" I shout back, my chest heaving even though I don't know why. "Are you *happy* now?"

Vicky steps back and I release a breath I didn't realize I was holding—that I didn't realize hurt so much as it escaped my throat. "Who?" she asks, but then her eyes suddenly widen. "Oh... you mean... the blonde girl? The one with the bow and arrows?"

I nod slowly, not trusting my voice at the moment.

"Why... why did you let her do this to you?" She's looking at me as if I just kicked someone in the shin for no reason.

I start, staring at her with furrowed brows. "Why would you think I would *let* her do this to me?" I ask angrily, pointing to my nose. "I'm not stupid, Vicky."

"I'm not saying that you are stupid, Xander, but when I see you with a bloody nose, I *do* ask questions—just like any normal person would." Vicky draws a shaky breath, trying not to look away from my face.

"Sometimes, Vicky, I don't like it when people ask me questions. *You* of all people should know that." I inhale deeply, trying my hardest to stay calm. "Why don't you just drop it and leave me alone?" I really hated the words as soon as they tumbled out of my mouth, and I know that I'm the idiot that can't turn back time—I can't take away the hurtful words I just threw in Vicky's face.

Vicky's lips part as if she is going to say something, but no words come out, and I don't blame her. She blinks a few times, eyes searching around my face. She turns away from me, says, "Screw you, Xander." She takes another step back, shaking her head like she can't believe I would *say* those words to her. She continues a few seconds. "Don't come running to me when something bad happens, Xander." She slowly walks away.

And I let her go.

It isn't until I hear the girls' bedroom door slam shut, that I actually start to feel my legs again. I fight the urge to collapse on the floor. I urge my body to stay upright.

I stare at the open bathroom door, waiting for it to suck me inside and slam the door shut behind it.

It doesn't.

I have to move my legs myself.

I push myself off the wall and force myself toward the bathroom, not even bothering to be quiet when I shut the door behind me, the only sound I can tolerate at the minute.

My heart is still pounding in my chest. I can hear it in my ears, can feel it in my throat. It hurts, but it doesn't compare to what I *really* feel. Everywhere.

The water splashes under my boots as I walk toward the only mirror in the room.

I wipe away the thin layer of dust with the palm of my hand. I use my other hand to run it down the length of my face, then through my hair, tugging it to the point where I want to rip it out.

I feel so sick that I want to empty the food in my stomach that I didn't even eat.

I stare at the boy in my reflection. I don't recognize him. The hollowed cheeks, the sharp jawline from not eating enough. Stubble growing on my face to the point where it looks like a beard, sort of.

The only things that look alive on my face are my eyes. So blue. Such a strange color. They look so unnatural on my face.

So many secrets in them.

So many tears that are just waiting to escape.

Except, I don't let them.

I let the warm water fill the palms of my hands and I stare at them for a few seconds, watching as the liquid overflows, spilling over the edge.

I splash the water on my face, sighing through my nose when I feel the sudden warmth on my skin.

225

No matter how hard I try, I can't wash away the feeling I have in the pit of my stomach. I can't wash away all the emotion swimming in my mind.

I so desperately want to wash away the last conversation I just had with Vicky from my mind, to block it out as if it never happened.

I dream so fictionally it's almost laughable.

With a quick pat on the face with a towel, I make my way out of the bathroom, halting for a split second before turning the doorknob, making sure no one barges in.

No one does. I step outside.

The dark hallway is empty.

Thank God.

I don't want anyone to see me like this. I don't want anyone to see me *at all*.

I rush inside the room, knowing for a fact that the room will be empty. I close it behind me, my back resting on the old wood.

I let out a long breath, closing my eyes when I feel my throat tremble.

When the back of my head hits the door, I can't help but let a single teardrop fall from my eyes. I can't help it. It started to hurt because I kept it all bottled up.

I flip the switch off, hoping that will blind my emotions, and I walk to the bed, sitting down on the soft mattress. When my head hits the pillow, I let exhaustion envelop me into darkness.

CHAPTER TWENTY-ONE

The next time I open my eyes, the boys are already asleep. It must still be late. I mustn't have slept for very long. I'm surprised I was even able to close my eyes and let the darkness take me under. I had so many thoughts in my head that it was starting to give me a headache.

My small fight with Vicky still weighs down on my shoulders, pulling me down onto the bed, trying to keep me there. The feeling is so strong that it starts to feel like it is crushing my chest.

I fight against the urge to stay on my bed, to stay a few more minutes lying where no one else will find me like this. I swing my legs over the frame, pulling my torso up from the soft mattress. The sudden movement goes straight to my head, and I raise a hand to ease the pain. I didn't bother changing out of my clothes. I didn't even take my boots off—I just climbed straight into bed.

My eyes scan over each person in the room. Drew and Kyle are sleeping soundlessly, but Joel is snoring quite loudly. Even in the darkness of the room, I can still see their sleeping silhouettes.

I don't bother to grab my bow and quiver as I make my way out of the room; being as silent as I can when I close the bedroom door behind me. I actually feel all the bottled-up air trapped in my lungs as the soft *click* echoes until it becomes nothing.

I can't help but feel a strain in my chest when I pass her bedroom. I feel like such an idiot. Why did I even open my mouth? Why couldn't I just tell her the truth at the start? I don't remember the last time Vicky and I had a fight. I hate the fact that we have tension between us; like the time she almost fell off the roof. I don't want things to always end up like this.

My tears have dried at the back of my eyes, and now it hurts to blink. It hurts to even move my eyes to look around the room.

I made sure that the boys didn't see me crying when they walked in the room. I tried my hardest to block the noise, to stop sniffing—to stop *crying,* but it just hurt too much.

I pull the old ripped curtain aside to let me through, letting it fall naturally back to its original position.

All the Wasters are still asleep.

I fumble with the hem of my shirt as I walk into the Mess Hall, feeling satisfied when it is dead silent. The material between my fingertips feels soft, almost as if I wasn't wearing anything at all.

I find a table at the back of the room, right in the corner; the furthest table away from prying eyes. I make sure it's dark enough, so no one can see me if, by some catastrophe, someone was to walk in.

Someone left their utensils on the table from dinner. They're clean—completely unused. I slowly slide the knife to the edge of the table, picking it up by the handle. I run my index finger along the round edge of the blade, squinting at it. A butter knife is a poor excuse for a knife; you wouldn't be able to cut anything stronger than meat with these stupid things.

I place the knife back onto the table and keep my gaze forward, watching as the very few Cooks move around the kitchen, making more noise than necessary as they clean the items.

My eyes land on Ponytail.

And I already feel my insides dying. My heart—broken, my limbs—numb, my head—gone.

All the emotions come rushing back to me so fast that I actually feel like I'm going to collapse right here, right now, on this floor, in this dark corner that nobody will ever look at.

I look down before any of that happens. I ignore the way her eyes are swollen, the dark patches under her eyes.

I ignore the way she—

"Hey."

I jump out of my skin and my bones land on the floor, the table, everywhere.

When I look up, my eyes meet a pair of black orbs, almost the same color as his shirt. His hood is down, showing more of his face, giving me a better view of the scar that travels from his cheek to his jaw.

"Thomas," I say quietly, clutching at my chest.

"Sorry I scared you," he says. "Mind if I sit?" He nods to the seat in front of me.

I shrug and he slides into the seat he said, folding his arms on the table. His tattooed arm is above the other, giving me a better view of the black and blue lines and circles. I'm still fascinated by them. I've never been this close to someone with a tattoo before.

"What are you doing up so late?" he asks, and I slowly look up to meet his eyes.

"I could ask you the same question." I cross my arms on the table, mimicking the way he is sitting.

Thomas looks down, the right corner of his mouth lifting upward slightly, giving himself a half-hearted grin. "Runners never really sleep. They have too much energy swimming around in their heads."

"You're a Runner?" My voice was so quick that I'm not sure if he heard me correctly.

He nods. "So?" he says. "Why are you up?"

I just had an argument with my best friend, and now I feel like an idiot, not a big deal.

229

"I just… couldn't sleep," I say instead, pushing the other sentence far, far away from my mind.

He sighs, looking down at the table. "Okay, I understand."

I want to ask how he understands, but I keep my mouth clamped shut. My eyes meet his scar and, I don't know why, but I almost regret the next question that comes out of my mouth.

"How did you get that scar?"

His hand slowly grazes the red line. He looks down again, pressing his lips together firmly as he thinks it through.

"It's okay," I say slowly, quietly. "You don't have to tell me—"

"Many years ago," he says, interrupting me, "I was a Hunter." He pauses. Swallows. "I was out with my group one morning, and I saw…" He trails off, staring at something, but nothing on the table.

"Thomas?" I try my hardest to get him to look up at me, to do anything.

His black eyes widen. He swallows, hard. "I saw the Shadows for the first time. My heart was in my throat. I couldn't breathe. I couldn't *think*." He doesn't look at me. He doesn't meet my eyes. "I watched one of them kill my leader. They stabbed him through the chest." His eyes have a faraway look, almost like he's seeing the leader's death all over again.

I know what that's like. I know that too well.

"Y-you know what?" He starts to get up. "It doesn't matter any more." He's walking away from me. "Goodnight, Xander."

"I know what that's like."

He halts in his stride, turns his head to the left slightly. "What?"

"I know what it's like to lose a friend to one of *them*."

He slowly turns around.

"I saw them kill one of my friends. I heard her last scream." I swallow, lower my voice to barely a whisper. "You never forget something like that."

My eyes travel over to Ponytail; she still hasn't realized I'm here, talking about the death of her sister.

Thomas turns around properly, never taking his eyes off my face. "Xander—"

"And the worst thing is, her sister now hates my guts because I couldn't save her." I meet his eyes. I lean forward, dropping my voice to a whisper. "And I don't blame her."

I can see something brimming his dark eyes. He steps closer. "How old was she?"

I lick my dry lips, swallow the lump in my throat. "About thirteen."

I can see his Adam's apple move slightly. "I'm really sorry."

I shake my head, shaking away the fresh tears that are about to spill out. "You don't have to be sorry; it's not your fault." I drop my voice even lower, so low it's hardly audible in my ears. "It's mine."

He sits back on the seat in front of me. "No, it's not, Xander," he says sternly. "You and I both know it's not. Stop telling yourself it is when it *isn't*."

I can see my reflection in his dark eyes, but I don't want to see myself at the minute. I look away. "I'm the monster that just watched her die, and I didn't do anything to save her."

"I don't believe that for a second." He shakes his head. "I know you would have saved her if you could."

"Then you should tell that to her," I say. "Because she sure as hell doesn't believe it."

"Well, that doesn't—"

"You still didn't answer my question." I try to keep my voice calm. "How did you get that scar?"

He is quiet for a moment. Then, "Let's just say one of the Shadows almost got me, and I escaped." Thomas shrugs, crosses his arms over his chest.

"So, one of the Shadows cut you?" I ask with a furrow of my brows.

"Yep." He nods. "Had to spend a week in the Infirmary."

"Damn," I breathe out. "I also… had to spend a long time in an infirmary."

Thomas tilts his head to the side. "What happened to you?"

It flashes before my eyes before I even realize it.

A white-hot pain rips through my entire body, snapping my eyes open. The world around me seems to slow down. The air around me starts to turn thick as I struggle to breathe. A flash of light crosses my vision, but I take no notice of it.

"Xander!" Vicky shouts from below me. Her voice sounds distant, like she is deep underwater, trying to shout my name, but it only comes out a mere echo. I think she says it again, but I can't tell.

Darkness has almost taken me fully. I fight hard to keep my eyes open just a few more seconds, but as the seconds tick by, I can feel myself dropping, dropping, drop—

A blurry figure is crouched next to me.

A cold hand touches my face, but I hardly feel it.

The sun behind the figure makes it look like a silhouette.

Vicky.

Vicky has come to help me.

I think she says my name again, then again, but everything sounds distant—even my own thoughts sound like an echo.

She grabs my face between her hands, keeping my eyes on hers. I don't want to look anywhere but her—I can't; her grip is too tight.

I can just make out the blue irises of her eyes, before darkness takes over.

I gasp and shoot up, eyes wide, searching around the room, blinking away the few tears before Thomas gets the chance to see them—before anyone sees them.

"Xander?" he says, worriedly. "Are you okay?"

"I..." I trail off, staring at the space between two tables. "I don't... even know." My throat is parched, my tongue is dry.

Sandpaper in my mouth.

Sandpaper in my mouth.

Sandpaper in my mouth.

I swallow more dryness in my throat. "I need... water."

In an instant, he's up, rushing to the kitchen, grabbing a glass full of something that doesn't seem real. I've completely lost my mind; I'm seeing glasses of water.

But it's real.

I swipe the glass from his hand, nodding my thanks before tipping the cold water down my throat, not even stopping to take a breath. I don't save it.

"Better?" he asks, crossing his arms on the table.

I don't say anything in return; I just wipe away some water dripping from my chin with the back of my hand.

"You don't have to tell me what happened if you don't want to," he says quietly. "I don't want you to go through that again."

I look down. "No." I slowly shake my head. "It's fine." I shift to a more comfortable position. "A few weeks ago, back in the Estate, I was searching around for supplies." I swallow. "I found this building that looked like it was under construction, and being the stupid idiot I am, I climbed up it." I bite my lip, continue to stare at the table. "About a minute later... one of the bars snapped clean off..." I trail off, trying my hardest to cover up the memory.

It doesn't work.

My throat starts to close up, and I wish I'd saved some of the water.

"The next thing I remember was feeling a sharp piece of the metal bar impale me through the side."

I see Thomas wince from the corner of my eye.

I laugh even though it's not funny. "I still have that scar to this day." I look up, into his eyes. "And it *still* haunts my dreams." I press my lips together. "I will remember that time until the day I die."

Thomas looks down, blinks fast.

I shake my head, fast. "I-I'm sorry, I'm depressing you." I slide out of the seat. "Goodnight, Thomas. See you tomorrow."

I hardly make it five steps away from him.

"I'm sorry this is happening to you, Xander," he calls out, making me halt in my stride.

I turn around slowly. So, so slowly.

"You're just a teenager, you don't deserve any of this."

I look into his eyes. "I've been through much worse than I care to admit."

I turn around and walk away.

*****

"Hold the knife in front of your face and keep the target in the center of your vision."

I hug the wall at the sound of Adam's voice.

I must be at the entrance.

Adam and Tessa must be on Security duty.

Adam's voice continues. "Don't grip the knife too hard, but not too soft, just enough so it doesn't slip out of your hand."

I furrow my brows.

"So... like this?"

I move to the corner of the doorway, peeking my head out ever so slightly, trying to see if my assumptions are correct. They are.

Adam is teaching Tessa to throw a knife.

She has her back pressed against his chest, his arms slightly wrapped around hers. He's holding her throwing hand and they are *very* close to each other.

"Don't be scared of the knife," Adam is saying. "Let it almost be a part of you. That's it. Like that. Perfect." His voice is so soft, so unnatural to my ears as he speaks directly next to her face.

My eyes follow the knife as it slips out of her hand, flying toward the wall in front of them.

The sound of the knife sticking in the wall echoes around the room, vibrating inside my body. Even though I knew it was coming, it still startles me.

"Perfect!" Adam beams and Tessa turns around in his arms, smiling such a big smile, that it almost makes me feel bad about what I'm just about to do.

The conversation I had with Thomas has finally disappeared as I pull my dagger from my belt, swiftly flinging it toward the wall behind them, startling them, making them gasp loudly.

"What the f—"

"Hey! None of that colorful language, Adam," I say, smiling. Adam stares at the knife, then at me.

They are both breathing heavily, turning red. They step away from each other.

I stride over to my dagger, wiping away the dust when I pull it out of the wall, securing it back into my belt.

"What the *hell* are you doing up, Xander?" Adam asks, his chest heaving, now a few good feet away from Tessa.

"Not bad, Tessa. Not bad," I say, nodding to the knife in the wall, completely ignoring his question. "Although, it would be a smoother flight, and it wouldn't vibrate as much if you just keep your wrist—"

"*Xander!*" Adam booms loudly, the sound echoing around the large space.

"Yeah?" I turn around to look at them, raising one brow.

"What. Are. You. Doing. Up?"

I sigh. "I just couldn't sleep, no big deal," I say, crossing my arms over my chest. "How's... *protecting* the entrance going?"

They both blush.

"It's going great, thanks," Adam says.

"Couldn't be better," Tessa says.

"Well, isn't that good?" I turn to Tessa. "Tell me, Tessa, because you would know more than Adam." I shift on the spot. "What would you do if one of those Shadow's hops down the rabbit hole?" I point to the sand slide that we slid down only a few hours ago.

Tessa shrugs. "You're asking the wrong person," she says. "I've never seen a Shadow come anywhere near here."

"Why is that?" I ask, furrowing my brows.

Tessa shrugs again. "Someone once said to me that they might be too scared to jump down here. Maybe they just don't know about the hole, yet." She turns to look at the hole. "We don't know exactly how many Shadow's there are, but we can never be too careful." She looks down at herself, then Adam, smiling. "That's why we're here, I guess."

"Well, then," I say, walking over to the knife Tessa threw, wiping the dust and dirt on my pants. When I get back to them, I drop the knife in her hand. "You're going to need to keep this handy."

She smiles down at the knife and Adam comes to stand beside her.

"Make sure you keep each other safe," I say, turning around, starting to walk away.

"We will," Adam says.

"Goodnight, you two," I say, smiling.

"Goodnight, Xander," they say at the same time.

I smile as I turn the corner, heading straight for our living quarters.

I don't really get why the Shadows never attack inside the Wastelands. When we were running away from them, when they got Blinky, they completely turned around and walked away, almost like they forgot about us. They could have killed us just as easily, so… why didn't they?

I pull back the torn curtain at the entrance to our living quarters, stepping inside, not bothering to look back as I make my way to the boys' bedroom.

Before I shut the door behind me, I swear—I swear I saw the girls' bedroom door crack open.

CHAPTER TWENTY-TWO

"Xander."

In my dream, Vicky says my name, so quietly, so softly. She's standing right in front of me, arms at her side, hair loose and draped over her shoulders. She's wearing the same thing she wore in the Estate, but there is something different about her. Something very, very different, and I can't seem to figure out what.

Maybe it's the way she's dressed, or the way she's standing. Maybe the way she says my name, like an echo— smooth, calm.

Or, maybe it's the way she's looking at me.

She's inching closer to me, taking small, tentative steps. So slowly, so carefully.

"Xander," she says again, but her mouth is hardly moving.

My back is pressed against the wall, hands stuck behind my back for some reason. I can't move my arms. I can't move anything. It's like an invisible rope has bond my hands together, and no amount of pulling will help them separate.

Vicky is in my face, leaning up, only an inch away. A breath away from my lips. Her eyes are a darker shade of blue than they normally are. Her eyes are searching down my face; from my eyes to my nose, my mouth and back up.

Then when Vicky turns away, then back to me, her eyes are hazel, green when in a certain light. A strange color. Beautiful. *Beautiful.*

This isn't Vicky, I keep trying to remind myself. It isn't, it *isn't*—

"Wake up!"

I bolt upright, chest heaving, eyes wide, gasping for air. I clutch madly for the dagger that is no longer tucked underneath my pillow. My *real* pillow.

"Whoa, whoa, whoa, calm down!"

I jerk my head to the voice, furrowing my brows tightly when I see Kara standing at my bed. Close, close, too close.

"What the hell are you doing in my room?" I snap, rubbing my eye with the back of my hand.

"Have you forgotten what time it is?" she snaps back, stepping away from the bed frame. "Or did you just need more of your beauty sleep?"

"I always need my beauty sleep, obviously." I yawn, swinging my legs over the bed. Kyle, Drew and Joel are nowhere to be seen. They must be at work. Typical of them not to wake me up.

I hardly flinch as a soft piece of fabric hits me in the face. As soon as it slowly lands in my lap, I realize that it's my shirt.

Kara stands there with her arms crossed over her chest. "Hurry up and get dressed." She starts to walk toward the door, stopping briefly to look over her shoulder, says, "Meet me in the training room in five!" Then she slams the door behind her.

I slip the shirt over my head; using my foot, with some effort, to pull my bow and quiver from under my bed. I sigh as I swing my quiver on my back, followed by my bow.

I'm too tired to do any of this. Back in the Estate, I could just about get up in the morning to scavenge, but the only reason I got up was because I had my best friend doing it with me. We had fun. This new job doesn't seem to be one where I can just wing it and do whatever I want.

Kara doesn't seem like that type.

The bathroom is surprisingly warm when I open the door. Someone must have recently had a shower—I can feel the steam on my face. I can smell the dampness in the air.

I don't bother to wipe away the condensation off the mirror, instead filling my hands with warm water, quickly splashing it on my face, rubbing in the corners of my eyes to remove all signs of last night. All signs of the dream. I sigh with relief when I feel the water drip off my chin, hearing the satisfying *plink* when the drop hits the pristine white sink.

I watch as the water fades into the drain, never to be seen again.

I run my hand down the length of my face, stretching my eyes wider slightly as my hands descend. I catch the water in my palm, letting it drop in the sink.

When I look in the mirror, I almost feel sorry for the people that have to look at me. Countless bags under my eyes, small red stains where my tears dried, and my hair is messy to the point where I hardly look human anymore. I brush it down with my fingers, but it still looks stupid. I brush it out of my eyes and forget it, moving away from the mirror.

Every time I touch the handle of this door, I keep thinking someone is going to burst in. My mind always thinks it's going to be Vicky.

But no one comes in; not Vicky, not Kara. Not *anyone.*

I step outside.

I silently make my way to the training room, trying my hardest to remember where it is—as Kara showed me. I didn't really pay attention to my surroundings when Kara guided me all the way here. I guess I just thought I would know it right off the bat.

Every door around here looks exactly the same; I can't tell if I'm near the training room, or back near the entrance.

As soon as I'm about to turn around and walk away from the door, I suddenly remember something about this door; the rusty handle, the fact that it looks older than all the other doors.

I'm at the training room.

I take a deep breath, stand up straight, square my shoulders, and walk through the door.

Vicky's on the other side of the room, staring intently, with furrowed eyebrows, at a small knife, using a rag to polish the silver instrument. She doesn't look up as I enter the room.

She doesn't even look up when I'm within hearing range from her. She acts as if she can't hear me. As if I was nothing. Like I'm *nothing* to her.

Maybe I *am* nothing to her anymore.

I step inside the target room, knowing that Kara will be in here, and I slam the door shut, startling her, making her miss the target by a few inches.

She clutches at her chest with her spare hand. "Damn it, Xander," she breathes. "Did you have to slam it?"

I step closer, shaking my head. "I didn't *have* to," I say, raising my eyebrows. "But I *wanted* to."

Kara rolls her eyes and turns around. "You're such an ass," she mumbles.

"I know." I swing the bow off my back. "So"—I crack my knuckles—"what are we going to do today?"

She uses the tip of her bow to point at the target. "Remember?" she says. "You're crap at shooting?"

"Oh, yes." I smile. "How could I forget?" I walk over to her, standing just a few feet away from where she was positioned. "And, uh"—I lean closer to her ear—"thanks for the moral support, teach."

She looks over at me, smiling, *actually* smiling. "Any time, friend."

I shake my head and smile as I pull an arrow free from my quiver, lining it with my bow. I notice her still staring at me. Maybe she's just seeing how my stance is, how I hold my bow. Yeah, that's got to be it. Am I holding the bow wrong? I can't tell.

"Okay," Kara whispers, stepping closer to me. She looks at the target, then me. "This time... don't rush."

241

I nod my head once, take a deep breath in through my nose, and pull the string back.

"Remember," she says. "Keep your elbow down."

I feel her push it down, slowly, slowly, so slowly. Like a breath of air—I hardly feel it.

I relax my elbow to let her push it down.

She places her hand on my side. "Stay rigid," she whispers. "Don't let the weight bend you out of shape." She looks over at the target, then me. "That's the bow's job."

I stare at the target, making sure that the razor-sharp tip is in line with the middle, before letting the string slip through my fingers.

Kara removes her hand from my side almost as quickly as the arrow impaled the target.

I look over at the arrow in the target, and I almost want to die inside.

I missed.

Again.

"This is a joke!" I look over at her, raising my brows. "How can I miss *twice*?"

Kara places a reassuring hand on my shoulder. "It's okay, Xander," she says. "You'll get better, I promise."

"If I can't hit a standing target from ten feet away, then how, exactly, am I supposed to hit a small moving animal from twenty feet away?" I look over to the target, over to her.

She looks at me. "You have so little faith in yourself, Xander." She points to the target. "If you don't *think* you're going to hit the target, then nine times out of ten you won't." She touches my arm. "Believe in yourself, Xander." She looks down, up. "You have potential."

They are such small words that mean so much, and a single fraction of myself almost, *almost* believes her.

"Try again," she says, speaking in a calm voice I've never heard before.

I squint at the target as I pull out an arrow from my quiver, lining it with my bow. I pull back the string, remembering to keep my elbow lower, to keep my body rigid.

Believe in yourself, Xander. Kara's words ring inside my head as the string passes my fingers, the arrow speeding toward the target.

The sound of the arrow hitting the target echoes inside my ears, vibrating around my head.

The arrow is protruding from one of the outer circles on the target. It's quite far away from the center, but at least I didn't miss completely.

I hit it, I think. That can't be real.

"Told you," she says, stepping in my line of sight. "I told you that you would hit the target if you believed in yourself."

"Thank you," I smile, "for believing in me when I didn't."

"You're welcome." She looks down, looks at the target. "Try again."

I spend the rest of morning missing the center of the target, cursing silently under my breath when I miss the target completely. Most of the time the string snaps against my forearm, but I just try my hardest to ignore it. I learnt a small thing to stop it happening, and it helps a lot.

Believe in yourself, Xander.

And yet, even after missing about a hundred times, I still believe her.

*****

"You're getting better."

Kara is sitting with her back against the wall, knees close to her chest, her arms resting on top of them. She's picking at her nail casually, every few seconds looking up at me to check what I'm doing. It's getting on my nerves.

She's trying to make me feel better, but I know I'm just shooting in the same space every single time.

But suddenly she smirks, looks down and then looks up as if she just remembered something.

"Why are you smiling?" I ask, eyebrows furrowed. "Is my failure funny to you?"

"Maybe a little," she says, her face emotionless now. She nods to the target. "Try again."

I roll my eyes, sliding my second to last arrow out from my quiver, lining it with my bow. I pull the string back to my jaw.

"Keep your back straight," she says quickly. She stood up and I have no idea when, but she is close, close, close. Very, very close.

I focus on the target.

"Lower your elbow," she says.

I sigh through my nose, trying my hardest to ignore her.

"If you hold it for a long time, you're going to strain your fingers, then you'll never hit the target in the center." Her voice has become harsher, more irritable.

What the hell happened to *you're getting better*?

Kara sighs. "Wow." She laughs. "I can actually feel myself growing a beard," she says. "Hurry up and release the damn string, already."

"Fine!" I shout, letting the string slip off my three fingers.

I don't bother watching where it goes; I turn around to stare at Kara, nostrils flaring.

She's still looking at the target, smiling—no, smirking. "Like a charm," she whispers to herself.

"What is?" I ask, getting angrier.

"Anger," she says. "Irritation." She points to the target, and I slowly look over.

I silently gasp.

My arrow is closer to the center than it ever has been, and I don't even know if it's real.

"I hit it." The words sound foreign to my ears. "I actually hit it." I look over to her. "What did you do?"

She shrugs. "I just got you angry enough," she says. "Maybe that's what you needed." She smiles. "A little push."

I half-smile at her. "Thank you."

"No, thank *you*." She shakes her head. "We're done." She turns around. "Let's call it a day, shall we?"

*****

The only thing I want is to get out of these clothes and into the shower.

I can't believe I needed a little bit of anger to be able to hit the center of the target. I need to stop treating the target as if it's a friend and I don't want to hurt it. I need to know, deep down, that the thing in front of me is something to eat. It's without feeling. Like it's fake. Almost like a life or death situation; I either kill the animal or go hungry for the rest of the night. I'm putting all the other Wasters at risk if I do that.

We Wasters need to eat.

The hot water from the shower almost makes me forget about the shot I did earlier.

I brush all my hair backward, letting the water drip down my neck and back. I let all the running water fall on to my face, down the sides of my face, wiping away most the sweat.

The shower finishes too quickly, and I stand here for a few seconds before moving. I grab the towel from the door, burying my face in it.

I quickly run the towel across my hair, messing it up, somewhat drying it. I can feel my hair sticking up in every possible direction as I pull the towel away from my head. I brush it down and move on.

Once my body is no longer wet, I pull my clothes back on, grunting in frustration when they get stuck because of my still-damp skin.

I put all of my weapons in my room, and all I have is my belt without a knife secured tightly inside. It feels weird. It feels lighter.

I open the cubicle door, trying my hardest to brush my hair down with my fingers, wincing when they get caught in a knot.

My damn thick hair is so unforgiving.

I don't go to the mirror to help me see my hair; I don't really care about it, anyway. I make my way out the door.

I almost have a heart attack.

Vicky is walking to her room.

Her long dark hair swaying from side to side, almost reaching her hips. She stops at her door, slowly turning around just to look behind her shoulder.

Her eyes meet mine, and I can't do anything but stare.

She looks away, closing the door behind her, and I release a breath I didn't realize was stuck in my mouth. That I didn't realize was trapped in my lungs.

I make my way out of the living quarters, and I wander around, burying my hands in my pockets as I walk down each hallway.

I don't know what makes me want to explore; a part of me wants to know what else the Wasters have around here, the other half of me just wants to crawl in my bed and sleep this all off.

It's a double-edged sword.

Maybe I think I'll meet new people. Maybe I want to see how Thomas is doing.

Maybe I'm just genuinely curious about everything.

I don't hear anyone speaking when I pass the entrance, I don't see anyone in the Mess Hall, which is surprising for this time of day. Maybe everyone is still at their work.

I climb some stairs that lead to a place I don't know. Even when I reach the top, it doesn't look like much. One of the four walls is completely open; I can see the sun as it sets over the horizon. I can see everything, even the Estate if I squint hard enough.

It's beautiful, so very, very beautiful.

I got so lost in the view that I didn't even see Kara sitting at the edge of the room, legs dangling over the side, her bow in her hand.

"You know it's considered rude to sneak up on people," Kara suddenly says, startling me.

"Oh—I, uh, sorry," I stutter, almost forgetting what I was going to say in the first place. I quickly turn around. "I'll just go—"

"No," she interrupts me. "Stay."

I slowly make my way to the edge of the room, peering down to look at the ground, a very high drop awaits me.

I drop down, shuffling closer to the ledge, dangling my legs over the side, resting my hands in my lap, intertwining my fingers.

"Did they forget to build a wall, or was it designed like this?" I ask.

My question wasn't meant to be a joke, but Kara laughs lightly. "No, Xander, they built it like this." She gestures with her hand around where she's sitting. "It's so people on Security can see if we are being attacked."

"Oh, that makes sense…" I trail off, looking out into the distance, thinking about the biting sand that was shooting up and down my body on our way over here.

My thoughts turn to Blinky. The Shadows. The sword that was driven in her chest… How could they just *stab* a small child like that without even hesitating? They killed a *girl* and didn't even think twice. There was no emotion in their eyes as it happened.

Monsters don't know a single thing about emotion.

"Thanks, again," I say after a while to distract myself, looking at the sunset. I look over at her. "For not giving up on me."

She smiles, that kind and genuine smile again. "You're welcome."

I bury my hand in my pocket and I immediately wish I hadn't. My finger catches the tip of the sharp instrument and I hiss, pulling my hand out of my pocket.

"Are you okay?" Kara asks, looking down at the tip of my finger, which is covered in blood. Dark red blood.

"Yeah," I breathe, wiping the red liquid on my pants, being careful not to pull the cut taut. I slide the arrowhead out of my pocket, curling my upper lip when I see my blood staining the sharp tip.

Kara reaches over quickly, pulling the metal from my fingers carefully as if she knows it will slice across my fingers. "Where did you get this?" she asks, even though she said it quietly, like a whisper, I could still hear her clearly.

"I found it back in the Estate," I say to her, looking down at the arrowhead. She twirls it around with her fingers. "Why? Do you know where this came from? Is this yours?"

She takes a short moment to answer, almost contemplating hard about what I just said to her. "My leader. It was his before he... before he died."

I stare down, not wanting to look up. "I'm sorry."

"Don't be," she says. "It was a long time ago. He died finishing what he always wanted to do, anyway." She presents the arrowhead to me, but I shake my head.

"You keep it." I smile weakly at her. "It belongs with you." *I'm sorry if you hate it* almost slips out of my mouth. I clamp my lips together, pushing those words out of my mind. *She's not Vicky,* I remind myself. *Kara is not Vicky.*

"Thanks," Kara says. She pulls it close to her lap, running her thumb across the smooth surface.

"How did he die?" I bite hard on my tongue, knowing I said the wrong thing. I *always* say the wrong thing.

But the look on Kara's face doesn't say that.

"He always wanted to go out there," she replies, looking up at me once, pointing to the Estate.

"The Estate," I say quietly, still staring at my old home.

"Yeah, that's it. He always wanted to go to the Estate." She breathes deeply through her nose. "So, one day, he decided he was going to visit it." She looks outside as her fingers graze over the arrowhead. "He never came back."

I want to say more. I want to ask questions. Why would he want to go to the Estate? What could possibly be out there that is so interesting? The two arrows I found, were they his?

I normally would say something like that. I normally would ask a lot of questions—maybe even too many. But I just keep my mouth shut, looking back over at her.

She goes back to running her hands on her bow, moving it this way and that, catching the light on the reflective silver surface.

She does it three times.

Once.

Twice.

My heart almost stops as she does it a third time.

My throat closes, my head and heart pound, my palms sweat, my eyes widen.

And I can only stare at her.

After all these years, I realize that it was Kara who was making those three flickering lights that I saw.

CHAPTER TWENTY-THREE

I don't know how long I sat there, staring at the silver surface of her bow, a stabbing pain clawing its way to my temple, but it felt like hours. My mouth slightly hangs open, a wheezing starting to sound near my ear.

All this time, *all this time,* it was *her* that was causing the flickers of light. For four years she's been doing that. For four years no one believed me.

And for four years, I thought I was going crazy.

It's like I'm seeing everything in a whole new light.

Kara—the person I've been trying to find for years.

She notices me staring at her. She looks over at me, smiles a small smile. "Are you okay?" Her eyes are trying to find the answer in my face; I can see it right in her hazel-green eyes.

I lift up the corner of my mouth. "Never better."

She looks away, looks down at the bow in her hand. "Then," she starts, "why do you keep staring at me?"

Because I seem to have the tendency to stare at people a second too long. Those were Vicky's words to me, and now she hates me. She can hardly look in my direction, let alone talk to me.

I laugh a little. "If I told you, you would think I'm crazy."

She looks at me, smiles. "I already do." She turns around to face me, resting her elbows on her knees, suddenly looking genuinely curious. "Tell me."

I look down, contemplating everything in my head, giving myself a migraine. How do I put it without it sounding like I'm crazy?

If I tell her, she will probably think I'm weird in some way. I just got her as a friend, I *don't* want to lose her.

But maybe she won't think I'm crazy…

I open my mouth to speak, the words ready to fall out of my mouth when—

"Kara!"

I'm not sure who was the first person to snap their head to the voice, but we are both staring at the stairs, wondering who it was who shouted her name. I hear the voice again, this time lower, calmer, almost like they think she's not going to be in here.

Kara must know who it is, because she starts smiling, wider, wider. "Will!" she shouts back.

Oh, crap.

His dirty blond head is the first thing I see as he ascends the stairs, then his thin, tall body follows. His face falls as he sees me sitting next to her. "Oh—hello, Xander." His British accent has never made me more frustrated before. "How are you doing, mate?"

I look away from his face, clench my jaw tight. "Peachy."

I think he detects the frustration in my voice, because he doesn't say anything else. I keep staring out to the horizon, watching as the sun disappears into the ground. Would it all hurt less if I just drop down from this building? I would just land on my legs, knowing me.

Every time I see Will's face, I keep picturing the way he looked at Vicky, how close they were in the weapons room, the way he winked at her.

I get up from the floor, brushing away some of the sand that has gathered there, and start to make my way to the stairs.

"Where are you going?" Kara asks, making me halt in my stride.

"To… bed." I hate the words pouring out of my mouth. I wish to swallow the words back up, to say something that doesn't make me sound like an idiot.

She shakes her head. "Xander, wait—"

251

"No, it's fine," I say, inching closer to the exit. "I'll leave you two alone." I don't give her time to respond—I make my way down the stairs as quickly as I can.

I try to walk as quickly as possible; I want to get as far away from Will as fast as I can. I go through several hallways, pass some old doors, see some Wasters milling around, enjoying the rest of their day, and I bet I look like I'm on some kind of mission.

My boots make the loudest noise you could possibly imagine as I make my way down each hallway, passing some Wasters who don't even look my way. Is it normal for people to run around looking like they are crazy? It doesn't seem like—

"—isn't fair, Johanna."

I almost slip and fall over as I skid to a stop, my hands gripping furiously for the wall to my left, hoping I didn't make much of a noise.

The Waster who was speaking is male, his voice rough, hoarse, and I don't recognize it. At least, I don't *think* I recognize it.

I creep closer to the door, press my ear to the old wood. I don't know what the penalty for eavesdropping is, but I don't care, because this sounds important. Serious, even.

"It is in all ways fair," Johanna says back, calmly. "They need to stay here, simple as that."

They? Who's they? Us?

"They," the Waster hisses, "are *not* Wastelanders, Johanna." A pause. "They will *never* be Wastelanders. The survivors out there will *not* be like us… ever."

"I am not saying they are officially Wasters, my dear friend," Johanna says, a chair scraping against the floor. "But they have nowhere else to go, so the least you can do is be a good host."

"How can I be a good host?" the male Waster asks, his voice rising as he walks over to the door, and I bolt away from it, not risking eavesdropping another second.

I try to jog as quietly as I can, but I know I need to get as far away from that door as possible. The Waster didn't sound like he liked us very much.

I just wish I knew who he was.

I don't know why they still don't like us. We do our jobs, we never take up any space, and we are always quiet.

In all honesty, I don't really care; he can hate us if he wants—it's one against one hundred. We are staying, period. It's Johanna's orders.

I don't exactly know when or how, but I end up at the Mess Hall, some people staring at me as I bend down, hands on my knees as I try to catch my breath.

Thomas suddenly appears in front of me, puts a hand on my shoulder. "Xander," he says. "Are you okay?"

I nod my head, my lips parted to let air in. It feels like I'm breathing in fire. "Yeah... I am."

I don't know when I got so unfit, but I need to start doing something about it. I want to do Scavenging again. I want to be a Runner. I want to do anything other than hunting.

"What happened?" Thomas asks, eyebrows furrowed. "Why were you running?"

I can't tell him that I was eavesdropping—I have no idea what he would say. "I-I—it... it doesn't m-matter." I hate the fact that I stutter when I lie.

I start to walk away.

"Yes, it does matter, Xander," Thomas says, catching up with me. "No one just runs around for no reason."

I stop in my tracks, look over at him. "Isn't that your job?" I ask, squinting my eyes at him, leaning closer, peering into his dark—almost black—eyes. "Aren't you a Runner?"

"Y-yes but... that's not the point—" Thomas says.

"Don't you run around, trying to look for things of importance?" I interrupt him.

Thomas sighs, runs his hand through his dark hair. "Yes, I do, but *listen to me.*" The words come out through clenched teeth. "The point is, Xander: I don't run unless I am on a job, unless I have to." A pause. "You looked like you were running from *something.* Maybe even some*one.*"

I shake my head. "N-no, I-I wasn't running away from... anyone." I wonder if he can tell how bad of a liar I am.

"You know what, Xander?" He holds up his hands, laughs a small laugh. "I believe you, okay?" He drops his hands, stops laughing. "I'm sorry I even asked." Then he turns around and starts to walk away.

"Don't be sorry," I call after him. "*I'm* sorry I was being such an idiot."

He smiles over his shoulder. "Don't worry about it, Xander." He looks down. "I'll see you later."

I'm still surprised at how horrible I can be when someone interrogates me. I hate it when people ask too many questions. I haven't known Thomas for very long, and I have already been horrible to him.

What is wrong with me?

My heart almost stops beating when I see Vicky sitting at a table across the room with Adam, Tessa and Kyle. She was the first person I noticed. She's *always* the first person I notice.

She's laughing with them, eating, talking, doing normal things. Like she completely forgot about me; completely forgot who I am.

Vicky will never forget you, Xander, I remind myself. I make too many mistakes for her to forget me.

With a deep breath in, then out, I start for the table, weaving through the small gaps between the tables, trying my hardest not to brush against any Wasters back, annoying them. The

Wastelanders always seem to get annoyed whenever you disturb their feeding time. Like animals.

I didn't even get within ten feet from the table when Vicky lifts her head, glances in my direction, locks eyes with me.

And I freeze. My legs, my arms, my feet, my blood. I just… freeze.

She looks away so quickly her braid whips around her neck. She says something to the group at the table that I can't quite understand, and gets up from the table, leaving her tray full of food.

It isn't the fact that she is leaving that hurts the most, it's not even the fact that she doesn't look back as she is leaving— it's the pained look in her eyes when she looked at me that hurt the most.

My heart shatters in my chest, the pieces fall all over the floor, and I don't have the strength to try to pick the remains back up. My bones have turned to stone. Everything inside me has passed the point where I can't feel anything any more.

I am numb. Everything inside my body is numb.

And it's happening right here—right in the center of the Mess Hall.

*****

I don't know when I left the Mess Hall. I don't know how long it took me to snap back to reality. I don't know how long it took for my limbs to thaw.

And I don't know why I ran after Vicky.

I'm running like my life depends on it. Like she will slip away from me and I'll never see her again.

I just run.

I run, and I run, and I don't care how much my feet are hurting. I don't care how much my lungs feel like they're about to explode.

I don't care that Vicky keeps trying to get away from me.

"Vicky!" I call out to her. We are in an empty hallway, so my voice seems to travel for miles, bouncing off the walls, vibrating inside my skull.

She heard me. I *know* she heard me. I feel like everyone can hear me.

She keeps her head down and walks faster.

I think that's what makes me want to run faster.

She is heading toward our living quarters. If she makes it to her room, I would be too late. She won't listen to me. I have a feeling she'll never listen to me again. A strong, gut feeling that's writhing right through my body.

We enter the hallway where our living quarters are. I'm running out of time. She's slipping away from me, and I can't get her back.

No, Xander. You *will* get to her. You *will*.

Either Vicky is speeding up, or I'm slowing down, because I seem miles and miles away from her. Her dark hair is the only thing I can concentrate on, the only thing to tell me she is really there, really is running away from me.

I try to call her one more time, but she doesn't look back.

She pulls the curtain back so hard that she almost rips it off completely. As she disappears inside our quarters, I push myself and go faster, wincing when my feet burn and burn and burn.

I reach my arm out to grab hers, but—

She slams the door in my face.

I almost drop to my knees. If it wasn't for the door right in front of me, I would have collaped in a heap on the floor. I can't feel any of my body parts, any more. Everything is numb, numb, *numb*. I'm glad it is, though—I can't feel my heart being torn from my chest.

I raise my hands, pressing my hands to the old wood. I feel the cool exterior under my palms, and I don't even know how—they are numb. *Everything* is numb.

I was too late. I can't believe I was *too late*.

"Vicky…" My voice is barely above a whisper. "P-please—" I can feel the tears forming at the back of my eyes. "Please… I'm so… so sorry." I don't think she can hear me. It doesn't even sound audible to my ears. I press my forehead against the wood, letting a drop fall from my eyes.

I can feel something forming inside my chest, and it doesn't feel good. It feels so bad that I do something stupid, something I never thought I would do.

I punch the door. Hard.

I don't feel the pain as I am numb. I don't think I will ever be able to feel pain again.

I slide down the door, letting anything fall from my eyes as I land on the ground, my back pressed against the wood. I let my head rest against the flat surface, and I wish, just for a moment, that I could see something, anything—everything is blurry. I wish I could feel something, and I don't care even if it's the pain in my right hand, or whatever might be in my chest.

I just don't care any more.

I let the sobs sound at the back of my throat because they can't seem to go further than that. Or maybe, I just won't let them go further than my throat. I think because it hurts, but I can't tell any more.

I can't do anything at the moment.

Nothing.

And I despise the moment when I will finally have to get back up again.

CHAPTER TWENTY-FOUR

A few years ago, I realized that tears are such powerful words that only come from the heart. Words that we can't say out loud. That's why sad people cry—they're trying to tell us what their heart is saying, why it's breaking, why it is shattered into a million pieces.

I wonder, sometimes, about tears.

Little beads of water that fall from your eyes, staining your cheeks. Water pours out of our eyes, and no one even thinks twice about it. When tears dry, people never stop to ask why you were crying. They always wipe them away before people can have a good look at them.

People say men shouldn't cry, but they do. They cry when people aren't looking. They cry when they see their mother in pain or distress. They cry when *they* are in pain.

They cry when their heart is broken.

I feel like I'm in that position.

I can't swallow anything in my throat as my mouth is dry, drier than it ever has been since I haven't said a word in a long, long time.

It feels like I've forgotten how to speak.

Vicky, I want to say, but I can't—my mouth won't move. I can't form the words on my lips. *Please—please. I'm... I'm so sorry...*

I've stayed in this exact position for a long time; back against her door, legs out in front of me, my hands clenched tightly into fists to the point where I feel my nails dig into my flesh.

It hurts, but I can't seem to release them.

No one else has stepped foot inside our living quarters. Or maybe they have, but I haven't been paying attention. I haven't focused on anything for a while. I keep staring at the same thing in front of me, but I can't seem to figure out what it is.

My mind replays the exact moment when Vicky slammed the door in my face. I can't get the way she looked at me out of my head. It will be printed in my mind until the day I die. It's just like someone got a scorching hot mold and pressed it against my mind, keeping it there until I scream out in pain.

Someone is crouching in front of me.

I can't see who as my eyes are blurry. It's male. It is definitely a male. Brown hair atop his head, tanned skin, a thin beard adorning his slightly hollow cheeks.

"Xander?"

I can't recognize the voice. It's deep—very deep, in fact, but it still manages to sound like melting butter; the way it flows from his mouth is almost mesmerizing.

And I still don't know who it is.

"Xander?" he says again, but this time it's different, less smooth, almost… croaky—hoarse, even.

I can hear you, I can't seem to say. My eyes travel up to where I think his eyes are, and they almost seem to be brighter than their normal gray color.

Kyle.

Kyle is crouching in front of me.

My mouth parts to let words out, but it seems like my throat has closed up, choking me, suffocating me.

And it still hurts less than what happened to me earlier.

I don't know when, but I'm suddenly on my feet, one of my arms wrapped around Kyle's neck, my legs struggling to keep me grounded.

I just want to collapse to the ground, never to get up again.

Every step I take is like a thousand needles stabbing me in my feet and legs. It doesn't even feel like I'm walking. It hurts so badly. I want to stop, but Kyle keeps pulling me with him.

"Come on, Xander," Kyle whispers, tightening his grip on my waist to keep me up. "Don't do this to us, now."

I think Kyle is struggling to keep me up, but my eyes are still so blurry that I can't see anything. I try to look back at Vicky's door, but my head won't turn past my collarbone.

She got out of my reach. She slid away from me, and I let her.

*****

"Here, drink this."

Kyle slides a glass half-full of water in front of me, trying to look up at me as he pushes it forward, forward. I slowly wrap my fingers around the cold exterior, watching the condensation drip off my fingertips.

At least I started getting feeling back in my hands.

Kyle slides into the chair in front of me, but I can't look up. He brought me to the Mess Hall, where most of the people have dissipated, leaving it completely silent.

I hear him sigh, folding his arms on the table. "Do you… feel like telling me what happened?"

I gnaw on my bottom lip until I taste a hint of blood, not saying a single word. Even though I know I can tell Kyle anything, this situation isn't something I want to share. Instead, I press the glass to my lips, trying to tip the cold liquid in my mouth. I wonder if I can continue to take the smallest sips and not say a single word at all.

Kyle stares at me, waiting for an answer.

So much for me drinking the water slowly, not being able to answer.

I shake my head. "No." My voice comes out barely above a whisper, but it still manages to feel like it's ripping my throat out. I take another sip of my water.

"You know, Xander?" Kyle shifts in his seat, but I continue to stare at the shimmering water in my glass. "When I see someone sprawled on the floor, staring blankly into space—I do ask questions. And I want answers to them."

I meet his eyes. "I was... tired, Kyle." My voice is hoarse as the lie pours out of my mouth. "I-I ju-just wanted to... go to sleep, but I-I couldn't make it to my room." Damn my stuttering.

Kyle laughs, looks down, scratches the corner of his mouth. "You see, Xander? I don't believe you."

"Believe what you want, Kyle." I shake my head. "I'm just telling you what happened."

Kyle laughs again. "You remind me so much of myself when I was younger, you know that?"

I give him a confused look; he's never told me about this— of all the years I've known him, he's never told me that I remind him of himself.

"I was in the same situation you are in when I was your age," Kyle's voice breaks through my thoughts.

My heart starts to pick up speed. He knows, he knows, he knows.

I try not to swallow hard.

"My... situation?" I ask quietly, my voice still sounding hoarse, and I drink the rest of my water.

Kyle half-smiles, dropping his voice lower. "With Vicky."

And my heart drops to my stomach so fast I swear it feels like I've swallowed it.

Kyle must have read whatever I was feeling on my face, because he shakes his head. "Don't worry," he says. "Your secret is safe with me." He presses his lips together firmly, running his thumb and index fingers across his lips, feigning zipping his lips shut.

"No—I-I… it's not like that, Kyle," I argue. "It's just… we had an argument, and now she hates me, won't speak to me, *or* even look at me."

"Give her time, Xander." He leans closer. "And if you ever get her back." A pause. "Don't let her go."

I lean back. "That's where you're wrong, Kyle." I swallow the lump in my throat. "I can't get her back." I swallow again, dropping my voice to a whisper. "I've already let her go."

Kyle looks down, presses his lips together. "That's not who you are, Xander," Kyle says. "You never give up on people. Never."

"Stubborn," I confirm.

"Yes," Kyle agrees. "Use that to your advantage." He leans even closer, drops his voice to a mere whisper. "Get. Her. Back."

I nod, swallowing the dryness in my throat. "I'll try."

And just this once, I actually will.

*****

"Xander? Hello? Xander? Earth to Xander!"

Kara snaps her fingers in front of my face, startling me. I blink, staring at her. "Y-yes—sorry, I was just… just distracted."

I drop the piece of rope that was in my hands, sitting straight up, stretching out my legs. Kara was teaching me how to trap an animal using nothing but a long piece of rope. I got about three minutes into it before my mind started to wander, thinking about Kyle's words before we parted last night.

Use that to your advantage. Get. Her. Back.

Right now, I have never been more determined to do anything in my life.

"You seem to be distracted a lot." Kara looks into my eyes. "Why are you distracted?"

I shake my head. "It doesn't matter." I fiddle with the long piece of rope, trying to tie it together.

"Here, like this." Kara quickly grabs my hands, showing me how to tie the proper knot, tightening it here and there, showing me where in the trap the animal will get stuck.

I try to stay focused.

At least, I try to *look* focused.

Last night, I got approximately half an hour's sleep before the sound of Kyle and Joel snoring woke me up. That, and another thing. Another thing I'll never say aloud to people.

"That's it." I drop the rope, starting to stand up. "How about we drop this and do something else?"

Kara stands up, leaving the rope on the ground. "Being a Hunter is not something you just 'drop' and leave, Xander. It's a job," she's saying, "and it's *my* job. I want to actually *keep* it." She stares me in the eye. "Okay?"

I stare at her back, leaning closer. "O-kay," I say slowly.

She shakes her head as she leans down, grabbing my bow and quiver from the floor, shoving them at my chest, making me stumble back slightly.

I've just slipped my quiver onto my back, bow in hand, reaching for an arrow when Kara stops me.

"Whoa, whoa, hold your horses." Kara grabs a few items scattered around the room, shoving them in her back pocket.

I eye her carefully. "What are you…?" I trail off.

"How are you ever going to learn when you hit the exact same thing every day?" she says, making me think. "When I throw *this*"—she lifts up a medium-sized object that I can't quite make out—"into the air, I want you to try and hit it. Easy, right? Good. Now try."

I pull an arrow from the quiver as quickly as my fingers will let me, lining it with my bow without looking down. I'm not even sure it's on properly, but I can't think twice about it—I need to hit the target.

I can see the object in the corner of my eye. Without a second thought, I raise my bow, pulling the string as far back as it will go. I keep one eye closed, the tip of my arrow following where the object will go.

I release the string.

I don't stop to see if I've shot the target when I pull another from my quiver, repeating the action over and over again until I'm out of arrows, and Kara is out of objects to throw.

I didn't even realize I was breathing heavily.

I feel like my heart might just fall out of my chest.

"Wow," Kara breathes, staring at the scene in front of her, which I turn to take a look at.

Scattered remains of whatever it was Kara was throwing lie across the floor. My arrows seem to have sliced right through the targets to the wall opposite. Some of them even managed to crack the wall.

I'm so shocked that I actually drop the bow to the ground, the clattering sound vibrating around the room.

"What got you so angry?" Kara's voice snaps me back to the present, and I look over at her.

"Why would you think I'm angry?" I ask, sweeping a layer of sweat from my forehead.

"Well… for one thing, you didn't look very happy while you were shooting the targets," she says. "The other thing is that you had a death grip on your bow. I mean, I could see the bones of your knuckles."

I was only thinking about one situation while I was shooting, and I must have gotten caught up in the moment.

Kara was right—anger does help, sometimes.

I just wish it was about something else.

"Kara," I call out to her, "is it okay if we take a rain check?" She looks at me weirdly. "I mean… I can hardly focus, and I'm shattered. Please?"

Kara looks over at the target, biting her lower lip. "Fine," she breathes out. "Fine. Have a good, and I mean *good* night's sleep. Try to focus. You will never hit the targets when you're not fully focused."

I nod along, wanting to leave the room as quickly as possible, and relax. "Okay."

I start toward the door, but Kara stops me.

"Are we ever going to talk about what happened yesterday?" she asks.

She's talking about the thing with Will. I know she is.

No, never in a million years. "Maybe one day we will," I say instead. I stride toward the door, heading out in case Kara stops me again. "See you tomorrow." I open the door.

I just about hear her say the words "See you tomorrow" before I close the door behind me.

*****

The fact that I still didn't know what was behind the only other door in the weapons room, was what made me walk over to it. I run my fingers along the length of one sword on the wall, picking up a small layer of dust.

The door is slightly smaller than the door to the training room; I have to stoop forward to be able to fit through as I slowly turn the handle. It squeaks quietly on its hinges as it swings open, letting out a cold gust of wind.

I step through into the dark room, the darkness slowly turning brighter as my eyes adjust to the dim lamp around a corner. I have no idea what is beyond that; I'm not really sure if I want to go further in and see for myself. The very small hallway leading up to the sharp turn has nothing else in it. Nothing. Just black on the floor, ceiling and walls.

"Hello?" I say quietly, listening for someone, some*thing* to respond. "Is anyone in here?"

Slowly, a blond head peeks out from the left side of the wall, and I start, almost jumping backward. The boy with the blond hair is looking at me as if I'm not really in here.

265

I wait, silently, for him to say the first word.

"Hi!" The volume of his voice makes me jump, and I clutch at my chest.

I step forward, the door slowly closing behind me almost as if it has a mind of its own. "What are you... doing in here?"

The boy looks at me like I'm stupid. "My job."

"Job?" I keep walking forward, the sudden smell of oil, grease and metal shooting up my nose. When I see what is behind the wall, my mouth actually drops open with shock. Broken pieces of metal—weapons, by the looks of them—are sprawled across the floor. A few swords and bows are standing upright against one of the four walls, looking old and new at the same time.

"Yeah." He scratches the top of his head. "This is my job. Pretty boring, huh?"

"What?" I look at him. "No—no, not at all." I pick a piece of metal up from the ground, rubbing my fingers against it. "Are you an Engineer?"

"That, I am." He flashes me a wide, white-toothed grin.

"How long have you been in here?"

He smooths down his shirt—one that looks like mine—as he stands up from a small stool next to a small desk. "All day," he replies, grabbing a small black rag from a hook on the wall. "Do you have anything that needs fixed?"

I stumble on the words that were going to fall out of my mouth. I don't really know what to say to that.

"You can say no." He looks up at me. "I won't be mad."

His strange green eyes stare straight back into mine as I find my next words.

"No, actually." I pull my bow off my back, crouching down to his height. "When I draw my bow, it creaks loudly right about here." I point to a spot just above where the string parts from the bow. "It's annoying me."

The boy nods quickly, grabbing the bow from my hand. "I can fix this." He slowly pulls the bow back to test where the noise is coming from, then nods to himself.

I stand back up, leaning against the wall as he wipes the same rag against the top of the bow. I have no idea how old this boy is; I'm not sure if he's the same age as me, or slightly younger or older. He's quite short—shorter than me, anyway. Although, saying that, I *am* tall for my age.

He brushes some blond hair out of his eyes as he works. His hair is long, but not as long as mine—slightly shorter.

"So," the boy starts, "what's your name?"

I look up at the ceiling, my eyes scanning each and every crack. "Xander."

"Hmm, interesting name." He stares intently at the bow as he wipes. "Is it short for something?"

I lick my dry lips. "Alexander." My full name sounds strange as I say it out loud to a person I hardly know.

"Oh—yes, of course it is." The Waster is silent for a moment. "Don't you like people calling you that?"

"No."

"What about Alex?"

I look at him weirdly. "I'm sorry, but that nickname doesn't suit me, at all."

He tilts his head at me. "You're right," he says. "Xander does suit you better. What about if I called you Xan?"

My heart gives a sudden lurch that I almost fall to the ground. I keep my face impassive, still staring at the wall in front of me. "My best friend is the only person allowed to call me that."

"Right, okay, I'm sorry." He draws my bow again, seemingly unsatisfied. "How long has he called you that?"

"*She.*"

"Okay, *she.* How long has she called you that?"

I shrug even though he doesn't see it. "Ever since she met me." I feel the pain again in my heart. I try my hardest to end this conversation.

"Cool," he says.

I guess that's one way to put it.

I look down at what the boy is doing. He picks up a rusting blue can with the name *WD-40* written clearly in the same blue against a fading yellow background. He sprays a small amount of the stuff on the bow, wiping it inside the creases. The boy draws the bow again, a big smile creeping onto his face. "All done."

I take the bow from his hands, thanking him while I draw the bow myself, feeling suddenly happier that the stupid creaking isn't bothering me any more.

"If you get any more problems, just bring it straight back to me. I'll fix it for you."

I smile kindly at the young man, swinging the bow onto my back. "Thanks again." I turn to look down the small hallway. "I got to go. I'll see you around."

The boy nods. "Goodbye, Xander."

I nod once before stepping toward the door, stooping down again as I step through the door, the door closing by itself again.

As I make my way toward my living quarters, it dawns on me that I didn't ask what the boy's name was, and I have no idea if I will ever see him again.

CHAPTER TWENTY-FIVE

Having a shower at this moment has never felt more appealing in my life. I need to melt away the stresses of the day. I need to loosen the tense muscles in my back.

I need to get the thoughts from the day before out of my mind.

The only way I can do that is to move on, no matter how much it hurts.

I pull back the ripped curtain, heading straight for the bathroom, trying my hardest to ignore Vicky's door. I try not to look where I wish I had just collapsed.

I push open the bathroom door, not really caring to be quiet as I slam it shut. Someone else is in here, having a shower, so they wouldn't be able to hear it, anyway.

The water hitting the floor silences my loud sigh as I grab a towel from the side, swinging open the cubicle door closest to the wall, closing it behind me. Turning the lock, I hang the towel on the door, starting to remove my clothes, untying my boots first.

I wait until I'm completely ready before hitting the *start* button with my thumb, jumping back slightly as the instant hot water hits my body.

I don't know what it is about warm water that always relaxes us. Especially when you're tense—you can actually feel it loosen all of your muscles.

I'm just glad it actually works.

I run my hands down the length of my face, catching a pool of water in my palms. I let the liquid soak my hands for a couple of seconds, savoring the feeling of water on my skin.

I don't feel it often.

The shower finishes too soon, and I internally curse this place for not having real showers, real running water. Sure, they're trying to ration the water, but at least give us longer than *five* minutes.

I stare at the water-soaked floor a second too long, knowing that the amount of water is probably enough to be able to have a bath. I start to turn around, blindly trying to reach for the towel hung on the door. I can't see a damn thing with all this steam. I can just about see the outline of the white door in front of me.

I run the fabric across my chest, drying it as best as I can, begging the towel to not touch the floor.

I leave my hair for last. It's the thing that takes the longest to dry, anyway. I place the towel over my head and ruffle my hair with the material, letting it stick up everywhere.

The other shower has turned off, and the person is moving around in their cubicle. I still have no idea who it is—it could be anyone. It could be the person I really want to see. It could be the person I really *don't* want to see at the moment.

The person's feet are padding against the floor. I can hear the water splashing around. It is a weird type of sound; it doesn't seem natural. The person exhales, and I swear my heart fell out of my chest. I'd recognize the exhale anywhere; I've heard it countless times before.

Vicky is in the bathroom with me.

Vicky doesn't know I'm in here.

I hold my breath and hope she walks out quickly.

Use that to your advantage. Get. Her. Back.

But I can't. I wish I could, but I can't. I don't know how. She won't even look at me, so how can I make her talk to me?

I'm halfway dressed before I even realize it. I pull the shirt on, making sure my knife is still tied on my belt. It's been so long since I used it, I really need to start using it again.

I place the towel on the hook at the back of the door, square my shoulders, lift my chin, and turn the lock.

Everything is silent for a few precious seconds. I can't even hear the splashes of water against the floor.

Maybe it is there. Maybe I can hear it, it's just I'm not registering it in my mind. The buzzing is starting to be the most comforting sound I've ever heard in my ears.

I push open the bathroom door and step out, making sure I keep staring at nothing but whatever it is that is in front of me.

I need to act as if nothing happened yesterday. I need to act as if she doesn't hate me.

So, I do the thing that I know will help.

I go and stand next to her at the mirror.

I can't stand to look at myself in the mirror right now. I can't look at the person I wish I had never become. Instead, I look at the cubicles behind me, avoiding my eyes, my hair, my *face* completely.

I hear Vicky take a sharp breath, slowly moving away from the mirror—away from me. Far, far away from me.

I take a chance to look at her from the corner of my eyes, and I see her blinking fast. She's trying to stop tears falling out, but I don't know why she won't just leave. Or, maybe, she's trying to see if I'm really in the same room as her, standing *right* next to her. I think it's the former. It's definitely the former.

It hurts to see someone cry, but what hurts even more is when you make that person cry. I didn't even know I could have the intention to make her cry, and the fact that I did rips my heart clean out of my chest.

"Vicky," I whisper, barely audible, just a breath of air.

She starts inching closer to the door, shaking her head the slightest bit.

"Please." I don't know if I just mouthed the word. I don't even know anything, any more. I turn to look at her; she's halfway to the door.

She shakes her head again, this time faster. "No."

She spoke.

She spoke to me.

It may have been one word with two letters, but it's more powerful in my ears than anyone else's.

I turn to look at her. "Vicky, please." I think my voice came out louder, but I'm still not sure. I reach for her hand, but she jerks away.

"No, Xander. D-don't... don't... do that." She's backing away from me, slowly.

"Don't do what?" My voice quivers slightly.

"Think everything will be okay." Her back is against the door.

Use that to your advantage. Get. Her. Back.

But I'm failing, failing, failing. I *can't* get her back. She won't let me.

"I'm... sorry." I don't think my voice will go any louder.

She swallows hard, moving her hand to the doorknob.

"Please, Vicky," I whisper. "Why... why won't you just... talk to me?"

She looks away, presses her lips together tightly. "I... I just can't."

I reach my hand out slowly, but she somehow manages to shrink against the door, almost like she is just getting farther and farther away from me.

She's turning the handle, and I back away, not wanting to make her leave.

"Please, just talk to me." I still don't know if she can hear me.

She must have because I can see it in her eyes, ones that are looking everywhere but at me. "I can't. I'm sorry." She turns the handle and slips out the door. I start as the door slams loudly in my face.

I let her go. Again.

What is wrong with me? What is *wrong* with me?

I release a breath I didn't realize I was holding, staring at the closed door for a few more seconds. I don't know why.

Maybe, subconsciously, I think she'll come back in and talk to me.

It's hard to believe that not even a week ago, Vicky and I were okay. We were the best of friends. We've never had an argument as big as this, or not that I can recall. She's never walked away from me without looking me in the eye.

I try to compose myself as I walk out the door, shivering when the cold air hits me in the face.

I quickly move out of the way as Joel walks out of the boys' room, a towel draped across his shoulder. His eyebrows furrow as he looks at my face. "Are you okay, Xander?"

I'm slightly taken aback. Joel—*Joel* just asked me if I was okay. That is not on my list of things Joel would say to me.

I try to keep my face neutral. Look normal. Look normal. Look normal. He won't suspect a thing.

I nod my head, crack the slightest smile. "I am," I lie. "Sorry for getting in your way."

Joel shakes his head. "N-no… it's okay," he stammers as I walk past him, closing the door behind me.

I'm glad no one is in the room to see me like this. I press my back against the door, flatten myself against it, lifting my head to rest against the hard wood.

I don't think anything has ever caused me so much internal pain before. Nothing has made me feel like my heart has just been ripped out of my chest.

I don't know how long it takes for me to finally peel myself away from the door, and over to my bed. It seems to take forever to finally get ready for bed.

Exhaustion creeps in, and I'm out when my head hits the pillow.

*****

She latches onto my neck before I can even comprehend what is happening. I didn't even see or hear her take those few steps to get to me. When I saw her, all my tears came rushing back, flooding my eyes—making them blur to the point where I couldn't wash them away.

She pulls me down to her height, and it's only then that I let my arms tighten around her waist. Her face is completely hidden in my chest. My head is resting softly on her shoulder.

I squeeze my eyes shut, letting a few tears to fall on the ground behind Vicky.

I can feel her warm breath hitting my chest as it passes through her bandana.

All of the feelings of loneliness slowly disappear as my grip on Vicky tightens, her arms tightening around me.

I wake with tears staining my cheeks.

Of all the things to think of, it was that *one* moment. It feels like it was years ago. I can't seem to forget that memory, but deep down, I *don't* want to forget that moment. It showed me how much she cared for me, even when everything was my fault. When *everything* was my fault. Everything *is* my fault, I correct myself.

But I guess that's what best friends do. They care for each other—no matter what happens.

I swing my legs over the side of the bed, using the palm of my hands to press in the corner of my eyes. When I remove my hands from my face to open my eyes, I start to see Adam sitting on his bed, twiddling his thumbs in his lap.

"Finally, you're awake," he says when he sees me sitting on the edge of my bed.

"What are you doing in here?" I yawn. "Aren't you supposed to be on Security?"

Adam shrugs. "We got the day off."

I shake my head. "You lucky little…"

"No, Xander. We've *all* got the day off," Adam interrupts me.

"What do you mean?" My voice sounds tired.

"I mean, we have all got the day off." Adam squints his eyes at me. "I don't know how to simplify that sentence."

It's too early for this. "No, that's not what I meant." I shake my head, releasing a breath. "I mean *why* have people got the day off?"

Adam shrugs, lifting his shoulders a bit too high. "Beats me."

I sigh. "You're no help, at all, Adam."

Just before Adam can reply to what I said, someone knocks on the door—three light taps.

Who could be at our door at this hour? I almost have an idea who it might be. "We're not in. Please try again later," I say, trying to keep my voice emotionless.

"Xander, I'm coming in now," Kara says through the door. "If you're not decent then you lost your chance."

The door cracks open and I slowly stand up as I see Kara walk inside, a small pile of clothes in her hand.

"Morning, boys." Kara smiles, but we just frown at her. It's too early for smiling.

"Morning," Adam and I say in unison, trying not to sound too frustrated.

"Did you sleep all right?" I know her question is directed at me. I know because she's looking into my eyes.

I nod slowly. "Better, thanks." Am I lying to her? I can't tell.

"Good," she replies, walking toward us. She hands me one of the items in her hand, then hands the last one to Adam.

"What are these?" I ask her.

"Shorts." She points to the clothes. "You're going to need these for our day off."

We both look up at her.

"So, you know about this 'day off', too, then?" I ask, knitting my brows together.

"Of course I do," she replies. "Every Waster knows about this day off. It's a tradition."

"Tradition?" Adam steps up. "Doing what?"

She turns to look at him, cracks a small smile. "You'll see." She turns around and starts walking toward the door. "Put them on, then meet me outside your quarters in two minutes."

I stare at the black material in my hand, turning it around to get a look at the back. The fabric is rough but soft at the same time. Durable, maybe. I can't really tell.

"Well," Adam huffs, "she isn't going to wait there forever." He starts replacing his pants with the shorts, and I do the same.

I leave my pants on my bed, tying my boots back on my feet. I can't remember the last time I wore shorts; I never wore them in the Estate, and I don't have any memories about wearing them before that.

I guess there is a first for everything.

"We look ridiculous." I look down at my legs, noticing how I look with shorts on as well as boots.

"Speak for yourself," Adam says. "I think I look rather amazing." He sticks his leg out, looking down at it, smirking a small smile.

"Okay then, Adam," I laugh and we both walk out of the door, heading toward the exit, where Kara is patiently leaning against the wall, her arms crossed over her chest.

"You ready?" she asks.

We both nod.

"More than I'll ever be," I say, and Kara leads the way.

"Where are we even going?" Adam asks eventually, breaking the silence. We just passed the Mess Hall, and I have no idea where we could be heading.

"You'll see," Kara says. "Man, you're impatient."

After what seems like an hour, we have finally reached somewhere I have never cared to venture. We are somewhere outside, but I'm not sure if we are where we came in, or the complete opposite side.

I'm thinking the latter.

"Damn, it's hot." Adam looks up at the sky, causing the sun to blind his eyes. He turns to look at me. "It never used to be this hot in the Estate. What changed?"

I shrug, not saying anything else as I keep following Kara's trail.

Kara pulls back one last ripped curtain, and what it reveals is what I never expected. Something I've never seen in real life. Something I've only ever thought or dreamed about.

An oasis.

A couple of trees line the perimeter of the water, but all I can see is the Wasters laughing and having fun inside of it. They are everywhere; in the water, out of the water. Some are even just sitting on the sand far away from the water.

"This is our day off," Kara's voice snaps me back to reality. "Enjoy."

"Don't mind if I do." Adam jogs lightly over to the oasis, being careful when he slides down the slide of sand. He must have spotted someone, but I can't make out who. They are too far away.

"Come on, you'll love it." Kara ushers me down the slide, and I lean back as I descend. The last thing I want to do is fall on my face.

I don't know why I feel nervous as I get closer to the oasis. Maybe it's because I have never seen a natural pool in my life. Maybe it's the smell of fresh water in the air, distracting my senses.

"Are you going to go in?"

I scan around the pool, seeing the different Wasters enjoying themselves. There is no way I can go in there with this shirt on, but there is also no way I'm taking my shirt off.

People will see the scar on my side.

"Umm…" I continue to look at the water, thinking of a way out of this. "I don't think so."

"Ah, come on. You're going to miss out. We don't get another day like this for another year." Kara's trying to get me to go in there, but I don't want to. I pull down the hem of my shirt, suddenly feeling exposed.

"Wait—a year? Why a year?" I ask, slowly moving away from the water's edge.

"Yeah, this is the Tenth Annual Day Off, let's say."

"You've only been doing this for ten years?" I ask.

"Yeah, that's when we decided to do this." She moves closer to the edge, ending the conversation.

"Oh," I say quickly, still trying to move away.

"It's not that bad." Kara guides me toward the edge of the pool, and the water is so clear that I can see the bottom of it.

It looks really inviting.

I shake my head.

"Suit yourself." Kara starts removing her clothes, leaving her in her swimming gear.

I try to look anywhere but her.

She wanders off into the water, ducking down so that only her head is dry. "Come on, it feels great!"

I look at the other Wasters behind her, seeing how much fun they are having. I spot Kyle, Adam, Tessa and Vicky in the distance. They look like they are having so much fun.

I really don't want to put a damper on anyone's day off.

I roll my eyes. "Okay, fine," I say. "Just give me a minute."

I crouch down and start unlacing my boots, slowly pulling them off my feet, stuffing my socks inside them, making sure they will stay safe and dry.

I'm already regretting it by the time I stand up. I swallow hard, grabbing the top of my shirt behind my neck. I hesitate before slowly, slowly, slowly pulling it up and over my head.

I try to hide my scar as much as I can, but I feel everyone's eyes on it, drilling holes into it. I pull my arms out of the sleeves, and fold it as much as I can, carefully placing it on top of my boots.

"You see?" Kara says. "No one is looking at you."

"Why do I feel like they are, then?"

"Who knows?" She shrugs. "Why don't you get in here if you don't want people to see you?"

She's right. I *can* hide in the water. I just hate the fact that I have to hide from everyone.

As I place my foot in the water, my stomach does flips. It's a weird feeling since I've never been in a natural pool before. I've never been in *any* pool before.

I feel myself sinking deeper and deeper into the water, and my heart beats fast against my chest. I sink further into the water, making sure that my scar is covered, and I stand next to Kara.

I think she sees the worried expression on my face, because she suddenly whispers, "You don't know how to swim, do you?"

I look down at my feet, bite my lower lip. "I was never taught." I never had anything to use to swim. Normally, your mother or father would teach you how to swim; they would bring you when you were a young child, but I never had that opportunity. I might never get that opportunity ever again.

She comes closer to me. "Maybe I can teach you."

I smile. "Thanks. Maybe one day."

She suddenly goes quiet, looking down at something on me, and I back away as I notice her staring at my scar.

"You never told me about that day," she says eventually, breaking the silence. "What happened?"

So, I tell her. I tell her all about me climbing up the scaffolding, and when it snapped. What I do miss out is what Vicky said to me back then. No one will ever know about that, other than us.

You need to stay awake. You can make it. Please. I can't lose you.

"Sometimes," I say after a pause of silence, "I still feel the piece of metal in my side. That feeling will never leave my system. Sometimes, I just wake up late at night thinking it will still be inside my body."

279

"I'm so sorry," she breathes out.

My fingers dance on the surface, causing ripples to circle around us. "It's not your fault, Kara."

She opens her mouth to say something, but I interrupt her, wanting to change the subject. "So... this is what you do on your day off?" I look around. "It's quite fun."

"Yeah, I guess so." Kara looks around as well, the sun reflecting in her hazel-green eyes. Her hair looks brighter out in the sun, her skin looks slightly paler.

The sun starts to feel like it's burning my neck, and I'm glad the water is cool. The weather has been so hot that I just wanted something, *anything* to cool me off.

Kara meets my eyes for only a second before I smirk at her.

Feeling brave, I dive under the water, holding my breath. I've only ever dreamed about what it would feel like to hold my breath underwater. It's weird—it doesn't feel like my lungs are about to explode, which is what I imagine could happen without air.

I push my hair backward as I re-emerge, releasing the extra air in my lungs.

"Did you enjoy that?" Kara asks, smiling.

I laugh, brushing away the water on my face. "I did," I say. "Thank you."

As Kara dives under the water, I take a look over at where Kyle and the rest of the guys are, but somehow, I can't seem to ignore the way Vicky is staring straight back at me.

CHAPTER TWENTY-SIX

When Kara re-emerges, she blocks the view of Vicky, and somehow—*somehow,* I'm almost grateful. I hate myself for saying it, but I don't really want to look at Vicky at the moment. It will just bring back too many emotions that I don't want to deal with right now.

"I didn't realize you could hold your breath for so long," I say, trying to distract myself, *and* to change the subject. It was the only thing I could think of to say.

"Well," Kara says, brushing some hair out of her eyes, "when you've been doing it for the majority of your life, then you kind of get used to it."

I nod along, even though I can't say I know what she means—until now, I've never been underwater. I've just tried to imagine what it is like. I've only ever *read* about what it is like.

The water ripples around us, and I look down, staring at the sand and my feet as they get covered with the small particles. It's weird how sand isn't irritating when you are in water; it just feels like it's washing away with every step you take. I guess it kind of is, though.

When I look up again, I notice Kara staring at me, and she doesn't even look away. She's very close to me, probably about a foot away. The water reflecting in her hazel-green eyes somehow makes her look more beautiful.

She smiles at me, so kindly, so genuinely, that I can't help but smile back at her.

"Hey, guys!"

My heart pounds against my chest as I step back, my head snapping toward the source of the voice.

Thomas swims into view, his whole body floating on the surface. He's looking up at the sky, making the sun blind his eyes. I can't help but notice something on his torso. A scar runs from his side to the center of his stomach. It isn't red, so it must not be recent. He doesn't seem to care at all if people see it, so I don't know why *I* do.

Maybe it's because it's my fault that I have this scar, and it's not Thomas's fault that he has his.

I'm starting to regret coming in here. I feel like every single Waster is suddenly staring at me, secretly talking about my scar and *knowing* that it was all my fault. I sometimes really hate my thoughts.

"—may be the best day of my life!"

I tuned in at the wrong time. I have no idea what Thomas was saying, but I doubt he directed it at me. There is no awkward silence following his statement, so I turn to look at Kara.

"I know," Kara says, moving her hands across the water. "It's the only day where we can actually *relax.*"

I take a peek over Kara's head, slowly noticing something that makes my heart drop to the bottom of the water.

Kyle, Adam, Tessa *and* Vicky are swimming over to us, and I've never wanted to scramble out of the water fast enough. I've never wanted to push myself away from my friends who haven't done anything to me. I just want to *go.*

But I stay put.

"So," Kyle starts, startling Kara and Thomas, "whose idea was it to have this day off?"

"We're not really sure." Kara turns to face the others. "We think it was Johanna, but we have been doing it for a long time."

Kyle doesn't seem that bothered, any more, so he doesn't continue with the conversation. He just gives a slight nod of his head and turns to look at something else.

My eyes meet Vicky's and I can't seem to look away. You know that type of feeling—like a force—when you look at something, and you can't seem to look away? That's how I feel. I can't look away from Vicky. My head won't turn away to look at something else.

She does the smallest smile you can think of, then finally, *finally* looks away from me. My lungs expand as I release a breath, my eyes looking away from her face.

I have no idea when I can talk to her again. I have no idea when we will finally get back to being best friends. Best friends always seem to make up—one way or another. I just don't know the *when.*

"So, what's the plan for later?" Adam asks, snapping me back to reality.

Kara and Thomas exchange a look I can't really place.

"Well, normally, we would do this for a few more hours," Kara says.

"Then we would just rest around a fire and chat," Thomas finishes for her.

A fire? Chatting? I thought this "Day Off" would last the *whole* day, doing different and random things for the day. But I don't know.

"When does this fire start?" I ask my thoughts out loud, finally speaking up. Vicky looks up at me, almost surprised that I spoke out loud, or even spoke *at all.* Almost like I'm just a part of this group to stay quiet and listen to the rest of them having fun.

"Normally around sunset," Thomas replies, even though my question was directed at Kara. He sinks his hands under the water, then back up to the surface. Out of boredom, probably.

We all look around at the different Wasters, watching as they laugh in the water. One male Waster laughs as he holds a female Waster on his shoulders, sinking lower into the water. A group of Wasters are swimming broad strokes around the whole perimeter of the oasis—they look like they are trying to race, but I can't be too sure.

We could have that much fun—if things weren't so damn awkward.

My eyes drift on their own, catching sight of a familiar blond head chatting with another Waster not too far away from where we are standing.

I excuse myself and brush past my friends crowded into a circle, the movement made difficult by all the water surrounding me. The water slowly lowers to my waist as I get closer and closer to the pair of younger Wasters.

The boy that fixed my bow slowly locks eyes with me, his face naturally lifting into a small grin. I smile back as he excuses himself from the other Waster who nods his head and swims away to another group of people.

"Hey, Xander." His smile grows wider. "I didn't think you would ever find your way 'round here."

His smile is contagious. I smile back as I incline my head backward to Kara. "Kara brought me here," I say, finally settling next to him.

He looks over my shoulder to my friends. "I saw you talking to the blonde girl a few minutes ago. Is that your best friend you were talking about?"

I shake my head. "No, it's not, but she *is* one of my friends. It's Kara."

"That's Kara? I didn't even recognize her. I *can* only see the back of her head, though." He nods toward the group. "Which one is your best friend?"

"The one with the long dark hair. You could probably see her blue eyes from here." I don't need to turn around to show him—I don't really want to turn around.

The boy nods, not saying anything else.

"I've never seen this place before. It's quite amazing," I say to change the subject.

"I know, it is pretty amazing, isn't it?" The boy looks up at the sky, the sun reflecting off his lightly tanned skin.

I study him for a moment, still trying to contemplate what the hell his name is, and how old he is. His face is too young and soft to be older than me, but he seems older than a child.

"Are you all right, Xander?" He looks up at me. "You were just staring."

I shake my head the slightest bit. "Yes—sorry. I just... I still don't know your name," I say. "Wait! How about a nickname? Can I call you Green Eyes?"

The boy—Green Eyes—laughs. "You can call me that if you want to, but"—he holds out his hand, dripping water—"I'm Levi."

I take his hand, shaking once, repeating his name just in case I misheard it. "Levi. That's a nice name."

"Thank you. It's nice to *officially* meet you, Xander." Levi drops his hand back into the water, the splashing sound the only thing audible in the silence around us.

The laughing slowly returns as I say, "You're a funny guy, Levi," I say. "Sorry, *Green Eyes.*"

We both smile as a few Wasters splash each other from behind Levi, their booming laughter echoing around the whole space.

"Thank you, again, for fixing my bow." It still amazes me how much he knows about engineering, and I don't know anything.

Levi waves his hands dismissively. "No problem. It's my job, I'm here to help."

I nod along, feeling a cold wind brush against my torso. "How long have you been an Engineer?"

Levi thinks for a second, staring at a point in the water a few inches away from me. "About two years now."

I didn't expect it to be *that* long. "How old are you now, then? If you don't mind me asking."

"I'm fourteen. I started doing this job when I was twelve."

Now that I know his age I don't believe him. He definitely looks older than *fourteen.* "You're fourteen?" I look him up and down quickly. "*Fourteen*? You look like you could be about... sixteen."

He looks down at his body, slowly knotting his brows together, looking up at me. "Really?"

I nod. "Really."

He shrugs half-heartedly. "Thanks, I guess," he says. "Let me see if I can guess your age." He looks me up and down, squinting his eyes slightly. I notice his eyes flick to my scar, then straight back to something else. I pretend I didn't notice. "You're... eighteen... nineteen."

I laugh lightly. "I'll take that as a compliment."

"You're not eighteen or nineteen?"

I shake my head.

"Wow! How old are you, then? If you say fourteen, I swear I'll just punch myself in the face."

I laugh. "I'm sixteen."

"Damn, dude," Levi replies. "With you being tall, longish hair, a slight beard on your cheeks and the fact that you're well-built, I thought you were older, but *c'est la vie.*"

I snort at the way he described me, turning around to look at my friends.

"It's true!" Levi replies, as if noticing my disagreement.

"Okay, thank you." I quickly look over my shoulder at my friends again. "I've got to go, but I'll see you later, Green Eyes."

Levi laughs as he says a quick, "Goodbye, Xander."

I turn around, trying to push myself back to the group, my feet burning up from the effort. I don't get how the water was shallower over there, but back where the group is, it's deeper.

When I make it back to the group, all eyes turn to me, and Adam, as if expecting all the questions, speaks up. "Man, I'm parched," he says, directing the attention back to him. "This damn heat isn't helping at all." I slowly nod, thanking him for taking the attention off me before it started.

Everyone agrees as they look up to the sky.

"I'll get you some water," Vicky says, walking toward the edge of the water. She turns around. "Anyone want a glass?"

Everyone except me nods. I do want a glass, I just want to go and get it myself.

She's already started walking toward the entrance.

I turn to everyone. "I'll go help her—," and I'm already off before I finish the sentence. My feet burn and burn and almost give up on me as I push myself out of the water.

I see Vicky grab a towel from somewhere on the sand, quickly wrapping it around her shoulders as she treks up the sand dune. The towel is really big. Even with it wrapped around her shoulders, it reaches to a point behind her knees.

I didn't even realize I grabbed my own towel, wrapped it around my shoulders enough so that my scar is hidden, and then walk up the sand slope as fast as my legs can.

My hair is dripping wet, but I push it back, letting the water drip behind my back, toward the ground.

I'm glad my hair isn't too long; it reaches the spot just before my shoulders. When it's wet, it reaches my shoulders, so it looks longer, but when it's dry, it goes wavy, making it look shorter.

In much simpler words: it's a complete and utter mess.

I pull back the ripped curtain and I'm inside, feeling great to have shade on my back. I try to adjust my eyes to the sudden darkness, starting to see the shape of the sun in my vision for a split second before it disappears.

I see Vicky's figure heading straight for the Mess Hall, and I wonder how she can walk so fast. I wish it wouldn't, but it reminds me of when I was trying to reach her, when she slammed her door in my face.

I push that thought from my mind and walk faster.

287

I see a few Wasters inside, sitting down at the tables, laughing, chatting, enjoying their day off as they ignore the two of us entering.

Vicky reaches the hole in the wall where we would normally get our food. She rests her elbows on the counter, smiling, tugging the towel around her tighter.

She doesn't seem to notice as I reach the counter, resting my right elbow and forearm on it. Ponytail is behind there, talking—well, listening—to Vicky.

I smile at her as she makes eye contact with me, and she gives me a small smile back. She turns away, grabbing glasses from the side, almost ignoring me completely.

I don't think things will ever be the same between Ponytail and me.

"Why did you follow me?" Vicky snaps, and I turn my head to stare at her, mouth slightly agape.

"Wha—I-I'm not following you," I say back, slightly offended. "I was just going to give you help with the water."

She turns away. "I don't need any help."

Well, at least we are talking to each other, but not in the way I wanted.

"You don't need help?" I raise my brows, even though she isn't looking. "To carry seven glasses of water?"

She laughs sarcastically, turning to look at me again. "There is a thing called *making a few trips.*"

"You don't have to any more, though." I shrug. "I'm here to help you."

She squints at me, presses her lips together, turns away from me, pulling the towel around her so she's clutching it together at her chest.

A small pool of water has formed on the counter from my hair and face, and I stare at it for a few seconds, trying to figure out what else to say to her. Maybe there just isn't anything to say anymore.

The sound of the glasses clicking on the counter startle me, bringing me back to the present.

"Could we have a few trays?" I ask Ponytail, and she nods, her hair swaying from side to side. She places two silver trays in front of us on the counter, and we both say a quiet "Thanks" at the same time.

I place four glasses of water on my tray, and Vicky places the rest on hers. "Thanks, again," I say to Ponytail before we walk away from the counter.

She waves at us—or just Vicky, I'm not sure—before we exit the Mess Hall.

"Thank you," Vicky says so quietly I almost didn't hear her.

I turn to look at her; she's got her head down, staring intently at the tray in front of her. "What was that?" My voice was also quiet, even though I didn't mean it to be.

She turns her head slowly, looks me in the eye. "Thank you," she says louder, but not so loud as to make her seem frustrated at me.

I smile at her for the first time in a while, and she *actually* smiles back. "You're welcome."

We're getting there. Very, very slowly.

Best friends always *make up*, I keep reminding myself.

I pull back the last curtain and let Vicky out first, for which she smiles at me.

I squint as the sudden brightness fills my eyes.

We both walk slowly down the sand slope, holding the trays in our hands as if we will drop them. I lean backward slightly, because, knowing me, I'll go tumbling forward.

I can feel my hair starting to dry under the rays of the scorching sun.

When we get nearer to the water, they all smile, pumping their fists into the air, whooping loudly.

I discard the towel, placing it where I think I found it. Vicky does the same, and we both slowly walk into the water, being careful with the trays in our hands.

I'm starting to get used to the feeling of water against my skin. The cool liquid feels refreshing after being out in the sun for a few minutes.

As we reach the rest of the group, they quickly grab hold of a drink from our trays, leaving two left on my tray.

Vicky tosses the tray onto the sand behind us, and I hand her a glass with a smile.

She quietly thanks me as she takes a small sip.

I throw my tray behind me, and gulp down almost half the glass in one go, enjoying the feeling of the cold liquid against my parched throat. I still don't think I've gotten used to the fact that we have *cold* water free for us to take whenever we want. We are really living the dream here, I guess.

"You guys are the best." Adam finishes his drink. "Thank you so much!"

Everyone else says their thanks, and we finish our drinks too soon.

*****

The sun has almost set.

Everyone started getting out of the water as soon as they saw it getting darker, but we were all so immersed in our conversations that we didn't even realize people started to leave the water *and* started to build the fire up.

But they haven't lit it, yet.

As I get out of the water, I grab hold of the same towel as before and start drying my hair. We are all too busy laughing and telling jokes for me to think about the scar on my side.

It takes me a few good seconds to put my shirt on, due to my damp skin, causing everyone to laugh at my struggle.

And I laugh, too.

Now, we are all sitting around a huge bonfire, waiting for a few male Wasters to light it. It's kind of fun watching them try to work with each other. They all just end up laughing at their mistakes, then laughing even harder when the sticks they were using to make the fire snap.

I lean my back against a huge tree trunk, my feet sprawled out in front of me.

Vicky sits about one person to my left, and Kara sits next to me, leaving about a foot of space between us.

Kara leans closer to me. "Normally they would have the fire lit by now," she says, her lips lifting to a small smile.

I laugh. "They look like they are having more fun making the mistakes, than actually making the fire itself."

She smiles. "Yeah, you're right..." She trails off.

After what feels like an hour, the fire is lit, warming my feet through my boots.

As the person to my left stares at the fire, I lean forward, glancing past him at Vicky. Her blue eyes are fixated on the orange glow for a few seconds before she looks over at me, her mouth lifting into a small smile.

Feeling brave, I mouth three words that I never thought I would say just now—words that I've only said in my head.

Are you okay?

She nods her head and smiles wider before looking back over at the fire, her face relaxing slightly.

I smile at the person to my left before sinking back against the trunk.

So, as far as I can tell, things are getting slightly better between Vicky and me. She's stopped looking at me as if I hurt her and stopped ignoring me. She smiles at me *almost* the same way she used to. *Almost.*

Things *are* getting better.

This is turning out to be the best day I've had since arriving here.

CHAPTER TWENTY-SEVEN

The heat from the fire is starting to burn my face.

The sun has fully set, and the air has turned bitterly cold. I can feel it through my still-damp hair, slipping down the back of my neck. I shiver, pulling my legs closer to my chest.

The male Waster to my left has joined a group of people that were sitting on the other side of the fire, and Vicky is sitting slightly closer to me, her knees against her chest, arms wrapped around them to keep her warm. I can see her shivering.

A deep part of me wants to scoot closer to her, to wrap my arms around her shoulders to warm her up, but the other part of me wants me to keep my arms where they are. I look over at her; she has moved her arms around her middle, suppressing her shivers. I have to *physically* stop myself from reaching out to her. Not yet. Not right now. Soon.

I nudge her arm lightly, and she slowly looks over at me, her lips slightly parted. "Are you cold?" I ask her.

She presses her lips together tightly, almost as if she knew they were parted, and nods. "A little bit." Her teeth chatter slightly as she speaks.

"Do you want to sit closer to the fire?" I incline my head toward the orange glow, the top of my head suddenly feeling hotter.

"No, it's fine." She smiles. "Thank you, though."

I smile back. "No problem."

We're getting there. Even though it is slow and tiring, we are still getting there.

The cracks and pops from the fire make me turn my head away from Vicky. I've never seen a fire so tall before, and it gets even taller when the Wasters throw old pieces of wood in there. The smell emanating from the fire is intoxicating; it shoots right up your nose and stays there, but I actually like the smell of smoke. No matter how strong it smells.

The atmosphere reminds me of the time we were in the desert, on our way to… here, I guess. It's weird how we never knew what was here, we just thought we would walk and walk until we found civilization.

For years, I thought we at the Estate were the only people left, the only survivors. I was wrong. I was *so* wrong.

I may have been looking for food and supplies when I was a Scavenger, but secretly I think I was looking for more survivors, even if I didn't realize it—even when I believed, deep down, there weren't any more. I was wrong again.

The majority of people around the fire are starting to get up, and I snap back to reality, whipping my head from side to side.

"What's going on?" I say to no one in particular. When no one answers me, I glance over at Kara, because she might know what's going on.

"They're wrestling," she says, smiling. "Want to go watch?"

"No." I shake my head. I don't want to be pushed into the ring again, but I don't tell her that. I can't afford another bloody nose. I don't want to see Blondie in the Infirmary. "You go if you want to watch."

"Suit yourself," she says, using the log to help her stand up. She walks over to where everyone is standing, getting lost in the crowd.

I can't help but watch as the two people in the ring are pushing against each other—I'm guessing trying to push the other out of the ring.

We would never do something like this back in the Estate. We wouldn't even think about it, but the Wasters are different; they aren't afraid to act crazy, to be wild. That's what I like about them.

They are free.

I turn to look at Vicky. "Don't you want to watch them?"

Vicky shakes her head. "No." She glances over at me. "I'm not really interested in wrestling."

I just realized how close we are sitting together, and I don't even know when that happened. No wonder she's stopped shivering.

"Me neither." A grin tugs at my lips. Changing the subject, I ask, "How's your work going?"

She bites her lower lip, maybe to stop her saying something? I don't know. "Great," she says through clenched teeth. "I'm loving *every* minute of it." She smiles sarcastically, and I don't even know how that's possible.

I guess I shouldn't have asked.

"Well," I say, resting my hands on my knees, "you're probably having a better time than I am." I laugh. "I just realized I completely *suck* at archery."

Vicky grins, turns away to try and hide it. "Have you even killed any animals, yet?"

"No," I say, smiling. "Kara's waiting until I'm 'good enough' with a bow and arrow." I lift my hands, using air quotes to emphasize my point.

Vicky opens her mouth to say something but promptly closes it when a loud series of cheers echo around the space. We both eye each other quickly, glancing over at the rowdy Wasters pumping their fists in the air. All of them are clapping a Waster on the back, a huge grin on said Waster's face.

Down on the ground is a male Waster of medium size, his entire frame being towered over by the Waster standing next to him, his foot resting against the other's back. The Waster on the floor has his face hidden in the sand, his hands clawing at the small particles to help get up, but nothing is happening. I've never wanted to push the other Waster off him so much. Then I realize this is all just a game—they do this every single year.

The referee from before—Ty, I think his name is—grabs the Champion's hand and raises it in the air. Just like he did when Kara beat me.

"Our Champion for the evening!" Ty shouts to everyone outside the ring.

Some of the people boo with their thumbs pointed down. Only a small percentage actually cheer at the victor.

Looks like this "Champion" isn't adored like Kara is.

The new Champion just ignores all the boos and walks out of the ring, brushing off his shirt with a flick of his wrist.

I watch as he walks back inside.

A loud series of cheers and hollers snaps my head to look back at the ring. Kara is in the center again, circling another Waster twice her size. I feel myself shrink against the log which my back is resting on, not wanting to be called to fight her again.

The bigger Waster lunges for Kara, but she smoothly dodges it, pulling her opponent by the arm, pinning it behind his back. The male Waster grunts as he has his back pressed against her chest—the same thing she did to me, and what I did to her.

The male Waster seems like he is in so much pain. Obviously, Kara isn't being as gentle with him as she was with me. But why? She had the chance to break—shatter—my arm in front of every single Waster in that room, so why didn't she take the chance? It doesn't make any sense. Maybe because I've never done something like this before? I don't know.

I swear I hear his arm shatter from here, and I flinch, looking away. I cringe as he screams out in pain, a loud *thump* telling me he collapsed into the sand.

The screams from the ring are deafening, and I have to start a new conversation with Vicky to distract myself.

The crowd from the ring slowly disperses, either coming back to sit down, or walking back inside.

Kara comes and stands a few feet in front of me, and I look up at her. "I'm going in, now," she says, eyes flicking back and forth between Vicky and me. "Don't stay up too late. Early training in the morning, remember?"

I nod slowly, trying not to roll my eyes. "Okay." I smile, but it feels fake. "Goodnight."

"Goodnight." She looks over at Vicky, nodding once before walking away toward the entrance.

"What time do you have to wake up?" Vicky asks after a beat of silence.

"Normally around the break of dawn," I say, a grin starting to pull at my lips. "*If* she can wake me up."

Vicky grins, brushing a strand of hair away from her face. "So, she has a very difficult time, then?"

I nod, lifting my shoulders for a half-hearted shrug. "What can I say? I'm not a morning person."

Vicky laughs. "I second that."

I smile wider. "What time do you normally...?"

Vicky cuts me off as she taps me on the arm, nodding to my right. Her eyes flick to the thing behind me, then back to my eyes.

With a furrow of my brow, I slowly turn to look in that direction, and I hesitate when the Waster to my right offers me something out of a bottle.

"Uhh... thank you." I take it slowly, marveling at the smooth texture of the dark green glass under my fingers. I've never seen or tasted wine in my life, so I have no idea what I'm getting myself into. I've only heard about it in stories people used to tell me. It was quite a popular thing in some books I used to read.

I bring the bottle close to my nose, instantly cringing as soon as the strong smell shoots up my nose. If it smells this bad, I wonder what the taste will be like. I don't really want to find out, but all the Wasters are staring at me, anticipation radiating off each of their bodies.

"Come on, just drink some, already," one of the Wasters snaps, starting to get irritated.

I try not to shoot the Waster a look as I wipe away whatever is at the top of the bottle. If all the Wasters have been drinking from it, I don't really want to put my mouth anywhere near it.

Where did they even get wine in the first place? I don't remember seeing anything near the Mess Hall. Unless, of course, they were saving it for this occasion, keeping it locked up until they needed it.

I press the cool glass against my mouth, raising the bottle up. Since it is almost empty, I have to raise it quite high for something to pour out.

I try not to choke as the liquid burns the insides of my mouth, and it's even worse when I swallow. I can't stop myself from almost coughing it all up.

I hand the bottle to Vicky without even looking in her direction, wiping some excess wine off my chin with the back of my hand.

She takes a quick drink of it without even thinking twice, and instantly almost coughs up the entire sip. She shakes her head as she reaches over to pass the bottle to the next person.

My head feels lighter as the burning sensation leaves my throat.

I smile for no reason as I look around the campfire, watching as the Wasters take generous sips of the somewhat… tasty drink.

Vicky and I both laugh a little too hard at something that wasn't even funny, earning grins from the Wasters around us—or was it funny? I can't remember. The bottle of wine comes around again faster than I thought it would, and this time I take a bigger sip of it, burning my throat to no end.

"Hey… guys!" A heavy arm plops down across my shoulders, and I turn my head to smile as Joel leans in-between Vicky and me.

"Hey," Vicky and I say at the same time.

"This is turning out to be… the *best* night of my… my life," he says, pulling Vicky and me closer together—closer to him.

I can smell the wine on his breath and I want to cringe away, but I can't. I can't stop myself from swaying back and forth, from smiling even though I wish my lips not to.

I was going to say something to Joel, but I completely forgot what it was.

"Oh, yes!" Joel almost shouts as the bottle comes back around to us.

How is it not empty yet? I remember it being half empty when I took a sip from it.

I decline the offer, which the Waster wasn't really happy about, but Joel gladly takes the bottle in his hand.

I take it from him, pulling it away from his lips. "I think… you've had enough, Joel."

"What? No!" Joel tries to get the bottle back, but I don't let him. "I hardly had any, Xander!"

Tell that to the smell coming out of your mouth, Joel.

Vicky takes the bottle from both Joel's hands and mine. "I think we've *all* had enough." She passes the bottle to her left, and the Waster tips most of it down his throat. "We need to… get some sleep."

I push myself up, almost crashing into Vicky when my legs buckle. Vicky has to guide me away from the fire, and I turn around quickly, waving at the majority of the people around the fire for no reason whatsoever.

We both have to hold onto each other as we climb up the sand slope, laughing very hard when we both slip and fall over.

I almost don't remember the rest of the way to our living quarters.

Most of the Wasters aren't around, probably since it's quite late. The few that are still around stare at us when we pass them, but we just smile widely at them and keep walking.

298

We're still holding onto each other tightly, almost afraid to let go.

"Hey, Tessa! Hey, Adam!" Vicky and I say as we pass them at the entrance, waving quickly.

How and when did we get to the entrance?

"Hey, you two," they say as we pass them, heading in the direction of our quarters.

"Be careful of that wall!" Adam says, pointing. "No, not that one! The one—the one I'm pointing to, Xander. Yes! That one. Be careful."

"We will do, Adam." I feel my hand graze along the wall, the irritating sensation sending shivers down my spine. When did Adam and Tessa leave to do this? They were in the water with us, I know that much, but I can't remember after that.

We both struggle with the ripped curtain as Vicky pulls it one way, and I pull it the other, but we both manage to slip inside, somehow.

"I'm sure you will feel better in the morning," Vicky says, still hanging onto me.

"Hey, you... you had the *same* amount as *I* did, Vicky."

"Maybe..." She shakes her head, blinks a few times. "I can't even remember..."

As we get closer to our bedroom doors, Vicky steps away from me, her hands slowly letting go of my shirt.

I turn around to face her. "Goodnight," I say, swaying back and forth the slightest bit.

"Goodnight," she replies, pulling me into a hug.

Startled and shocked, I wrap my arms around her back slowly, resting my face in her shoulder. I don't know whether my fast-beating heart is because of the drink I had, or if it's the situation I am in at the minute. I tighten my arms around her, closing my eyes.

Her hands linger on my chest as she pulls away, but then she slowly pushes me closer to my door, eyes never leaving mine as she smiles before closing the door behind her.

I can't believe Vicky hugged me. I can't *believe it.*

I step into the room faster than necessary, closing the door behind me without even bothering to turn the light switch on.

I blindly walk toward my bed, cursing when I bump into something on the floor, and when I *finally* reach my bed, I sink down onto the soft mattress, letting the material of the covers run through my fingers.

The last thing I think of before I fall asleep is Vicky's arms wrapped tightly around my shoulders—something I never thought she would do again.

CHAPTER TWENTY-EIGHT

I'm never drinking wine again.

The pounding in my head started before I was even fully awake. It feels like someone is reaching into my eyes and pulling on my brain, tugging and tugging to the point where I actually feel like screaming until my throat hurts. I rub at my temples as I walk down the halls to soothe the feeling, but it doesn't do any good.

And I didn't even have that much to drink.

I enter the Mess Hall quickly, cringing when all the laughter rings loudly inside my head. I shove my hands into my pockets as I head toward the huge hole in the wall, smiling weakly at Ponytail as she scoops beige colored… something into my bowl.

I push my tray to the side so I'm not in anyone's way, curling my upper lip as I dunk my spoon into the thick liquid.

"It's called oatmeal."

I jump out of my skin at the sudden voice near my ear. I turn in the direction of the sound, keeping my face emotionless.

My eyes widen at the Waster to my left. He's standing so casually, grabbing a spoon from the side, placing it next to his bowl on his tray. He's not looking in my direction, but I know he was talking to me; I'm the only one next to him.

I note a sheen of sweat dotted around his dark skin—maybe he was doing his job before he came to get food. Maybe he's a Runner. His clothes look exactly like mine and every other male Waster around here. It's hard to tell what jobs we all have when we wear the *exact* same clothes.

You could probably recognize the Hunters because they have a few scars littered around their arms. Well, Kara does, anyway; I haven't actually met any other Hunters, yet.

He blinks his dark brown eyes at me, and I snap back to reality.

"I'm sorry—what did you say?" I hate how tired my voice sounds, the way it still sounds slurred—just like it was last night. Never again.

"Oatmeal," he repeats, nodding down at the food inside my bowl.

"Oh," is all I manage to say as I step away from him, grabbing hold of the tray by my hands.

"Despite what it looks like, it is actually pretty good," he says. "And trust me." He leans slightly closer. "I'm a picky eater."

I'm starting to like this guy, already.

I laugh, and he smiles, looking back at the food on his tray. "I don't think we've ever really met before." He extends his hand toward me, palm pointed to the side. "I'm Sam."

I stare at his outstretched hand for one whole second before grabbing it, shaking once. "I'm Xander."

Sam nods. "Yeah, I think I saw you around the campfire yesterday." He eyes me carefully. "You're the new guy, right?"

"The one and only." I jerk a thumb at my chest, and Sam laughs.

"So, what job did they give you?" Sam lets go of my hand, gripping his tray with both hands.

"A Hunter," I reply with a shrug, trying to keep my voice emotionless, hoping that it doesn't sound like I hate the job.

"Really?" He looks down at me, then up. Nods. "Who is training you?"

"Kara." I look at him weirdly, wondering what he was thinking. "You know her?"

Sam nods quickly. "Oh, yeah, everyone knows her." He scratches the back of his neck. "She's like some kind of legend around here."

"Really?" My voice is quiet as I look around the Mess Hall, trying to find a specific blonde head.

"Do you like the job?"

I turn to look at him. "It's all right." I'm lying, I'm lying, I'm lying. "It just gives me something to do, I guess."

Sam nods, thinking it over. "Well, it was nice chatting with you, Xander, but I better get going." He grabs his tray, stepping away from the hole in the wall. "I'll catch you later."

"See you later," I say as he turns around and walks toward a table with a group of Wasters sitting around it. Probably a couple of his "Runner" colleagues.

I spot Vicky across the room. She's eating alone at the end of one of the tables. I can't see Kyle or Adam anywhere; I can't even find Joel or Tessa. Where is everyone?

When I get to Vicky's table, I slide in the chair, leaving the tray a few feet in front of me. "Morning," I say without any emotion in my voice.

She looks at me for a few seconds. "Wow," she says. "You look like hell."

I rub at my temples harder. "I *feel* like hell." I squeeze my eyes shut. "Where is everyone?"

"I don't know." She shrugs. "Probably working."

"Why aren't you working?" I quirk an eyebrow at her.

"Because I'm eating." She scoops up some of the oatmeal, tipping it back into the bowl. "Very, very slowly."

"I'm sure Will wants to know where you are." I hate even saying his name. "Doesn't he?"

Vicky furrows her brows. "What? No." She looks down at her food. "Will isn't a Weapons Cleaner," she says. "He doesn't do it with me."

"But I thought...," I start. Will helping Vicky flashes in my mind, and I hide my fist under the table. I could have sworn

303

that was his job. He was helping her like he knew *exactly* what to do. I'm sure Johanna said he was...

"No, no. Will wasn't doing that because it's his job," she says. "He was doing it because he was showing me what to do."

I don't have any words. I think Vicky can read the expression on my face, because she just shrugs.

"So...," I start, drilling a hole in the table, "what *does* Will do?"

Vicky shrugs again. "Who knows?" She swirls her oatmeal around with her spoon, staring intently at it. "After you went into that room with Kara, he left." She looks up at me. "He said to me: 'You are doing great, Vicky. Keep up the good work' and scurried out of the room."

I have to stop myself from laughing too hard when Vicky imitates Will's British accent. "That accent was terrible, by the way," I laugh, making her glare at me.

"But I got my point across, didn't I?" she asks with a smile, and I nod.

I'm glad Vicky and I are on speaking terms, now. I'm glad we can just have a joke without it sounding like we're arguing. Everything is slowly getting back to normal. She's becoming my best friend again.

I spoon some of the oatmeal into my mouth, burning the back of my throat as I swallow, but I don't care, because the food is delicious.

Sam was right; despite what the food looks like, it *is* pretty good.

Vicky turns the ring on her finger over and over again, staring intently at it. I almost forgot that she wears it. She smiles the slightest bit as she runs her thumb across the smooth surface. She switches between her ring and the braclet I gave her recently, keeping a smile on her face.

I remember she wore the exact same expression every single day after I gave her the ring. She's never taken it off. I think she really likes it.

I lean forward. "Hey, Vicky—"

"Xander?"

I snap my mouth shut as I look over to the side, staring wide-eyed at Kara as she leans her hands on our table, her eyes flicking between Vicky and me quickly.

"Uh... hi," I finally manage to say.

Her eyes settle on me. "Are you ready to get to work?"

I stare down at my food, then back up to her. "Sure." I look over to Vicky for a split second. "I'll just finish my food quickly. I'll be five minutes."

She nods slowly. "Yeah... o-okay," she says. "See you in a few minutes."

I don't watch as she turns around and walks away. I turn back to my food.

That was weird. Normally she would drag me by my hair to get me to go to work. So... why is today different?

I look over at Vicky to see if she might know the answer to this conundrum, but she just has her head down, staring intently at the food in her bowl. Slowly—very, very slowly—spooning food in her mouth.

She really doesn't like her work.

I know this because she has hardly eaten her food; and is still eating it. If she really *did* like her job, then she would have inhaled all her food and would have been over there right now.

I swallow the last bits of my food, pushing my tray to the side—away from me. Vicky doesn't look up as I push myself away from the table, my chair scraping against the floor.

I hate seeing Vicky upset. I need to do something about this.

"Vicky?"

She slowly looks up at me, raising her brows. "Yeah?" she whispers.

I try to word what it was I was going to say correctly in my head, making sure I don't tumble over the words. "If you don't like your job, then maybe you could talk to Johanna," I say. "She might be able to change it for you."

She shakes her head. "You know Johanna won't, Xan." She looks down again. "You heard what she said to us."

I shrug even though she isn't looking. "I don't care." She looks up at me. "You're upset with your job, and I'm going to help you change it."

Vicky starts to protest, shaking her head. She opens her mouth to speak.

I hold up my hand to stop her. "No, no, Vicky, I *will* do this. I hate seeing you like this." I look her in the eyes. "Maybe I can make you a Hunter with Kara and me."

Vicky looks at me as if I had said the world's dumbest thing in the world.

"What?" I say laughing, feigning being offended. "You never know what she will say." I press a hand to her shoulder, brushing my thumb against her shirt. "Just… trust me, okay?"

She smiles up at me, nodding just once. "Okay."

I let go of her shoulder, stepping away from the table. "I'll see you soon, yeah?"

"Yeah." She smiles wider, watching as I back away from the table, toward the training room.

*****

My fingernails claw at the rough metal as I ease myself up onto the platform. Kicking frantically against the metal bars below, I use my forearms to hoist myself up, rolling in a mess on top of the small wooden platform.

It feels good to be in my own nature, again, but not in this situation.

My chest rises and falls as I stare up at the ceiling, trying my hardest to fill my lungs with what I hope is air, but it feels like fire.

My hands burn, and my feet are blistered, but I still stand up, leaning against the railing. The whole climbing frame looks out of place in this room. They designed it to look almost like a tree, but to me, it looks like an old scaffolding—much like the one that stabbed me in the side.

I push that thought away from my mind.

"Tell me again, *why* I'm doing this."

Kara's arms are crossed over her chest as she thinks over my sentence. "Because," she finally says, still looking up at me, "Hunters need to learn how to climb trees in order to see the targets easier."

"Well, when you put it *that* way..." I trail off, looking away from her.

"Come on," she says, stepping to the side. "Get off there and try again."

I suppress a groan, rolling my eyes as I duck under the railing. I lower myself down onto the ground with a *thud*, brushing off imaginary dust from my shoulders and pants.

I crack my neck as I get into position, my foot in front of me, ready to go—

Kara stops me, handing me my bow. I eye it carefully, flicking my eyes to her.

"You'll need it when you are out *there*," she says, pointing to a random direction on the wall. Outside. Hunting outside seems so far off from what I can actually do, which isn't a lot.

I nod and swing the quiver onto my back, securing it, making sure that no arrows will slip out while I'm running. The bow sits comfortably against my back as I slip it around my shoulders. The string rests diagonally from my shoulder to my chest, to my stomach—and it feels really comfortable.

I quickly calculate the safest way up to the top with the extra weight on my back, before a jolt of energy kicks in.

Before I even know it, my legs are moving—heading straight for the makeshift "tree". I kick against the ground as hard as I can, trying my hardest to grab hold of the metal bar closest to me, pulling myself away from the ground with all the energy I have left.

My muscles strain with the effort, and I start to feel a vein popping out of my forehead as I heave myself over the metal bar, trying my hardest to hear any strain from the metal as I use my weight against it.

Hearing nothing, I kick my feet against the metal bar, jumping up to grab the next highest one. I don't know where this sudden power came from, but I don't have time to contemplate it—I need to get up there quickly.

There is only one more bar to grab hold of. If I just push myself hard enough, kick against the bar at my feet with enough force, then maybe I can reach it. Maybe I can—

I miss the bar by an inch.

My heart jumps to my throat, suffocating, suffocating, suffocating me as I fall. Everything turns silent as I feel everything slip away from me. Seconds merge into minutes. Minutes merge into hours, but it is all in my head. I'm not falling. I'm *not* falling.

I *am* falling.

The world around me blurs into one color, and I'm ready for it all to turn to black, when—

My hand grips one of the metal bars, feeling like it's pulling my arm from its socket. I cry out in pain, the sound muffled in my ears. I keep swaying from left to right, and I want to drop down, but I can't.

I want to give up, but I can't.

I want this all to end, but it won't.

I don't want to be a Hunter any more, but I'm still here.

I grab the bar with my other hand, gritting my teeth hard as I heave myself up. My breathing is heavy, my heart is beating too fast, but I still grab the next bar up.

Just before my heart feels like it could just explode out of my chest, I grab hold of the flat platform, pulling myself up, my teeth still clenched together tightly. I kick my feet against the metal one last time, slowly hauling myself up, and over the platform. My bow hits against the railing with a loud *clank* and I find myself going forward. I brace myself for the fall, but I hug my arms close to my chest, and roll forward, the world doing a quick three-sixty before I land in a crouched position.

Before I even realize what my hands are doing, an arrow is slipped out of my quiver, lined with my bow, then shot straight for the target down on the floor.

I think I surprised myself more than I surprised Kara because I didn't realize I could do that. I guess when the moment is right, you just have to believe you can do it.

Then you *can* do it.

My breathing comes out hard and quick as I stare at the target on the floor. I don't know if I'm just seeing things, but I swear I see the arrow a few inches away from the center. But I *could* be seeing things; I might have hit my head on the scaffolding without even realizing it.

Maybe I *did* hit my head while I was falling; maybe all this is fake. I *haven't* shot the arrow. It *isn't* a few feet away from the center.

The silence that follows tells me I'm wrong.

I hop down off the platform, still staring at the arrow inside the target, then over to Kara who has her mouth agape, wide eyes.

I smile as I walk over to her, leaning my elbow on her shoulder.

Looks like I *did* surprise her more than me.

"So...," I say, snapping her back to reality. "What do you think?"

She looks over at me. "I think," she says, cracking a small, small smile, "you might be ready to go out into the real world."

CHAPTER TWENTY-NINE

"There's no point in waiting," Kara says as I pull my arrow free from the target. "We might as well get out now while there is still daylight."

"Sounds like a good plan." I smirk at her as I slide my arrow into my quiver, hearing the satisfying *click* as it sets into place. My heart is still beating fast from the fall, now even faster because of the shot.

Kara rolls her eyes as she crosses her arms over her chest, fighting the urge to smile. "Come on," she says, turning to her side, inclining her head toward the door, "we're losing daylight."

I swing the bow onto my back, blowing out a puff of air between my teeth. I stalk my way toward the door, trying to ignore the sudden feeling of nervousness deep in the pit of my stomach.

I swallow my nerves and swing open the door, enjoying the quick sensation of the cool breeze brushing against my sweaty skin.

Kara propels me forward with a touch to the back, and I say a quiet "Sorry" under my breath, knowing I was walking too slow. For someone with long legs, I sure walk a *little* too slow.

Vicky looks up as we pass her station, and I stop at the table she is working at.

She places down her cloth and the knife that she was cleaning. "Hey," she whispers, slowly smiling.

"Hey," I say back, smiling. "How are you?"

She looks down, nods her head slowly. "All right." She looks between the two of us. "Where are you guys heading?"

Kara doesn't reply to Vicky's question, even though we were both looking in her direction. I turn back to Vicky. "She's taking me hunting for the first time."

Vicky raises her brows at me. "Oh, really?" she says. "Are you scared?"

"Absolutely terrified," I say dryly. "We'll see how it goes. If I come back with an arrow in my foot, just laugh along with me." I flash her a toothy grin and wave, and she shakes her head, rolling her eyes before going back to cleaning her weapon. "I'll see you later."

"Bye."

I look over my shoulder as I walk away, catching her eye. I see her smile at me before I turn back around, following Kara out the door.

Very few Wasters are about. Most of them are probably working—just like I am. Only the odd one or two are milling around the halls, their conversations echoing around the cramped space.

I don't know what Kara and I look like with our quivers strapped to our backs, and our bows gripped tightly in our hands, but I would hope—somehow—we look like Hunters.

It takes me a moment to notice a mop of blond hair and a pair of all-too-familiar eyes. "Green Eyes," I say as Levi gets closer to Kara and me.

"Alexander." He nods in our direction.

"Hey!" I point a finger at him, trying not to smile. "Don't call me that."

My warning falls on deaf ears as he ignores me, turning to look at Kara with a smile. "Hey, Kara." He steps closer to her. "It's good to see you."

"Hi, Levi." She pulls him into an embrace. I'm taken aback by how affectionate she's being. "It feels like it's been ages since I've seen you…"

Her voice trails off as I half-listen to the two of them exchange pleasantries. In my mind, I'm playing out scenarios of what will happen while we are out there hunting animals, even though I have no idea how to. I kick around a small ball of dust, hoping my nerves aren't radiating off my body.

It feels like it takes an hour for Levi and Kara to hug goodbye.

"We'll see you later, Green Eyes," I say, turning around with Kara to walk in the opposite direction.

"Green Eyes?" she questions, now walking side by side with me.

I shrug. "He has green eyes." I look down at her. "I didn't know his name at first, so I just called him that. It stuck." I look back up, dodging a few Wasters coming our way. "It kind of suits him, actually." She still looks confused. "Forget it. It's an inside joke."

"Right," Kara says, ending the conversation.

As we get closer to the entrance where Kara took Adam and me for our day off, (which, supposedly, could be known as a back door) I see a group of Wasters talking and laughing loudly, holding weapons tightly in their hands.

More Hunters.

My nerves suddenly come creeping back inside my stomach, writhing to the point where I feel like I'm going to be sick. Now, at the moment, I don't care if my nerves are radiating off my body. If I focus hard enough, I think I can feel the nerves traveling around the room from the other Wasters standing around.

But there is something that makes my nerves dissipate slightly, *only* slightly. The familiar tall frame and dark skin.

"Sam," I say as he makes eye contact with me.

He smiles wider as he turns away from the group of people he was having a conversation with. "Xander." He slaps me on the back as I step up next to him, Kara only a few feet behind me. "How are you doing, mate?"

"I'm doing great," I say, half-meaning it. "But... I thought you were a Runner."

"Oh, no." He laughs. "But every morning I go for a run just to wake myself up a bit."

Well, that makes more sense. Now I know why he was in the food line with a sheen of sweat on his forehead.

"Whoa." A girl sidesteps from behind Sam's back, slowly looking me up and down, her arms crossed over her chest. "Who's the new tense guy?"

The girl looks as scary as she sounds. Half of her white blonde hair has been shaved off completely, leaving the other half longer, waving past her shoulder. Her strange brown eyes look light next to her olive skin. A few scars litter across her neck, but none that look too serious. Not in this light, anyway.

"Xander," I finally say, extending my hand.

She looks down at my hand for a second, scoffing at it silently before grabbing it tightly. "Scarlett."

"A pleasure," I say sarcastically, shaking her hand once.

Scarlett laughs. "He's got some sass." She looks over at Sam, keeping her smirk planted on her face. "I like him already."

I look over at Sam who is hiding a smile, then back to Scarlett, but she has already started to walk away.

"We are about to go soon," Sam says, and I look over at him. "I'd better go. Don't work too hard." He taps me on the shoulder twice before walking off to another Waster.

A male Waster steps above everyone else on some sort of platform, high enough so we can see him. "Okay, everyone." His voice seems to echo around the large space. "Get into your pairs and get ready!"

"Pairs?" I question quietly to Kara, who has stepped closer to me. "Who am I paired with?"

"You're looking at her." She glances down at the ground, then back up at me.

I nod my head slowly as I sweep my eyes across the Hunters, taking in their stances, the way they hold their weapons. They look like they've been doing this for years.

313

The only exception is a young girl—probably a few years younger than me—visibly trembling. She grips her small bow so tightly that you can actually see the bones of her knuckles. She exhales visibly, rolling her shoulders backward, forward.

At least I'm not the only one who's scared.

My ears ring slightly as the male Waster tells us to go, and I hesitate as I see all of them rush out the door like this is a big game they are all trying to win.

"Come on!" Kara shouts at me. I tie my bandana around my neck, pulling it up to cover my mouth. "First one down the sand dune wins."

My feet shuffle, and I grip the bow tighter as I follow her out of the door, not bothering to look back.

*****

The sun feels too hot against my neck.

My bow hand is starting to sweat to the point where it feels like I'm going to drop it. Blisters cover every fraction of my hands that you can think of, and it's starting to hurt to even curl one, two, three of my fingers together.

My lungs feel like they're about to explode as I follow Kara up a sand dune, and I urge my legs not to give up on me.

My fingers dig inside the soft sand as I try to pull myself up the steep dune. I end up using my forearms to glide along the rough sand, each and every particle creeping their way to my skin.

Kara's waiting at the top, her bow tightly clenched in her hand, her golden hair brushing against her back in one long braid. She doesn't look in my direction as I sit next to her, my chest heaving up and down like it's about to burst.

I pull the flask of water they gave us from my belt, taking a generous amount from it, sighing loudly as the cool liquid quenches my thirst. "How you do this every day is beyond me."

Kara doesn't reply, only saying a quiet "Shush" under her breath, and I follow her line of sight. The hare she was spying is hardly moving, only pushing its nose into the soft sand underneath it. It's smelling around for food, but the poor animal won't find a single thing.

"That's not going to be big enough to feed the Wasters," I say, turning to look at her. "I mean, have you *seen* how much they eat?"

"At least it's *something*," she hisses, looking over at me. "We can always get more if we need to. Plus, don't forget all the other Hunters; they'll get food, as well."

I look back over at the hare, knowing that this poor animal has no idea what its fate will turn out to be. it has no idea an arrow will be shot through the other side of its body, ending its life before it even realizes it.

This is making me feel sick, and we haven't even done anything yet.

When I look back at Kara, I notice she's still staring at me, never wavering, completely stock-still.

"What?" I ask, wondering if I have something on my face.

She inclines her head toward the animal, raising her brows as if telling me something important.

"Me?" I ask. "Why me?"

"Because otherwise, all your training will be for nothing." She looks over at the animal, tilting her head to the side. "I believe you can do it." She looks back over at me. "I *know* you can do it."

She really believes that someone who has never held a bow before in his life—until now—can kill an animal from ten feet away, and I guess, just for the moment, a small fraction of myself also believes it.

I keep one eye on the animal as I pull an arrow free from my quiver slowly, without a sound, lining it with my bow. Kara keeps her eyes on me as I pull the string to my jaw, keeping my breaths even, slow. In through my nose, out of my mouth. Twice. Three times.

Keep the arrow in the center of your vision.

Kara's words ring inside my head as the point of my arrow wavers slightly, and I try to hold still.

Lower your elbow slightly.

My elbow moves before I can even think about it.

Keep your body rigid, but straight.

I remember Kara's hand placed just where my scar was, and she had no idea about it. I straighten my back. Inhale—

And shoot.

My heart hammers in my chest, and I don't register the slight pain shooting up my forearm. I don't feel anything; I don't even realize that my arrow has shot clean through the hare, a small pool of blood leaking from underneath the dead animal.

"Nice shot," she says, bringing me back to the present.

"Th-thanks, I guess," I say, working up a small smile, wondering if it's real or not. "I... didn't realize I had that in me."

"You never do until you try." She looks at the dead animal. "Come on, let's not let it rot away." She pushes herself down the slope, leaning back as she takes each step forward, and I follow behind her, trying not to tumble down the dune.

She carefully picks up the dead hare, smoothly pulling the arrow free from its limp body. I cringe as she passes it back to me.

She shrugs at my disgusted expression and tells me never to waste an arrow if possible.

I wipe as much blood as I can off the arrow, sliding it back into my quiver, watching as Kara ties the dead hare to her belt, pulling her bow from her shoulder.

"My turn," she says with a smirk, grabbing an arrow from her quiver.

"Don't enjoy yourself too much." I step back slightly, giving her room to pull a single, perfect silver arrow from her quiver.

"I'll try not to."

She's already found her target. She's eyeing it as if it will disappear right in front of her eyes. I turn around to look at where her eyes are fixated, and my assumptions are correct: another hare, hopping aimlessly around the desert.

She crouches down, just low enough so her knees are slightly bent, and starts toward the animal, readying the arrow on her bow.

She doesn't hesitate as she releases the arrow, impaling the animal, sending it flying a few feet away from where it was positioned. She blows out a puff of air, moving a strand of her gold hair away from her eyes.

I compliment her shot, and jog over to the animal, pulling her arrow from it. I tie the new weight to my belt and hand her over the arrow, which she just slides into her quiver without washing.

She's probably done it a hundred times.

"So, what now?" I ask when I finish tying the hare to my belt. "Do we just go back?"

She shakes her head. "Not yet." She turns around, peeking over a low dune, then nodding in the direction of where she was looking. "Come on."

And I follow her, letting the dead animal slap against my thigh as I trek up the small dune. I sigh as I see a flat expanse of sand on the other side, which I'm sure is where she was looking.

"What are we doing?" I ask as she grabs dried bits of... something on the ground.

"Having lunch," she replies simply, kneeling down on the ground.

"Won't we get into some sort of trouble for doing this?" I ask. "I mean, the food is for *all* Wasters, not just us, right?"

317

"Then it's a good thing we shot two then, isn't it?" She smiles, and I crouch down next to her, not saying another word. She points to the hare tied to my belt. "We'll eat that one."

I listen carefully to Kara as she tells me how to handle a dead carcass like this. She motions for me to remove all entrails, leaving the blood to drip onto the soft white sand, and I almost gag.

Kara starts building a small fire just a few feet in front of us, using the dried objects for kindling tinder.

My knife carefully removes all the unwanted skin and fur, leaving it in a light pink—almost gray—undercoat, and Kara uses two long sticks to ignite the fire. We let the blood drain from the hare for a good few minutes, making sure there is none left.

I lay the hare on my thigh as I cut away two equal chunks of the uncooked meat, laying them on a small rock about the size of my hand, if I was to curl them into a fist.

Kara hands me a long, thin stick which I kindly take, piercing the meat with it, hanging it a few inches above the now-roaring fire. Kara does the same, and we both sit side by side in silence as we watch the pink meat brown ever so slowly.

Kara takes hers out of the fire, picking at it slowly, but I let mine linger a few seconds more, browning it to perfection.

I ignore the scorching feeling in the tips of my fingers as I pick small chunks from the meat, chewing on them slowly, relishing the taste of cooked meat—something I don't ever remember having in my life.

I look into the distance, seeing who I think might be Sam and Scarlett hunting just a few yards away from us. They are actually doing their job, but I haven't seen any of them pull an arrow from their quivers yet.

They haven't been lucky enough to find an animal.

"Just out of curiosity," I say once I swallow, getting her attention. "If someone wanted to change their job, can they do it?" The conversation I had with Vicky suddenly comes rushing back, and I tread carefully, not wanting to push her under the bus.

Kara slowly shakes her head. "No." She looks down at the ground, pressing her finger in the soft sand. "They will never allow it, Xander."

"Can't you just ask Johanna?" I really don't want Vicky to stay at a job she hates, so I keep prodding.

"*She* will never allow it," she replies, and I drop my head. "She's very uncompromising with what jobs we have here."

"What about Will?" I ask. "Can't he talk to her? I mean, he *is* her son..." I trail off. "Or you could talk to Will. I mean, you two are..."

"Xander, please," Kara says calmly, and I shut my mouth, pressing my lips together firmly. "You know the answer will be no, so just stop asking. Please."

I nod slowly, looking back down at the fire. "Okay. Sorry."

Seconds stretch to minutes, and the minutes almost stretch to an hour without Kara and I saying a word, enjoying the food in comfortable silence, listening to occasional animal noises, the sound of wind—calming sounds that fill my ears and make the tence muscles in my shoulders drop.

We've both finished the meat, and are now sitting near the fire, enjoying a relaxing moment we might never get again.

It almost takes me an hour to finally speak up. "Thank you."

Her arm brushes against mine as she turns to look at me. "For what?"

I pull my legs up near my stomach, resting my arms on my knees. "For all this." I look around. "For teaching me archery. To hunt." I look back at her. "I wouldn't even be here if you had never taught me." I smile, lowering my voice. "So... thank you."

A smile pulls at the corners of her lips. "You're welcome."

I look back at the fire, letting the flames engross my eyes, and I close them for a good few seconds, inhaling the intoxicating scent of the smoke around us.

I open my mouth to say something to Kara, turning my head to look in her direction, but I promptly close it. Her eyes are boring into mine, and I get lost in the color of them. Such a strange, but beautiful, color, and when she looks a certain way her eyes are green, then back to hazel.

My heart, my head, my thoughts, and time stops as she leans forward, pressing her lips to mine. I instinctively close my eyes, doing something I never thought I would do, something that never seemed to cross my mind all the time I've been here.

I kiss her back.

CHAPTER THIRTY

Kara presses her hand to my jaw, and I break away, eyes wide, wondering what the hell just happened. She leans her forehead against mine, but I move back, trying to get as far away from her as possible. Her eyes slowly travel up to mine and I bolt upright, jumping as far away from her as my legs can.

She blinks blue eyes at me which aren't hers.

And I snap.

I scramble away from her, squeezing my eyes shut. Opening them again, I stop dead in my tracks.

"What's wrong?" Vicky says, but it's not her, it's not her, it's not her. It looks like Vicky—her dark hair in one simple braid over her shoulder—but it sounds like Kara. I squeeze my eyes shut, trying to snap back to what is really in front of me.

Kara's blonde hair swims back into view, and I relax… only slightly, only to stop acting like I've gone completely insane. "Are you okay?" she asks.

Yes? No? I don't even know how I feel any more. Nothing is making sense to me any more. Nothing. Nothing. *Nothing.*

"I…," I start, staring at the expression on her face, which I'm sure doesn't even compare to what my face holds. "I… I d-d…" I have no clue what I'm trying to say. It just sounds like inhuman noises trying to fight their way through my throat.

She starts to stand up, and I do the same, moving farther and farther away from her, my feet sinking in the soft white sand below me. The sand is too bright. The sun is too bright, and I feel like I've gone blind.

She slowly walks toward me, but I try to step away from her, almost stumbling backward on the soft sand.

"Xander?" she says, her eyebrows furrowed. "Are you… okay, Xan?"

"No!" I shout, making her jump. "D-don't… call me that." I start walking backward up the dune, trying to get away from her as quickly as I can. "Don't… don't…"

The heat from the fire makes me want to crawl into a ball; to never get back up again.

I just want to get away. Away from everything, *everything*—

"I have to go," I say, watching her figure getting smaller. I'm sure I sound and look crazy, but I don't care. "I have to go," I repeat as I turn around, jogging back to the entrance, seeing if I remember where to go.

*****

I almost rip the curtain off the ceiling as I enter the building.

I don't exactly know where I'm going. I don't even know why I *am* running away. I just know I need to be alone. When I saw Vicky's blue eyes on Kara's face, something inside me just exploded, and I don't know what to do about it.

I ignore the Wasters' eyes on me as I speed walk to nowhere in particular, trying to find somewhere where there is no one to bother me.

I only know a couple of places that I could go to— somewhere no one would want to disturb someone else.

Our bedroom.

The oasis.

And the shower.

I decide to go with the latter, so I head straight there as quickly as my legs can carry me, silently praying no one will be there. I have a high risk of someone entering my bedroom, and more than likely some of the Wasters will be at the oasis.

I pass the Mess Hall quickly, not looking up at the Wastelanders as they cast glances in my direction. Maybe some of them are looking up because they know what I'm thinking—no. *Don't be stupid, Xander.* They don't know. Maybe they are looking up just out of curiosity. Yeah. That's got to be it.

I don't pass anyone I know as I head toward our living quarters. I'm really glad that all of them have work to do because I won't have any awkward encounters with people I know, trying to explain why I look crazy, why I *always* seem to look crazy. Why I *am* crazy.

I stop a moment to hear if anyone is in the bathroom, listening out for the water running, the splashing sounds of feet against the wet tiled floor. Hearing nothing, I step inside, checking over my shoulder for anyone, anything. Nothing.

I shut the door behind me. I exhale, leaning my head against the cool door, hardly caring about the small droplets of water seeping into my clothes and hair.

Pushing myself away from the door, I head straight for my usual cubicle—the one closest to the wall on the far left, trying my hardest to lock the door behind me as fast as I can.

My eyes scan around the familiar space, my nose suddenly picking up the scent of recently used water. It's a calming type of smell—relaxing, familiar; like I've known it for years.

Whilst I'm in here, I may as well have a shower. I need to try to forget the events of what happened only a few minutes ago. If I *can* forget. Knowing me, I won't be able to. You never forget something like that. I *never* seem to forget *anything*, any more.

I strip my clothes off, not really caring at the moment if they get wet when they are dropped on the floor. I kick my clothes closer to the door, so they don't get soaked from the shower; I *do* have to wear them later. I hang the towel back up from where it was dropped on the floor, making sure it will stay dry.

323

The water runs down my back as I turn the shower on, and I sigh quietly as the hot water loosens my muscles.

I keep seeing Vicky where Kara was supposed to be every time I close my eyes. Her blue eyes were boring into mine as if it was *Vicky* staring straight back at me, but it wasn't—it didn't even feel like it was Kara. I don't know who it felt like.

I shake the images out of my head, running my hands down the length of my face, catching a pool of water in the palm of my hands. My wet hair is covering my eyes to the point where I can only see the wall through the small partings of my hair. I run my fingers to the back of my neck, pushing my hair back, causing all the water from my hair to drip down behind me, allowing me to see better.

I wipe as much dirt and sweat from my skin as I can before the stupid five minutes is up, and the shower slowly turns off, leaving me dripping from head to toe, staring at the floor as if it will have all the answers to my dilemma.

I shake as much water as I can from my hands and arms as I carefully walk toward the towel, unhooking it from the door, slowly wrapping it around my waist.

As I dry myself, I think of different things to say to Kara the next time I see her. What could I say to her that won't make me sound like I'm crazy? Every possible scenario of what she will say back runs through my head. I have a few ideas about what she would say to me if it was the time when I first met her. The other ideas are what she would say to me now—now that we've had time to get to know each other.

None of the scenarios make me look like a normal person.

My shirt gets stuck in the middle of my torso, and I get so frustrated pulling it down that I almost rip it at the seams. I tuck my knife inside my belt, making sure it's secure as I buckle up my belt. I don't bother to tie my laces as I pull my boots on, leaning against the wall for more balance.

I quickly towel dry my hair as I unlock the cubicle door, a cool breeze suddenly snaking its way up my neck to my damp hair.

I make my way over to the mirror, placing down the damp towel. I brush down my hair with my fingers, wincing when they get snagged in a small knot, which I just break away. Every time I look in the mirror, I wish, somehow, that I looked... normal. I definitely don't look like a sixteen-year-old—I could probably pass as eighteen just like Levi said. Maybe I could pass as being a little bit older since my hair is longer and thicker than normal. I'm just glad my hair doesn't reach past my shoulders.

I don't even know how, but I think my eyes have gotten duller; not as bright as they used to be. The shape of my eyes is still the same, with the exception of a slight bit of darkness underneath them.

I turn away from my reflection, walking straight out the door. Normally, I would wait a beat—or two—to see if anyone would walk inside, but I don't bother this time; I just leave.

I pass nothing and no one as I walk inside my room, trying not to slam the door with the frustration still writhing through my body, but it slips past my fingers, the sound echoing around the larger room.

I sit on my bed as I tie up my laces, pulling them harder than necessary. It feels like I haven't slept in my bed for ages, but in reality it has only been a few hours. That's what happens when something big happens in the morning—it makes it feel like you've wasted the whole day.

I don't know where I'm going as I walk out my door. I don't have a specific place in mind. I've already been to two of my places of solitude, and the last one might have some Wasters there, so there's no point.

Before I even realize it, my feet are dragging me toward the training room, even though I wish them not to. Vicky's

325

station is there, so it won't be too bad, but if Kara's there, then the day will have just gotten a whole lot worse than I thought it would be.

*****

Vicky isn't even in here.

I don't even know why I thought she would be; it's lunchtime anyway. She's probably in the Mess Hall enjoying her food alone, oblivious to what just happened a few minutes ago.

I stare at the door to where Levi's workstation is, wondering if I should go and bother him. I can't read minds, but I feel like I annoy the hell out of Levi sometimes. That's why I sometimes hate meeting new people; you never know what *they* think of you. Like they know something is wrong with you.

I don't know if Levi feels like that about me. He's a very nice guy; he's never been rude to me.

I'm so paranoid that I'm starting to get a migraine.

I place down the dagger Vicky must have been cleaning and head for the main door, almost collapsing to the floor as Kara walks into the room, both of our bows and quivers slung over her shoulder.

"Xander, I need to speak to you," she says quickly, and I back away, wide-eyed.

I don't want to speak with you, I wish I could say, but I wouldn't. I don't want to speak to anyone. I just want to be alone.

You can never truly be alone in a place full of people. Someone will always find you, one way or another.

Kara tugs on my arm, pulling me toward the weapons room, and I follow behind her, wishing, *begging* my legs to stop, to run away, to do *anything*.

But I just follow behind her.

326

The only audible sound I can hear is the *click* of the door behind me; not my heavy breathing, not my footsteps, not even Kara shuffling around. She's probably saying something to me right now, but I'm either not listening, or can't hear her.

I want to say it's the latter, but deep down I think it's the former.

"What happened back there?" she asks. "You completely freaked out." Her voice sounds calmer than normal.

I don't like it.

And I don't know why.

No words are coming out of my mouth. Sentences that don't make sense are forming inside my head. I open my mouth as if to reply to her, but I just close it straight back up. I have nothing to say to her. Nothing.

She steps closer to me, pulling my bow and quiver from her shoulder, slowly handing them to me. I take them carefully, eyeing them as if they might suddenly spring to life and shoot me straight through the chest.

It would probably be less painful than right now.

She suddenly walks around me, turning around to look into my eyes, blocking the door, dissipating all my chances of running out of here if I wanted. "You went really pale... after we... you know—"

We both know exactly what she is talking about. She just doesn't know why I went pale; neither does the person I saw. No one else will know why.

"I... I don't know why, Kara." I'm surprised my voice still works. I'm surprised an actual *sentence* is coming out of my mouth. These words coming out of my mouth are no longer my own. I don't know which part of my brain I'm picking them from, or how I've managed to create a sentence when my mind feels like a dark void I can no longer get out of.

"It wasn't..." She steps forward, coming very close, too close to me. "It wasn't *me* was it?"

I look down at her. "I-I... I think it was."

327

Her arms slowly wrap around my neck, my eyes widening as her chest presses against mine. I try not to push her away too hard, but she won't be discouraged by anything. "I know you liked the kiss, Xander." She leans closer. "Didn't you?" Her voice has dropped lower, to a whisper. I can feel her breath on my neck.

I keep my hands tight on my bow and quiver.

I tell her the complete truth as I say, "No." I say, "No, I didn't."

She slowly reaches up, placing her mouth close, close, close to my ear, dropping her voice even lower. "I don't believe you, Xander," she says slowly. Her lips slowly press against my neck, and this time I don't try to be soft—I just push her away from me. Far away from me.

I don't know what shuts down in my body first. It may have been my hearing, my sense of smell, the feeling in the tips of my fingers, but it definitely wasn't my eyes—which happen to catch Vicky's at completely the wrong time.

I watch her face phase through completely different emotions: shock, dread, confusion, sadness, anger, but mostly sadness and anger.

Her grip on the door handle is so tight that her knuckles are actually white. Her mouth is slightly agape, and she backs away, slowly, so, so slowly, eyes flicking between Kara and me and her hands near my chest.

"Vicky, wait!" I say, trying to step forward, but it's too late—she's already slamming the door in my face.

Again.

I push Kara out of the way as I step toward the door, willing my legs to run after her, to tell her it wasn't what it looked like. How much of *that* would she believe?

I hear Kara laugh quietly to herself, and I've never been angrier in my life. I spin around, letting the bow hit against my side, hard. "Why are you laughing?" I shout, but she doesn't take any notice, which gets me angrier.

"Because, Xan." The use of Vicky's nickname for me makes me grit my teeth to the point where I want to shatter them. "I got what I wanted."

"Then tell me. *What* was it you wanted?" I don't think I've ever spoken to her with that much anger, not even when we first met.

She points a finger toward the door. "*That*," she says, and I follow the point of her finger.

"Why?" I whip my head back to her. "She never did anything to you—"

"After I made you a Hunter, I knew it was just too easy, so I waited it out for a little while longer, see what else I could do." She crosses her arms over her chest, smirking.

"Wait—*you* made me a Hunter?" I can't believe any of the words coming out of her mouth.

"Yes," she says. "And I also made *her* a Weapons Cleaner to get what I wanted."

The conversation I had with Vicky comes rushing back. Why would Kara want Vicky to be a Weapons Cleaner if she knew she would hate it?

I ask my question aloud to her.

"Because, *Xander*, I wanted a very specific thing, and I needed no distractions."

"And what is that?" I'm getting more and more irritated with each passing word from either Kara or me, I can't really tell any more.

Then she says it. One word. That's all it takes for everything to come crashing down.

She says, "You."

Everything suddenly makes so much sense. She wanted Vicky to be a Weapons Cleaner to get closer to *me*. To make a move on *me*. She's never liked Vicky, I know that much, but I need to do something about all this.

I need to find Vicky.

"I can't believe you did that." I slowly back away toward the door, trying to look anywhere but her face. "I need to get away from here. I need to get away… from *you.*"

"Don't do this, Xander," she says, shaking her head. "If you leave now, you'll never be a Hunter again. I'll make sure of it."

I inch my way to the door, catching her eyes.

She shakes her head, uncrossing her arms, then crossing them again.

I almost laugh at her sentence. "You don't have to go to that much trouble, Kara," I say, "because, I quit."

"You… you *can't* quit," Kara argues.

"Then watch me," I say. "This is me"—I drop the bow and quiver on the ground, watching as her face hardens as she follows them—"*quitting.*"

I slam the door behind me.

CHAPTER THIRTY-ONE

I have no idea where she might be.

My mind can't register the fact that I'm running, and I'm running fast. Every single one of my thoughts are scattered, everywhere at once, and I don't have the energy to sort through them. The only thing I know is I need to get to Vicky—and I need to do it fast.

The conversation I had with Kara swims into my mind, and I smile inwardly at the way I spoke to her. She deserved it. I've never been angrier at one person before, and the fact that I found out about her making me a Hunter to get closer to me—and for Vicky to get away from me—gets me so angry.

I ignore the looks the Wasters are shooting in my direction. I ignore someone shouting my name. I pull away when someone grabs my arm to stop me. It might have been someone I know, but I didn't care enough to look. I only care about one thing at the moment.

I had a look at where her station was when I first left the weapons room, but she wasn't there. This place is huge—she could be anywhere right now.

I stop in front of the entrance, hunched over, breathing heavily. I spot Adam and Tessa, watching me with worried eyes.

"Are you... okay, Xander?" Adam asks, stepping up to stand next to me.

I give him a small thumbs-up as I straighten, blowing out the biggest puff of air. "Yeah... I'm... great." I can feel my pulse in my throat. "Have you guys seen Vicky anywhere?"

They look at each other, both silently saying the same thing. "No, we haven't," Adam says. "Sorry, Xander."

I shake my head as if to say it's fine, but no words come out of my mouth. Only air.

"What about your quarters?" Tessa pipes up, stepping to my line of sight. "She might be there."

I nod. "Yeah, okay. I'll try there now." I turn around on the ball of my foot. "Thanks, guys." I don't listen to their response as I push myself toward the one place she might be.

I quickly glance inside the Mess Hall to see if she's in here, but I don't catch her bright blue eyes anywhere.

I slow down my pace as I near our quarters, brushing past the curtain with one quick swipe. I check down the hall, but only see three tightly-shut doors.

I stop in front of the girls' bedroom, and I knock three times, silently hoping it didn't sound rushed—like it could be me behind this door.

No answer.

I knock once more before giving up. I quickly check inside the boys' bedroom, and I have no idea why; she won't be in here.

I check the last room in the hallway, and this time, I actually step inside, searching top to bottom to try and see if she's in here, but no luck. I get so frustrated that I actually kick the door, making it slam into the frame, echoing around the room, but I hardly hear it.

I lean my back against the cubicles, facing the door. The time when I saw Vicky in the Mess Hall comes to mind, and I squeeze my eyes shut to stop it, but it does no good. I see her tears glinting in her eyes. I watch her face phase through all those emotions that broke my heart, all of them... about *me*.

I watch as she slammed the door in my face, and I had no time to reach her.

I can't let that happen again. I *can't—*

The door opens, and I almost have a heart attack. I don't know who it is, but I don't want to lift my head to find out.

Maybe they will just brush past me and forget I was ever here. Maybe they will just turn around and walk away.

The person gasps, and my heart falls to my stomach. I slowly look up, locking eyes with Vicky.

She looks terrified. She looks sad. She looks angry.

And it's all because of me.

"Please, Vicky," I say, making her eyes widen. "Please wait. I need to speak with you."

She looks back toward the hallway, her grip on the door handle tightening so her knuckles are white.

"I'm... I'm really sorry." My voice is barely above a whisper. "What you saw... I didn't have anything to do with it."

"Really?" she suddenly says, and I start at the volume of her voice. I can see the anger clear in her eyes. "And do you expect me to believe that? You say you hate her, but then the next minute she's all over you... and you're loving it."

"I didn't want her close to me!" My voice has risen slightly, but it doesn't sound real in my ears. "Didn't you see me push her away?"

"That's not the point, Xander!" she shouts, and I wince, wanting all this to be over. "I saw *her* lips on *your* neck—" Her face suddenly falls, almost as if everything is washing over her in a big wave. "Did... did..." She can't seem to find the right words. "Did you... kiss her?"

I can't lie to her, and if I open my mouth to speak, I'll stutter, and she knows I only stutter when I'm not telling the whole truth.

But not saying anything is worse.

Her hand slowly comes up to cover her mouth, and she takes a small step back, trying her hardest to get as far away from me as she can.

I reach my hand out to her, but she shakes her head, fast. "No, no!" she shouts. "Don't... touch me!"

"Vicky..."

"Don't speak to me!" she says, and it feels like a knife gets lodged deep in my chest, and I can't seem to get it out—no matter how hard I pull. But it doesn't feel like Vicky is on the other end of that knife, and I have no idea who it could be. "I... never want to... see you again, Xander."

All at once, words fail me. I can't form a response in my head for what Vicky just said. She's never spoken to me with that much anger, not even when she saw my bloody nose back when Kara punched me. That seemed like years ago.

She slowly starts to back away from me, taking shaky breaths, her eyes glistening with new tears.

And I still can't speak.

She turns around slowly, letting go of the handle, taking a few steps forward, but I don't let her get that far away.

I swallow the rock in my throat as I reach forward, grabbing hold of her hand, pulling her back toward me. I silence whatever she was about to say with my lips, moving my hands up to cup her cheeks, then behind her neck.

I don't know what is running through my head—it's all just too many words, such loud sounds, and a headache is working its way up to my head. I can feel the tension disappearing from my body now that I've finally done what I wanted to do for years. I don't get much time to get used to it, though.

She pulls away from me as if I burnt her, and I take a step back, bracing myself for the slap I'm sure to get from her... but it doesn't come. Nothing comes; only a deafening silence that seems to settle everywhere around us. I look up at her, but not really wanting to meet her eyes.

The urge to kiss her again is almost overwhelming. I have to bite my lower lip hard and step back to stop myself. It felt natural to kiss her, to hold her close in my arms.

But she doesn't feel the same way.

I look down at the ground, suddenly feeling very numb. "I-I'm... sorry I did that." I don't even know why I'm speaking—it hardly sounds like me. It won't make this situation any better, so I don't know why I can't keep my mouth shut. "I… I don't know why I—"

She steps forward, grabbing the sides of my face, pulling me down to meet her lips.

I'm startled and shocked for a moment, completely taken aback. I slowly wrap my arms around her waist, pulling her closer, closer to me, not wanting to be an inch apart.

My thoughts are just mere echoes now.

Her arms snake around my neck, carefully weaving her fingers through my hair, then grabbing a fistful of it, tugging slightly. Only slightly. I don't even think she realized she did it. That small gesture made me break away for a second before I press my lips against hers again with more force this time. Now that I've got her with me, I don't want to let her go. I pull her closer to me again by the small of her back, pressing her in the curve of my body.

She fits so perfectly with me it's almost like it's not real.

I rest my forehead against hers as I pull away, trying to catch my breath. Our faces are so close together that my lips lightly brush against hers. The slight touch of them is killing me. She cups my cheeks in her hands for a moment, eyes traveling to mine, never leaving them.

She moves her arms to my shoulders, slipping down to my chest, her eyes finally breaking away to watch where her hands are traveling. Her hands move to my scar, lingering there, tracing around it almost like she's memorized what it looks like in detail. My breath catches in my throat and I almost cough.

I can't believe I've got her here in my arms. For so long I've been waiting for this moment—even if I didn't really believe it before. My fingers thread into her long hair, slightly pushing her head closer to mine.

She looks up at me, her gaze moving from my eyes to my lips. "Took you long enough, Xan," she breathes.

"I was an *idiot* for not doing that years ago." I rest my forehead against hers again. "Forgive me?"

She reaches her hand up, and brushes her fingers through my hair, moving it out of my eyes. I lean into her touch as she rests her hand on my cheek, brushing her thumb against something on my face.

"Of course I do," she replies quietly, keeping her hands on my face.

I slowly open my eyes as her thumb brushes against my bottom lip, parting it from my top lip, and the urge to kiss her again overpowers me. I lean down to brush my lips against hers slowly, but she wraps her arms around my neck, and my lips crash against hers with more force, taking my breath away.

I press my hands against her back, using my palms to pull her closer to me—if that's even possible. My back rests against somewhere on the cubicles, letting Vicky rest against my chest.

After a while, Vicky breaks away, her chest heaving. "We have… to speak about this, Xan."

"I know," I say against her neck, my nose skimming the soft skin. I don't really want to speak, but I know it's for the best. I just want to stay like this forever, for everything around us to become distant memories.

For everything around us to just be… *us*.

I can hear her breathing heavily in her throat. I plant a kiss there, and she gasps quietly, moving her head to expose her neck. I kiss her there again, then again. "I… can't do it like this, Xan. You know I can't."

I can feel her melt against my body, pulling me closer by the neck. I kiss her a few more times in the same spot before I groan and pull away from her, slowly grabbing hold of her hands, slowly lacing our fingers together.

She steps between my legs so she's closer to me. "So," she starts, looking down at our hands, "the thing with Kara…"

I nod my head slowly. "She kissed me," I confirm, though saying it aloud to her doesn't make me feel any better—it makes me feel worse. I don't want it to be real. I don't want *anything* with her to be real. "But I truly didn't want to. I got away from her as quickly as I could." I watch her head drop down to avoid looking at me, to avoid looking into my eyes. "I only wanted to ever kiss one person, and you know who that is." I lean down to look up at her, and she smiles, brushing her hair behind her ear. "I was just a fool for not doing it back in the Estate, when we were kids."

"Why would she even kiss you? I thought she hated you?" She slowly looks up at me, her eyebrows furrowed.

I shrug half-heartedly. "I guess not." I squeeze her hands, pulling them close to my chest. "She told me she made me a Hunter to get closer to me. To try and make a move on me, I think." I kiss her fingers. "I guess that's why she kissed me."

"Well, I can't blame her, to be honest." She looks down at me, then up. "I mean, have you even *seen* yourself lately?"

I look down and pull her closer, laughing as I kiss her forehead. "I hate her so much, Vicky," I whisper against her hair. "I've never hated anyone this much." I sigh, letting Vicky rest her head against my neck. We stay in this position for a long while before I say, "I never want to see her again."

Vicky pulls away from me to look into my eyes. "You know you'll still have to be a Hunter tomorrow," she says, keeping her eyes on me. "You can't exactly stay away from her when it's your job, Xan."

I lift her chin up with my thumb and index finger. I shake my head, giving her a small half-grin. "I quit."

She furrows her brows. "I thought you couldn't quit your jobs," she says. "That's what Johanna said to us."

"I don't care what Johanna said." I look up at her, brushing a strand of her hair away from her eyes, tucking it behind her ear. "I don't want to be a foot near her any more."

She pushes our hands to my chest, lightly punching me. "But you could get kicked out, Xander."

I lean closer to her, our foreheads touching. "Then I get kicked out." I lean back slightly. "Or, I could be with you as a Weapons Cleaner."

Vicky laughs lightly, her eyes looking down at my chest. "You'll be bored within five minutes. Trust me." She picks at a piece of thread on my shirt.

"Well…" I pull her slightly closer, putting my lips near her ear, dropping my voice to a whisper. "I'm sure we'll be able to make it fun." I wink at her as I pull away, causing a slight color to rise to her cheeks, and I push away from the sink, heading straight for the door with Vicky by my side.

*****

I don't care if we look like idiots as Vicky and I laugh and talk our way to the Mess Hall. I guess that's what's good about being… more than best friends, now; we already know everything about each other, and we can just have a joke that we both get.

"Do you want anything to eat?" I ask Vicky as we both sit down at a table near the back.

She shakes her head, giving me a thankful smile. "I'm not very hungry. Thank you, though."

"That's fine." I look toward the food line, scanning how long it is. "Well, I'm kind of starving so I'll be right back."

"Okay," I hear her say as I turn around, walking straight for the food line.

About two minutes later, I've managed to grab a tray and I see Ponytail on the other side of the wall, and this time—weirdly—she smiles at me. I give her a small smile back, looking down at my food.

Tonight's serving for dinner: brown soup with pieces of what I can only guess is a type of meat swimming in it. Very appetizing.

"You caught that, you know?"

I scoff loudly at the voice behind me, knowing Kara is the *last* person I want to see today, or for the rest of my life, for that matter. I turn around to look over my shoulder, not actually looking at Kara's face. I turn back around, not saying anything to her.

She doesn't say anything back for a few seconds. "Didn't you hear what I said, Xander?"

I shrug, still not turning around. "Temporary deafness, I guess."

"What—"

I start to walk away, grabbing a spoon, and heading straight for the table, ignoring the way she almost silently screams at me. I smirk to myself, keeping my gaze straight ahead even when I feel her hateful gaze burning a hole in my neck.

"What did she want?" Vicky asks curiously as I take a seat next to her, my arm brushing against hers.

"I have no clue," I say. "But I may or may not have told her I went deaf while she was speaking." I look in her direction. "And... *not* in the nicest way."

She places her hand on top of mine, squeezing softly. "You didn't have to be rude to her, Xander. She was probably trying to clear the air between you two."

I place my hand on hers, rubbing my thumb against the back of her hand. "Vicky, sweetheart, be honest with me right now." I lean down close to her ear, smiling with satisfaction as she shivers slightly. "You would punch her in the face if you had the opportunity to."

She leans back, hiding a smile, pulling her hand away from mine. "*Maybe.*" She leans her hand against her chin. "But I wouldn't say it out loud."

I laugh and wrap my arm around her shoulders, pulling her against my side.

*****

No one is in the hallways as we make our way back to our quarters, but we still speak in hushed tones about our job situation.

"I bet there are *loads* of Wasters that slack off during the day," I say, still trying to keep my voice low. "I don't see why *we* should be the ones doing the jobs. I've had enough of it."

"I have too, Xan." She looks over at me. "But what are we going to do for the rest of the time here?"

I shrug. "We could do anything. This place is huge," I say. "We could go to the oasis, stay in our bedrooms, anywhere!"

We were so caught up in our conversation that I didn't even realize we'd made it back to our quarters and stopped right in between the boys' and girls' bedroom doors.

I rest my back against the wall, pulling Vicky closer to me by the hands. She rests her hands on my shoulders, stepping closer, closer to me. "Are you even tired?" I ask, keeping my eyes on hers. I place my hands around her waist, wrapping my arms around her.

"Not really." She rests her face against my neck. "Why?"

I squeeze her waist lightly. "No reason. Just wondering if you were tired."

She presses her lips against mine softly, lingering there for a few moments. "I can tell you are, though, Xander." She brushes something off my face, moves my hair away from my eyes, cups my cheeks in her hands. "Get some sleep, okay?"

I nod slowly, pressing my lips against hers again as I let go of her waist slightly. "In a minute. Just be with me now."

She looks up at me. "I'm right here with you now. Forever."

She rests her forehead against mine, not saying anything else for a while. I just stay here with her; her in my arms, pressed against my chest—always just a breath away.

I close my eyes for a few minutes, enjoying the silence around us.

"Xander?" Vicky says after a while.

"Mhm…"

"You're falling asleep."

I raise my head slightly, eyes still closed. "No, I'm not." When she doesn't say anything for a while, I open my eyes, seeing her watching me with raised brows. "What?"

"Go. To. Sleep."

"Fine. I'll go to sleep," I say, yawning. "I guess today has been quite a long day." Vicky steps away from me, and I inch my way toward the boys' door, never taking my eyes off hers.

"Try to have a good night's sleep. And If you don't get up in the morning, I'll throw water on your head," she says, smiling.

"You always say that." I quirk an eyebrow at her, and she looks down, blushing.

"This time I mean it?" She says it as if it was a question.

I laugh. "I'll look forward to it." I turn around. "Goodnight, Vicky."

"One last thing," Vicky says, and I turn around, suddenly shocked as she grabs a fistful of my shirt, pulling me down, crashing her lips to mine.

I pull her against my body, but she pulls away too quickly, and I can't help but stare at her. "Goodnight," she says, trying not to smile too wide as she lets go of my shirt, smoothing it back down before walking toward her door. She gives me one last look before she shuts the door behind her.

CHAPTER THIRTY-TWO

I'm thirteen years old in my dream. I think it's more of a memory rather than a dream. Everything around me seems... new.

I remember this day like it was yesterday.

It had been almost a week since meeting Vicky when I had my first real injury. While scavenging, I managed to scrape a sharp piece of what I thought was metal—turned out to be wood—against my back.

A large part of the roof was coming down, and I managed, just in time, to move out of the way, resulting in the wood cutting across my back. It wasn't too deep, but it managed to slice through my jacket *and* my T-shirt.

It was a good thing I was only a couple of houses down from ours. If I wasn't... I don't know what would have happened to me.

I don't really remember much after that, other than Vicky guiding me all the way back to the house, whispering reassuring things in my ear that, to this day, I can't seem to recall.

The next ten minutes were torture as Vicky helped Kyle clean up my wound, wiping an alcohol-soaked rag across my back, washing away every last bit of blood that he could see. I kept biting hard on something Kyle gave me, so I wouldn't scream out in pain, but I felt all the screams bubbling inside my throat, just waiting to escape.

"He's almost done," Vicky said, handing me a small bottle of water, which I downed within a few seconds. "Just a few more minutes. You're doing great." She pressed a hand to my bare shoulder and gave me a smile. Her hand felt warm against my cold skin, and it was very relaxing.

Kyle wrapped a bandage around my back and chest three times to keep it clean, then secured it with a piece of tape. "All done," he said from behind me. "See? It wasn't so bad, now, was it?"

"Mentally, it felt worse," I said as I slipped my ripped T-shirt over my head, being careful so I didn't touch the newly wrapped bandage. I winced as I straightened my back, feeling the cut strain under the pressure.

Vicky slowed me down with her hand. "Take it slow, Xan," she said, and I nodded, guiding the fabric carefully over my skin.

The only position I could have stayed in, and to be comfortable, was to lay on my bed on my stomach, leaving my back to get fresh air. I leaned my cheek against my forearm as I watched Vicky sit down on her bed, elbows propped up against her knees.

"Thank you," I whispered after a long beat of silence.

Vicky looked up at me, never taking her chin off her hands. She smiled. "You're welcome."

After all of this, she stopped being skittish around us. She started to talk to me more, and we joked back and forth while we were the only two Scavengers.

Vicky knelt down next to my bed, crossed her arms on top of the rock-hard mattress, leaned in close to my face.

The hours after that were filled with light-hearted chatter about everything and anything, joking around with Kyle as he came in to check up on the bandages.

He looked so much younger then.

His hair was slightly darker, except for a slight bit of silver lining his temples. His beard was shorter, showing more of his cheeks and chin. Most importantly, his gray eyes were brighter, showing us that he still had a lot more years left in him.

After he left, Vicky and I stayed up all night learning more and more things about each other, not once checking to see what time it was, or realizing how late it was.

It was after all that, that I knew she was going to be my best friend—no matter what.

*****

Vicky wakes before me this morning.

Her fingers are running through my hair, moving it to one side, then the other. I have no idea if she's moving it out of my eyes, or just running her fingers through it, but I've never felt more relaxed before in my life. I sigh through my nose, moving my head to the side.

She presses a single, soft kiss against my lips, and I slowly open my eyes, groggily seeing her watching me with a smile on her face. She's crouching down next to the side of my bed, showing only her head and shoulders; just how she always did it. Like she did in my dream.

"Good morning," she whispers slowly as if it would startle me.

"Morning," I say, reaching out to brush a strand of her hair behind her ear.

She leans against my hand, and I brush my thumb against her cheek, making her open her eyes, brighter than ever.

"Why didn't you wake me up earlier?" I ask, rubbing the sleep from my eyes.

"Because you looked so cute while you were sleeping. I didn't want to disturb you." She smiles widely as her eyes search around my face.

I shake my head as I rub the sleep from my eyes. "I'm not cute."

She moves my hands away from my face, her brows furrowed tightly as she leans closer to me. "You're funny, Xander." She pulls me closer by the chin, her lips almost

344

against mine. "But you're a liar." She pecks me on the lips. Leaning back slightly, Vicky pulls her fingers out of my hair. I want to protest, but she won't listen to me. She starts to stand up, leaving me on the bed.

Suddenly feeling cold, I grab her by the waist, pulling her onto the bed so she's lying next to me—her back against my bare chest.

"Xander," Vicky says through a laugh. "I have to go to work."

I shake my head against her neck. "No, you don't," I say, closing my eyes. "You have to stay with me, wasting the day like I am probably going to. We're going to play hooky together."

"We can't play hooky, Xander." She shakes her head.

"Can we at least pull a sickie, then?"

Vicky turns around to face me in my arms, snuggling against my chest. "No. I'm not going to let you stay in this bed all day, Xan. You're *going* to do some work with me today." I can tell she's not being serious because she can't stop laughing.

I smirk and lean down to press my face into the crook of her neck, trailing my nose down slowly, toward her shoulder. "Really?" I mumble softly. I press my lips against her skin slowly, hearing her breath quicken slightly. "How are you going to do that?" My kisses start to get slower as I travel to her jaw, feeling her grip on my shoulder tighten, tighten, and I break away for breath.

"I... I don't know." I think she tries to say something else, but it won't pass her lips. I press my lips just below her ear, but she suddenly moves back, pressing her index finger against my lips to stop them from moving forward.

"If that's your way of keeping me here, Xan," she says, "then it's not working." Her words may be convincing, but her eyes betray her; which are flicking to my lips. I rest my forehead against hers as her finger slips from my mouth.

I didn't want to move, and now Vicky doesn't, either.

I must admit, it doesn't feel real. It just seems like a dream where I have Vicky in my arms, her chest pressed against mine; my lips against her skin.

Her finger outlines the shape of my eyes, and I resist the urge to close them from her touch. "You have such beautiful eyes."

I stare deeply into her's. "They are *nothing* compared to yours." I keep my voice low, knowing she will be able to hear me either way.

She blushes as she looks away from me. Her hand suddenly moves to my chest, and so do her eyes. Her finger grazes over something, going back and forth slowly. It's only until I look down do I realize it's one of my scars. She's furrowing her brows at the heinous mark, and I don't know why.

"How have you been hurt so many times?" she whispers, still tracing over my scars.

"I don't know. It doesn't matter, though." I place my hand over hers, making her look up at me. "Because I'm still here." I press her hand against my chest, making sure she can feel my fast-beating heart. "See?"

She kisses me again, her hands still pressed against my chest. She pulls away to slowly move out of my arms, trying to pull me with her.

I pull her back toward me. "Don't you want to stay with me, here?" I ask, keeping my eyes on her.

"Of course I do, Xander. You know I would stay here forever." She keeps her hands on my chest. "But if someone were to walk in, and they saw us like this, they would get the wrong idea." Vicky struggles to roll out of my arms because of my grip around her waist, but she manages to pull away, getting off the bed. "Come *on*, Xan." She pulls at my arm. "Just get up."

I groan. "I'm too tired, Vicky," I mumble, moving my arms around my middle, missing her warmth. "Just… come back to—"

Vicky suddenly pins my shoulders down on the bed, and I don't have time to snap my eyes open as Vicky's lips crash against mine. I can't move my arms as she's pinned them down, and I try to get them out of her vice-like grip, but she's too strong.

I suddenly feel awake as she pulls away, standing up straighter. I tried to keep her lips on mine, but she moved away too quickly. My eyes are wide as I stare at her, making her laugh.

"Better?" she asks, and all I can do is nod slowly, blinking with my mouth slightly parted.

"That was evil," I mumble.

"I know," Vicky says, grabbing my hand, which looks big compared to hers. "Let's go get breakfast."

*****

The Mess Hall is a mass of voices as we walk inside.

Most, if not all, of the Wastelanders have filled the tables. Some of them have even resorted to sitting *on top* of the tables, laughing with the others around them. The majority of them are just standing around, talking intently to one another.

The amount of food on the floor is enough to feed all the Wasters twice.

Vicky and I make our way to the food line, saying a quick "Hello" and "Goodbye" to Ponytail as she scoops oatmeal in our bowls. She nods in our direction as we turn to leave, filling her large spoon with more oatmeal for the next person in line.

The only two seats available that I could spot are the ones opposite Adam, Kyle and Tessa, all talking to each other, but looking up and smiling as we walk into view.

"Morning, all," I greet the three as I set down my tray, sitting close to the person to my left without touching him, hoping Vicky will have enough room to be able to be comfortable.

"Morning," they say in unison, all looking as tired as they can be.

Adam suddenly springs up at the sight of Vicky. He turns to me, points to Vicky. "Hey, you found her, Xander."

I smile at Vicky as she slides into the chair next to me. "Yep," I say slowly, "I found her."

Adam eyes the two of us carefully for a few seconds, slowly going back to eating his food. I don't know if Adam has figured all this out, but even if he has, he doesn't question it, which is why Adam is the best person in these types of situations.

Tessa leans forward slowly, staring intently at something on, or near Vicky's face. She points to her neck. "Where did you get that?"

I squint at the small mark on her neck, so faint it might as well be invisible, but the slight bit of purple tells me something is there for the world to see.

"Where did you get that hickey?" Tessa asks, and I smirk at the faint bruise.

Someone chokes on their food.

Someone holds back a laugh.

I just continue to stare at it.

Vicky punches me in the leg, and my smirk drops. I turn back to my food, casually mixing around my breakfast, hoping against hope I don't seem suspicious. I probably do because I'm such a bad actor.

Vicky laughs nervously. "You know what?" she says. "I must have got attacked by something." She flips her braid over her shoulder, half-covering the purple mark as much as she can.

"By what?" Adam asks. "Someone's lips?"

I try so hard not to laugh.

Vicky shoots him a dark look, and he goes back to eating, laughing as he spoons food in his mouth. Adam doesn't care what he says to people; he doesn't care what people's reactions would be. That's why I like him so much.

"Who gave you that hickey?" Tessa asks again, her interest piqued.

"No one did," Vicky says too quickly, looking over all of us, eyes not meeting mine. "Please, can we just drop it now?"

Everyone mumbles their own "Okay" to themselves, silently picking up their spoons.

I look up, over Vicky's head to Kyle, who is staring at me with the ghost of a smile on his lips as his eyes flick to Vicky, then me.

He must know it was me.

I nod my head the slightest bit, looking back down to my food.

"You asked the wrong question, by the way, Tessa," I say after a short period of time, making everyone look up at me. I turn to look at Vicky, trying not to smile too wide. "Was he a good kisser?"

Vicky's face turns white, and I smile wider. Her cheeks then turn red as she looks down.

"Is that a yes?" Adam says before I can.

She looks over at him, presses her lips together firmly. "I'm not saying anything, you assholes," Vicky says, still eating her food. We all continue to laugh, despite Vicky's groans.

Vicky kicks me in the leg as if to tell me off, as if she wants an apology.

But I'm not sorry, at all.

The rest of breakfast is filled with listening to Adam and Tessa flirt with each other as if we weren't on the same table, directly in front of them. I don't mind it, though; it's almost amusing to watch the two of them flirt.

I don't know when Vicky wants to tell the others about our... new situation, but I'll let her decide because I don't really know what our current situation is, exactly.

I guess when the time is right, we'll know.

"You are going to pay for saying that, Xan," Vicky says quietly so only I can hear.

"Am I, now?" I smile.

She nods slowly. "Yep."

I lean down, putting my lips near her ear, making sure it looks innocent to the rest of the guys. "I can't wait."

As soon as Vicky and I are finished, we head straight for the weapons room, dropping our trays off on the way.

"Okay," Vicky says as she pushes open the door, walking straight for the table. "Do you want me to show you what to do?" She picks up a knife and rag and presents them to me.

I laugh as I pluck the knife from her fingers, marveling at the way the shiny metal reflects the bright lights in this room. "It's cleaning, Vicky," I say. "I think I'll get the hang of it."

She plucks the dagger from my hands and carefully sets it down. "It's not as easy as that, Xan," she says, handing me the rag. "They are much sharper than the ones we found back in the Estate. You've got to remember these are *knives,* not toys, and they can *stab* you."

I look down at the rag, picking it up, dropping it back on the table. "Isn't that what *Will* taught you?" I mumble sarcastically under my breath.

She ignores my sarcasm as she says, "As a matter of fact, yes he did." She hands me the knife, and I take it slowly. "Here, like this." Her hands softly grab onto mine as she swipes the rag across the smooth surface, and I am slightly mesmerized at how softly she does it. "See? You don't have to be aggressive with it."

I look down at Vicky as her hands move from my arms to my waist, slowly, slowly moving to my side, tracing the pattern of where my scar would be, and I lean down when she looks up at me.

"You're not cleaning any more, Xander." I don't know how she can know—she's not looking at the weapon.

"No," I say, "I'm not. Not any more." I slowly lower the rag, slowly, slowly lower the knife, not letting go of it.

Her hand moves, coming to rest on my shoulders. Her forehead touches mine. "You're... you're distracting me... from my work."

"Am I?"

She nods slowly, pressing closer to me. "Y-yeah." Her hands slowly move around my neck, pulling me closer to her. Her breath feels hot against my skin as—

The door slams open.

We both jump away from each other, making me almost cut myself with the side of the knife. I place it down on the table, turning around until I'm facing the door.

We both watch with wide eyes as a Waster walks into the room, completely ignoring us as he grabs a random weapon from the wall, then swiftly leaves with it at his side.

"That was... really weird," I say out loud, furrowing my brows at the door that the Waster left open.

Vicky steps forward. "Yeah, it was—"

Another Waster walks into the room, grabbing a weapon, leaving with it gripped tightly in his hand.

Then another.

Another.

Two more.

Three.

The next thing I know, the Wasters are filing into the room, grabbing the first weapon they see from the wall. They don't argue about who gets what weapon; they just grab one and go.

The last Waster is running, and it turns out to be Levi as he steps out of his little room with a big sword clasped between his hands. A small sheath full of daggers is tied around his

351

waist, resting against his hip. I step forward and grab his arm before he can leave. He whips his head in my direction, his chest heaving, almost like he didn't see me here. He looks down at my hand on his arm, eyes traveling to mine.

"What is happening, Levi? Why is everyone grabbing weapons?" I ask, finally letting go of the younger Waster's arm.

Levi manages, with some difficulty, to suck in a lungful of air before speaking. "Because, Xander," he pants. "Because we're…" He breathes slowly again, and I lean closer, eyes never leaving his bright green ones. "We are being attacked by the Shadows."

CHAPTER THIRTY-THREE

The Wastelands is nothing but panic.

Every single Waster is moving somewhere; in every direction possible. Most of them have weapons slung across their backs, scared and angry expressions written clearly on their faces. Some push passed us, nudging Vicky and me in the shoulders with their bulky frames.

All I can do is stare at them, watching as they slowly blur into one color.

I can't feel my limbs, any more. I can't feel Vicky pulling on my arm. I can't hear her say my name. I can hardly hear my own thoughts any more.

Blinky's death flashes across my vision, and I gasp—or at least, I think I gasp; I can't feel anything. Air won't seem to fill my lungs.

Levi's scared words echo around my head, bouncing around my skull as if they are trying to find something.

We are being attacked by the Shadows.

The Shadows?

The exact same savage group of monsters that killed one of my friends? Killed a thirteen-year-old girl? Almost killed *us*? Me, as well?

Spots of red fill my vision, and I blink to remove them.

"*Xander.*"

The voice. It sounds so scared, so familiar it snaps me back to reality.

Curling and uncurling my hands, I look over to Vicky whose blue eyes are searching mine as if she's lost me, as if she is *desperately* trying to search for me.

But I'm right here.

"Xander?" she says again. "Can you hear me?"

I nod slowly, looking back at the Wasters as they run toward the entrance; some of them running, some sprinting. Some look as confused as we do.

The entrance. Of course. That's where the Shadows will be. That's where I'm going to go. That's where I *need* to go.

"Come on." I pull Vicky by the arm and she follows me. I stare intently at the back of a male Waster's head, briefly considering turning back, but I don't.

We make it to the entrance quickly.

Every single Waster is here, it feels like, and I have to weave through them to get near the front. Some of the Wasters are blocking the front row, stopping people like me from getting past them. A few Wasters press tightly against my side and I try to push them off, but to no avail.

Hushed whispers are the only thing I can hear now. We are all packed tightly together, forming a shield from the Shadows, even if we don't realize we are doing it. I keep Vicky as close to me as possible, her chest pressed against my back. I can feel her heartbeat pounding against her chest.

My pulse quickens, and I have no idea if it will ever go back to normal. My breathing is fast, and I'm trying to calm it down, but with everyone around me, pressing, pressing, pressing in, I feel myself suffocating.

Everyone's heads snap toward the hole.

We suck in a tight breath in unison as dust and rocks fall to the ground, the only sound in the entire room.

They don't even let the dust settle as bows, swords, and every single weapon rises toward a pair of legs dangling from the hole, suddenly dropping to the ground with a *thud*.

I hear all of them release a loud breath as the figure stands upright, a long sword clenched tightly in each hand. I recognize this person; he's the Waster who shouted for all of us to get ready for hunting. He's the leader of the Hunters.

"Don't worry, guys," the male Waster says, breathing heavily. "I didn't see them. I think they might have—"

His eyes bulge, and his mouth parts. He starts to sway backward and forward, suddenly looking down. He slowly falls forward, and that's when we see the arrow protruding from his back.

Multiple screams reverberate around the room and inside my head. Vicky's grip on me tightens, tightens, tightens… but I can't feel it. I can't feel anything.

Then the first Shadow drops from the hole.

I don't have time to study what he or she looks like as I stumble back, taking Vicky with me. She keeps me upright as we try and fight our way to the back of the crowd, weaving through the tightly packed group.

I can't see if the Wasters shoot the Shadow. I can't see the dead leader of the Hunters. I can hardly see the backs of the Wasters; it all just looks like a smear of color.

All I can see is the Shadows dropping from the hole; one by one, their booted feet keeping in time with the sound of my heart beating.

We finally push our way out of the crowd, running straight for the one place that could help us. I don't turn my head to see the Wasters and Shadows fighting. I try to ignore the cries of pain as we both run away.

We can help them, I know we can, but I don't want to do it empty-handed.

I push open the weapons room door, checking left and right before heading straight for the room where I left the weapon I had to use; the same one that I threw on the ground when I quit being a Hunter.

The one that is now right in front of me.

When I left the room, Kara must have put the bow and quiver on the table near the door. I thought she would put it back on the wall, or even use it for herself, but she didn't.

Maybe she thought I was going to come back as a Hunter, leaving the bow ready for me.

She would have thought wrong.

The material of the bow is cold as I grip it tightly in my hand, shaking slightly as I study it carefully, feeling every curve, every fraction of it.

Was it really only yesterday? The last time I held this bow? Shot this bow? It feels like it's been years. Holding this bow doesn't make me want to go back to being a Hunter; it just reminds me of the time when I quit. The time I said I was never going to use it again.

"What are you going to do?" Vicky asks, bringing me back to the present.

I wait a beat before answering her, sliding a medium-sized sword in my belt, making sure it's within easy reach. "I'm going to fight."

"No." She steps up, grabbing hold of my arm as if it would change my mind. "This isn't your fight, Xan. You've got to remember that."

I swing the quiver onto my back. "But it isn't the Wasters fight either, Vicky."

"They can protect themselves, Xander," she says. "They've been doing it for years." She steps forward. "You don't know what it's like to be in a real battle."

"I can imagine it, though," I say, walking toward the door.

"Xander, this isn't funny, any more," Vicky says. "You could get *killed*."

"I'm not trying to be funny, Vicky." I'm walking down the hallway, heading directly for the entrance. "They need all the help they can get. I'm going to be that help."

"Why are you... *doing* this, Xander?" Vicky asks, still trying to keep her voice calm.

"I just...," I start, feeling my heart thumping in my chest. "I just have to, okay?"

"You can't save everyone!"

I stop, turning around to face her. Her hands are trembling at her sides. I step up, grabbing the side of her face with my only free hand, and pressing my lips to hers.

It's the kind of kiss that I never thought was possible; one that takes your breath away and breathes life back into you at the same time. It's a hello and a goodbye wrapped up together, just waiting to be said, waiting to pass through someone's lips.

But neither of us have the courage to say it.

She wraps her arms around my shoulders, pulling me closer, preventing me from leaving. With her arms tightly around me, around my shoulders, I can tell she really doesn't want me to go, doesn't want me to risk my life like this.

But I *have* to.

I slowly start to pull away from her.

"No," she says as she cups my cheeks to pull me down to her lips.

I can literally *feel* how much she doesn't want me to go with just one kiss. I know what she is saying—and doing—is right, so I don't know why I can't just... stay out of it.

Vicky is right.

I *can't* save everyone.

But I'm right too.

I can at least *try*.

I pull her as close as I can before slowly detaching our lips, resting my forehead against hers. "I'm really sorry, Vicky," I whisper, finally breathing in air. "But I have to do this. I *can't* let them kill any more of our friends. They have done enough to us; it's time they were stopped."

She squeezes my shoulders hard, as if that would change my mind. She swallows. "Please be careful, Xander." I can hear the sobs forming at the back of her throat. "Please. I can't... I can't almost lose you again."

"You won't." I nod once, pulling her closer. "I promise."

I grab Vicky's hand as I step away from her, biting my lower lip to keep the tears at the back of my eyes. "Go to the quarters," I say. "You'll be safe there. I promise." I pull the dagger I got from the Estate out of my belt, pressing it into her open palm. "To protect you."

She eyes it carefully, nodding once as her fingers slip out of my reach. She turns around, heading straight for our quarters, turning around once to look at me over her shoulder. "I love you, Xander."

My heartbeat thumps loudly in my chest as her words echo in my head. I have to stop myself from holding her in my arms again, to never leave her side. It kills me that I have to leave her, but she can't be put in the middle of this fight. She *can't*. "I love you, too, Vicky."

She presses her lips together tightly to stop herself from crying as she slips through the door, shutting it behind her, the only sound echoing around my head.

I blow out a puff of air between my teeth, hoisting the bow and quiver higher on my shoulder.

I can hear the battle cries from the Mess Hall. They are so loud, so intense, that it makes me want to turn back around, but I can't—I can't turn away now.

My heart is in my throat as I make it to the entrance. The sound of metal clashing against metal echoes around my skull, making me dizzy. I pull my bow from my shoulder, trying to line an arrow in it with my shaky hands, aiming it in every single direction.

A Shadow and a Waster cross my path, and I step back, trying not to get hit by the sharp, sharp metal. The Shadow has pushed his sword down hard against the Waster, making him—or her—lean over the Waster.

I aim my arrow toward the first place I lay my eyes on, and shoot.

The Shadow cries in pain as the arrow lodges in his shoulder, the sound muffled by the black bandana wrapped tightly around his mouth.

The wound is gushing blood, dripping to the floor. The Waster butts him in the head with the back of his sword and the Shadow collapses to the ground, unconscious. The Waster nods his thanks before clashing with another Shadow.

I knew, deep down, where I wanted to shoot the arrow. I don't want to kill any of these people. They are still human just like us—even *if* they kill their own kind. The shoulder wound won't kill the Shadows, but maybe just slow them down a bit.

Someone pulls me backward, making my quiver rip off my back, and I swipe blindly at the figure behind me with a new dagger that I didn't realize I picked up. I think it was the sharp one Vicky was helping me clean, but I can't be too sure now; it has some blood stained on it, and I can't tell if it's his blood or mine.

My forearm has been cut, and I have no idea how.

With no more arrows to reach for, I swing my small dagger at the Shadows in front of me and behind me. Just before the Shadow can swing his sword at me, I pull mine from the back of my belt, protecting myself just before my opponent's sword slashes across my neck.

I clench my teeth as I stare into the dark eyes of the Shadow, trying my hardest to push myself upright, but my attacker is too strong.

I'm pushed into a nearby wall, the edges of our swords dangerously close to my neck. I keep my face impassive, contemplating all my options to stay alive before the edge of my sword makes contact with the skin on my neck. I throw myself to the side, somehow able to duck underneath both swords. I kick as hard as I can into the knee of the Shadow, and he collapses to the ground. He tries to swing his sword at me, but I push it out of the way with my own sword, sending it somewhere far away from us.

Just before I can move away from the Shadow, an arrow flies toward us, landing deeply in the back of the neck of my former attacker. I gasp and jump backward, staring at the arrow, hearing the horrified sounds of coughing and spluttering, then a second later, nothing.

Arrows fly overhead, and I have to stop myself from looking at where they will end up. One of the arrows lands in the wall right next to my ear, and I duck down as fast as I can, my hands making contact with someone's blood.

My attacker's blood.

Dead and unconscious bodies lie on the ground; some covered in blood, some of the injured are still trying to fight, some leaving the entrance, leaving a trail of blood behind like a snail. I can recognize some of them as Wasters, but the Shadows can't seem to escape and heal—no matter how hard they try.

The Wasters won't let them escape.

I don't know if it's frowned upon by the Wasters to leave a battle like a coward, but maybe it's every man for himself. Maybe it's like: "Thank you for your help. You've played your part, now leave."

I can never tell with the Wasters.

The number of Shadows is dropping, and I see something that makes my blood run cold, my head spinning, my vision blurry, and I want to empty my stomach.

Kyle is swinging left and right at a couple of Shadows in front and next to him. He's backed up against the wall, trying his hardest to keep his sword in front of him, protecting his chest. The veins in his forehead are popping out from his struggling. He's fighting them off, but they are too strong for him to hold on forever.

I grab my bow from where it was knocked to the ground, tightening my grip on it. I didn't realize I stopped fighting, staring intently at Kyle, half-wishing for him not to be real, to not really be here, for him to be in our quarters safe with Vicky. He shouldn't *be* here.

But he's here.

He's fighting.

And he's losing.

One of the Shadows fighting him gets distracted by another Waster, and I'm very much grateful. Kyle pushes the Shadow away slightly with his sword, but the attacker will not be discouraged, he will not stop. He goes straight back into the fight, raising the sword high above his head, and just as Kyle raises his sword to protect himself—

The Shadow stabs Kyle in the stomach.

It's like everything is in slow motion as someone screams, and it's only until my feet propel me forward that I realize it was me, my throat ripped clean out from the cry.

I yank an arrow from the quiver which belonged to a Waster to my right, and shoot it straight at the Shadow—who just stands there until the arrow lodges deep in his back. The Shadow's body jerks quickly as he falls to the ground, and by then I've pushed him to the side roughly, dropping the bow to the ground, and crouching down beside Kyle, cradling his head in my arms.

Everything goes silent.

I feel like I've smashed into a million pieces as tears stream down my face. My heart lurches and breaks all at once, all at the same time, and I can't keep track of it. I can't do anything to stop it. My hands are shaking, but I can't tell whether it's from anger or sadness or guilt—I can't tell any more.

I can't feel anything after that.

Kyle looks up at me with his suddenly darker gray eyes, but I can't focus on his face, I can't focus on anything, anything, *anything*—

"Xander?" Kyle chokes, and I have to peer down to hear him. "I'm... I'm... s-sorry." Blood dots the corners of his mouth, trailing down to his chin. "I... I tried my... h-hardest..."

"N-no," I breathe, but it doesn't sound like me, it doesn't sound like anyone. "J-just... keep your... e-eyes on me, Kyle.

Focus on my face. P-please... you can't... you can't leave me. You can't leave *us*."

His hand reaches up to press against my cheek. His eyes start to close, the life slowly escaping them. "Take... c-care... of... them..."

And I break everywhere as his head rolls backward, his hand slipping from my face.

"No," I breathe. "No!" I shout, shaking his shoulder hard. "No, Kyle!" This can't be happening. This isn't happening. It isn't, it isn't, it *isn't*—

Someone is pulling me backward, and I don't have enough willpower to fight it, to do anything but watch Kyle slowly slip to the floor, his head hitting the ground.

Kyle is gone and there is nothing I can do any more. I have no one to look up to any more.

I have *nothing* like that any more.

He is gone.

My vision blurs, then stops as a sudden sharp pain slices across my back, then everything goes dark.

CHAPTER THIRTY-FOUR

I come to slowly, to a bright white light piercing into my eyes like tiny daggers.

I have no idea where I am. I have no clue how long I've been unconscious. I don't even know if I'm still alive. It would probably be less painful if I wasn't alive. It would probably be best for everyone if I wasn't alive. I'm more trouble than I'm worth.

The last thing I remember was watching Kyle slowly pass away in my arms and being dragged away from him by a Shadow. I remember being slashed across the back before I blacked out.

My back suddenly explodes in pain, reminding me that I'm still alive, and I lurch forward. The pain secretly tells me that I can still survive, that I can keep going. But I sometimes don't want to. I just... I can't any more.

Something forcefully pushes me back down, on what I can only assume is a bed. I don't know who it was that pushed me down, and I don't really want to find out. I hardly want to be here. I can't stop the pained feeling in my heart, my stomach, my *head*.

Kyle flashes across my vision, repeatedly being stabbed by that one Shadow who fell down when I shot the arrow in his back, his body jerking uncontrollably.

The realization hits me all too soon.

I killed that Shadow.

I *killed* him.

I didn't know his name. I didn't even know if it was a male or female. I didn't know if he or she had a family, had friends, had people that loved and cared for him or her.

But then I remember he or she didn't know us, didn't know our names. This person killed Kyle. *Killed* him. People that kill for no reason don't deserve to live.

Kyle shouldn't have died—no one should die.

Something catches in my throat, and I don't know what it is; maybe it's the tears that are threatening to spill, maybe it's just air.

But it still doesn't feel good.

The figure to my left moves over to look at something on, or near my face, and I don't have any power within me to turn away, to raise my hand to wave them away from me.

He, she, shines something in my eyes, and this time I actually do turn to the other side, trying to lift my hand up in the air to get them away from me, but to no avail.

"Xander?"

The voice sounds so familiar. So much like home, it makes new tears swell in my eyes. My immediate thought is *Vicky,* but then I think otherwise—it was too deep of a voice. I want to respond to the voice, but my mouth can't move; I can't form sentences to say out loud to myself or to anyone.

"Xander, please turn back around."

I oblige because I know this voice. The voice is soft, is kind, doesn't have any anger in it at all.

The light shines in my eyes, and I resist the urge to move, to shut my eyes, to run away—

But I can't.

Drew's ash blond hair and dark, dark brown eyes come into view, and I have to blink a few times to make sure he's really there, really crouched down beside me.

"Drew?" My voice sounds hoarse, so unlike me; so unlike… anything.

"It's me, buddy. It's me," he replies, placing a reassuring hand on my shoulder.

My gaze travels across the room, and they land on the people who I never thought I would see again.

Adam and Tessa step up next to Drew, and I squint at them to avoid the bright light.

"Hey, Xander," Adam whispers with an apologetic smile. It's unsettling—it's not the type of smile Adam would throw out to people willingly. "How are you feeling?"

"I feel like it would hurt less if I was just dead." Actually, I feel worse than that. Much, much worse. I don't know how bad I actually feel.

"Don't say that, Xander," Adam says quietly, looking down at the ground. "Please don't say that."

I look down at what I'm lying on—the white sheets, the uncomfortable pillow, the slight smell of antiseptic.

I'm in the Infirmary.

A large bandage is wrapped tightly around my middle, covering every inch of my chest, stomach, and probably back, too. The bandage feels like it's putting pressure on my chest, and I can hardly breathe.

Drew pulls my arm closer to him, wiping an alcohol-soaked rag across my cut, but I can't feel the pain. Even something that I know hurts so much is almost bearable. Slowly, Drew wraps a clean white bandage around my forearm a few times before securing it with a piece of tape.

My eyes land on Ponytail, who slowly steps up next to me, placing her small hand on my shoulder, giving me a kind and genuine smile—one she hasn't given me... for what feels like years.

My eyes scan each corner of the room. "Where's... that blond guy?" I ask, not really caring about where Blondie really is, but I just have to know.

Drew looks down, smiles the slightest, slightest bit. "I really, really hate myself for smiling." He looks up. "But he's dead, Xander. He died while fighting near the entrance."

Even though I really hated Blondie for always being horrible to Drew, he shouldn't have died. He was just an innocent person who wanted to help people get better.

He, plus many others, shouldn't have died.

No matter how hard I look or move and almost fall off the bed, I can't seem to find the one pair of blue eyes I've been wanting to see since waking up.

I sit upright, ignoring the strain in my back. "Where's Vicky? Where is she? I can't find her. Did she come in earlier? Is she outside?"

No one answers any of my many questions.

Drew pushes me back down, but I shrug him off a little harder than I wanted to. "Where is she?" My voice has never sounded like this—it scares me a little. "*Where?*"

"Xander, please, just... just calm down." Drew keeps trying to push me down, but I get so frustrated as I ask the question again.

When no one answers again, I swear my heart drops to my stomach, and I can't breathe, I can't breathe, I can't *breathe*—

"What has happened?" I ask, my voice lined with so much concern, so much anger, so much frustration... it doesn't sound like me—not like me at all. "Drew?" He doesn't answer. "Anyone?"

"It's Vicky," Adam says quietly, just above a whisper, and I turn to look at him, still trying to breathe. "She's... She's..." He swallows hard, removing something in his throat. "She's been taken, Xander. She's been taken by one of them."

I didn't think it was possible for a single word to push me over the edge.

Taken.

Vicky can't be taken. She can't, she can't, she can't be. She should be safe. She should have been safe in our quarters. She *is* safe. She hasn't been taken. They are all lying. They are *lying* to me.

This is all a joke. Vicky is going to come bursting through the door, wrapping her arms around my shoulders, pulling me closer, telling me how much she missed me, how much she thought I was dead.

But the faces around the room tell me otherwise.

I can't speak. I can't form a single sentence in my head. All the words and sounds are merging together to create a headache at the back of my mind. I think I'm hyperventilating, but I can't be too sure of what I am doing any more.

Anger replaces the sadness, and I've never wanted to rip the heads off the Shadows before. They will pay for what they did to her. They will pay for taking her.

They will regret what they did to my friends.

It was after the word *taken* that I knew, somewhere in the recesses of my mind, that I needed to get Vicky back. It wasn't something I thought twice about—I knew it as soon as it came to mind.

She's strong. She's stronger than she cares to admit, and I know she will fight out of the reach of those Shadows.

I will find her; I will search every *single* inch of the desert if I have to.

The Shadows think they've broken me in some way, made me weaker. They've just given me the opportunity to get the person I truly care about back. To get stronger. To know what I truly need to do. For everyone.

And I'm ready.

I'm ready for whatever will come next.